My Luck

TWISTED LUCK BOOK 1

TERNION UNIVERSE

Mel Todd

Bad Ash Publishing
86 Desmond Court
Powder Springs, GA 30127
www.badashpublishing.com

Publisher's Note: This is a work of fiction. Names, characters, places, and incidents are a product of the author's imagination. Locales and public names are sometimes used for atmospheric purposes. Any resemblance to actual people, living or dead, or to businesses, companies, events, institutions, or locales is completely coincidental.

Book Layout © 2015 BookDesignTemplates.com
Cover Art - AmpersandBookCovers.com

My Luck/ Mel Todd -- 1st ed.
Paper ISBN 978-1-950287-04-8

Life goes on, love reminds you of where you've been.

Author's Note:

Hey everyone, I'm Mel and I'm super excited that you picked up this book. This is book 1 of the Twisted Luck series. If you'd like to see what I'm up to you can sign up for my newsletter here. There are free short stories in my newsletters, updates as to what I'm working on, and occasionally recommendations for other books. You can find the Facebook Group for this series here.

Just a reminder here's the blurb for My Luck.

Coffee and my BFF are all the magic I need.
I see dead people. No, really. I find a disturbing amount of dead or dying people. It's just my luck - if something freakish happens, I'm usually in the vicinity. Prime example: The body I found on the way to work this morning that's now making me late. I can't afford to lose my job at the coffee shop. College is expensive for non-magical folks like me.

Except things have gone wonky around me most of my life. I can't possibly be a mage, though. I would know something like that. Right?

My best friend Jo is the only person I've let myself depend on the last several years. But when my name is found in the pocket of the latest dead body, I discover I have more friends than I thought. I'm going to need them all to graduate. I am determined to complete my certification program no matter what obstacles get in my way.

I have plans for my future: enjoy life, be a great EMT, and keep looking for the reason my twin died. If life is a series of steps, this is step one. With my luck, anything could happen.

My Luck – the first book in the Twisted Luck series, an Urban Fantasy you didn't know you needed. A found family, non-romantic urban fantasy with a smattering of magical beasties.

Thanks everyone, you see you at the end!

Mel

be the paramedic. Not that there was any chance of helping this guy. Not even a merlin could save him, though they might be able to figure out what killed him. Because I couldn't see a darn thing that might have separated his head so decisively. The left side of his head facing me didn't have a mage tattoo on it, but most people had them on their right side. I couldn't see any jewelry, but all of that meant nothing. Hedgemages didn't have to wear markings.

"Only you, Cori." Hazel heaved a sigh. "Do you know him?"

"Nope."

"Did you see what caused the death?"

"Oh heck no. If I had, I'd still be running." Well, probably. With my life I might have stuck around to watch.

"I think that's all, as the police will be there soon. You need me to stay on the line, or are you fine?"

"Right as rain," I chirped back, but there wasn't a smile on my face regardless of my peppy voice.

"Talk to you later, Cori. Gotta go." The disconnect tone rang in my ear. I resisted scratching my head. Leaving my damn dandruff here would make my life even more complicated. In my world, I'd scratch my skull to get rid of the dandruff and a gust of wind would blow and coat the dead guy with my DNA. Not what I needed.

I slipped my smartphone, the cheapest one available, back into my pocket and looked glumly at the dead man. "You are really messing up my routine you know? I'm supposed to be at work—" I paused, pulled my phone back out to check the time, and heaved a sigh—"in five minutes. I can guarantee that I won't make it. Oh well. Maybe Samuel will give me a ride. Might make my boss less annoyed. Oh, crap, Molly!"

With the sirens getting louder I rushed off a hurried text to both my boss, Molly, and my coworker, Kadia.

Found dead body. Waiting for cops. Will be late.

I hit send as the flashing blue lights of the cop car pulled up on the street next to me.

"See what you did? Distracted me," I told the body. Too much time alone had me talking to anything and everything. Maybe I should get a pet. Or at least work on talking to living people? I stared at the body, resisting again the desire to go investigate, to find out something about him. Dig through his pockets, at least get a name to call him. But leaving traces of myself on a dead body would be stupid. That lesson I hadn't had to learn the hard way. Cop shows are excellent for teaching you some basic crime scene protocol and the consequences for breaking it.

Slipping my phone back into the pocket of my thrift store jeans, I stood up, brushing off my butt as Samuel Clements got out of his squad car. We all gave him a bad time about his name, but right now my mood was more on the snarky bitter range of things rather than the peppy teasing. I'd heard rumors he was a Pattern hedgie, but I never saw anything to give credence to it, so I didn't worry about it.

"Corisande Munroe, what trouble are in you this time?" He, too, had that exasperated tone. My goal after I graduated was to have people talk to me without sounding exasperated. That would probably never happen, but I could try.

"I'm not in any trouble. I was simply doing my civic duty and reporting a dead body." I didn't say murder victim or accident victim; that had been beat into my head by my third dead body. Don't assume you know how they died or anything about their death, even if you watched them die. Those were the worst. And why I was striving to make sure I'd never need to just stand by unable to save or even help someone again. But this guy had not been dead for a long judging by the few insects that were just now beginning to be attracted to his corpse.

"Again? I swear, Cori, you attract trouble more than any kid I've ever seen." The tone and frown got my hackles up even more.

"And this is my fault how? You know I don't ask for it. And don't call me a kid." I regretted the words the second they left my lips. Protesting you weren't a kid always made you sound like a kid.

Samuel held up his hands in mock surrender as the ambulance, with flashing lights and wailing siren that made me flinch, pulled up behind him. "Yes, ma'am."

I bit back a retort; I really did need him to give me a ride to work and being snarky wouldn't help that. I'd turn twenty-one in April, but he'd known me for a long time. At the ripe age of twenty-eight, he'd always seen me as a kid. As much as small towns rocked, they also sucked. Once you were notorious, you were always notorious.

The EMTs got out of the bus pushing a stretcher and came up alongside of us.

"'Ello, Cori," Jeff Pierson said, his soft southern drawl pulling out the syllables until it almost sounded sensual. I rolled my eyes. With his long lanky body, dark brown eyes, and light brown hair, half the women under thirty lusted over him. I wished I did.

The thought at least snapped me out of my stupid look, and I smiled at him and Sally Chang. "Hey, guys. Come on, I was just about to show Samuel where the body is."

Sally nodded, her long black hair twisted up in a series of intricate braids, each one with beads sectioning off an inch. I looked at her, always marveling how even in a uniform she looked stylish, smart. But then most mages always seemed to. Her tattoo gleamed on her temple, black with solid red showing her as strong in Pattern. Rather than hash marks she had little dots in Air and Transform. I frowned when I noticed that her right hand was missing her normally beautiful long nails.

"What did you run into that needed that much offering?" I nodded at her hand.

She glanced down comparing the two hands. Her left hand had nails about an inch long, painted with protective gel, the right looked like they had been bitten to the quick.

"Bad car accident. Child involved. Idiot parents hadn't buckled her into the child seat." Sally shrugged and grinned at me. "Worth the offering. Kid should be fine, and the parents will be in jail for a while. DUI."

I nodded, the familiar mix of envy and relief washing through me. I wanted to help people, save them. Magic would have made it possible for me to be better, more powerful. However, magic scared me on a level I didn't know how to address. It wasn't an issue. None of my family had ever emerged. I'd never be a mage so worrying about it was a waste of time.

"Enough chit-chat," Samuel said. He was prickly about magic too; his dad was an archmage and Samuel, as he lacked a tattoo, obviously wasn't. Or at least not above a hedgemage. "Where's the body, Cori?"

"I said I'd show you," I huffed. "It's not like waiting is going to make a difference."

"It might," Sally said mildly and I fought not to bristle. I really needed some food; my temper was way too short today.

"Trust me, it won't." I turned away from them. "This way."

"Lead on, mi'lady," Jeff drawled again. I ignored the groans from Samuel and Sally. Jeff was an unrepentant flirt, but I just found him amusing.

"Down there." I pointed and under the shade of three pink azalea bushes and a tall magnolia tree lay the body of a man in a dark brown almost black suit. A few feet away lay his head, eyes closed, much to my relief. Blood covered the area, sprayed around in streams of red turning to brown. The amount of blood implied a lot of things, but unless I got closer, I couldn't figure out where he'd been standing or sitting when he'd been killed. I'd been studying him since I stumbled upon him, literally. I pegged him as out of town businessman, as I didn't recognize him and he was too old to be here for the college. No matter how badly I wanted to know his name, all his information, everything, I had not gotten any closer than this. I can act with restraint. Sometimes.

The three looked at the body, hidden by shadows and the slight slope of the ground away from the road. Away from where anyone would notice.

"Cori? Why were you here and how in the world did you notice this body?" Samuel asked.

After so long with all the 'incidents' surrounding me, I didn't even try to make up anything believable anymore. "I was walking to work, the long way," I interjected before anyone could point out this path was a mile longer than a direct route from my house. They didn't need to know why I wanted the long quiet walk to think. "A white cat chased a squirrel across the road, catching my attention. Pretty sure it was Mrs. Hansen's Mortimer. I stopped to watch, not sure which of them I was rooting for, when the squirrel did a ninety degree turn and ran up my body. The cat followed, claws and all." I pointed at my jeans and the holes with drops of blood creating dark spots on the legs. "I fell backwards

7

Mel Todd

and tumbled as they finished running over the top of me. When I sat up his head was the first thing I saw." I waved at the rest of the body. "I came back up to the sidewalk and called 911."

None of them even blinked at my story. This was just proof of how weird my life was.

"And you didn't touch anything, right?" Samuel asked, even as Jeff and Sally made their way down.

This time I didn't restrain myself. "No, I crawled all over the dead man, licked him, then decided to play with whatever killed him because it was my first time seeing a dead body and I couldn't resist." My arms crossed over my chest as I stared at him.

Screw it, I'd walk.

"Point. Sorry, Cori. Habit. I forgot you're you."

"Gee, thanks." I didn't even try to keep a civil tone. That had been uncalled for.

"I said sorry," he muttered as he turned back to look at Jeff and Sally coming back up.

"Very dead. Nothing we can do. You'll need to call the coroner. He'll want to see the body in situ, so no reason for us to stay," Sally stated as she pulled the gurney back towards the ambulance.

"Thanks, guys," Samuel said, his tone distracted as he pulled out the radio.

I walked a few feet away giving him privacy to do what was necessary. But he'd have to stay here and wait for the coroner. I might as well just walk to work. I kept looking back at where the body lay. Death fascinated me. It was the greatest mystery and the one I wanted to stop from taking people. Which meant the desire to poke and prod at dead body number thirteen was tangible. My phone vibrated, distracting me, and I pulled it out of my pocket.

*Another one? Cori, your luck. Fine. Just get here

8

soon as you can.* This was from my boss.

Oooh, was it gory like the last one? You need to give me all the deets when you get in. That was from my coworker Kadia.

I just shook my head and put my phone away. Jo, my best friend, was probably already at work, but no reason to distract her with this. I'd tell her later tonight. See if I could talk her mom into feeding me again. I was very tired of microwaved dinners, but every time I tried to cook something it went wrong. I'd given up.

Samuel was walking back towards me. "May I head off to work? I'm late as it is. You know where to find me."

"True. You are predictable. Either work at Grind Down, school at West Georgia, or at Jo Guzman's place. Last ditch your apartment over the garage," he rattled off. They'd gotten good at finding me over the years.

"Hey, at least you know I'm not trying to avoid you."

"Ha, I almost expect you to start a social media account logging all of this." He paused and looked at me suspiciously. "You haven't, have you?"

"No, I haven't." Like I had any desire to document just how screwed up my life was. Before I could say anything else another car pulled up next to where we were standing. We both turned to look at it and I silently cheered as the coroner stepped out. Maybe I would get my ride to work after all.

Chapter 2

Each class of magic has four branches. Chaos is composed of Entropy, Fire, Water, and Time. Order has Pattern, Air, Earth, and Transform. Spirit (the rarest of the classes) has Soul, Relativity, Non-Organic, and Psychic. Every non-merlin, even the lowest rank, hedgemages, are strong in one, pale in two, and null in the final branch. ~ History of Magic

ORDER

Why is there so much bureaucracy surrounding death? How long can he ask us questions? I didn't touch the damn body.

The coroner started out with a string of questions and I began to feel like I was the one under attack. Once he looked at the body he calmed down, but it took another fifteen minutes before he let us go. After a brief discussion with Samuel, the coroner called in a forensic unit. Samuel called in another officer to watch the scene, then gave in to my completely unsubtle hinting.

"Get in, Cori. I'll drive you to work and let Molly know why you were late." Each word sounded like it had been pulled out of him, but I didn't care. I slid into the front seat and pretended not to see his glare of exasperation. That was becoming my new goal in life— to not exasperate people. Or maybe I'd keep that as my life goal, to exasperate everyone. I rolled the word around in my head, but the excitement of being a pain faded fast.

"Molly knows. Sent her a text, but she'd probably like to know I wasn't making it up." I didn't really look at him as I talked, or even listen, too wrapped up in my own thoughts. I glanced in the rearview mirror at the receding vehicles, all my questions unanswered. My amber brown eyes stared back at me and I swore I could see the hole in my soul. The missing half of me. I pushed it down. Study, work, Jo. That was all I needed. Someday I would have answers about why Stevie had died. I had to find them.

"Cori!" Samuel all but shouted and I jumped, looking at him, my heart racing.

"What?"

He shook his head at me, trying to give me the "I'm disappointed in you" look that Laurel did so well, but he didn't have the age to pull it off. "I've been asking you a question."

"Sorry, was lost in my head. Thinking about that guy."

"Don't. He isn't your issue." He said it like that should be enough to shut my mind off.

I shot him a glance, but didn't argue; what good would it do? "What was the question?"

"Did you notice anything else weird as you walked? Any cars or anything else?"

"Besides the cat and squirrel running up and over me?" I watched him out of the corner of my eye and saw his mouth twitch a little.

"Besides that."

I closed my eyes and thought, but I really had been oblivious to most everything. My thoughts were stressing over graduating, finding a job, and getting the hell out of this town. But that meant leaving Jo and her family. That thought made me want to cry.

"I wasn't paying attention really. The cat was white, so it caught my eye and I stopped to watch. The rest of the time I was more focused on my own thoughts." I hated admitting I couldn't provide a clue, that I didn't have any information to give him.

"With your luck that's a bit dangerous, isn't it?" The smirk was back. I ignored it. Just because he'd known me as a little kid didn't mean I had to put up with him being a jerk. I felt myself flush with annoyance but pushed it away.

"Let me out up here. I'll slip in the back. They're already open and probably slammed."

Samuel nodded and turned to go up the back alley when there was a bang and the car shook. I froze, hand on the dashboard as I quickly scanned for bullets or another car or something. A beeping came from the console and Samuel started to cuss softly.

"I swear to the Merlins, Cori. Something always goes wacky and I'm not always positive you had nothing to do with it." He pointed accusingly at the light flashing on his dash. I leaned over and peered and it and fought a smirk.

"That's what you get for being a jerk. Have fun changing your tire." This time there was a smile on my face as I chirped my goodbye at him and opened the door. I ignored his muttered response, shutting the door and looking at the very flat front passenger tire. At least it had waited until I was almost at work.

I headed down the alley to find the back door wedged open, probably for the deliveries. With a tug I pulled it wide and headed into the back of the already busy shop. I glanced at my watch; only forty minutes late. The big rush would just be starting. Darting to the back I washed my hands and face, stopping for a moment to look at the image of me in a mirror. Did it look like I'd seen another dead body?

Please, like that is anything unusual. Get to work before Molly kills you.

12

I bent over at the waist and spent a minute running my fingers through my short hair briskly, trying to shake out the ever-present dandruff. It was annoying. No shampoo would cure it, it was always bright white, and it was so fine it almost looked like dust. With a shake of my head, the short strands flying back into place, I turned and stepped into the hustle while mentally asking for nothing else weird to happen today. Not that I was ever that lucky.

Kadia was cranking out drinks, chattering with customers and flashing her trademark grin. She loved showing off her mage status through jewelry or clothes. When she emerged, two candles bursting into flames and a rush of dizziness had been the only indicators. But she'd rushed in to be tested, coming back with Fire hedgemage status. It didn't seem to upset her she was so low. It meant she'd never need matches if she wanted to smoke and could warm up her coffee if it got cold. But there was no draft, no mandatory college for anyone lower than wizard ranking. Kadia being Kadia, just said it would help her be a great chef. She'd be graduating from her culinary classes this summer, and already had a job lined up.

In stark contrast to Kadia's grace, Molly struggled to handle the register and socialize with the people waiting for her. Molly Carter was a great boss and a good businesswoman, but a deplorable counter person. She could juggle the business stuff in the quiet of her office on her computer, but having people rattling off orders at her, paying in multiple ways, and trying to fill the easy drinks in between made her panic and become even more stressed. I'd always thought a customer-centric business was a weird choice for someone with social anxiety.

"Here, I've got it," I said stepping in behind her. I

liked this job. By the end of the first month I had figured out how to troubleshoot the equipment and fix it if needed. We kept extra cleaning supplies for all the weird accidents that happened. Molly had kept me employed almost full time for three years now without any complaints. Best part is she rolled with all my schedule changes. In return, I worked my ass off for her, looking for anything I could do to make the shop and our lives better.

"Thank Merlin. All yours." Molly stepped back with a relieved look on her face. "You okay?"

I smiled at the customer and nodded. "Yep, just the usual."

"Only you, Cori. I'll be in back. Don't need me. This morning has peopled me out." Molly babbled as she backed out and all but ran to the back office.

Trying not to laugh, I turned to the waiting customer and took their order. Kadia and I meshed well, switching between the register and pulling drinks. The day went well until a double ring of the bell after the morning rush caught my attention. Looking at the door, I sighed as Shay stood there glaring at me.

O'Shaughnessy Sato had copper red hair, Asian features, a lean body, and chin length hair. Together they created an exotic picture of a man and a first-rate pain in my ass. Then there was the merlin tattoo that gleamed on the side of his face. It almost touched his right eye in swirls of red and yellow, triple symbols proof he was a Chaos merlin strong in Earth and Time.

Sally was a Pattern wizard, pale in Transform and Earth. Which meant she couldn't use Air magic at all. But merlins were different. Powerful. Scary. Stories and movies revolved around them, as the heroes or the villains in everything.

Me? The only merlin I knew was a confusing jerk.

Shay?. I always thought it was weird a merlin would live here of all places.

Why do I always get Shay on my shift? Why?

He felt the same as he stalked towards me, the last customer turning away as he got to the counter. "Why are you here?" he demanded, glaring at me as if I'd caused him some personal affront.

"Because I work here? I have for the last three years. Something you should know as you see me every time I'm at work."

"You were not on the schedule. I checked. Three times!" He all but shouted.

"Lori called out. I said I'd cover as school hasn't started up. I'm working a double today." Normally on Wednesdays I only worked from noon until four, but hey, extra money.

Shay glared at me and I glared back. The other nice thing about small towns was, if you were a jerk to someone who deserved it, no one complained to your manager. Or if they did, the manager laughed. Molly had, multiple times. The best one had been when she told a customer, "If Cori dumps a hot coffee on your head, I'm going to laugh and say you deserved it."

But Shay never crossed that line. Our altercations were always verbal and I had no idea why he found my existence such an affront. Part of me wanted to figure out why, quiz and assail him with questions, but after three years I mostly wanted him to quit being a jerk.

Shay huffed. "Damn probability factors. Just because all the threads point to convergence in your presence doesn't mean I want to be there when it happens. Maybe I should give up coffee."

He didn't seem to be talking to me, but I answered anyhow. "There's a Waffle House down the street. Feel free to get your fix there."

Shay wrinkled his nose. "Not even probability convergence is worth their coffee. Double espresso almond milk chaser." He tossed the money at me and stalked over to the other side of the counter where Kadia already had his order waiting. Shay was predictable, but he also tipped well. I dumped the two dollars into the tip jar and put on a smile as another person came up.

Three hours later my feet were sore; it had been a busy day. The lull before lunch had occurred and the only people still in the shop were a pair of retired teachers who met twice a week for a social hour. They were so cute and fragile I always made sure Kadia served them. If my crazy attacked while I was serving them and they got hurt, I'd never forgive myself.

Kadia yawned. "That was quite the morning. But now that it's calmed down a bit – tell me what happened?"

I shrugged. People thought it was neat finding a dead body. When the first one shatters you, the rest quickly become annoying. More people needed to die at home quietly in their beds.

"Just a dead guy. Business suit."

"Ewww," she squealed shaking her head, causing her long braids with beads on the end to clack. But her avid eyes told me she was fascinated. I wasn't, but this was a conversation I had with way too many people every time something happened. "So how did he die?"

"Don't know. They yell at me if I say anything about cause of death." I dropped my voice, not wanting anyone to hear me, or at least not clearly. "But I will say his head wasn't attached to his body."

Her eyes went wide. "We have a serial killer?" Her voice squeaked and I rolled my eyes.

"Here? In Rockway, Georgia? Please. That's an Atlanta thing. Probably going to be something stupid

16

and boring." Unfortunately, most of the bodies I found were rarely stupid or boring.

Kadia started to say something when one of the women called for her. As I busied myself restocking muffins and cookies and cleaning up the espresso machine, my mind wandered off, going through the list of dead people.

I don't talk about the first death, the one I can't forget. That was at twelve. It was the one that drove me to find answers. My brother, Stevie.

When I was thirteen Mr. Johnson, had a heart attack out walking his dog. I found him but didn't know how to do CPR. He died while I watched. Useless again.

At fifteen it was a couple that had a car accident while I was home alone. They slammed into the light pole outside the house. I called 911 but they had been killed on impact. Nothing I could have done.

At least I wasn't alone with the death that happened at sixteen. Our English teacher had a stroke in the middle of class and dropped dead. I was just the only one sane enough to call 911 and the office.

The year I turned sixteen was busy. A piano being hoisted into an office building fell on one of the workers, killing him. I was ten feet away. Being splattered with blood was not fun, but again I called 911.

At seventeen I found a really weird and creepy death. Guy fell out of the sky on to a picket fence as I walked to school. By then I had my first aid training, but when I touched him, his body was mush. He died as I called for help. Turns out he'd been parachuting and in a freak accident his harness broke, dropping him at my feet. That had been gross. Bone should not be mushy.

I kept cleaning and restocking, still going over each face, each death in my mind. If I got my degree and my job, would I save enough to erase them from my mind?

Would I figure out the reason for the first death? Would it solve anything?

Too many questions, too many missing answers to things I needed to know. I started back on my list; it had become a habit, a comfort I sank into. When I needed to prove to myself that I hadn't forgotten. That I would never forget him, I went over the deaths. Every time asking myself what I could have done differently. The death at eighteen was the worst. It would have taken a merlin to save him.

Merlins.

The word rang in my mind. The hope and bane of most people, everyone wanted to be one. No one wanted to need one. The highest rank magic user there was. They didn't have limits. They could do almost anything. Yet Shay came in regularly like anyone else. Only his ability to annoy me seemed epic in any way.

Why in the world was this what I was thinking about? My family wasn't magical, at least nothing recent. Family legend, well that went back to Spain centuries ago and only my grandmother even remembered the stories her grandmother had told. But that was of a kid, well before the ruptures that let magic into the world occurred. Besides, grandma died ages ago. So, not like I could ask her.

Why am I thinking about this? I should be thinking about school next week.

A flicker of color caught my attention and I glanced up at the TV and everything clicked into place. A news story about the emergence of a new merlin and a recap of the history of the Emergence of Magic. Like anyone who lived today didn't know about magic. It was embedded in our world. The speaker did better than my high school teacher did, making the emergence of magic in the early 1800's sound interesting and exciting. All

Mrs. Roulf had ever done was bore us to tears. It took talent to make magic boring. The reporter continued, talking about the various ranks of magic users and reminding people of the laws surrounding mages.

I pushed the overview of magic out of my mind and finished up my work. The lunch crowd would want stuff to ward off the January cold, if you called high fifties cold. The clatter of the bell had me glancing up in time to see the door fall off its hinges and crash to the ground with a horrendous explosion. I looked up to see Laurel Amosen staring down at the door, the look on her face one of startled shock, a normal reaction. As she looked up at me her face hardened and her uniform echoed her focus, all sharp and crisp.

Watching Laurel stalk towards me, military training dripping off her like water with her short cropped black curly hair and purposeful stride, it became apparent I was the goal. I had no desire to be the goal of the chief of police. She came to a precise halt in front of the counter, mouth opening.

Before she could say anything, I did. "So, are you going to reimburse Molly for tearing her door off the hinges, Chief Amosen?"

All mages are broken into four groups. The lowest are hedgemages, those with little power. They aren't required to be marked, and many live out their lives without making offerings and rarely use magic at all. Then you have magicians, wizards, archmages, and of course merlins. All of these ranks are part of the draft. ~ History of Magic

SPIRIT

Huh, apparently giving the chief of police attitude isn't a good way to start the conversation. Lesson learned.

Sitting in the interrogation room, alone and a bit freaked out, I stared at the mirrored glass and tried to keep a smirk on my face. I still thought my comment was funny and if I kept thinking it was funny maybe I wouldn't break down in tears. Too bad Chief Amosen hadn't. Her lack of humor probably contributed to my riding to the station in the back of her squad car and why I now fought worry and fear. I had no idea why I was sitting in the police station.

After waiting what seemed like forever, at least ten minutes, the chief walked in. This time she flashed me a smile that wasn't completely fake. Her tat glinted at me. Somehow hers was outlined in gold, the Water section a bright yellow. It looked good on her.

"Your mouth fires off when it really shouldn't," she commented as she sat down in the other chair.

"Defense mechanism," slipped out and I clamped my mouth shut. The last thing I needed was to tell her anything about my internal woes. She wasn't interested.

"So why am I here?"

She gave me a long look and I shrugged; my conscience was clean. While weird things happened around me, I didn't get in trouble, not really. Last run-in with the cops had been at least three years ago, a high school egging prank.

"How did you know the victim?" Her voice remained flat and she watched me like she might pull the answers out of my head. I didn't think Water wizards could do that. Not that I had any answers for her to pull out.

"The who? You mean the dead guy from this morning?" At this point I was lost, what was she talking about?

"Yes, the man from this morning. How did you know him?"

My reflection in the mirror showed my jaw hanging open. I snapped my mouth closed and stared at my image as if there might be an answer in my reflection. The panicked look in my eyes and the oversized dark grey t-shirt displaying the Grind Down's logo in bright blue, which seemed almost garish under the florescent lights, held no answers.

"Um, I didn't. I told Samuel that. What's going on?" I resisted scratching my head. White on grey would stand out way too much.

"You didn't talk to him at Grind Down, run into him at class, hire him to do something?"

"Not that I know of. I mean I might have served him and not noticed, but I didn't recognize him. Granted, dead you look different." That comment made me swallow as Stevie's image flashed in my mind. Dead, lifeless, looking nothing like how he had just moments before. I pushed the image away; it never changed, so dwelling on it until I had answers was useless.

"So, you are sure you don't know," she paused

glancing down at her notes, "Harold Court Jr?"

I riffled through my memories, but nothing about the name seemed at all familiar. "I don't think so. Look, Chief Amosen, should I be calling a lawyer or something?" I had no money to pay one. No idea what one would do, but for the first time in a long time I was scared. Why was I here? They had to know I had nothing to do with his death. Didn't they?

My heart raced as she looked up and locked eyes with me. The camera in the corner exploded in a shower of sparks. We both whipped around to look at it, wisps of smoke rising up from it.

"What is it with you and crap happening?" Laurel sighed and dropped the badass attitude, which didn't make me feel much better. "For the record, you have never met Harold Court Jr., never hired him, or asked him to do something for you?"

"For the record, no. I have no blasted idea what you're talking about." I tried not to panic but being in the police station like this was stripping out my bravado quickly. I wanted my own little sad world back. I knew I wouldn't get to keep it for much longer, but while I could, I wanted to hold it close.

She glanced at the camera, sighed again, and stood. "Come on. Let's finish this in my office. The smoke is giving me a headache."

Standing took me a second as my knees trembled. She waited at the door, holding it open for me. As we walked out, she waved at another officer. "Go check on that camera. I want to know why it exploded."

The officer smirked at me. "Catastrophe Cori struck again?"

"No such thing, just crap made in China. Get it taken care of. Come on, Cori. I'm sure you'd like to get back to work." Laurel turned and headed down the hall at a quick pace, annoyance in her every step.

I nodded, silently following her. The nickname usually made me smile, mostly because it was accurate. Things happened around me. The urge to scratch my head gnawed at me, but I followed, still unsure as to the whole reason I was here. I needed to quit reporting dead bodies if they were going to think I had anything to do with their deaths.

She went into her office, dropping into her chair with a sigh. "Sit, Cori. You don't need a lawyer. You're not in trouble."

I didn't particularly believe her, I mean she had dragged me into the police station, but I sat in the chair and looked at her warily.

"Do you know any reason why a private investigator from New York would have your name, or a variation of it, in his wallet?"

My jaw dropped back down.

She snorted. "I'll take that as a no."

"Wait, what?" There were so many things in her question it took me a bit to unpack them. "Private investigator? My name? Variation?"

She pulled out a sheet of paper and slid it over to me. On it was a photocopy of something that looked like a sticky note in a baggie. Written in blocky letters was a name, my name, well kinda. It was spelled with a K, not a C and the last name was spelled different.

Kory Monroe.

"That isn't my name," I pointed out. It was a lame comment, I knew that, but it still freaked me out. Because it sounded like my name if you said it.

"Which is why I asked. You don't know of any reason someone might be looking for you?"

Without conscious thought, my head was shaking back and forth. "No, ma'am." My snark was all gone. I'd

Mel Todd

lived here most of my life. My parents lived here.
Everyone knew me and my oddities. So why would
someone have my name in their pocket?

"I figured as much. Okay. You need a ride back to
work?"

They'd taken my phone, but my watch told me it was
after noon. Kadia and Molly would be dying. Both of
curiosity and worry.

"Yes, please, ma'am."

She waved me out of the office and fifteen minutes
later I was in the back of a squad car, again, being driven
to work.

"Just drop me a block or so away?" I asked from the
back. I got a grunt of agreement as a response, but I
didn't care. I had my phone back and I needed to call Jo.

The cop let me out at the corner. There was a small
green space and a bench, and I dropped on it, hitting the
first name in my favorites list, "Jo-Jo Guz".

As it rang, I sat on the bench watching cars going by,
but all I could do was try to figure out why anyone
would be looking for me. And I failed completely.

"Yo, Cori. What up?" Jo's bright voice, with the lilt of
Spanish still in it and the background of power tools
whirling. A bit younger than me, Jo planned on working
in her dad's shop until she reached twenty-four or
emerged. I'd been the oldest kid in my high school class;
missing a year of school does that. But in nine months
she'd be twenty-one. If you turned twenty-four without
emerging, the odds were you'd never become a mage,
especially girls. Magic showed up when puberty ended.
Lots of young adults went into the military or civil
service until they turned twenty-five, then they decided
on a career. Magic could and would affect your choices,
so why spend time and money on something magic
might completely change.

24

I knew Jo was getting stressed about not emerging. Most of her family were hedges or wizards, her dad was a Pattern wizard while her mom was a Fire wizard, not that she did much with it besides be the best cook ever. But either way Jo'd have a job at the shop, something she enjoyed even if she didn't emerge. I still looked for a place to belong like that. But I knew she had other plans. Other hopes and dreams.

"I found another dead body today."

"Eww. Why can't you ever find money or winning lottery tickets?" Jo must have walked outside as the noise level dropped. "Was it gruesome?"

"Not really. Just odd, I mean I've never seen a head separated from the body before."

"Oh, gross. Mi amiga, you have issues that a body like that doesn't affect you," she said, her accent getting more lyrical.

"That isn't the important part," I blurted, my fingers tingling 'cause I was clenching the bench and my phone so hard. I wiggled them as I watched a repair company truck pull up next to Grind Down, probably to fix the door.

"Okay? What's the important part?" She sounded confused and I didn't blame her. I was confused and a bit weirded out.

"He had my name!" I didn't quite screech that last part, but it was close. With a forced cough I cleared my throat and continued talking, this time trying to keep the hysterics down. "He had a piece of paper with my name on it, well sounded like my name. He spelled it with a K and M-o-n-r-o-e instead of M-u-n-r-o-e."

Jo was silent on the other end. "What do you want? I can come get you. We can track him down. Do you need to stay with me?"

Something in me melted and I wanted to sob, but

that would be silly. "Thank you. Can I come over after work? Maybe get dinner?" I hated to ask, but while the job covered school and my phone, it didn't leave much left after. My parents paid the utilities, and I got health insurance through them, but otherwise, nothing. Besides, the Guzman's made me feel like family. Like I was wanted.

"Cori! If I told mom you asked that, she'd have your hide. You are family. You know that. Get over early and you can help her roll tamales."

My mouth watered at the thought. Marisol Guzman still made them the old way, with cornmeal and corn husks, and they were so good. "Will do. Thanks, Jo-Jo."

"Stop it. We're family. Now you get to work and I need to get back before Stinky throws a fit."

I snickered and said goodbye, then headed back to Grind Down. The handymen were re-securing the door as I slipped in.

"CORI!" Both Kadia and Molly yelled as I walked in. They all but swarmed me, ignoring the customers wanting their afternoon caffeine boosts.

"Are you okay? What did they want?" Molly asked, her eyes worried. She checked me over as if expecting to find out that I'd been roughed up or something.

"What did you do? Do they think you murdered him?" Kadia asked, the picture of small-town gossip.

"Nothing. They just needed to ask me some more questions about the guy this morning. I suspect Chief Amosen would have asked me here, but—" I paused and nodded at the fallen door—"my mouthing off annoyed her." Suddenly I didn't want to tell anyone but Jo. I felt like I had a target on my back and that made no sense. Who would be interested in me?

I continued to assure them it was routine, just some standard questioning and after a few minutes the crowd of people encouraged us to get back to work. I did it with a fervor. Anything to keep me distracted. It didn't work.

After we closed at six, I spent an hour cleaning and prepping, mercifully alone, I had worked myself into a nervous wreck.

Lost heiress

Kidnap victim

Identify fraud

Serial killer target.

The possibilities and reasons spun in my head until, "ARGH!" I screamed it at the top of my lungs in the empty shop. In response a can of coffee beans slipped off the counter and spilled all over the floor. I slumped over my broom, looked at the beans, and started to clean them up. "Catastrophe Cori, indeed."

Chapter 4

The magic wave that appeared in the 1850s seemed to come from nowhere, though later studies showed it rippled outward from the tears between our reality and others. The location of these planar rips was discovered in what is now Area 51. The US government put it under top secret security prior to World War I. But some information was verified before the true understanding of it registered. Three rips, one to each plane labeled Chaos, Order, and Spirit hung in the middle of the Nevada desert. No one discovered what it meant until the 1950s when they closed for a decade. ~ History of Magic

CHAOS

It took me another fifteen minutes to get all the beans cleaned up and finish locking up. I stepped out into the cold night air and pulled my jacket tighter. With a sigh, I started walking to Jo's. Only two miles, I used the time to think. But all I could do was wonder why my life was so blasted weird. People asked me if I'd get magic tested, but you knew when you emerged, and it was always after puberty. I hadn't, so why bother? I didn't need one more thing to tell me I'd failed. Each step seemed heavier and slower than the one before. Even the thought of tamales couldn't get me to pick up the pace.

The winter sky had reached full dark as I trudged up the street to Jo's. Jo or any of her family would have come and gotten me, but it felt like I asked them for so much. So, I refused to ask them for more if I could avoid it. Food was always my weakness.

Usually my disasters didn't directly affect me, or even hurt me, and all of them were things that could, and occasionally did, happen to others. But when I tried to cook meals, everything went wrong. Hence my dependence on either food I could microwave, or Jo's mom.

I turned the front door handle and called out as I stepped in. "It's me!" Shutting the door behind me I slipped off my coat and wandered towards the kitchen.

"My Cori," Marisol exclaimed from the counter. "I would hug you, *mi pequeño*, but..." She held up her hands—they were both covered with cornmeal. My mouth started to water just thinking about it.

"Jo said you were making tamales. Want help?"

"From you? No. I like my kitchen in one piece. Set the table, *por favor*?" She had already gone back to expertly making the delicious treats.

"How many?" Their family was liquid; I was proof of that. Paolo, Jo's oldest brother, had his own place, but since he still hadn't found a girl who could handle the Guzman's, he often came to dinner. Marco was in constant demand by the various girlfriends he had; they all knew each other and usually ate out in a big group. Sanchez, or as everyone called him, Stinky, would be at dinner. He'd rather be playing video games than anything else, even though he worked for his dad as a tow truck driver and provided roadside assistance for most of the insurance companies in the area.

"Oh, just five. Marco and Paolo are out tonight." Marisol shot me a wicked grin. "It's the fifth date with the same girl for Paolo, so maybe I might get to meet her soon."

I laughed. Marisol wanted grandkids but not until her children had steady jobs. Paolo, at twenty-five and with his certifications in car mechanics, would most likely

Mel Todd

take over the shop when Henri, Jo's dad, retired. What Sanchez wanted to do was still up in the air.

"Don't count the grandbabies until after the wedding."

"Oh, I won't pressure him but that doesn't mean I can't hope. The chips are in the cupboard." Marisol finished making the tamales and tossed them in the pressure cooker to finish. I helped until she shooed me out of the kitchen.

I grabbed a few chips and collapsed on the couch, exhausted to the point that my anxiety over the PI had faded. Pulling my phone out, I glared at it, then texted Jo.

Where are you? I'm here. Need food.

I stared at the phone as if that would make her respond faster. Instead the back door to the garage opened.

"*Mi carino*, I'm home," Henri Guzman called out. I had to fight a smile. They were so cute. A flash of sorrow washed through me as what I'd lost when Stevie died hit me again. There were quick footsteps coming down the hall and Jo tore into the living room.

"There you are. Come with me while I change, and tell me everything," she ordered, grabbing my hand and pulling me up and with her.

Jo was a force of nature and my best friend. Her long black hair had been pulled up in a ponytail and her jeans curved her ass in a way that made every man look at her. Too bad she preferred girls and we both felt too much like sisters to ever date each other. The second her door was closed she began stripping grease-covered clothes off, revealing the heart on her hip that matched the one on mine. Her heart said 'BFF – Cori' while mine was 'BFF – Jo-Jo'. I hoped it would never change.

"You aren't talking. Why aren't you talking? I can't

30

help if I don't know what is going on." She shot me a glare as she pulled off her shirt.

"You're going to jump into the shower in a second, and I hate yelling over the water. Wash and then I'll tell everyone at the dinner table." I flopped down on her bed, feeling morose and unloved. It was a good thing school started in a week; I thought too much when not drowning in deadlines and homework.

"Wow, you must be worried if you're telling *Mami* and *Papi*," she said, pausing with only her underwear on. She naturally posed, emphasizing her round full breasts, at least two cup sizes bigger than mine.

"You trying to get me to date you? It didn't work, remember? You kissed me at sixteen and you said it was worse than kissing Stinky."

Jo glanced down at her body and unconscious pose and laughed. "No. I'd rather keep you as my heart's sister. Maybe I can trade Stinky for you? *Mami* likes you better anyhow."

I rolled my eyes. It wasn't true. Her mother just adopted strays, and I was one of them. "Get. I'll tell everyone in a bit." Jo stuck her tongue out at me and headed to her private bathroom. That was a luxury wrested from her parents at sixteen after her brothers walked in on her showering, four times. They were jerks.

I stared at the ceiling trying to get my thoughts ordered. I'd almost succeeded when Jo came out dressed in sweats and a t-shirt. I levered myself off the bed and we headed down to dinner. Henri was there just settling into his chair. Henri's tattoo used to fascinate me as a kid. He'd had it done in a rich gold outline, then filled with a turquoise color that matched Marisol's favorite stone. His magic, Pattern wizard, worked well with his chosen profession as he could see where the cars broke and sometimes see better ways to repair them. He had served his four years of mandatory service at the Georgia State Department of Transportation after getting his degree. All mages at magician rank or higher were required to go to college and get degrees and the government paid for it. Your minor was always your strongest magic class. They taught you how to control it, make the offerings and the various spells, but then took the equivalent in work as payment.

Henri had his degree in Mechanical engineering with a minor in Pattern, but he didn't care enough to make magic his primary focus; it was a tool like anything else. He loved working with his hands so used his knowledge of mechanics and willingness to work to start his own business. Marisol on the other hand was a Fire mage, and personally I thought that was why she was such a good cook. She taught math at the local middle school and most everyone liked her. Her tattoo was red and black, and I always expected it to flicker with flames, especially when she was mad. It never did, to my disappointment. But then I didn't usually see her mad.

We settled in, saying grace, which still made me uncomfortable, then started passing around food.

"So, Cori, how was your day?" Henri asked once people had food on their plates. My appetite disappeared and I sighed.

The table went quiet and everyone focused on me, even Stinky. Jo elbowed me in the ribs. "Tell them. Heck, tell me. I still want the details."

Though being in the spotlight was something I'd almost gotten used to, it still felt uncomfortable to have my second family staring at me like this. Even Stinky. I cleared my throat and explained everything. The dead guy, calling the police, the chief coming to get me, the questioning, and the fact that he had my name.

"That is not good. I'll help you figure out who he was and why he had your name." Jo's declaration made me smile. She always had my back.

"Well, we do have a name. He's a private investigator from New York. Harold Court Jr. And, to be accurate, the name was Kory Monroe." I spelled it out so they could see the difference.

"That sounds too close for comfort. I could see hearing your name and spelling it like that. I do not like this." Henri frowned and turned his gaze towards Jo, who had an intent look on her face. "I will not forbid it, I can't. You are both adults. But be careful, and if you are out at night, call one of the boys." He gave Stinky a look. "Sanchez, that means you and your brothers will not have an issue going somewhere with them."

My worry spiked when Stinky didn't protest. He nodded and looked at me. "This doesn't sound good. No going off on your crazy adventures by yourself. Either of you."

Jo sighed, but I felt warm. They weren't my family, but they made me feel like I was theirs. Some days it was the only thing that kept me sane.

"Thanks. But I wanted to ask if anyone had asked about me. I don't have a picture of him, but maybe someone was around looking for someone by my name?"

They all looked at each other and then shook their heads.

Henri said, "Not that I would have told them anything, but I also would have let you know." He frowned as he ate, using the chewing of his food to give him time to think. I'd seen him do this over the years and it still made me smile every time. "Why would someone be looking for you?"

"I don't know. I've thought of everything and I can't figure out any reason." I hated admitting that, but it was true. I was a young woman in rural Georgia, not anyone famous. I had decent grades, was non-magical, with average looks. I wasn't good enough at sports to be on any of the pre-professional teams. So why would anyone want to find me? Either way it was time to change the topic of conversation.

"Jo, you still putting in your applications for trade schools?" I knew the answer to that, but I knew her parents didn't. My smile was beatific as she glared at me, then ducked her head.

"I thought you were going to wait and see if you emerged?" Marisol sounded confused and vaguely hurt. "Then you could go to college and have a guaranteed job after you got out for four years."

"I know. But the odds are if I emerge," she was interrupted by both parents saying "will emerge" and continued after a soft sigh. "If I emerge, I'll be a hedgie. So, I'd rather go and get my Associates Degree with something that will help dad with the shop. There are lots of certs I can get after the AA that mean we can repair and work on more cars. I like working on them, it'll be a way I can help us all. It's smart." Her voice almost pleaded at the end and I reached over and squeezed her hand. Jo shot me a relieved look. We had spent many evenings discussing future plans. I understood her practicality, and I shared it. It drove my need to go to college immediately instead of waiting until after all possibility of emergence had passed. I knew I'd never emerge, and I needed the skills to get a good paying job now. The possibility my parents, landlords, could rip the apartment away from me at any moment was just one more thing that drove me to become independent.

Marisol and Henri looked at each other, an entire argument being conducted with looks and head gestures. Then Henri nodded to his wife.

"Very well, Josefa. If you emerge and are less than a magician, you can continue with your plan and get the certifications you've talked about. I won't deny it would be a help as two of your brothers don't want to stay in the car repair business. But if you come out at magician or higher, you are guaranteed a degree. One that lets you follow your dreams. Promise me, Josefa. I know you don't mind working on cars, but that isn't what you dream."

Jo didn't look at anyone, her fingers fiddling with the corn husk wrappers discarded on her plate.

I nudged her with an elbow. "Tell them. Or I will."

Jo huffed out a breath and glared at me sideways. "Traitor."

"Nope. I just know what you really want."

"Fine." She pouted, but I knew she was relieved to actually tell her parents. Normally she hid her own wants so that she could help everyone else. "I'd really like to be some sort of mechanical engineer. I love engines and electricity and how to generate it. I want to figure out how to build better cars and make it so they're safer for everyone. But without it being paid for, I, we, can't afford it. So, I was going to work on cars. Because I do enjoy it. "

I kept my eyes on my own food, not wanting to look up. I might cry if I did. She'd mentioned it before, but she'd always said doctor before. As always, Jo wanted to help me figure out the thing that haunted my soul. I could feel her parents' eyes on me. They knew. They'd always known.

"I think that is an excellent idea." Marisol's voice was warm. "I do wish, Cori, you had waited to see if you emerged. Both of you going to college together would have been perfect."

Lifting my head, I managed to smile. "You know I won't. Parents are both non-magical." I hated the term norms—it implied mages weren't normal. At this point they were more common than blue eyes, though merlins were still as rare as truly violet eyes and just as noticeable. With a shake of my head, as if I could rattle my thoughts back into the dark corners of my mind, I smiled. "We'll make it work. I'm not letting her go that easily."

Stinky mock leered at me. "I'd date you, Cori. Then you'd really be family."

"Ewwww," Jo and I said in unison as Henri reached out and bopped his son on the back of the head. Sanchez was a good young man, but he'd been the annoying older brother stuck watching his sister. And the thought of dating him made my stomach turn. I'd rather date Jo. It wasn't anything personal, just that he was Stinky. The childhood name had stuck when as a tween, he'd picked up a skunk by the tail on a dare. The expected happened and he had a nickname that years later still stuck to him the way that stink had. But Sanchez and I were not couple material.

Stinky pouted at me and reached over to pick up the pitcher of water to refill his glass. As he lifted it up to pour the water out, the handle snapped off and dumped the water into his lap.

Now soaked, he looked at all of us, eyes wide in surprise. We broke into laughter as Stinky mock scowled at us. I got up and grabbed a towel so he could wipe up. He might be a pain and care too much about his computer games, but he was a good brother and would be there for us if we needed him.

Chapter 5

While mages pulled in by the draft are given the leeway to decide what degree they choose, often they are encouraged to the point of being told to follow degrees that mesh well with their strongest branch. For example, if you are a Fire wizard, then you'd be encouraged towards things that use fire: industrial engineering, cooking, solar physics. Someone strong in Transform is pushed towards medicine, biology, or chemistry. What you are pale in can be taken into consideration, but a good mage learns to combine all their branches for the best effect. ~ History of Magic

ORDER

True to his word, Stinky drove me home. Jo and I had plans for tomorrow to start researching who this guy was and see if we could figure out anything about it. Worst case I'd go down to the police station and see what the two of us could wheedle out of Samuel. Even though Samuel knew Jo liked women, he still could be swayed by her teasing. It was her superpower—neither men nor women could resist her.

I walked up to the detached garage and started up the steps. Between all the walking I did and these stairs, I didn't have to worry about staying in shape, though I really needed to put on some weight. A burst of laughter grabbed my attention and I stopped at the landing, leaning on the railing looking down towards my parent's house. From the landing leading to my apartment over the garage I could see through the large picture windows into the living room. They normally kept the curtains closed, but today they were open. I watched, riveted by what I saw.

In the living room my younger brother Kris, he had to be eight or maybe nine by now, ran around the living room shrieking in laughter as my dad chased him around. Mom leaned in the doorway, arms folded, an amused look on her face.

My heart seized as I watched, missing that, remembering what it had felt like for them to pay attention to me. Before. Someday I'd find a way to make them ... what? I didn't know what I wanted to find. Something that made them proud? Happy? I think they loved me. Maybe I was looking for something that would let them forgive me, and maybe I could forgive myself. Pushing it down, (that problem wouldn't be solved tonight,) I turned and headed into my apartment, locking the door behind me.

Originally built as a way to make extra money from the local college students who wanted a place close enough but not be part of the campus life, it became mine at 14. I guessed I was that college student it had been built for, not that they charged me rent. Everything was paid for and they left me two hundred a month to help with bills in an envelope under the mat.

Walking in I flipped on the lights and headed for my computer. I had some research to do. The clock on the wall stopped me. Nine o'clock. And I needed to be up by five am to get to work by six.

Thirty minutes. I can take that long to see what I can figure out.

I sat down in front of my laptop, one I'd bought with money from the Grind Down and used for all my schoolwork. It sat on an anti-static pad, had a surge protector, and was secured to the desk. I strapped an anti-static strap to my arm before I even lifted the lid.

With all the damage that happened to things around me, I couldn't afford to lose my laptop. I'd already had to replace my cheap microwave twice.

Pulling up the search engine, I typed in the guy's name and "New York". A minute later I found his website, his smiling face looking out at me. It fascinated me how different yet the same you looked when you were dead. Something was missing from the eyes after you died.

Clicking through the website didn't tell me much other than he specialized in missing persons. But I wasn't missing. I'd seen my baby photos. Heck, the doctor that delivered me came into the café sometimes, so it wasn't like I'd been stolen at birth or anything. And my name was on the birth certificate all spelled out. Corisande Lorelei Munroe. My grandmother's name had been Lorelei, not that I'd ever met her. She'd died a year before I was born, but Mom had wanted to honor her.

With a sigh I closed the laptop. There wasn't much that I could figure out or even find out. Maybe I'd call his office in the morning and see if I could find out anything. Disconnecting carefully, I stood up and stepped away. Exhausted from the day, I headed to the bedroom, only to trip over the rug in the hallway and slam into the bookshelf at the end of the hall. It tipped over and a cascade of heavy medical books, textbooks, school awards, and notebooks pummeled me.

Instinctively I covered my head. This wasn't my first time being attacked by inanimate objects. It happened pretty often. When the shower of objects stopped, I raised my head slowly and peered at the disaster.

So much for getting to bed on time.

I stood up and began putting things away. Leaving it would bug me so much it wasn't worth the effort. As I sorted and re-shelved, I wondered what else would happen with the dead guy and if I could make it to work on time.

Twenty minutes later, because there were a lot of papers that had fallen out when the notebooks popped open, I finished cleaning up. Ready for bed, a peal of laughter, oddly familiar laughter, caught my attention. Unable to resist, I walked to my door, opened it, and stepped out onto the deck. Pain wrapped my soul tight as I looked out on the scene.

Shrieking with laughter Kris ran around the lawn, a cape streaming from his shoulders, waving a sparkler in the dark January evening. They had the yard lights on, and it gave me a crystal- clear view of everything.

"I am Batman!" he shrieked. Mom and Dad stood on the porch watching, trying to convince him to come in, but neither were trying too hard. Instead they had looks on their faces I hadn't seen in longer than I could remember. Warm, caring, loving. My chest hurt and I fought to swallow as I watched him. He looked like me. Same dark hair and smile. I couldn't remember the color of his eyes. What were they? Brown like mine and Dads? Or more hazel like Mom's? So many questions that shouldn't exist.

Watching him, watching them, the family I didn't get to have, was like poking at a wound to see if it would start bleeding again. It didn't, but the pain spread out through every inch of my body. My head itched fiercely and I reached up to scratch, scattering that blasted dandruff everywhere. Something behind me in the apartment fell, but I didn't turn or even think about what disaster awaited me inside. I couldn't look away from them. An image of Stevie laughing popped into my mind, and for a second I saw him running around the lawn. I bit my lip hard as the memories spiraled through me.

Maybe I could go down there, get to talk to them. Maybe the pain had faded. Maybe they could look at me again.

Mom stepped off the porch, a smile making her look younger than the last time I was close enough to really see her. Kris had been about two then. She'd handed me the keys to the apartment, told me it was my place now. They'd pay for all the utilities and provide grocery money. That everything was explained in the envelope. All my stuff was already there. She'd turned and walked away, leaving me standing there. My brother babbled at Dad, looking at me as if I was a stranger. Which I guess I was.

I choked on the emotions in my throat. I should go in. Standing here, watching this hurt too much. As always, I searched my heart for anger or even resentment, but all I could find were questions. Why? What should I have done? Would they have been happier if I died instead? Did they blame me?

The reasons were obvious, but I shied away from that memory.

Why court pain? Instead I watched as Mom reached him, grabbing his arms and swinging him in a circle. He was getting big. He might be taller than Dad by the time he became a teenager. They looked so happy. I remembered that happiness. I'd been part of that once.

I couldn't tear my eyes away, wanting, needing, pleading to be there. Maybe I moved, or maybe the keening in my soul was audible. Estella, my Mom, looked up and her body froze, face staring in my direction. Her voice, sharp and high, emerged, though I couldn't make out what she said. My dad glanced up and he stiffened too. Kris looked up at me, a grin so wide I could see it from there, and waved at me. He kept waving even as they dragged him into the house and shut the door, locking me out.

41

Story of my life, always on the outside looking in.

I shook my head and went inside. I needed to get to bed so I could get to work tomorrow. The more I worked, the more I could save, and the sooner I could get away from here. Away from Jo? That hurt but compared to what happened every time I saw them, at least Jo would still talk to me.

Chapter 6

The rank of merlin, based on the legends of Merlin, was originally set as another word for mage. But over the years the meaning has changed. It is a title, a rank, but also the person and a favorite to use as an oath. When magic first arose, most mages were called merlins. But over time, as science and our knowledge about magic expanded, we saw there were different ranks to them. Now only those beyond our ability to measure are afforded that title and rank. ~ History of Magic

SPIRIT

I woke to my alarm blaring. With a groan, I struggled out of bed and over to the alarm clock to shut it off. The cute little mechanical alarm was a present from Jo a few years ago. The electric ones seemed to die, lose time, or just not go off. And if the clock was near me, I would somehow knock it off or have it break during the night. Having it on the shelf on the other side of the room worked well and I hadn't managed to kill it yet. That was impressive. The only other things that I'd kept for more than two years were my phone and laptop, but my paranoia about them might have been called excessive if the person saying that had never been in my presence for more than a few hours.

Mornings suck. Why do we have mornings? Thank the laws of magic we have coffee.

I stared bleary eyed at myself in the bathroom mirror wishing I'd already had a cup of coffee. With a groan I started the process of getting ready for the day. A quick shower in my tiny bathroom, hair and teeth brushed, I headed out the door and stopped at the envelope peeking out at me. I stood staring at it, the cold air stinging my face. I reached down, picked it up, and stepped back inside. The door closed to trap the heat inside, I opened it, wary and curious at the same time.

Five hundred dollars in hundred-dollar bills lay inside. A slip of paper fell out onto the counter. With fingers that I refused to let tremble, I picked it up. There, in my mother's handwriting, were two words. "I'm sorry."

Guilt, shame, sorrow, and bewilderment hit me all at once and I didn't know if I wanted to scream or cry. Instead, I put the note with the blank birthday and Christmas cards I'd gotten for the last seven years, always pretty, always containing money, never with anything else. Storing them away with care, I took a deep breath and headed out the door. I still needed to get to work. School started in a few days, so I needed to get in as many hours as I could. I glanced at my watch—five-thirty. It would take me ten minutes to walk to work, which gave me about twenty minutes to deal with any oddities.

With a forced grin I locked everything away, setting out to see what would attack me today and maybe get some answers about the private detective.

It turned out to be a quiet day. My walk in found two unscratched lottery tickets. Those I saved for Jo. If I scratched them, they would have no value. If she scratched them, she'd get about a hundred and we could probably go do something fun. I saw Mortimer the white cat again, this time observing a bird with a fixed stare. Deciding I didn't need a repeat of yesterday, I kept moving and got to work before anyone else.

It will be a good day. I need a good day. One full of answers and lacking any disasters. I want too much. I know that. The universe will dash my hopes, but until then I can dream. Can't I?

It was not a good day. That would have been too easy.

One espresso machine jammed, and it took me an hour to fix it. Then a grinder lid hadn't been put on fully and it blew coffee grounds everywhere. The capper was a customer who came in and got two carry trays full of drinks and they both collapsed as she lifted them off the counter. Coffee drinks everywhere. We spent ten minutes remaking them all, and a half hour cleaning up the mess.

Then, because life hated me, Shay walked into the cafe. Glaring at me as usual. "You were supposed to be off at three. You have classes at four."

"I had classes at four. School doesn't start back up until next week and I'll find out the new schedule then. And how did you know that? Are you stalking me Shay? So bored you need to torture a poor student?"

"I don't need to. I can't not intersect with you. Someday there will be purpose in our meetings. Today is not that day." His tattoo glinted at me and I wondered why I still gave him so much shit, knowing he was a merlin.

I rolled my eyes and stared at him. "Does that mean I don't need to serve you? Cause really, I can go back to do other stuff."

"Of course not. I'm here, therefore I need to be caffeinated."

Kadia slid his drink on the counter. Even her normally bubbly personality had been dampened by the day. The clock read four-thirty. Soon the day would be over.

He glanced at both of us, our wet aprons, flat hair, and exhausted looks. Shay sighed and put a five in our tip jar, taking his coffee over to his usual corner, then disappeared into his laptop for all the attention he paid to the world around him.

I looked around the café then at Kadia. "Ready to clean up? I'll kick Shay out last."

Kadia nodded. "Yes. I'm exhausted. This has been a day."

That was hardly the word. In silent unison we cleaned, stocked, and got ready to go, even as my mind spun. I started classes in a few days, so my time to figure out what the PI was looking for was running out.

"Shay, we're closing," I called out. Shay grunted in response, but a minute later he'd gotten up and headed to the door, tossing his cup as he went.

Kadia left via the front door and I locked it behind her. Flipping off lights as I went through, I tried to make a game plan for when I got home. Stepping out the back door, I thumped into someone. A scream ripped out of my throat and the light at the end of the alley exploded in a shower of sparks.

"Whoa! Cori, it's me, Sanchez." His voice, adult rough, cut through my fear as he grabbed my shoulders, stopping me from falling backwards and probably breaking something.

"Yeesh, Stinky, you trying to give her a heart attack?" Jo's voice came from further down the alley and I craned my head to see her sitting in his truck. "Come on. Mom's waiting for us and we have research to do, *chica*!"

"Marisol sent you to get me?" I asked, my heart still feeling like it was about to shred into a million parts.

"*Si.* No going by yourself. You should have had me drive you to work," he muttered as we walked back to his truck and I tried to get my breathing to even out.

"Sanchez," I said. He was being nice so he deserved his real name. "I'm not going to expect you to get up that early and drive me to work."

He cast me a funny look. "You do remember who my father is, right? I'm up and in the shop by five-thirty. Heck, if I take you to work, I can get good coffee and not that crap he drinks."

"You have a point there. Fine. Tomorrow I open, then again on Sunday. But then I won't know for sure what my schedule will be. School starts on Monday and all it says for my practicals is To Be Determined. Which tells me nothing." I climbed into the truck, a mixture of relief and worry clashing in me. I had kinda wanted to go home and research more. I never had time to do what I needed. How in the world did single parents survive? It increased my lack of desire to get pregnant, not that anyone was even interested in me. No one wanted to get too serious until after about twenty-two. You would want to emerge if you were going to before getting pregnant. Emerging while pregnant meant the death of the infant, if you were lucky.

"To what do I owe the honor of both of you picking me up? And was I supposed to come over for dinner?" Not that I minded. But still, I didn't want to wear out my welcome. If I did that, it might kill me.

"No, but you're always welcome. Nah, *Papi* said he wanted to talk to us," Jo said as she pulled her coat tighter. "Now come on, Stinky. I'm ready for dinner. *Mami* is making enchilada lasagna, and I'm starving."

Stinky grunted and started up the truck as I buckled in. The ride was quiet, mainly because Jo was focused on flirting via text with a girl she'd met at the shop. Sanchez didn't talk much, and I was too wrapped up in my own dilemmas. Odds were Jo would date her a few times and then find a reason to not continue. I couldn't figure out if she was waiting for something? Or just not ready to have to decide on anything right now. Maybe

47

both.

The questions were spiraling and about to drive me crazy. To my relief, we arrived at the Guzman's house before I lost my tentative hold on sanity.

The cold January air nipped at my cheeks, making me glad I wasn't walking home. I needed to get a better coat, maybe with the extra money. I wanted to probe at that too, but there was only so much I could do in a single day. And not talking to my parents usually was at the top of my list.

The smells and lively conversation wrapped around me as I stepped inside the house. Shucking our coats, Jo pulled me into the dining room where a rich bubbly pan of enchilada lasagna was being set down.

"Grab glasses, Josefa. Everyone else sit," Marisol ordered. I followed the orders gladly, my stomach rumbling at the smell. Marco was there flashing a smile at me. I nodded back. He was handsome, and a flirt, and just not anyone I was interested in.

Jo set the glasses on the table, filled them up with water, then dropped into a chair. Her eyes were locked on the enchiladas too. There was also salad, tortillas, butter, and beans. But they all paled compared to that smell.

"I really need to learn to cook," I muttered as we all got servings of rich cheesy goodness put on our plates.

"You can cook just fine, Cori," Marisol reproved. "You just don't pay enough attention and accidents happen."

I felt slightly wounded. Some of my incidents really were about my not paying attention, such as my tripping last night. "Hey, I didn't cause the microwave to short out." But using salt instead of sugar and setting the oven to 450 instead of 350 I couldn't deny as my fault.

"Accidents happen to everyone. You just don't pay

attention and hence Murphy's Luck follows you like a lost cat."

I didn't roll my eyes—it would have hurt her feelings—but I did internally. Though I wouldn't have minded a cat. Something to keep me company in the evenings that wouldn't require me to walk it. Maybe after I graduated I could get one.

That thought worried me. Graduation. How would I stay close to Jo and everyone? But I couldn't stay here. One more semester and I'd graduate with my AAS in Emergency Medical Technologies, Criminal Justice, and Medical Assistant. Which should guarantee me a job and ensure I never had to watch someone die again while I was useless. I hoped. I still needed to pass the tests, but I wasn't worried about them. The college offered practice tests and I'd aced all of them. I just needed the degree and I'd get a job somewhere away from here.

The dichotomy pulled at me. Away from my parents and the memories was a positive. Away from Jo, the Guzman's, the Grind Down? That registered as a solid negative in my book.

My thoughts disappeared with the first taste of cheese and spices. The entire table fell silent, everyone focused on food first, conversation later.

When the first round of inhalation had faded, chatter slowly started up, first with Marisol asking about the girl Jo was flirting with. Jo for her part played it down, but I could tell she rather liked this one. Stinky and I exchanged amused glances. Jo fell hard, burned fast, and then walked away. Someday she'd find the one to stick with forever. I'd search for the person that matched with her if I needed to. I didn't want her to have an empty life like me.

I didn't need to go down that thought trail and I grabbed some *frijoles negros* to give myself something to do. Well that and they tasted incredible. I really need to learn to cook, or at least not screw things up in the kitchen.

"Cori?"

I jerked my head up at Henri calling my name. My mouth was full, so I just nodded at him instead of saying anything. I'd learned not to eat too fast. I had a tendency to inhale food into my lungs if I did. Lying on the floor gagging from coughing so hard ranked very high on my "Don't Repeat" list.

"The chief came by the shop today."

The table went silent. Even the clink of silverware halted. I choked on my beans. Five minutes later, finally able to breathe again and with most of the tears wiped off my face, I looked at Henri.

"And?"

"Laurel wanted to know if anyone had been by the shop. Showed me the picture of the man. Harold Court. I looked at it a long time, but I told her I hadn't seen anyone like that."

"She asked me and Sanchez too," Marco put in, an odd, grave look on his face. "But we didn't remember seeing him, and I can guarantee that we didn't talk to him. I'd remember anyone asking questions about you," he assured me.

I forced a smile but remained a bit confused. "That doesn't surprise me, and I still want to know why he was looking for me or someone with something like my name. I mean if my name was Mary Williams, maybe it wouldn't be so odd. But Kory? That isn't any more common than Cori is." I drew out the letters in the air as I spoke, to make clear which one I meant.

"Which is why I think Laurel is following up on it." Henri frowned and my gut curled in on itself a bit more.

"Right, so while I'm glad you told me, I'm not sure

why you told me. I mean, I figured she would, but why make it such a big deal?" I knew that sentence sounded awkward, but how do you explain the complexity without sounding like a babbling idiot? Then again, they knew me inside and out, so I doubt my confusing explanation bothered them.

Henri took a deep breath and the yummy enchilada threatened to turn into acid in my stomach.

"We talked for a while, and she mentioned she'd swung by and talked to Estella and Rafael to see if they'd seen or talked to anyone about you." His voice had gotten cold as he said that.

The names of my parents fell like explosions into the quiet room. Jo and Stinky erupted into yells.

"Why would she talk to them? They don't even talk to Cori." That was Jo, at least I thought it was. The room seemed to have receded a bit from my awareness.

"Like they'd care if someone was looking for her. Not that they'd admit to knowing who she was!" Sanchez shouted. He'd even stood up from the table.

Marisol was muttering in Spanish under her breath and I could catch various words casting aspersions on Laurel's intelligence, but more about my parent's lack of parenting.

"Shush, shouting doesn't change anything. Laurel mentioned she wanted to make sure they weren't involved in some way. Asking seemed the most direct path." Henri sounded calm and logical, and that made it hurt even more.

I bolted down the hall to the bathroom and everything came back up. It didn't taste as good the second time. Why would they have been involved? Was talking to me so hard? I lived less than a hundred yards from their house. If they needed to talk to me, to see me, couldn't they walk up the stairs?

Tears threatened, but I fought them back. Instead I focused on the last time I'd actually spoken to my parents. I had to think about it, but it was my eighteenth birthday. I'd run into them at the grocery store. My mom had looked at me, Kris in the grocery cart. She'd reached into her purse and handed me a prepaid debit card. I still remember her words, "Here. Buy something you want." And she turned and pushed the cart away. Dad had stood there looking at me then he'd said, "I'll send you the paperwork you need now that you're an adult." And with that he'd turned and followed Mom out. I walked out of the store, crying so hard I almost got hit by a car. It was the last time I'd let myself cry for them.

Which meant I wouldn't cry today.

I washed my face and walked back out, but this time the food smells assaulted me, threatening what little remained in my stomach.

"I'm sorry, Cori. I thought you should know." Henri looked so apologetic and worried.

"Not an issue. Thanks for telling me. Sanchez, could you give me a ride home?" I knew I was running, but this time no one blamed me. Nor tried to stop me.

"One minute, Cori. Let me send you home with something." Marisol was up and bustling in the kitchen and before I could come up with the words to protest, she handed me an insulated lunch bag. "Here's some left over enchiladas, fresh tortillas, and homemade salsa. I know you have chips. This is for later when you decide you're hungry." I didn't try to refuse—I would be hungry later.

"Thanks, Marisol." I sounded weepy. I wasn't weepy.

She pulled me into a tight hug. "You are family, *mi hija,* just like Josefa. You always have a home here."

Dammit, I will not start crying here.

I hugged her back hard, then pulled back. I needed to think about this bombshell.

"Thanks. Stinky? Ready?"

"Sure, Cori." We were out the door and driving, Jo recognizing I needed space. I'd text her later or even call, but right now I needed to think.

The great thing about Stinky, he didn't pry. But as I got out of the truck at my apartment he spoke, surprising me.

"Hey, Cori?" I turned back to him, curious. "You need anything, you get scared, or you think something's wrong, call. Mom and Dad weren't happy when your parents moved you to this place and Jo told us. For days there were arguments about you moving in with us and rooming with Jo. They almost did. But you act fine, real good, even when you aren't. We should have done more, but you'd been dealing with them for years and you seemed happier there. So they didn't." He cleared his throat, not looking at me, but at the house where my parents and brother lived. "Look, I'm trying to say, I know you're an adult, and I know I was a shit kid to you. But if you need something we're here. Got it?"

"Better watch it, Stinky. I might start to like you." I smiled to show I was teasing and he flashed a smile at me.

"Just don't forget. Now get going. I've got a raid later tonight."

I rolled my eyes. "You and your video games. You ever going to get a real life?"

"Why? I like my fantasy life just fine."

With a laugh I headed up my stairs. I heard his truck pulling away as I shut the door. I leaned against it, the choice bouncing in my head. Go talk to my parents or not? Ask them what they know or not?

I stared at the cup laying shattered on the floor.

Closing the door must have jarred it enough to fall off the shelf.

I had to talk to them. I had to know. I was already upset, why not get it over with now? With a sigh I turned and went back down the stairs and headed towards the house I'd grown up in.

Chapter 7

Emergence is what the appearance of magic in any given person is called. It generally has been described as a warm flush, then everything imploding and exploding in you at the same time. An intrinsic understanding of what offerings are and how much is needed to do any amount of magic is embedded, though training and practice are required to make coherent sense of choosing what genetic material to lose. ~ Magic Explained

ORDER

They're my parents. They'll let me know if they were involved in this. Right?

I felt like I was facing my worst fear and steeling myself for war at the same time. It felt wrong to confront my parents. We'd spent the last six years avoiding each other, trying not to admit the other existed, or at least that was what I assumed. They'd never said, they just faded away from me and did everything possible to make sure I didn't need them.

Was it even worth the effort? Why would they be involved? Everything there was to know about me they either knew or could have found out just by asking. I didn't know if I'd open my heart to them, but maybe.

No, I have to know. They need to tell me.

Marching up to the front steps I knocked on the door. My knock rang in my heart and mind like the warning bell at school. Was it warning that my family was about to get the death knell? Or that maybe something would change for the better?

Mel Todd

I heard steps approaching and was suddenly aware of my grimy condition. Between working all day, then getting sick at the Guzman's, I looked and smelled a wreck. Why hadn't I changed first?

The doorknob turning and the door pulling open shut down my internal flailing. I looked up as my dad's gaze locked with mine. His eyes went wide as his face paled. He took a stance at the door as if I was trying to break in or might charge him.

"May I help you?"

The overly polite formal voice wasn't any more than I had expected, yet it still hurt. "I wanted to talk to you and—" I hesitated unsure what to call her anymore. I cleared my throat. "—you and Estella about what the cops asked. I need to know about the private investigator."

"We didn't know anything and told the chief that." He started to close the door when I heard Estella's voice behind him.

"Who is it, Rafe?" Even as she spoke, I saw her approach the door and pull it open. Rafael let her, even as his body stiffened even more. She flinched when she saw me. "Why are you here?"

At this rate the blows to my soul would kill me. "I'd like to talk to you both? Please? Did you know the investigator? Why was he hired to find me? Did you do it? Is there something going on I should know about? Are people looking for you? For us?" The questions spilled out of me like a stream of over-caffeinated coffee and I wanted to sew my mouth shut. I didn't need them, but I needed answers.

"Hey, Mom! Are we having pizza rolls?" The question was shouted behind my parents and a moment later a head peeked between them. "Hi! You're the student renter? Wanna come in for dinner? Mom made pizza rolls. I seen you around. You're pretty. Mom, you letting her in?" The stream of questions sounded so much like mine I had to smile. Both of my parents flinched, and my smile faded.

"Kris, she can't come in. Our renter just needed to ask us a question about a report. Go get your homework and what book you want to read." Estella's words, dismissing me as a renter, not even admitting that I was her daughter caused another sharp pain to stab through my chest.

"Okay, Mom. Bye, lady." His head pulled back, the brown hair ruffling just the way Stevie's had. I closed my eyes for a minute, listening to the pounding of his feet as he sped away.

"Really? You aren't even going to admit you have a daughter? Are you ever going to tell him that he also had a brother?" My throat choked up. "People will ask when he gets a bit older. They know me. They knew Stevie."

My parents exchanged an odd look that I couldn't interpret. "We didn't talk to, or see, the man the police showed us. Nor do we know of anyone that could be looking for you. As you know, we are both only children. If we knew anything, we would have told the police." Estella said all this not looking at me, though if she turned any paler, I'd start worrying she was bleeding out somewhere.

"If you need any help with the apartment or if something goes wrong, please use the email address for the apartment. Now if you would excuse us, we need to go to dinner." Rafael stepped back from the door as did Estella, almost as if they had practiced the maneuver. In a smooth motion the door shut in my face, leaving me standing there, none of my questions really answered and even more spiraling through my brain.

I don't know how long I stood there. Rage and

sorrow waged a war in my heart. I raised my hand to pound on the door but froze halfway through the motion. What good would it do? Would it change anything if I threw a fit? Would it hurt Kris?

I don't need them. I haven't for a while. I need to walk away.

My arm ached from holding it there. It was that pain that finally let me turn and head back to my apartment, my fingers and arm numb from the cold. The heat inside my apartment came as a welcome relief. Standing inside the door, I stared at the card, the one holding the five hundred. I needed to get it into the bank, but a part of me wanted to tear it into pieces and dump it in front of them.

The light bulb over the stove fritzed out with a crack. I didn't even bother to sigh, just went over and replaced it with one from my stash. I purchased cheap bulbs in very large packs. That replaced, I put the money in my purse. I'd walk to the bank at lunch.

The clock glared at me. After eight. I needed to talk to the chief, to find out if there was any progress. I should move, research, do something. Instead, I stood in the middle of my kitchen and let the last few dreams I had of my parents coming back into my life fade away. I gave in and scratched my head, ignoring the white particles that cascaded down as I headed to bed. Nothing else mattered now. School started Monday and then my weeks would be full of work and study. Now was my only chance to find out the answers I craved. I still wanted to be a doctor, but I'd never make it through the course, and didn't have the funding to afford that level of schooling. Besides, the idea of something weird happening during surgery scared the daylights out of me.

I shook my head. I needed to chill out and focus. My

parents were nothing new; that had been going on since
- well since Stevie died. Me crying over it now would
not change it. Someday I'd be able to think or say that
and truly mean it. For now, I kept trying to pretend. Six
more months - I could make it. I had to make it.

That thought, or was it a dream, followed me to bed.

Chapter 8

Magic strengths are denoted by pale or full. Many people think this comes from the idea of being a pale comparison – i.e., a lighter shade of something darker, more full. In truth it comes from the phases of the moon; full, waxing, and waning in light and power. Originally you were full of Air or full of Spirit, and waning in Water or Transform. But people wanted it associated with positives, so strong took the place of full. But the moon terminology held on with the idea of a pale moon. Hence secondary skills are still regarded as 'pale'. ~History of Magic

SPIRIT

I should never hope for a good day—it's guaranteed it won't be.

Stinky picked me up at five-thirty on the dot and I was at work in record time. I treated him to the best coffee I could make and filled up his cup. Though if he survived after drinking 32 ounces of my high-octane brew, magic was good for more than I thought. From there the day went downhill.

Kadia called out. She had gone out for sushi last night and got food poisoning. I could have told her any place around Rockway wasn't a good place to get sushi. But that meant I had Molly as help for the morning rush, which meant I had no help at all. Molly struggled to such a point that in the chaos of Friday morning orders, I gave in and asked her to just restock. It was less stress to just do it all. By nine-thirty most of the crowd had disappeared, Molly had come back to help me clean, and things were just settling down when Shay walked in.

I didn't groan. I didn't. But I did steel myself as he walked up to the counter, his odd green-gray eyes locked on mine, contrasting to his red hair.

"Disaster follows you like stink on a skunk. But your time here is winding down. The paths that lead you away will make you grow in ways you never wanted."

I blinked then frowned at him. Yes, the shop looked a bit rough—I needed to finish picking up, not to mention get things restocked. "Hey, Molly?" I asked, but I kept my eyes on Shay. For some reason he always reacted to me, and I didn't understand why. I knew he was a merlin—that shouted out at everyone who glanced at his face—but I had no idea what he did or who he worked for. He always worked on his computer, and traveled a lot, but that was the extent of my knowledge.

"Yeah?" I could sense her behind me, watching.

"Are you going to fire me in near future?"

"Hadn't planned on it," she replied. "If I did that, I'd run myself out of business before I got someone to replace you."

"Well, I am graduating this summer," I responded, smirking at Shay. He didn't look impressed.

"Don't remind me. I'm in denial, thank you very much." Molly groaned. "The floor is sticky, let me go get the mop. And I really need Carl to show up for his shift. Early would be nice."

I heard her move away from me and I looked at Shay. "I think I'll be here for a bit. So what can I get you? Your usual?"

"Time is relative and paths twist, but yours are all going away, never to be here for long again. Yes, my usual." His tone didn't change, and it took me a minute to realize he had answered my question. And to convince my skin that crawling in reaction to his words was ridiculous.

I fought to shake the feeling off as I made his usual drink, then started to put all the baked goods into the display tray. Molly left them there as she went to get stuff to mop up the spilled drinks. Nothing major, but coffee always spilled when you moved as fast as I had been moving that morning.

That notion made me realize there hadn't been any disasters today. Maybe this odd effect was starting to dissipate. I handed Shay his drink and he headed to his favorite corner table and chair. As he sat, the chair collapsed underneath him.

That's what I get for thinking things were going well.

The frantic thought ricocheted through my mind as I tore towards Shay. If he'd been hurt, I'd never forgive myself. The chair lay in pieces under him. To my utter relief he'd set his coffee on the table before he sat down. Hot coffee dumped on him would have made it worse. Our coffee was HOT.

"Shay are you okay?"

He seemed a bit dazed and looked up at me, a strange expression of exasperation on his face. "I should know by now your effect on the entropy lines. I just hadn't expected it to be this blatant. I shouldn't be surprised. All the lines are being pulled towards your vortex, regardless."

I had no idea what the meant, but as he was standing slowly and brushing himself off, I figured it meant he'd survive. I pulled out another chair for him and went to work collecting the pieces of the chair that used to be there. It looked like the chair had been infested with dry rot and when he sat down it basically disintegrated.

"Everything okay?" Molly asked, coming out of the back, holding the mop, a worried look on her face.

"Yeah, but we should probably get the rest of the chairs checked. Shay, are you sure you're okay?" He drove me crazy but that didn't mean I wanted him injured.

He waved his hand, shooing me away. "Fine, fine. Entropy and convergence have been, and always will be, my bane."

It made no sense to me, but I slunk back to the counter. How in the world had that happened? There were days when I felt like I should be the one in a bubble, but everyone knew these weird things weren't my fault. I'd never emerged, and they'd been going on for years. So not me, but that didn't mean I didn't feel guilty. I went back to work, trying to shake the feeling of unease and focus on the issue of my name.

It must be me, right? I think Jo is right and it has something to do with family. But then why wouldn't they have talked to Mom and Dad? Or heck, knocked on my door?

That line of thought didn't make sense as any family investigation would start with talking to my parents. And while they might have lied to me, they would never lie to Chief Laurel Amosen. My head itched so badly I had to clench my fists to not go and scratch it. I hated the stupid dandruff. Like I didn't have enough other issues.

I feel like a character looking at a tantalizing quest object, but I can't pick it up because it isn't mine.

The image of me staring at the grail just unable to touch it made me snort at the same time the bell to the Grind Down rang. I looked up to see the person I'd been thinking about walk in.

"Well think of the devil and she appears." The words slipped past my lips before I could think better of them. What was it with me and the chief where I seemed determined to always be at my worst in front of her?

No, I knew the answer. It just was all in that same

bucket of stuff I refused to think about, except that I always thought about it, about Stevie.

"I'd like to talk to you, Cori," Chief Amosen said, her voice hinting at her annoyance.

"Sure. Molly?"

Poor woman is going to have a meltdown having to deal with the front again.

But before she could emerge from the back, Carl waltzed in. Carl was nineteen, waiting to see if he emerged and frankly didn't care either way. Mostly he wanted to hang with friends, but the rumors were his parents were getting tired of him not doing much and this job was the only thing keeping him from getting kicked out on the street. Luckily, he actually enjoyed being a barista.

"Hey, Carl, will you take over for a bit? Chief needs to talk to me."

"Sure thing, dudette," Carl drawled and I rolled my eyes. He was back on his surfer kick and called everyone dude or dudette. We were at least six hours from the ocean and his pasty white skin and light red hair meant if he got on a surfboard he'd turn into a lobster. Whatever. At least he worked, mostly. Cleaning the bathroom was not one of his strong points.

"Thanks. This way, Chief." We didn't really have a break room or private area outside of Molly's office, and it was too tight for me to squeeze us in and not feel crowded, so I pulled her back into the store room. "Need me to close the door?"

She shook her head, her tight cropped curly black hair reminding me I needed to get the next batch of beans grinding for the afternoon caffeine crowd. "No. I'm sure this will become public knowledge soon enough. I got a call back from the secretary at Harold Court Investigations."

I went still—everything leaving my mind except what she said.

"She went over his cases and found out that he was fulfilling a case for the estate of Merlin James Wells, a Spirit merlin in New York. His estate is looking for an emerged Spirit mage. Probably a merlin."

I felt my heart sink as she talked. "The merlin died soon after the hunt started, but he felt the emergence of a mage about nine or ten years ago. He got the impression of a female and the name Kory Monroe or something like it. There is a big reward to find the mage. So Harold was following up on any women with a name even close to that to see if they might know or be the woman he was looking for."

"So not me," I said and poked at the sense of disappointment. It would have been nice for someone to want me.

"No. Figure she'd have to be in her very late twenties or early thirties at this point. From the gossip the secretary told me, they figure she must be dead as the Office of Magical Oversight has no record of any spirit mages with any name even remotely like that. Which means it's a ghost chase."

OMO was a global agency where all mages were required to register. While the US instituted a draft of all mages at magician rank or higher at the beginning of World War I, regardless of gender, other countries had different ways of dealing with their high-rank mages. Regardless, everyone registered, and all the countries worked together. The consequences of not, well I didn't really know. Too much protection and benefit came with registering, not the least of which was a free college degree.

"Oh." It came out dejected and sad and the chief arched a brow at me. I ducked my head, thinking through it. "I guess I figured he had to be after someone alive. Maybe he really was looking for me, wanted me." I managed to cut off the rest of my sentence, but she nodded.

"I get that, but no, he was looking for a woman almost a decade older than you. She would have emerged before you even became a teenager."

I had to admire her diplomatic way of framing the time for me. But it didn't answer all the questions. "So how, or why, was he killed? I mean there was a lot of blood there on the scene, so I don't think his body was dumped."

The chief gave me a look that if I'd been up to something would have made me quail; as I wasn't, I just looked at her. "You been watching crime shows again?"

I almost ducked my head, there'd been a time back in high school where I'd gorged on them non-stop. But this time I lifted my chin and gave her a flat look. "No, my homework. Remember what I'm going to school for?"

She leaned back, pressing against the bags of used ground beans—we sold them to the local plant place where they made it into a soil nutrient. I almost told her to be careful, the beans would stain her light khaki uniform, but I didn't. What can I say? I occasionally hold grudges and Laurel Amosen was easier to blame than myself. Some days I think she knew that. Some days.

"Ah yes. Your need to save and fix. Triple AA I believe? Paramedic, Criminal Justice, and what was the third?"

I swallowed. Her knowing so much about my plans made me uncomfortable. "Medical Assistant. The max degrees I could get at the community colleges. Figured someone would hire me even with me not being a mage."

Laurel waved her hand, dismissing it. "Believe it or not, being a mage isn't the end all and be all of everything, regardless of what they like to pretend. Be good and work hard and no one cares." She touched her tattoo. "And sometimes being one causes more problems than it solves."

I nodded, but I didn't really believe her. Everyone wanted to be a magic user; it made life much easier, even if doing the right or wrong thing could kill you.

"But back to your question - how did he die." Her voice turned suddenly stern and her eyes locked on mine, no give to them. "This is not to get out. Do you understand Corisande Munroe?"

The lump in my throat took me three tries to swallow past. "Yes, ma'am."

Laurel softened. "Okay. You may tell Josefa, but the rest stays silent." I nodded rapidly, needing to know. "As is usually the case with those you stumble across, it was a freak accident. One of the guidelines on the telephone pole near where you found his body apparently snapped as he was walking by. It flicked up and through his neck, severing it. He would have died almost instantly, if that's any help." She must have seen my stricken look or remembered the other times I felt useless. "Even if you or a mage, possibly even a merlin, had been standing there, he still would have died. There wouldn't have been any pain."

I studied my feet, thinking it through. He'd been dead for a little bit before I found him, so Laurel was correct. There wasn't anything I could have done. No matter how hard I studied, I'd never save everyone, or have all the answers. But I could keep looking and maybe someday I'd figure out why Stevie had died.

"Thanks for telling me," I manage to say finally. When I looked back up at her, she had an expression I couldn't interpret.

"You earned it." She pulled away from the stacks of grounds. "Good luck with your classes."

"Thanks," I muttered and watched her leave, smirking a bit at the brown spots on the back of her uniform. Some days I really was a bitch.

Chapter 9

Merlins are the scary bad guys, but a smart person is scared of a hedgemage. They aren't branded and it doesn't take much to stop a heart or create a blood clot in a brain. ~ Freedom from Magic tweet.

CHAOS

How sad is it, I'm so desperate to be wanted that I want a private investigator to be looking for me? I have mental issues.

Jo took the news they were looking for someone at least a decade older than me with a relieved sigh, even if she understood why I was upset. Maybe better than I did. I suspect she told Marisol something, because when Jo pulled me over to her house for dinner Saturday, they surprised me with tres leches, my favorite dessert. I ate three pieces. Gaining weight was never an issue for me. I'd been the same size ten since high school. Which, given my weird life, was just one more thing. Non-stop dandruff, hair that wouldn't grow, and I never gained weight. Oh well, I guess it could be worse.

With the death being explained away as a weird incident I went back to walking to work, though that was only over the weekend. I arrived bright and early for the first class of what I hoped would be my last semester of college.

The class changed constantly as students came in and rolled out, but I was one of ten in a special program. Aimed towards those who either weren't mages or, like me, didn't think they'd be one, it was a three-year program to get a triple certification. When we walked out, we'd be eligible to apply for the police academy with our Criminal Justice associate's degree, work as a Medical Assistant, or get hired as an EMT. I'd taken the extra course load to qualify as a paramedic. My skill test was scheduled for the day after graduation. With those certifications I shouldn't have trouble getting a job anywhere. At least that was the hope. While no one could legally discriminate against people without magic, the unemployment rate for anything other than blue collar jobs for the rest of us was three times as high as it was for tattooed mages.

Sitting in the classroom, I pulled my coat a bit tighter around me. It was cold and my jacket had seen better days.

One more semester, then you'll have a good job and can get some of the things you need, you want.

That was what I held on to. I didn't have much else besides Jo to give me hope for the future.

Others started to drift in and I recognized most of them. Friendly, but not friends. Between work, study, and taking public transportation, I knew their names and not much else. Oh well, I had Jo and the Guzmans; that would be enough for anyone. We nodded cordially and people took their seats. I didn't look at Monique. Every class had one, and she was ours. Always complained about everything and acted like she was better than the rest of us. She annoyed me to no end, and I tended to let it show.

One minute before class officially started our teacher, Bruce Marxin, strolled in. About my dad's age, he had dark brown hair with a few streaks of silver that seemed to draw the attention of the female students. I cared only that he was a good teacher. At twenty, I was the youngest person in class—the others were between twenty-four and thirty, some starting a new career, most making the best of no emergence.

On the dot of nine a.m. Bruce snapped his fingers for attention. Even after two years of him, I still didn't know if I liked or loathed that habit. Either way, I only had to deal with it for this last semester. I'd make it.

"Welcome to the Spring semester, people. This is your practicum class and the most important class you have." I rolled my eyes at that and he must have seen me. Sitting in the front row was never smart but being able to move when something went wrong made me feel better. "While I know many of you think your other classes are just as, if not more, important, I am here to correct that misconception. We will only meet in this classroom weekly but if you flunk this course, you won't be graduating." I wanted to cheer about the once a week part—maybe I could get more hours—but the second part of his statement had me freezing in place, eyes locked on him as he moved back and forth.

"This is a practicum and has been developed to make sure you know how to use the skills you spend so much time studying. As we all know, there is a world of difference between studying how to do something and actually doing it. Tomorrow you will all have to take tests which will give you partial certification – think of it as the equivalent of a learners permit for the Medical Assistant and Police Intern. We are one of the first colleges in the country, and the only one in the state of Georgia, to offer this. While you can't work independently with this cert, you can work as interns. What that means is each of you will have a five-week ride-along in each specialty that will be thirty-two hours a week. It will be added as work credits to your degree if you wish to pursue a bachelors in any of these areas." He stopped and scanned the area, a grin crossing his face that was half amused, half cruel. "Come on, smile. This is what you've been studying for. To be out in the field and dealing with the realities. If you hate it, well aren't you glad you'll learn this BEFORE you get the job?"

The half laughs and mutters just made him smile and he flipped open his power point. "Well, since this is the beginning of your last semester, let's get going. This is all about paperwork and regulations, which are not only common, but the three job tracks have similar forms, though of course they all go by different names. We will be starting with medical assistant paperwork and move on from there. Expect a lot of reading and tests on the material weekly. You'll get your reading assignment at the end of each class." With that he launched into it, but I barely registered what he said.

My mind was still locked on losing thirty-two hours a week. I worked at Grind Down about thirty hours, mostly weekends and noon to close, as all the classes seemed to require mornings. I did homework in the evenings and took one or two online classes for the more basic stuff. I needed to sleep and eat; commuting here via public transportation both ways easily ate up two hours a day.

I frantically tried to figure out how to deal with the ramifications. If I cut hours, I'd be short on money. I already ate most of my meals at the Grind or at Jo's, so I didn't need to buy food. Right now, all my money went to tuition, my cell phone, and buying necessities like hygiene supplies, the local transit pass, and other things. Parents still paid my health insurance, but unless I thought I might die I never went. The copay hurt too much. After taxes, I made just under nine hundred a month. Between December and January, I'd been making closer to twelve hundred with the extra hours. It would give me a cushion for the next few months, but my mind flew back to the five hundred from the other day. That might be enough to get me through a month, maybe two. While I had some in savings, that was my escape from Rockway money.

Oh gods, I'm going to have to ask them for money.

My stomach clenched at the thought and I thought I might be sick. My scalp itched so fiercely I couldn't resist clawing on it, ignoring the white dust drifting to my shoulders.

"Yo, Bruce. Is the clock supposed to be doing that?" one of the students called out, pointing up at the clock on the wall.

I looked up to see the hands on the clock spinning backwards. Bruce had stopped talking and looked at it also. "Interesting. Wonder if there was an electricity surge." As the words left his mouth the projector connected to his laptop sparked, sputtered, and smoke drifted up from it. He stared at it and sighed. "They have got to get the electrical system in this room fixed. This is the third projector in two years. Okay peeps, you know how to be adults. The pages are from this textbook," he said and patted a new book. "This one and this other one,"—he paused for a moment and pulled another textbook out—"are the required books for this course. Only two of them, but they will be where all your classwork comes from. I know the paramedic track will have some supplies you'll need to purchase. Check the bookstore for the bundles you'll need. Now back to the fun world of HIPAA regulations." He continued to talk, telling us what to read and reference and what the test would be on in a month.

I took notes, making sure I had everything, but the other part of my mind, the one trying not to have a meltdown, started going through options. There weren't that many: parents, teacher, Molly. I swallowed down my panic. No need to start swimming across the rivers until I figured out if there was a bridge.

Bruce Marxin wrapped up the class early and most of the students streamed out, but I lingered and walked up to him, trying very hard to keep any hint of whining out of my voice. Maybe I'd get lucky and this wouldn't mean I'd be eating nothing. I hated asking Jo for food, no matter how often she invited me over.

I cleared my throat and he looked up at me. "Yes, Miss Munroe?"

Not wrinkling my nose took effort, I hated people calling me that. It felt wrong. "Mr. Marxin, I had some questions about the ride-along internship things."

He paused what he was doing and looked at me. "What about them? I don't believe you're feeling squeamish. You've gone through all the stuff without blinking. Heck, I think you were the only student not puking at the cadaver trip."

"Oh, no, I don't have an issue with any of that." I didn't want him thinking I was a wuss, I wasn't. Blood and gore didn't even register with me most days. "It's more the hours. Are there any restrictions as to when you are expecting us to do this or how many days a week?"

He tilted his head and his eyes drifted down and back up. Part of me wished he was ogling my chest and butt, but I was a B cup and had slim hips and a small butt. Definitely nothing there for anyone to lust over. And while I might qualify as cute, any guy with brain cells would take Jo any day of the week if she liked men. But I knew he was registering my clothes. My worn, out of style, clothes. "This is the trial run of this program, so I'm sure the various groups that have volunteered to help will be open to flexible schedules to accommodate work. But you may have to make some sacrifices." He managed not to sneer or sound pompous as he said all of that, but I still couldn't see how I wasn't going to take a major hit. Molly only stayed open until four. Maybe I could do all evening shifts?

"Okay. When will we get the list and how do we know what we're doing first?" I didn't think my voice quavered, but I never could tell.

"It should be out this afternoon. Everyone will be emailed their schedule. We are rotating you through the positions." Maybe he saw how stressed I was because he gave a little. "I think there may be weekend and evening work available. This program is supposed to make life easier by giving you a very strong skill set, not force you to flunk out. And we will be asking for advice and suggestions when you graduate as to how it could work better."

I nodded, a jerky motion as my head felt like it might fly off. That unexpected money from my parents might be the only thing to make it so I didn't end up dropping out because I couldn't pay. "Thanks."

"You got down what you need to study for next week?" he asked as he closed the laptop.

I had no idea if I did or not, but I nodded. While none of us were friends in class, we had exchanged email addresses and I could shoot someone an email if I couldn't read what I scribbled down.

"See you next week." He strode out without looking back. I trudged out of the classroom, the weight of financial worries dragging me down. I needed to go to the bookstore and buy the two books and other stuff I'd need. My mind went in loops as I walked. This was the only morning class I had, and now that it was monthly, that meant I could work the rest of the weeks in the morning. My other classes were all late afternoon. But the ride-along terrified me. Working through the money, I tried to convince myself I'd be able to do it. At least I didn't have to pay rent too. Most of the other students had a few years on me and qualified for scholarships and loans. I didn't because I hadn't passed the maximum emergence age and my parents made plenty of money. They figured we were too likely to change our minds if we emerged with different skill sets than what we were studying for. Idiots. Only forty to fifty percent of people had magic. Which meant most of us just wanted to have a life and live.

That brought me back to Molly. I needed to see where I was. I knew she couldn't afford to pay me more, so I'd either need more hours or come up with an idea for something other way to make money. And all the while knowing I was leaving her for another job, one that I could live off of, as soon as I graduated.

There was a line in the bookstore—there always was. Small town and no one else would ever carry the weird things they came up with for classes. Even online I couldn't find them sometimes. I headed towards the area that should have my stuff and found the kit. Both textbooks, a practicum for the paramedic stuff, and a bag with supplies. We went through a lot of supplies practicing how to take care of someone. At least it was a decent quality bag. Then I saw the total price and my eyes started to water. The light two rows over exploded in a shower of sparks and people screamed, startled. I didn't even move just staring at the black letters. Three hundred forty-eight dollars and thirty-two cents before tax.

Can't I ever get a break?

OMO - the Office of Magical Oversight. Established in 1937; became a global entity in 1954. The idea for the OMO started in Russia of all places by Vladimir Ilyich Ulyanov, better known as Lenin. Haunted by stories of Baba Yaga, the Snow Queen, and the reality of Rasputin, plus having lived through multiple revolutions and World War I, he felt all mages should be recorded and controlled. Originally, he wanted all mages to serve at the will of the state or face imprisonment, but cooler heads prevailed. However, multiple governments agreed being able to track more powerful magic users had its uses. Thus, the OMO first started in Moscow, was moved to Paris, then eventually had its own building next to the United Nations building in New York. Now it is the controlling bureaucracy for all mages. ~ History of Magic

ORDER

I spent the ride back to Grind Down trying to figure out if I could get the books and supplies cheaper online. I could find one book cheaper, but when I added in the supplies, it always came out to more. In a weird turn of events the bookstore had it for cheaper than I could piecemeal it together, and as a bonus had the nice bag that I couldn't get anywhere else. No matter how hard I looked, there wasn't any other option.

Maybe Molly can give me a few more hours, or we can do a weekend thing that goes later. Mix in some end of winter stuff? Something, as I'm about two hundred short no matter what I do to afford everything. Or, I drop my savings to under five hundred, which means I'll have a hard

time affording an apartment anywhere.

Getting out at my stop, I slogged my way up the street toward the coffee shop, my bag weighing nothing compared to the burden of worry and stress that dragged at my every step. Approaching the front door, I forced myself to stand up and put a smile on my face. Maybe I could still salvage this. Pushing the door open, the familiar smell of coffee and baked goods filled my senses and it made smiling a bit easier. How could you be sad when you could all but taste pumpkin pie scones?

Carl stood at the counter cleaning while Kadia was picking up things from one of the tables.

"Yo, dudette. You on shift?" Carl asked, his voice lazy, as if it really didn't matter either way.

"Nah, well not yet. Molly in?"

"In back. Muttering 'bout numbers." He nodded to the back then turned to deal with cleaning out the bakery display, already dismissing me from his attention.

"Thanks. Hey Kadia, feeling better?"

"Yeah. So sorry about calling out, but trust me, I couldn't get more than five feet from the toilet. You didn't want me here." She still looked a bit pale, but her smile was back, and she wore yellow beads in her braids today. Each bead had a chaos symbol on it.

"No, I didn't. But glad you're feeling better. I'll talk to you later." I headed into the back as I said the last. My proposal for staying open later on the weekends would give me more hours and hopefully make money for her.

I reached the back room and knocked on the door jamb to her tiny office. Molly lifted her head and smiled at me, though I could tell from her wrinkled brow she had a headache. Too bad none of the mages had ever come up with a way to completely prevent headaches. Now that would have been worth a fortune.

"Hey, Molly. Got a minute?"

"Sure. Take a seat." She waved at the only available chair in the tiny office. "You aren't on shift, are you?" Molly looked up at the calendar on the wall where we all kept our shifts listed and if we needed to swap with someone, we would update.

"Nah. Class got out early today. Hey, I wanted to talk to you about maybe staying open later on the weekends. I was thinking maybe we could do some book clubs or something to draw people in later. Drum up evening business. I could run it, probably by myself." That was the truth, but it also meant whatever tips were earned would be all mine. And right now, even an extra ten dollars would make a difference.

The lines around her eyes and mouth grew deeper. "I actually needed to talk to you. I've already told Carl and Kadia. I need to cut back hours on the shop."

My throat went dry and what little wisps of hope I had vaporized in that instant. I made myself listen as she continued to talk.

"The profit in the afternoons isn't there, and actually I'm losing money at this point. After running the numbers, I've decided I'm going to start closing at two every day." Molly forced a smile. "Look at the bright side. You'll have more time to study."

The smile I forced onto my face felt more like a grimace than anything else, but I kept it there and nodded. "That makes total sense. Not worth staying open if you're losing money."

"But I think your weekend idea is a good one, just not right now. I'll look at it later in the year." She gave me a sad smile. Molly knew I'd be gone by then.

"Not an issue. Just random ideas. When does the shift change take effect?" I asked as I rose up, trying to keep my panic at bay. Maybe I could find a second job. I could do with less sleep. Lots of people didn't need more than five hours or so. I could make myself do it. Only six months. I could pull it off.

"Next week. So normal schedules this week. I need to get the new signs up so people know about the change." She sounded apologetic, but at least she was doing it for the right reasons. If she closed, we'd all be out of work.

"Okay. I'll see you tomorrow morning at open."

The ringing of her phone distracted her and she just nodded at me, reaching for it. I let myself out of her office and headed to the front. So much for getting out of here. I didn't have a choice anymore. My mood darkened like the skies outside. Another winter storm coming in. Maybe I'd get lucky and it would snow.

Waving at Kadia and Carl, I stepped outside, avoiding their concerned looks. Most people in town knew something about my past, but right now their sympathy would kill me. I started towards the bank. I didn't have a choice. I'd need to deposit the money and then go back to the bookstore. Might as well do it today while I had the time. Tonight I'd figure out just how bad my life was about to be.

Wrapped in my own stewing, I didn't notice anything until the horn yanked my attention to my surroundings. I spun trying to figure out what the issue was. The streets had gotten icy as the temperature dropped, something I had noticed as I walked. People were yelling now, and I looked to see a car spinning down the road. An older model family SUV was literally spinning on the icy streets down the road. I could see the terrified look on the woman's face as she gripped the wheel, then she was gone as the car spun, heading right towards the big light pole at the intersection.

Oh crap, please hit it with the rear end of the car, please hit it with the rear end of the car.

The thought spun in my head as I ran that direction. There was no way for the car to miss it, and as I watched, it slammed, passenger side first, directly into the huge pole. The sound of the impact exploded like a death knell in my mind and I pushed to run faster. I slid to a stop by the car, not bothering to call 911. Not this time. I could see others with their phones out, taking pictures, calling, someone would have already called.

I went to the driver's side first, calling on my lessons so far and wishing desperately I had already bought the damn bag. I dumped my backpack and grabbed the small emergency kit I kept in it. Disposable glove, CPR shield, pads, and inflatable splint, nothing major but enough that maybe I could help until the professionals arrived. I pulled out the gloves and slipped them on, then turned to the door. I pulled on the handle and it opened. First major hurdle down.

"Ma'am, can you hear me?" The air bag had gone off, leaving white powder everywhere. Her nose was bleeding, but she blinked her eyes and looked at me. Good, she was alive and conscious. Win! Relief started to soothe across the scorched earth of my panic.

Her eyes fluttered open and closed, then she frowned at me, turning her head a bit looking around. "Wha?" Her voice trailed off and all the head injury options rippled through my mind.

"The paramedics are on their way. Stay still and they'll get you out." As I spoke, I ran my hands quickly down her arms and legs, checking for any obvious injuries. She shifted her feet a little, which was a great sign.

"Bobby?" She said, looking around, confusion fading from her face replaced instead with worry. "Where's Bobby?"

I knew I needed to keep her calm. I placed a hand on

her shoulder, causing in her to look at me. "Who's Bobby?"

Let it be a dog or she got confused.

As she blinked at me, I glanced at the seatbelts again, all slack and no car seat in the back or front.

"My son. Where's my son?" Panic spiked in her tone and she started to struggle. I really didn't want her to move—I still had no idea what internal injuries there were—and while it didn't seem like her spine had been damaged, that didn't mean she should move until they got her strapped to a board. Car accidents did weird things. I knew she'd have bruises, but she could have also done real damage to her organs.

"Ma'am, there's no one else in the car. Are you sure?" Confusion was often present after head injuries, and if she was my patient I'd suggest a CT.

"In the back, I picked him up from school. He wasn't feeling well. He was laying in the back." She started trying to get free but gasped in pain.

Fudge, she's going to hurt herself.

"Stay still. Emergency personnel will be here shortly. I'll look, but you need to stay still.

"Where is he?" her frantic voice cut deep.

I swallowed and forced a smile. "Give me a minute and I'll check. Just don't move. You need to make sure you stay still."

"Look for him, he has to be there." It was obvious she didn't care about herself and that worried me even more.

Keeping the forced smiled on my face I rose up and moved to the back driver's-side door. I still didn't see anything, but I pulled open the door and peered in. The world around me vanished as I saw a crumpled figure laying in the space between the seats. The figure didn't move and the cold in my veins had nothing to do with the temperature outside.

I crawled in. His head nestled near the passenger side, his body wedged in tight on its side, his nose against the seat. By crawling, I could get there. I scanned as I moved across the seat but didn't see any blood or broken bones. I still didn't let myself wish or hope, just scanned. I positioned myself so I was mimicking his form laying on the seat. "Bobby? Can you hear me?" My voice low, but his mother still heard me.

"Is he okay? Why isn't he talking?"

I ignored her, focusing on the boy even as the icy feeling in my soul spread. He was about twelve, the same age Stevie had been. With a boy's soft features and his haircut, it all brought back images I had tried to block for so very long. I fought to focus and pay attention to the boy. To my patient.

Blood trickled from the ear facing the ceiling. His eyes fluttered open. I saw his throat move and I saw the vertebra that were out of alignment with his spine. His mouth moved again, trying to breath, but he couldn't move his lungs to get oxygen in. Choices slammed at me. If I pulled him out, I might be able to breathe for him, but his spine was severed, I could see it. If his heart quit beating, I wouldn't be able to do anything. And moving him might make it worse.

What the hell do I do?

Part of me already knew. It had been at least two minutes since the accident, probably close to four. His body was already ravaging itself for oxygen, and the blood from the ear indicated brain damage. He was going to die and there was nothing I could do.

Well, there is one thing I can do.

I got closer and laid my hand on his face, his eyes widened as he focused on me, his mouth still gasping for air. I smiled at him, letting him feel my hand on his face,

83

and watched the life fade as I lay there, the sirens of first responders creating a death song that escorted his life away from me and my uselessness. The tears running down my cheeks were the only parting gift I could offer.

Chapter 11

One of the core things taught in magic classes, and a lesson that the OMO tries to push, is that mages are not gods. They can't stop death, turn back time, or make the blind see. They can do powerful and wonderful things, but they, like the rest of us, are bound both by the laws of physics and their knowledge of various sciences to control what spells they wish to cast. ~Magic Explained

SPIRIT

And once again I let someone die.

Afterward the paramedics assured me there was nothing I could have done to save him. They were surprised he lived as long as he did, but he'd been dead the second his neck snapped. The mom was inconsolable, but she was mostly okay. A fracture in one hip and lots of bruising. And grief. Oh, she would have grief and guilt until the day she died. I knew that better than anyone else.

They let me go about three hours later and I snuck out, grateful no one I was friends with had seen that. I didn't need the extra pressure. The effort to grab a bus seemed too much and I walked home, lost in guilt and frustration. Between my money worry, the look on Bobby's face as he died, and being emotionally exhausted, I didn't even remember the walk home, though by the time I got there and climbed my stairs it registered that I was freezing.

Getting inside, I checked the time, not even one in the afternoon. Great, a day's worth of drama and I couldn't even justify going to bed. My shivering made it hard to think, so I headed to the bathroom. I tripped once trying to get out of my clothes, but whether that was part of Catastrophe Cori or the fact my hands were too cold to grab my clothing correctly was anyone's guess. I made it into the shower and stood there, letting the heat blunt the sharp edges. I don't know if I cried. I refused to pay attention, just letting the water beat down on me like a thousand tiny lashes against my skin. When it started to run cold, I got out and pulled on comfort clothes; sweats, tank top and fuzzy socks.

I shuffled down the hall to my living area, thinking I might gorge on popcorn, I still had some. I drew to a halt when I saw Jo sitting there.

"Heya. Shouldn't you be working?" I wasn't really surprised Jo was there. Somehow it felt inevitable. I'd given her a key years ago. We used to have sleepovers, but lately we were always working or going to school. If I'd had another bedroom, I'd have asked her to move in with me. I missed her bright cheery presence as a daily spark.

"Samuel called. Explained what happened. What you did. Dad kicked me over here with that." She nodded at the large bag sitting on my counter, the closest thing I had to a table. I arched a brow and moved over to open it. Every step, every movement felt like my body weighed a thousand pounds. I recognized the signs of depression. Been there, done that, and nothing changed so I refused to give into it. Depression didn't mean I didn't have bills to pay and goals. My parents had already given up on me—I refused to give up on myself.

Trying to shake off the mood, I opened the huge reusable bag and shock rippled through me. Not only was there enough food to feed me for the next two weeks, all nicely packaged in meal containers for me, but a fifth of rum and a two liter of Coca-Cola. I looked at Jo, confused as I pulled it out. Neither of us were old enough to buy liquor and her brothers had proven remarkably resistant to our requests.

"No one should have to be alone after watching someone die, even when that person is a stranger." Even those simple words brought the image of the dying boy back into my mind, overlaid with the way Stevie had looked.

I must have faded out for a second, swamped by memories new and old, because when I refocused Jo was standing next to me. "Dad said there were some days that a good drink was the only way to make it through. Mom heard about the cut in hours from Kadia and made all the food for you. Dad told me to spend the night here." Jo looked at me and smiled. That smile had always been there for me. "Oh Cori." She pulled me into a hug and I sank into it, just letting her hold me. I didn't have any more tears, but her arms and her love helped push a lot of it back to bearable levels.

After I pulled away, Jo helped me put all the food away, glaring at me as she took in the quantity of ramen and cheap canned soup I had in my cupboards. I ignored it. Her mom fed me at least half the time, so it wasn't like I was strictly living off that. Jo poured us two rum and cokes, and we curled up on the small couch.

"You want to watch something?" I tried to sound interested, but right now I really wished I had a tub to soak in. I wanted to hide.

Jo looked at me as she sipped her drink. I sipped too, enjoying the sweet spicy mix of rum and coke sliding down my throat. "What I would like is you to tell me what's going on. I can't help if you don't share."

I shrugged. Just because I didn't tell her all my money problems didn't mean I actively lied about them.

Mel Todd

"School stuff is really expensive this year and they have
started a new program that might make it harder than
ever to work. And then I talked to my parents, and then
today..." My throat grew tight and I took another
desperate mouthful of the drink, trying to stave away
the emotions, the realization of failure again.

"Do you need money? I ca-"

"No!" I cut her off. "I'm not about to take your
money. You'll need it. I know you want school and it
isn't cheap when you aren't a mage. I refuse to take any
from you. Heck, the only reason I accept your mom's
cooking is 'cause I can't cook anywhere near as well as
she can." I reached up and scratched my head. My scalp
bugged me as usual. I ignored the white flecks that
settled on my shoulders.

Jo sighed. "If I emerge as a high rank mage, I won't be
able to get my mechanics cert, so the money wouldn't
matter. But, okay. You know I'll do whatever you need."
Her look of concern warmed me. What would I do if
our lives dragged us in different directions?

"I know. And I treasure that. But I won't be a burden
to you or your family. I'll figure it out. I just may need to
stay here longer than I thought. My parents will have to
live without the rent from this place for another few
months while I get my savings built back up."

Jo looked like she wanted to protest but she needed
the money she was saving up. Mages got free rides over
a certain rank – though they paid in years of draft
service, but that meant the rest of us paid a bit more.
Trade schools, like Jo wanted, were popular, and a good
value. But they were still expensive.

"I worry about you. I really don't like your parents
some days."

I shrugged. "I'll live. I'm good at making money
stretch. Want to hear about the new program that has

88

me all stressed? Though after today I wonder if I'm making a mistake going into this profession."

"Cori." She sighed out the word and I swallowed at the amount of love and worry in her voice. "You can't save everyone. You aren't a merlin, and even merlins can't save everybody. You did everything you could. You were there. He didn't die alone."

That almost broke me and I had to swallow rapidly multiple times to push the tears back. "How do you know?"

Jo gave me a funny look, then her eyes went wide. "You haven't seen, have you?"

"Seen what?" I clasped the coke in my hands. A bad feeling, like the worst catastrophe yet was coming at me, swam in my stomach.

"There were lots of people taking pics. It made the news. I thought you knew. One of them has a picture of you laying on the back seat of the car with your hand against the boy's face."

I went white. "They what?" I thought back, but I couldn't remember anything except crying and watching him breathe his last. I hadn't realized the paramedics had shown up until they encouraged me to leave the vehicle. They'd taken my recitation of events, but I'd barely registered anyone except the body of the child. I'd grabbed my backpack and disappeared as soon as they were done with me. I didn't remember anyone paying that much attention to me.

"Yeah. Not sure it's made national news or anything, but I wouldn't be surprised if reporters call you."

That thought filled me with horror. I'd been through it once—never again. "I'm not picking up the phone if I don't know who it is." My statement came out fervently as I set my Coke down and scrambled for my phone. I had it silent for class and then hadn't paid it any attention since the accident. Sure enough, there were four missed calls, but no voicemail. I pulled that up.

"This is Cori Munroe. If this is in regard to school please leave a message, including a number and why you are calling and I'll get back to you as soon as possible." I hit save, checked it, then dropped it on the table. One more stress I didn't need.

I looked at Jo. "This, this sort of crap is why I don't know how you can stay my friend. Disasters follow me. Bad things happen."

Jo groaned and took a big drink, then let her head fall back against the sofa. "Because I love you, idiot. You're my best friend. I'm never going to let you be alone." She lifted her head and stared at me. "I expect us to get jobs, live together, date people together, build houses next door, raise our children together, and eventually grow old and sit there having marshmallow wars with each other."

A spurt of pure joy washed through me and for a moment I felt hope, unfortunately reality, jobs, and our lives would probably tear us apart. For now, I'd just enjoy it.

"So, what about money? Want me to go talk to your parents?" Jo got an evil look on her face. "Or I could ask *Mami* to do it."

The thought of Jo talking to my parents filled me with nerves, but the thought of Marisol? I blinked, then blinked again. "You think she would do that?"

Jo jerked up straight on the couch and looked at me, her mouth dropping open. "Are you kidding? She's been waiting for YEARS for you to ask her to talk to them. She's wanted to give Estelle a very large piece of her mind. She's so mad at your mom I'm pretty sure she's been cooking so much just to keep her temper in check. And it's just getting worse." Jo bit her lip then shrugged.

"I don't think Mami will mind me telling you. We moved here when I was what, eleven?" Her brows furrowed as she thought.

"Eleven and a half. It was the week before my birthday, and I begged Mom to invite you. You were the toughest girl in class and I wanted you to like me. Of course that party was canceled when Stevie died."

Jo blinked, and nodded. Then a laugh slipped out. I didn't mind. "I remember that. Mami asked why when I'd only been in school a week I already had a birthday invitation. But we were still moving in so she couldn't take the time to get me over here. And then well," she flashed a sad smile at me and once again I couldn't imagine my life without her. "But what we never talk about is she had one miscarriage when I was seven. We were so excited about that baby. It was going to be another girl. I couldn't wait to have a sister. But something went wrong, if I knew what then I don't remember. She lost the baby. Then apparently, I had an older brother, a year before I was born, that died at six months. A SIDS death."

I knew my face reflected my shock. SIDS or Sudden Infant Death Syndrome was something awful. They did an entire class on it and things to look for that implied child abuse instead of SIDS.

Jo shrugged and drank a bit more, snuggling down into the couch. "*Mami* gets grief. She knows what it is like to lose a child. She's lost two. But she never gave up on the rest of us. Never threw the rest of us away because she was grieving or guilty."

I didn't know what to say. Defending my parents wasn't anything I could do, yet I couldn't just stay silent. "Yeah, but I killed him."

"No!" Jo's voice snapped out at me like a spark of electricity and I pulled back a bit, surprised by her vehemence.

"He died in your arms. You were twelve. They still don't know why he died, what happened, nothing. Probably a fluke medical issue and even if you had been the best surgeon in the world, maybe even if you had been a merlin, you wouldn't have been able to save him. I know you blame yourself, but you didn't kill him."

"Okay. But you don't know there wasn't something I could have done that would have saved him."

"And neither do you. None of that justifies what your parents did. They abandoned you. Not physically but emotionally and I think that hurts worse. At least if they had just left you could be angry at them." She shook her head and brushed it away. "How much do you need?"

"You have to promise neither you nor your parents will pull it out of your savings. You will only get it from my parents."

"I swear. Though we would give it you. Cori, you're the sister I always wanted. I'm never giving you up. Though I really wish you did it for me." She wiggled her eyebrows at me at the last statement and I snickered.

"I'll keep my eyes open for someone you'll like. Speaking of which, kids? Since when did you decide you wanted kids?" I didn't. The risk of losing them? To do what my parents had done? No thanks.

She glanced away and shrugged. "I like kids. And I could just see kids with my hair. But you tend to need sperm to pull that off and guys don't give me the warm fuzzies. Maybe I'd find someone who ..." She trailed off and shrugged. "There are ways. From artificial insemination to adoptions to getting it on with a guy. But I'm not doing it solo, so it isn't in the cards right now. Back to money. How much?"

I sighed, knowing she'd never drop it, and pulled out my phone. I'd made my notes in it. "Assuming I lose about ten hours a week dropping me to twenty-five?" I typed in the numbers I'd been avoiding. They made me sick. "I need about 1500 this month to cover all the supplies and fees they added for this quarter. At least we aren't having to pay malpractice insurance for the ride alongs. To avoid tapping into my savings—I have three thousand to move out and get an apartment saved—I need at least—" I swallowed at the number—"three hundred a month to bring me back up to what I was. But that 1500 is what is killing me. If I watch what I eat I might be able to squeak by."

Jo glared at me and pulled out her phone. "Hey Stinky, will you come get us? We need to talk to *Mami* and *Papi* and we've been drinking." She paused and groaned, flopping her head back on the couch again. "Yes, he knows. He bought it. Come get us, we need to talk to them soonest." She listened for another few seconds, still in her poise of annoyance. "Stinky, I swear if you don't get over here pronto I'm calling *Mami*. I don't care if you're raiding. It doesn't take that long to get here and back." Jo hung up staring at the ceiling. "I swear he's still twelve. He's older than we are, how can he still be twelve?"

I took another big sip of my coke. I hadn't really drunk before and wasn't sure what to expect. Jo hadn't made that strong of a drink and mostly I just wanted to not stress. It seemed like I'd been searching for answers forever, and all I found were more questions.

"Come on. Get up. We'll put all this away. I texted that we are coming over. You know she'll have food waiting for us."

I finished my drink, feeling a bit calmer, though was that because Jo was getting me help or the booze? Either way I wasn't going to complain.

Stinky was banging on the door before we were

ready to go and he glowered the entire time. Which just made Jo move even slower to the point that Stinky's annoyance radiated from him as he drove us back. Before the rumble of the engine died, he'd bailed out and raced into the house and back to his game.

"See? Twelve, I swear. Come on." Jo winked at me as she headed into the house, her walk suspiciously steady.

Does that mean she's been sneaking drinks or that she didn't drink as much as me?

I shook my head. I wasn't dizzy really but I didn't feel like my world was about to crumble either, which had to be an improvement. Trying not to be apprehensive, the rum helping, I followed her into the house. The scent of spicy peppers and broiling meat wrapped around me and pulled me into the house like arms of welcome. The stress lifted up a bit more as I shut the door behind me and the smell and warmth lifted up my heart.

"Come on in, Cori. I've got *chili rellenos* cooking and mini *quesadillas*." Marisol called to me from the kitchen and I could hear Jo already putting bowls on the table. I knew they would be full of salsa and chips. The Guzman's never had fries, always chips and salsa. It made my stomach very happy.

As I stepped into the kitchen, I could see Marisol putting the last of the fluffy battered *chili rellenos* in the pan." *Hola, mi hija,* grab the rice and beans and put them on the table please."

I did as she asked while Jo put out some cheese and sour cream. My mouth watered as the spicy chili, cumin, and frying fat smells invaded my nose and mouth.

"STINKY! *PAPI*! Dinner's ready!!!" Jo shouted and Marisol turned around to glare at her.

"Was that really necessary?" Marisol's tone was chiding but her mouth tilted in amusement.

94

"Yep. I'm hungry and Cori needs to spill the beans."
Jo flashed a grin at her mom, but she frowned and
rubbed her head as she headed to her seat.

Stinky stomped in, glaring at his sister. " I missed the
raid because of you," he grumbled as he sank down in
the chair.

"Oh well. You would have had to bail for dinner
anyhow," she replied, but her jabbing wasn't as amused
as normal. That was a standard rule at the Guzman
house. Everyone in the house came to dinner, no
exceptions.

He sighed and waited for Henri to take a seat, not
wanting to admit she was right. Their constant
squabbling amused me to no end. It also made me
wonder what Stevie and I would have been like. I
pushed the thought away—it had no purpose but to feed
my already precarious emotional balance.

"How are you doing, Cori?" Henri asked watching me
as he loaded up his plate.

I shrugged, not sure how to answer that. "I'm okay, I
guess."

"Tell them about the money," Jo ordered. She hadn't
reached for any food. I cast her a funny glance—my
stomach was doing a happy dance from the smells alone,
but she looked off.

Before I could ask her a question Marisol spoke.
"What's this about money?" She passed me the plate of
rellenos as she spoke.

I took two, they were so good, and tried to figure out
how to explain everything. It came out halting and
awkward. Jo prodded me twice to keep going. She'd
taken one *relleno* and poked at it, though she grabbed
some chips and salsa.

I gave her another look—lack of appetite was never
her issue. She hadn't seemed drunk, but then what did I

know. We'd talked about our twenty-first birthdays, but we had months to go.

Once all the money information had been laid out, Henri and Marisol exchanged those lightening glances, then Marisol focused on me. "What would you like us to do?" There wasn't anything in her voice, just the gentle question, and that made me feel worse. I stared at my plate, the cheese and pepper now sitting like a lump in my stomach.

The elbow in my ribs wasn't unexpected, though it hurt less than I had expected. Jo didn't do subtle. "Jo suggested I ask you if you'd speak to my parents about getting me some money or something," I admitted. I had no issues throwing Jo under the bus, the traitorous wench, but I didn't want to see their faces when I asked.

"Yesssss." The word hissed out and I jerked my head up to see a wide grin on Marisol's face, and a resigned one on Henri's. "I've been waiting five, almost six years for you to ask me to do this. I hinted that I would but you never took me up on it. Now I can. I promise, you'll get the extra money you need."

I blinked at her, trying not to let the moisture that pooled in my eyes escape.

"I feel strange," Jo muttered and I spun to watch her head flop backwards, nose towards the ceiling and eyes rolled so only the whites showed.

Chapter 12

The symbols for magic, Chaos, Order, and Spirit, are the same across all cultures and governments. It must be noted however that while the symbols are identical, thanks in part to the formation of OMO, the names of the classes can vary by language, culture, and government. For instance, France refers to Spirit as Esprit with the connotation of mind and intellect, not the same way the English language means spirit. ~ History of Magic

ORDER

Not again, please by all the Merlins, not again.

I didn't know where that thought had come from as I sprung to my feet and pulled her out of the chair, laying her down. Her skin, normally a dark tan, had flushed red and heat was washing from her. Her eyes showed only the whites as I laid her on the floor, and her body arched back.

"Call the OMO," I said, my voice calm, distant from my thudding heart.

"What? Really?" Her mom's voice broke on the two words even as I caught Henri pulling his phone from his pocket.

"She's emerging. Give her space. Remember it looks scary, but it's just the body adjusting to the sudden influx of power and adapting." I sounded like a damn recording, my voice calm and matter of fact, even as I saw the damn magic stealing my friend. We'd seen videos of emergences in training. Everything from a hedgemage who got a bit flushed as if with a mild sunburn to a merlin who damn near took out his house. Jo was coming in hard and fast. My hand tingled and I looked down.

"Close your eyes." I barked out the order as I squeezed my eyes tightly closed. Different mages emerged different ways, but it always traced back to their primary skill set. The burst of light, bright enough I could see it through my eyelids, didn't click with anything I could think of. A gust of wind would have been Air. A burst of heat, Fire. Sweat drenching us? Water. But light and a strange tingle across my skin? I couldn't think of anything. At least not until I opened my eyes.

"Oh." My voice lost its calm as I glanced around the room. Where it had once been a dining room with a sturdy hardwood table and warm colors, now it was the same shape and size, but the colors had gone to Jo's preferred greens and blues and the table was made of a glossy wood that looked the same, but different. I reached out and realized the wood had petrified.

"I suspect she's a strong Pattern mage, though effects created during initial emergences are rarely repeatable." My voice remained distant and calm, shoving all my terror and the realization my world was crumbling around me behind a very strong wall. I looked at her parents who had recovered their poise, though Henri still spoke to the operator. OMO or Office of Magical Oversight had worldwide jurisdiction for the registration and testing of mages. Which meant they had offices everywhere. While you dialed 911 in an emergency in the US, in every country you dialed 999 for emergences.

"They will be here in a few minutes," Henri whispered, dropping down next to his daughter. "So strong. None of the boys were like this. They were a wave of air or heat washing through us, maybe a moment of disorientation. Nothing this drastic."

I nodded. This was something they hammered into us. Emergence was usually scary to anyone not realizing what was happening. Even when you did understand it, you needed to recognize that a high rank or merlin could get people killed.

"So, she might be a high rank, maybe even archmage." I forced a smile at Marisol, hoping it didn't look as fake as it felt. "It looks like you might get your college wish after all."

Her smile was wan. "I haven't seen a higher-rank emergence, I didn't realize they were so..."—she looked around the room—"dramatic."

That did get a real laugh out of me. "You need to go to the vid channel. There are a few of merlins where they're lucky no one was killed." Sirens sounded, causing me to drop that line of conversation. They would be here soon and get her tested. Next time I saw Jo, she'd be a mage. Have her tattoo.

I am happy for her. I am.

I didn't know if I was lying or not—all I could see was her being pulled away even faster than I already feared. Pounding came from the door and Stinky raced to open it. A moment later, either seconds or eternity, I wasn't sure which, three people came striding in. The lead, an older man with a bit of salt in his dark brown hair graced everyone with a kindly smile, one that screamed practiced. He looked around the living room, and the obvious change in appearance. As he turned his head, I saw his tattoo, bright in the light. He must have paid extra to have metallic ink, or he could change his own. A Fire mage, probably an archmage. Part of me wondered if you had to have special skills to be part of the OMO response teams. Most of me tried not to grab

Jo and hold her close to me.

"I'm Warrick Jones. I'm the archmage for this office." He continued his survey of the living room as he spoke. "Interesting, I haven't seen that before. I'll send someone out to reverse it." The two people following him both had symbols too, letting me know they were mages. I had always found it funny that a mage and an archie would have the same tattoo, so you never knew if they could give you a hot flash or melt your bones. But merlins? With their triple tattoo they were always recognizable.

"Leave the table. I rather like it," Marisol interjected, before he could keep talking. "It will give us something to tease her about."

The man smiled again, an easy smile that didn't reach his eyes. We probably bored him to tears, but oh well.

"As you wish. I see you are both mages, as is your son, Sanchez, though only a hedgemage." His eyes flicked to me then past. I didn't have a tattoo. I'd rarely experienced discrimination because of my lack of magic but some people were born assholes. "My people will take her to the local center, we are affiliated with the hospital." He said it as if imparting great information, but everyone knew where the local OMO office was. It was a small building adjacent to the hospital. Not all emergences went smoothly. "We will make sure she is okay, rate her, register her, and provide her with her required identification." Warrick waved his hand at his wallet then his head. Must be nice to create IDs on demand. I just hoped they had a good tattoo artist, but since you had to be registered with the OMO to apply mage tat's they were rarely bad.

Marisol took a deep breath and stood, stepping away. "Let her know I'll make dessert for her when she comes back."

I couldn't bear to leave Jo quite yet. Unconscious or close enough, stepping away seemed too much like abandoning her to strangers.

Again, he flashed that smile, oh so friendly, and oh so false. "Of course. It should only be two to three hours. This is a routine process at this point. I'm afraid the ratings are private and can't be viewed."

I really wanted to roll my eyes. Everyone knew that, but they were also recorded and sent to you as soon as you were registered. It was a standard practice, though the methods used to rate mages were still super hush hush and no one had ever been able to explicitly explain how they did it. Whatever, I guess it didn't matter.

He signaled the two others with their gurney to come in and I had to unclench my fingers from Jo's hand and slide backwards. My legs wouldn't have supported me. One of them, a friendly smile white against dark reddish skin, took my place and they lifted Jo onto the gurney.

Her limp body drove panic reactions in me as I wanted to demand to go with her, to protect her.

Deep breaths. They won't allow it. She'll be okay.

Warrick approached, handing out a piece of dark colored paper to Marisol. "Here is my card. Please let me know if there are any complications at a later point. A representative from OMO will be by tomorrow to reverse anything you don't want to keep this way." He glanced around once more. "She has quite the personality, doesn't she?" It was a meaningless statement and he proved it by walking out before anyone could have responded. I watched them with my eyes, refusing to admit the burning behind them as they disappeared down the hall. I heard the door shut. It sounded like the death knell of my dreams of a possible future.

Mel Todd

"My baby is a mage." Marisol sounded relieved and I flinched, but I don't think she saw it as when I looked at her, she was facing Henri. "College, a degree. Maybe if she is high enough a doctorate?"

"Don't go counting the degrees before we get her back. A lot will depend on where and what she rates. While they don't require specific degrees, the government leans awfully hard to make sure you go the way they want you to go."

"True, but it doesn't mean I can't hope. My baby girl a doctor of science." Marisol all but whispered the word and I fought not to smile, but it was dashed as I remembered that no one would ever think that about me.

"I suppose this means we need to get her presents now?" Sanchez didn't say it sourly, but he was gazing in annoyance at his food. Which had also been petrified. I hadn't noticed that before.

"Sanchez Alfonso Guzman. Do not take that tone with us. Or do I need to remind you, your emergence got you the gaming rig you love so much?" Marisol snapped at her son, who just shrugged, but I could see he was kinda happy about Jo. It made parents happy to have their child emerge as a high-ranking mage—so many more doors opened to them. "So, the answer is yes." She paused tapping her finger on the table. "Don't tell anyone yet. Let her get home and see what her ranking is. Then we will decide. I so hope she is higher than a wizard. I want to rub Analise's face it in." She and her sister had a long-standing rivalry, always trying to top each other with the things their children had done. Analise's last child, a son, had emerged as a respectable wizard.

"Now, Mari. No reason to be catty. This is about Jo, not you. Why don't we pull up the listing for what we

102

thought about getting her?"

"Really? You still want to get that for her?" Rather than excitement, I heard worry in Marisol's voice. That surprised me. What in the world could they get Jo that she would have trepidations about?

"You know she'd love to restore it, and she's a good rider. Besides, if she has Air, even as pale, she'll never have to worry about a severe accident. School will teach her to respond in a fraction of a second."

Marisol crossed her arms, staring at her husband for a long moment, then sighed. "Fine, but Sanchez, you are getting her the helmet as your part. The nice one with the highest ratings and built in Bluetooth. If we are getting her a motorcycle to rebuild, she is going to be as safe as possible."

Stinky winced but nodded. "*Si, Mami.*" He disappeared into the kitchen, then came back out with a small plate of things that hadn't made it onto the table and promptly been petrified.

Henri pulled Marisol over to where they had their household computer, a compact thing, used strictly for web surfing and a few simple games. And just like that they had all forgotten about me. I fought down any emotional reaction and made my way quietly to the front door. Grabbing my jacket from the hook and slipping on my shoes, I went out the door shutting it as quietly as possible. The cold air slapped me and helped to stave off any tears. Shoving my hands in my pockets I started home. It was at least a three-mile walk. I'd use the time to think, or maybe try not to think. At least there was still rum and coke at the house. Suddenly getting drunk sounded like the best idea I'd had in a while. Get drunk and not focus on anything. Maybe I was overreacting and everything wouldn't be as bad as I thought. But in my experience, it was best to expect the worst and then be surprised by it not being as bad.

I reached into my pocket to pull out my phone, and to my complete lack of surprise, it had been turned into wood. Petrified wood.

Huh, that's impressive. I'll have to remember to tell her.

With a sigh I put the useless device back in my pocket. And started to regret my decision to walk home. Her transformation splash had not only changed my clothes to bright blue and green, but my jeans were now thin blue slacks. Linen maybe? And my cotton sweater was now silk? That was a lot of effort. I hoped the offering hadn't been too bad. I paused and closed my eyes for a minute trying to remember. She had flushed red, so probably analogous to an all over sunburn. Indicating a medium level offering, depending on how deep the destroyed cells went. They'd slough off first chance. Her nails were always short, side effect of working in a car repair garage. Hair? I frowned trying to remember. Maybe, I seemed to remember a white powder on her arms when I grabbed her hand, but most of the hair on her head had been there. She would be so pissed if she fried her hair, but then transforming required control, not always a large sacrifice. That meant it might be okay.

I kept on my walk, trying not to pay attention to how cold I was. Winters, even the relatively mild winters in Georgia, were enough to make me wish I kept my hair long, but that was a mage status symbol. While some liked to flaunt what they weren't, I wasn't interested. Besides my hair grew so slowly I almost never had to get it trimmed. That odd thought made me frown. It seemed like once upon a time my hair had grown so fast I needed to cut it almost weekly.

The honk of a horn pulled me out of my spiraling thoughts, and I looked up to see a car pulling up to me. I recognized it. Chief Laurel Amosen. It was her personal car and I'd seen it when she came to get coffee or had done a talk or two at college. Those classes I'd always sat far in the back and tried to be invisible. She'd never mentioned she had seen me, so maybe it worked. Or she just didn't notice.

Her window slid down and she peered out at me. "Cori, what are you doing on the road at this time of night? And looking like you're freezing?"

Until she said it, I hadn't realized I was shivering. Oh well, it kept me warm, right? I couldn't even lie to myself, shivering like that was not a good sign. And while it was only thirty-three degrees out, the wind was making it even colder. Just what it needed, hypothermia or frostbite.

"Well?"

Oh, I should probably answer her. "Out enjoying the wonderful night air to escape my adoring fans."

"Really?" She made a show of looking around. "I think you've managed. You get dropped off or something?"

If her tone hadn't been curious and worried, I might have taken offense. As it was, she just sounded worried. I sighed and toned down my attitude. "The Guzman's. Jo emerged. They're a bit distracted right now."

"Ah." Her tone held a wealth of understanding and I sank down a bit further into my coat, wishing it covered more. "I take it your clothes are the result of that."

I nodded. There wasn't much else to say. Weirder things happened when the magic snapped into someone the first time. "Get in." She nodded at the other side of her car. "I'll give you a ride home."

"I'm not a charity case, you don't need to rescue me." My protest was instant, and I didn't know why. I was freezing.

Mel Todd

"Yes, I do. You die and I'll have to write up the police report. Trust me, the two minutes out of my way it will take to drive you home is worth it to avoid that paperwork." Her dry humor elicited a bitter smile from me, but I didn't argue again. Climbing into her car, the warmth wrapped around me and I sighed with relief, holding my hands out to the heater. Sometimes I didn't think things all the way through.

I react too much, always worried about crap. About bugging people. I really should stop it.

"She okay?" It was a valid question, the OMO office was attached to the hospital for a reason.

"Think so. Looks like a strong Order mage if the transformation effect is any indication."

"Good for her. I bet Marisol is delighted. How are you?"

I didn't look at her, but I pulled up my lying face. "Fine. My best friend just won the lottery in magic. High rank, college paid for. I'm excited for her. I can't wait to see what she does next."

"Leave you? Like your parents did?"

Any other time I might have snarked back, done anything to deflect the attention. Tonight, it just didn't matter. "That was always going to happen. Now she can get a degree and have an incredible life. I'll be fine. I'll get my degree, pass the tests. I'll get a good job. If I'm lucky we'll stay in touch."

"I think you might be underestimating Josefa Guzman. She loves you. She won't walk away or let you go."

"I'm not gay. She'll find someone else."

"I didn't say she was in love with you. That girl is a spark of fire. But she loves you and she'll remind you of it." Laurel sighed. "There are days I could beat your parents for what they did to you. But turning you over

106

to Child Protective Services would have been worse. I wish I could have changed how they treated you."

My jaw dropped open as I stared at her. I had no idea what to say or how to respond. I knew the Guzman's hadn't been happy, but Chief Amosen?

"We're here. Cori, if you need something call. You've earned a lot of credit over the years. You've got a smart mouth, don't think things through, and charge into situations always looking for something. I don't know what you're looking for, but people care about you. You're a hard person to get close to. But if you need something, ask."

I didn't know how to respond to that, so I didn't. "Thanks for the ride, Chief." I got out of the car and climbed the steps, my breath steaming in the cold. She didn't drive away until after I shut the door behind me.

Chapter 13

The tales of Baba Yaga existed before magic was recorded, but in the steppes of Russia, planar rips could have gone unnoticed for years. The witch's recorded magic, granted all via stories and old folk tales, align directly with a Chaos mage strong in Fire. She disappeared from the records in the late 1800s, but it is possible she decided not to mess with people anymore as more and more were coming forward with magic in their own right. Unless someone finds her famous hut, she is recorded as probable mage, rank unknown. ~ A Study of Magic throughout History

SPIRIT

When I get a job as a paramedic, I'm taking swing or graveyard. I hate mornings.

Staring at my coffee pot didn't make it brew any faster. I finally pulled away and finished doing a bit of cleaning while I waited. I couldn't set the auto time because it failed, sometimes with spectacular results. Which meant watching it to make sure it didn't do anything unrecoverable. Having the cheapest and simplest coffee maker in the world helped. And I had two spares, important in my life. When they died it was never worth the money to fix them.

I thought about what Jo had changed my clothes into. The shirt, originally a thick cotton button up over a tank top still had the same style, except now it was a brilliant green silk. If I'd bought it in a store it would have cost me a fortune. I'd made sure it had no stains and hung it up in the closet towards the back. At least if I ever had a date, I'd have something to wear. The tank top had changed to a lacy material that obscured nothing. That I left stuffed into the back of my dresser. I couldn't think of anyplace, or anyone, I'd wear it for.

Occasionally I wondered about the fact that I didn't go ga-ga over anyone, male or female. But mostly I chalked it up to stress and trying to keep everything going. I'd have more time to pay attention to people when I had a steady job and didn't have to always wonder what next? Though the idea of my weirdness following me gave me nightmares. Mostly I just planned around it. Always have extras, allow extra time, and don't overreact to anything.

The production of coffee prevented the coffee maker from being reduced to basic components. I poured it into my travel mug, the largest Grind Down carried, doctored it with some heavy cream, cinnamon syrup, and a touch of ginger. It was weird, but it really did taste good. Smooth, not super sweet, and caffeinated like crazy. I only bought coffee from work with our discount. I'd miss that.

All packed up and ready, I headed out the door by six-thirty.

I needed to get a new phone, more money I didn't have or at least I couldn't afford to spend. But it was my lifeline and sanity. Luckily Androids were relatively cheap. I made my way to the bus stop. It was cold enough that I moved fast, but I just missed the bus.

I resisted the urge to cuss. It never made a difference. Even getting up early I still seemed to miss the bus more often than not. With a resigned sigh I huddled in the small bus shelter and focused on my coffee.

Its heat helped ward off the chill. That, and this time

I was dressed appropriately. Wearing actual jeans with a pair of long johns under them helped a lot. I couldn't decide if the destruction of my phone was a good or bad thing. Bad, because Jo couldn't get a hold of me. Good, because this way I didn't have proof Jo hadn't gotten a hold of me. I pushed it away. This was her time and she deserved the joy. I wasn't about to ruin it with my moping. I focused on my to do list. School, bookstore, class, discuss schedule, then phone. I was worried I hadn't seen a schedule in my email and without a phone I couldn't check during the day. But knowing Bruce, he'd have copies to go over with us, so I wasn't going to stress over things I couldn't control.

The rumble of a diesel engine pulled me out of my fog and I looked up to see the bus coming. I was usually the only other person at this stop, so I was a bit surprised as someone came walking up quickly to me. He was bundled up, so I couldn't see anything about him, but he came to a stop a few feet from me, obviously glaring.

"Of all the people, why you? Why does the Murphy link to me so hard? Whomever fucking cursed you must have had it in for you. I swear, I'm moving to Atlanta just to avoid the ripples you create by existing." It all came out in a muttered rush, and I didn't have to see one hair on his head, or the merlin symbol at his temple to know who it was.

"Oh Shay. You missed me so much you got up early just to ride the bus with me? How sweet. Come on, you can sit with me and tell me all about what you have planned for today." I said it in my super sweet voice, making sure I smiled wide.

He grumbled and stomped onto the bus and I followed, fighting laughter. I didn't know if I'd ever figure out what Shay's problem was with me, but he kept me from getting bored. Besides, snarking at him had become a mandatory response.

Shay found a seat on the all but empty bus. Rather than sitting beside him, though I was tempted, I plopped into the seat in front of him and turned around, smiling at him. "Tell me Shay, what's on your agenda? And since when do you take the bus? Or did you decide you couldn't live without me another minute?"

He had pulled down the scarf that had wrapped around his face. His hat was still low covering the red hair and tattoo. I might actually miss him. That thought caused my mood to sour, but I had a role to fill, and I wouldn't want to let my audience down.

"So, what do you do all day? You're an Earth merlin, with strengths in Time and Order. So how does that relate to a career?" Part of me was curious, most of me was being a pain.

Shay glowered at me from under his brows, though they were black not red. I just smiled wider. If nothing else, he was a distraction from my thoughts.

"I'm a geophysicist. I run computations for earthquake risks in the Ring of Fire. I did my ten years with the USGA." He rattled it off as if it was a common question that he found terribly boring.

I hated being boring, so I narrowed my eyes, trying to think of something that people didn't usually ask him. My eyes drifted to the lower part of his tattoo. Pale in Transform.

"So how much energy does it take to transform something from plastic to petrified wood?"

He blinked and I smirked. "What? You thought I'd ask if you'd ever caused or stopped an earthquake? Pfft, like I care. So spill. How much sacrifice would it take?"

"Body parts. That is high rank and you'd have to rearrange the entire thing from the molecular level.

111

That isn't a simple transformation."

I felt the blood drain from my face and went over everything in my head again. She'd had all her fingers and her hair, but what about her toes. I'd never wanted my phone to work so bad in my life. I'd thrown it in my pocket, thinking maybe I could get a discount when I showed them what happened. Couldn't hurt to try.

But his words had me scrambling to tug it out of my pocket. My fingers were stiff with my worry and it took forever for me to grab it so I could pull it out. I shoved it in his face. "Body parts, for this? She turned a table and food petrified too. I didn't see anything missing." My voice shook and I realized my hand was shaking too.

"Murphy cloaks you. You'd think you had suffered enough," he muttered as he reached out and took the phone from my hands. I wasn't sure what that meant and ignored it as I stare at him, the thoughts of Jo foremost in my mind.

He grunted and handed it back to me. "Emergence?"

My head felt like it bobbled I nodded it so rapidly, then I paused as pain lashed through me.

Stop it. The last thing you need to do is give yourself a concussion.

"Don't worry about it. What happens in emergence may be an indication of a new mages' power. May," he stressed. "But the sacrifice never matches. It's as if during that moment of the magic settling into you, you're a merlin with a familiar and five yards of hair all at once. Very few people ever die during their emergence. More people die when they are accidentally killed by the mage emerging." He shot me a look, sighed. "She's fine. Don't worry about the sacrifice. Really, you need to get your facts straight, especially if you're going to be a paramedic. Jumping to conclusions might get people killed." He reached up and pulled on the next stop cord.

"Don't forget," he said. "You need to figure out your own path. You've been looking for the wrong thing."

I blinked at him. What did that mean? I was looking for why my brother died. I was looking for a way to make sure no one else died. I was looking for answers to why my parents couldn't love me enough to forgive my failure.

Before I could say anything, he stepped out and disappeared into the trees.

"ARGH!"

The bus driver turned and looked at me. "Are you okay? Did he hurt you?" Alarm and worry coursed through his voice.

"No. I'm fine. He's just annoying." I sulked for the rest of the trip trying to figure out what the heck I was supposed to be doing if not what I was doing. And his comment about jumping to conclusions had a sharpness of truth that stung. I knew better, but it was Jo. I tended to worry over much about losing her.

At the campus I headed to the bookstore, already in a bad mood. I swear Shay was the most annoying person on the face of the earth. There were only two bags left and I felt my heart lurch as two other people headed that way. I sprang towards the bookshelf as someone else grabbed one of the kits. As they reached it, it collapsed and tumbled the second one to my feet. I swooped down and grabbed it, ignoring the look of disappointment of someone that I didn't recognize. I didn't care. This was now my bag and I'd be damned if I'd give it up.

I turned and stalked towards the cashier, ignoring the protest behind me. This was mine. I paid for it and cringed at the mental drop in my bank balance. But whatever. I needed this.

Dragging the heavy pack to class I almost regretted getting it. But I had a suspicion it might have given them a reason to flunk me. And that wasn't ever going to happen. Getting into the classroom I dropped the bag with a sigh. I'd need to work on my stamina and strength if I needed to get around with that hanging off of me. Oh well, I'd have time with my hours getting cut. Maybe start jogging? The idea made me nauseous. I hated running, but joining a gym?

Huh, wait a second. I pay that damn athletic fee every quarter. I can go work out there. Once I get the ride along schedule and the new hours from Molly.

The idea of doing something that might actually be a good thing after all the bad things made me a bit more upbeat. It didn't last long.

"Okay, listen up everyone. We had an issue with the servers last night, which is why no one has their schedules. I have them here. Remember we have thirty students total in this program. This is just one class. It took a lot of juggling to work with the groups that were willing to support us and help you get your triple degrees. So I don't want to hear anyone whining about the schedules or anything else. What you have is what you have." He seemed to look at me as he said that, and I glared back defiantly. I wouldn't apologize for trying to save my life. Six months. I could live off ramen if I needed to for six months.

Bruce walked up and down the rows handing out the schedules. Well to be exact he laid one face down in front of each of us. I glared at it, halfway expecting it to blow up. People around me were flipping them over and exclaiming or groaning, but I only knew of two of them that were in my boat, working while finishing school, and they were both three years older than me. Ones who never emerged.

I flipped it over and stared at it. Waiting for the text to make sense to my stressed-out mind. When it did, I wanted to cry. But you never ever showed weakness. People used it against you. I folded it up and stuck it in my pocket then directed my attention to the front of the class where Bruce stood.

"As this is your final semester and your practicum you will report to the contacts listed and work as an intern for them. They are covering your malpractice insurance and will sign off on your credit hours. Try to impress them. They are the ones you will be turning to for letters of reference after you graduate and take the certification exam. They will also assess you and provide input to your final grades. I expect you all to pass with flying colors."

I swear he always seemed to stare at me when he made these pronouncements. But then maybe I was just paranoid at this point. Either way I stared and waited for the next shoe to drop.

"This is our last Tuesday class—as you can see most of you will have a practicum at this time next week. Mondays are the only days you will spend in class and you should expect a full day in class from now on. We will meet weekly to test on material I've given you the week before, then present the new material. Figure the test from nine to ten, then a break. New material presentation from ten-thirty to one, a break of an hour. I do expect you to eat. Then we'll have class discussion and go over what the reading is and an assignment to ask during your internship. I'll try to kick you out by four each day. Any questions?"

I had tons of questions, but no one would care, so I sat mute as he looked at us all, waiting.

"Good. Then get out of here and contact your first rotation. Remember to ask basic questions like what is

Mel Todd

suitable attire, any supplies you might need, and when you should be there. Remember, even if this is the south, showing up late means you might fail. Keep that in mind. Good luck and you damn well better be shining stars. I want this program to work. Get going."

Everyone streamed out and I hung back, in no major hurry. Besides I had to go get a new phone before I could call anyone. More money. I just closed my eyes and heaved myself to my feet, plotting out my path. Phone store, then Grind Down. Make calls. Talk to Molly and try to hope it all worked out. So damn close I could taste it. I wouldn't fail now.

"Miss Munroe?" I turned to see Bruce looking at me and waving me over.

What now? Isn't there enough going wrong in my life?

I headed towards him. Smiling was more than I could do, but I forced my face into a neutral expression. That much I might be able to pull off.

"I talked with the registrar. They confirmed you are paying on the payment plan and everything seems to come from your own accounts. They refused to confirm, but you have no assistance documents filed?"

I didn't know whether to snarl or cry, so I fell back on my default. Snark. "Do you really think if I had anyone else supporting me, this is what I would be doing? Not all of us have silver spoons in our mouths to compensate for no magic." The silver spoon was a direct jab at Monique, but it made me look petty.

He flushed but I didn't back down. There wasn't a blasted thing he could do to me. My grades were good, and I would succeed. Everyone else could take a flying leap.

"Point. I made the assumption that..." He trailed off and shook his head. "Never mind. Hopefully I'll learn not to assume. That being. I talked to the sponsors for

116

Police and EMT. They apparently know you?"

At that I snorted. I'd think so. Lord knows I'd called them enough.

Huh, maybe I can be a 911 operator if things get bad. I know most of the steps already and none of the mage gifts help. When you're talking on the phone there isn't much magic can do.

"Yeah. I seem to end up in weird situations. Most of them know me personally at this point."

"I suspect there is a story behind that, but regardless. They seem to have a great deal of confidence in your ability to, and I quote, 'not fuck things up too badly'."

That did cause a laugh and the spurt of amusement helped make the day not quite as frustrating. "I'll take that as a compliment."

"I would. Better than they say about most newbies that have passed the tests. But I mentioned you might be short of funds doing this at the time you were scheduled. Others had childcare issues and they trumped your situation. "

I fought back the lump in my throat and just smirked. "See, you get punished for not sleeping around and getting pregnant."

Bruce made a weird sound in his throat. I chose to pretend he was choking back a laugh. After a minute he continued. "Be that as it may. They agreed you might not be the normal intern, though they did mention a catastrophe quotient, but I wasn't sure what that meant."

From the amount of heat that it felt like my face radiated, I was sure I was the same shade as a Red Hot candy. "Just a thing at home."

Bruce gave me a long look and shrugged. "Either way, they agreed to pay minimum wage while you are working for them. You'll need to fill out W-2's and be in the 'cadet' program. Both people I spoke to didn't seem to think there was an issue with it. "

I grabbed the table, sure my knees would buckle. It would still be tight, but the schedule had eaten every time I was supposed to be at Grind Down except the weekends. And I only had hours from six to twelve those days. The schedule had me working Monday to Friday, a realistic thing, but if I thought about it too hard I'd panic. This, this meant everything. I didn't want to count on Marisol talking to my parents. But being paid might make it so I could survive without doing anything too stupid.

"Thank you so much. You have no idea."

He gave me a considering look. "No. But I suspect I should have. You've been in this program two years. You're smart, sarcastic, but damn good, and I rarely see you overreact to anything, no matter how strange things get, unlike some students."

I shrugged, not wanting to get into my record of weird things happening around me.

"If nothing else, I promise to pay more attention. While everyone works very hard to not be biased against mages, I need to make sure I support the students in my program to the best of my ability and not assume anything. Most non-mages tend to stay in family groups for money and support. And I assumed. I won't do it again."

I tossed him a wan smile. "Then my job here is done. I shall continue on to educate the opinionated."

This time he did laugh. "Well then, carry on in your mission. I should hate to dissuade you."

Maybe he didn't suck as much as I thought he did. "Thanks again."

"Get going. You have people to call."

"First I need a phone." I pulled out my petrified phone. "Mine is a bit dead."

He looked at it, did a double take. "How in the world?"

"Emergence." I'm not sure what my tone conveyed, but his eyebrows crept up towards his hair line.

"Transformation mage, obviously. Hope that person gets a handle on their powers."

"Yeah." I shoved the object back in my pocket. "Thanks again."

"Good luck, Miss Munroe. I have faith in you."

I was glad he did. I didn't have any at all.

Chapter 14

Emergence is one of the most mysterious and least understood aspects of magic. While most mages emerge when puberty has ended, the history of magic is long and varied. It is possible that we don't yet know everything about magic, but the consensus is that the rampant hormones in the body need to be settled before the confusion of magic is added to the mix. But remember people once thought the world was flat too. ~ Thoughts on Magic

CHAOS

I will not kill phone reps, I will not kill phone reps.

If I kept chanting that in my head, maybe I might emerge from this without committing a felony. Maybe.

"I understand this isn't covered by my warranty. I just need a new phone. What is the cheapest full function – data, voice, messaging, you can sell me?" I didn't know how many times I'd said that already. If I said it again, I might snap.

"I just don't think I can give you any credit. This qualifies as mage damage and that isn't covered." The sales rep was a skinny Hispanic kid who made me look overweight, and that was saying something.

"I'm not asking you to. Just sell me a new phone so I can move my number over!" My voice might have spiked a bit and I saw his eyes flip to my temple before he relaxed.

"Fine, but you're going to have to pay full price for the phone. This can't be traded in." The snooty tone had returned and I resisted the urge to leap over the counter and strangle him. For a few reasons: One, I'd probably face plant doing that. Two, it wouldn't be a good way to start an internship. Three, then I'd never get my new phone. I fell back on the only thing I could do and not get arrested.

"What? You mean you can't give me a free phone because my old one was destroyed? Wow, that never occurred to me. I mean, here I thought you'd give me a free phone because my old one got all magicked up. Who would have thought?" I let my annoyance and sarcasm coat every word, and that seemed to finally register with the kid.

"Fine. Yes. What phone did you need? We have the newest and—" I cut him off. Like I had the money for the best and brightest.

"No thanks. Same model that I had before. I think it's what, ninety?"

The kid looked at me sourly—that phone didn't get him a nice commission.

Sorry, but some of us can't buy all the sparkly stuff.

"Yes, a bit more with tax."

"That one please. Activate it with my number." I backed up religiously to the cloud, so everything should sync back down but my frustration level was causing me to itch all over my body.

He huffed a sigh, then flinched as his computer monitor sparked, cracked, and a wisp of smoke trailed up out of it. "Umm... I've never seen that happen before. We'll need to do this over here."

Managers were rushing towards us and my head itched so badly I wanted to scream, but I gritted my teeth. I'd give in after I was outside and could get rid of the dandruff.

It took another twenty minutes, mainly because the SIM card flipped out of his hand once and we couldn't

Mel Todd

find it, then the second one snapped in half as he tried to punch out the SIM card. He'd started to look a bit frazzled, so I had mercy on him and kept my mouth shut.

"Here you go. All set up and ready to go. You can log into your account and it will sync all your contacts."

I didn't grab it from him, quite. Either way, he widened his eyes a bit at how fast it appeared in my hands. "The voice mail will transfer, right?"

"Yes, that is on the switch. If you had any it would sync down."

The indicator above the voice mail showed nothing. My heart seized with a pain I didn't want to face. "Thanks." I headed out, mentally counting the money and not thinking about no frantic notes from Jo.

What if she did die, what if?

The thought wracked me, so I figured it'd be easy to figure out. I called the shop. On the second ring Marco answered. "Guzman Auto shop, how can I help you?" His friendly tone had no hidden depths, they weren't closed and he didn't seem upset. I hung up.

See, she's fine. Go do what you need to do.

Lugging the heavy bag, I headed to the bus stop. I might as well make all the calls from home where I could be assured of at least eating for a while. Eating at campus cost way too much. Besides, I had homework I needed to do.

The ride back was blessedly uneventful. I needed something to be unexciting. As we rode I called and asked Molly if she needed anyone today. I'd take any hours I could get, but she was already completely covered, though that didn't surprise me. I told her I'd email her with my new available hours that afternoon. First, I had people to contact.

Settled in my apartment, the huge bag taking up a

122

spot on the couch, I pulled out the sheet and looked at my schedule. The first five weeks were with an Urgent Care that was subsidized by Healthstar, the local health care system, and they needed a Medical Assistant. My least favorite thing to do, but for the most part it should be basics. Taking temperature, blood pressure, weight, verifying why they were there, getting them into the room and then entering the notes. Basic stuff, and from the notes they would fully train me on EPIC which never hurt.

"Rockway Urgent Care," a brisk voice answered when I called.

"Hello, this is Cori Munroe. I'm with the triple cert program. I was assigned to this center and I'm supposed to speak to Melanie Strickland?" I kept my voice as calm as if I was calling 911 again. No reason to get agitated. Just my future depended on this.

"Ah, yes. We were told they were handing out the schedules. I'm Melanie. So here's the rundown – and don't be offended if I sound rude, but you're the third person and we are swamped today, so I want to get through it quickly."

"No, I respect that. Please go ahead."

I had a notebook and started writing as she spoke. "Your shift is Tuesday through Friday eight hours a day which puts you at thirty-two, creating enough practicum hours to qualify." My pen snapped. I dropped it and picked up the next writing implement. I always had three or four ready to use. "Hours are from seven am to three-thirty pm with a half hour lunch. Please wear sensible closed-toe shoes and dark blue scrubs. We'll issue you one set when you arrive, but you are expected to buy at least two more sets to be able to change out." My throat clenched at the idea of more money for clothes I'd hopefully never wear again. The pen's tip

Mel Todd

broke. I kept my groan to myself and grabbed the next one. Cheap pens were easy to find. "Expect to hit the ground running, though you have paperwork to fill out first. Any questions?"

The list of notes made sense, only the scrubs made me nauseous, but that was what it was. "No ma'am. I'll be there bright and early tomorrow."

"Excellent. I'll see you then." She hung up before I could say anything else. I grabbed a few more pens from my stash and laid them out. I'd need to get more soon. With a deep breath, I called the one for the police internship, a bit of hope in my heart. A tiny bit.

"Chief Amosen." Her crisp no nonsense voice answered the line and I cringed. Of all the cops who could be running the program I was in, it had to be her. And someday I'd have to let why I didn't like her go. It wasn't her fault she had to take Stevie from me.

"Chief, it's Cori. I'm calling about the internship?"

"Ah, Cori. Yes. You know we specifically requested you, right? And I know this screws up your work schedule, but we wanted you with Sam."

My breath caught, nothing making sense in my head. They had requested me? But why. And why hadn't she mentioned it the other night.

"I don't understand." And I didn't, though the statement came out blunter than I probably intended.

Laurel laughed. "I know we have issues between us, and I know why. I can't change that any more than you can. But we, meaning most of the department, know you seem to be a trouble magnet, not that you cause it. You just find it like a damn dowsing device. As such, we'd rather have you with us than have you end up in another department that might not react as well to what happens around you."

Huh. I hadn't even thought about that. She's right. Me

124

with another department might have gone very sideways.

The program was tapping three different police departments and one sheriff's, so no one had to deal with too many interns. All of a sudden, I felt like maybe this might be a good thing after all.

"Thank you." I swallowed. Why was I so emotional? I really needed to get a grip. "So, what do I need to know?"

"Show up wearing black slacks, closed toed comfortable shoes, a dark simple t-shirt. We have some cadet in training shirts from an old program that should fit you. Bring your phone, but not much else. Sam is almost excited about this. He says his shifts are never boring when you're around."

"Sam barely tolerates me," I blurted. Then I felt my face heat. Sometimes my life would be easier if I kept my thoughts to myself.

The chief started to laugh. "He said you'd say that. Cori, he thinks of you as an annoying little sister. And worries about you. People do care. There just hasn't been much we could do. Show up at seven, in what, five weeks?"

I looked at my schedule and calendar. "Yeah. My Mondays are spent in class and my first rotation is as a medical assistant. They are five weeks each rotation and keep us at thirty-two hours."

"Excellent. We'll be ready. Stay out of danger, Cori."

"What? No telling me to stay out of trouble?"

Argh there goes my attitude again.

"You are almost never in trouble, just in danger. See you." She hung up with that leaving me staring at my phone. That conversation had not gone the way I expected, and it felt like the ground under my feet was shifting. I just didn't know if it was a good or bad thing. My eyes went to the voice mail indicator again, still it showed no one had called for me.

I forced everything down again. I could deal with my feelings in a bit. Right now I needed to deal with the last call. The number was listed as Captain Martin Martinez and I frowned. While I didn't follow all the interpersonal relationships, I was pretty sure that was Chief Amosen's husband. That couldn't be right. What were the odds?

Shrugging, I dialed the number.

"Rockway Fire, Captain Martinez speaking."

"Yes, this is Cori Munroe. I'm calling about the internship."

"Ah yes. You're the young woman Laurel stresses over so much. Sally said she wanted you on her rig. Let me see if she's available." I could hear the phone being muffled as I felt rocked again. Laurel talked about me? Why? Why would she even care? And obviously this was her husband. It was beginning to look like I'd been played. But was this a good thing or a bad thing? I wouldn't know unless I played it out. But still, couldn't they have talked to me?

Reality sank into me. Probably not. I was prickly at the best of times and even asking Jo for help seemed like an imposition. My eyes grew wet and I blinked rapidly, forcing myself to focus on the issue at hand.

"Yep. She's available. Let me transfer you through. I look forward to meeting you, Cori." Before I could say anything, I heard a beep and then the sound of road noise.

"Cori? You there?" Sally's voice came through the speaker.

"Hey Sally. So, what is going on?"

"Well, we all knew you were going through this new program and decided you needed to be with us. Which means, you get me last as you'll have taken the last of the courses by then and be about ready to take the certification test or have taken it. Jeff needs to have some minor surgery, so you're going to be my partner for most of the last five weeks. You ready?"

"No. But I'll try. What do I need to do, or bring?"

"Well I'll have moved my schedule by then so four twelves and then three off, then three twelves, four off. You will be contracted at an odd rate. You'll get more than thirty-two hours, we can't afford to have someone work half shifts, but that's all in the paperwork. If you can swing buy the fire department sometime and fill it out, it'll make sense then."

"I can do that. Clothes? What do I bring?"

"I've got two jumpsuits that should fit you. You can wear those. So closed-toed boots, something warm and soft to wear under the jumpsuits, your bag, and you should be good. This will be fun." Her voice seemed bright and real. And I really thought they were all insane.

"Will do. See you then, Sally."

"If not sooner. I know your luck." Her voice held laughter as she said it. We hung up and I stared. Not only did I need scrubs, but shoes that would work for all three places. And I knew very well that you bought good shoes, even if you couldn't afford them. I swallowed and added another thing to my list of items I needed to buy in the next day. At least for this week I could limp by on the work shoes I had and the single pair of scrubs. But this weekend I'd have to go shopping.

My fingers dug through my hair releasing a cascade of white flakes and I sighed. I didn't know how to reach out to Jo. I didn't want to impose, but I ached to see her, know how she was doing.

My eyes drifted to the bottle of rum still sitting on the counter. With a determined clench of my jaw I got

Mel Todd

up and made myself a strong drink. I sat back down on the couch and downed half of it. The burn of the alcohol mixed with the sear of carbonation on a throat that had been more parched than I realized hit me hard. I sat there and my mind went back to that day. The day I lost Stevie. The day I lost everything.

As if watching a movie I could rewind and fast forward, I relived it again, searching as always for an answer as to why he'd died. What had happened? And why had I lived?

While Air and Fire rage, the smart man looks at the soul to see the truth - Mao Sun Lun (Pattern merlin of Qing Chinese Dynasty)

ORDER

Why not torture myself and go back to that day and see if there is anything I never saw before?

I'd never mentioned to anyone that I could take this one memory and manipulate it like my own private video player. I'd heard of other people, not mages, but just people, who had perfect recall, so I didn't think much about it. Most mage skills they talked about were big, showy, things that created impressions. This was trauma and a single hour's long memory. I kept drinking as I started the memory once again. If it had been a vinyl record, there would have been a groove in it that threatened to snap it into pieces. My mind didn't break like that. The wound just dug deeper each time I looked and didn't find an answer.

The sun shone brightly. It was a few days before our twelfth birthday. A Saturday. The image of the park, the blue sky, the warmth in the sun, and the cool in the shade, the temperatures felt so real that I could almost hear the other kids in the park playing, feel the sun on my skin. Mom had dropped us off while she ran to the post office to mail something. What had it been? Oh yeah, taxes. Our birthday was April 15th, Tax Day. She was mailing stuff early. Stevie loved the swings more than anything, always chasing the ultimate high of flipping over the top.

I preferred playing on the monkey bars, hanging upside down and seeing the world from different angles. I was hanging there, my long hair almost touching the ground as I studied how different trees looked driving into the ocean of sky, when Stevie screamed.

He yelled and laughed a lot, much more exuberant than I had ever been. But all I had to do was think back and I could hear that scream ripping me in two. This is where the memory gets funny. Minds are odd places and they do weird things. For me, everyone else around seemed to freeze. They just didn't move.

Over the years, researching what could have caused it, I read other people describing traumatic events, and they would mention the rest of the world going away, or everything moving in slow motion. Even the birds seemed to hang in place as I flipped off the bar and ran to him. Now looking back, it was a good flip. I nailed the landing, but I only cared about getting to him. This quirk of my memory was just one more thing among many that didn't make sense that day.

He lay there under the swings, the one he'd been on hanging broken above him like a sad flag pointing to the fallen figure. He lay there and a gust of wind knocked my hair into my eyes. The seat pointed at him. I still avoid playgrounds and the associated panic attacks.

I sat there on my couch, taking another large mouthful of rum and coke, even as in my memories I watched myself peer at him. Shake him.

Huh, I never noted before his eyes were rolled back up in his head. He kinda looked like Jo did. But you don't emerge until after puberty.

Thinking back, I remembered I'd started my first period the month before. It sucked and I was still whining about how unfair it was boys didn't have to deal with this. I felt myself smile at the memory. Stupid kid complaints.

Heat seared me as I reached for him and I flinched back. That was another clue I'd searched for, rapid onset high temperature. Though if his body was that hot with fever, he would have already had irreversible brain damage. I watched my body react to the heat. It was like something had hit me too. A pain to the heart and mind so great that I blacked out for a few seconds. I remember feeling like my inner self was being attacked, that I fought with everything in me to break free for what felt like an eternity. Then the ribbon of power collapsed, sinking into me, pooling, merging with my very essence.

From all witness accounts nothing happened that day at the park. Stevie had collapsed and I ran over to him crying. Nothing more was reported. My fear and trauma were creating false memories, nothing else made sense. I'd probably never know for sure what happened, but I always figured it was me feeling my twin die or at least start to die. Maybe it was his soul pulling away from mine. And that was my psyche dealing with the breaking of our bond.

Stevie and I had been best friends. I always knew when he was lying. He always could time things to make me smile. Sometimes I thought we'd both grow up to be mages as we could almost hear each other's thoughts. But that didn't happen and would never happen for either of us.

I never knew how long I was out. It was probably just a few seconds as I was still kneeling and panting for breath as if I had forgotten to breathe for too long while running. He lay there, limp; his body now cold instead of burning hot. I remember pulling him into my arms, screaming his name, screaming for help. At this point the world always seemed to kick into gear. I heard other children scream, parents yelling, the creaking of the swing as it moved in the wind, but all I could see was his limp body.

There were strange marks all over his face and arms. Then I just thought they looked like little sunbursts, now I know they were petechiae. Pulling him even tighter, I begged him to wake up and look at me. His eyes fluttered open for the briefest moment, eyes the same amber brown as mine looking back at me.

Pausing the memory, I looked deep into his eyes, noting the pupils dilating as he stared up at me, the frown creasing his brow, and then he closed his eyes and was gone.

It started up again with me screaming, sirens, people talking to me. I stopped it again. I drained the coke, wanting more rum, but drinking while lost in my mind was too easy. Getting up to make more took too much effort. The booze swirled around my system as I looked at the stopped picture.

How did they get there so fast?

I'd never asked that question before, but it had been a few years since I let myself fall into that day. To relive everything. I had learned response times down to the minute for most people in our town. Why hadn't I ever asked why they got there so fast?

Time distortion in traumatic events is normal. There isn't anything odd about it. I'd learned from the autopsy report that something hit Stevie so fast and hard the cells in his body burst. Overwhelming catastrophic cellular failure.

I still had that report. I'd stolen it from my parents. Not that they would have cared. That thought pushed me up and moving to pour myself another drink. I could see the exploding blood vessels in his eyes. He'd looked like a failed zombie makeup. After making my drink, I curled back up, taking another large gulp. The strength of it made me gasp, but I welcomed the sting as I got pulled back into the memory. I had held him screaming. Even in the memory I couldn't figure out what I said. Help? Don't die? Maybe I just screamed. Any or all of them were correct. I could see them rushing towards me. Police, EMTs, fire. They tried to pull him from me, but I had him locked so tight to my body they couldn't get him.

"Corisande Munroe? That's your name, right?" In my memory, I turned and looked. Laurel Amosen knelt there. Talking to me in rapid words as people around us shouted for a backboard and stretcher. "I know this is your brother. We need you to let him go so we can help him."

Even then, days before I became an almost teen, I knew there was no help for him. No reason to let him go. The memory, the emotion slammed back into me and I took another swallow trying to drown the emotions. The tears.

"We need you to let him go. Please Corisande. We need to help him." Watching again, her hands seemed to move in slow motion but I knew they were fast, strong, needing to pull him from me. She did, she reached in and pried my hands apart. Others grabbed him and pulled him away. I lunged forward trying to grab him, but Laurel was there. I saw her insignia bars. I hadn't realized she was only a lieutenant back then. I had known she'd risen through the ranks, but I'd always thought she'd been the captain then. I blamed her for making me let him go. I watched again, the memory and feelings overlapping in my heart. She'd held me tight as I'd screamed and struggled while they loaded him on a gurney and raced away. The next time I saw him was in the funeral home during the viewing. The south had traditions that even growing up here I hated. Seeing him lying there; still, dead, not the brother I had loved so badly.

The memory dissolved. After that my parents withdrew into themselves unable to look at me without crying. After that everything crumbled away.

A drop of wetness hit my hand. Touching my face, I realized I was crying again. Why? It wouldn't change anything. I chugged down what was left of my drink and grabbed the new phone. Twenty minutes later I had multiple reminders set, my clothes laid out for tomorrow and was as ready I could be.

I headed to my room and set the mechanical alarm Jo had given me years ago, ignoring the emotional pain as I put it down on the other side of the room.

It had been such an exhausting day I should have passed out the second I laid down. Instead I looked at the ceiling, my mind caught on two memories from that day. Stevie laying there, body arched, eyes rolled back in his head, and the strange heat. It felt almost textbook emergence. But that wasn't possible. While there were certain physical conditions that might cause puberty to start or end early, neither of us suffered from them. So why did that image tug at me? It just had to be a coincidence. Strong physical damage or poison could cause similar reactions or damage to the body. There could have been something. After all, I knew how he died. I just didn't know why.

Everything I did was to gather more information, to figure out why he died. Why he had died and I didn't. I snorted a bit to myself. I'd keep looking, but I suspected I'd find out who the detective was looking for before I ever quit looking for the reason my brother died.

Whatever. I need to get over this tears crap. I can't

bring him back. Nothing I do will change anything.

And that thought hurt worse than anything else. I didn't remember falling asleep.

The next thing I knew I was back at that moment, reaching out towards his limp body, but this time there was more. That endless moment of blackness, of a struggle, wrapped around me. I felt myself pushing and pulling on a thick stream of swirling light connected into me as it was being pulled out of me. It hurt as it tugged and pulled, emptying me out. Somehow I knew it was a dream, but it wasn't a dream. Confused, I watched my dream-self as she grabbed that stream and pulled. Like a tug of war that pulled at my very essence. I panicked and yanked hard, every bit of me in the fight to stay whole. Something snapped on the other side, I felt it reverberate through that solid yet flexible stream. The end, much longer and larger than I could have believed, came flying back through the void towards me. It impacted with a resounding crash that had no sound, but I felt in every cell of my body. The feeling shocked me out of my sleep, and I woke up laying there - panting, heart racing, and sweat pooling on my body. I knew if I had stayed, I would have ended back next to the swings at the moment I woke up from blacking out.

I tried to slow my racing heart, but what I couldn't manage to push out of my mind was the vague impression of a figure at the other end of the stream collapsing as it snapped back into me.

It was just a dream. Right?

If you think you might be a mage, get tested. Always free, and knowing is better than not knowing. ~ OMO Advertisement

SPIRIT

Second shift, I swear by all that is holy, I'll do anything for second shift.

The chant stayed in my mind as I slogged through the pouring rain to the bus stop at six in the morning. The urgent care clinic I had been assigned to lay on the other side of town. With the bus route I should get there at least fifteen minutes early.

I didn't even bother to look around as I huddled in my coat under the flimsy protection of the bus stop. You would think, given that it rained as much in Georgia as Oregon some years, they'd build better bus stops. My coat didn't keep all the water out and umbrellas were a recipe for disaster for me. It never failed but something freaky would happen if I used one. My old coat, way too short, was better and safer for everyone around me. The rumble of the bus had me stepping to the edge and looking forward to the warmth and dryness inside. The pouring rain obscured my vision and I hadn't been paying attention to anything except trying to stay warm and relatively dry, which meant I didn't realize there was a puddle there until the wave of water from the bus pulling up soaked me from the waist down.

My eyes closed and I heaved a big sigh, then dragged myself onto the bus.

"Oh crap. Did I do that?" the bus driver asked,

looking at my now soaked pants and shoes.

"Yes," my voice dull as I tapped my pass on the reader.

"I am so sorry. Here, sit in that seat. It has the heater blowing on it directly. Again, so sorry." The poor man was almost babbling.

I just nodded and sat down, clutching my coffee. It had to be my salvation.

At least with this much going wrong, maybe I'll get to work early, if not on time.

The second the thought finished, I cringed and waited for the world to end.

To my vague relief and surprise, it didn't. The bus pulled up at my stop, one block from the clinic door.

"I am really sorry, ma'am," the driver said again. I just shrugged. If I got mad at this stuff, I'd live my life mad. I didn't need any more negative karma in my life.

A quick glance out the bus doors showed it was only drizzling. Good, I'd make it to the front door without much trouble. I stepped off the bus onto the sidewalk. The doors closed behind me and as I started towards the front door, the sky opened. Between one step and the next, the rain started to fall so hard and fast I couldn't see in front of me. I felt the water seep into everything else that wasn't already wet.

"Really? Really?" I couldn't even muster up the energy to get upset. Instead I just splashed my way to the front of the clinic. As I stepped under the overhang the rain lightened up, back to the drizzle it had been. I cast a baleful look at the sky and pushed my way in. Melanie Strickland had asked me to arrive at seven and it was six forty-five. I'd wanted to be earlier, but the bus had been a bit slow with the rain. The waiting room was empty and there was no one behind the glass at the reception desk. I walked over and knocked on the door.

Mel Todd

Loud enough that anyone back there should be able to hear me, but not so bad as to be obnoxious.

"We don't open until seven. Please wait and we'll be with you shortly," a voice snapped back, annoyance clear in the tone.

It took me back a bit, but I replied, trying to sound like something other than how I felt, a drowned wombat. "It's Cori Munroe. I start my internship this morning?" At this point I wasn't sure about anything and it showed in my voice. There was a heavy sigh from the other side of the door, and I straightened trying to appear... something. Less bedraggled wasn't going to happen. The only reason I wasn't panicked about my phone was it had a waterproof case, and I'd put it in a plastic baggie when I put it in my pocket. Some lessons I didn't need to learn twice.

The door slammed open, and the only reason it didn't hit me was I stepped back as it unlocked. In front of me stood a slim girl, with a figure that I knew men drooled after. Slim with large breasts, dark hair colored red and yellow in beautiful braids that hit just past her shoulders. Large brown eyes, with makeup that made them dark and mysterious and skin a dark nutmeg. She was stunning and I immediately felt even more plain and unkempt.

"Wow, we got a real prize with the first one. I hope the rest are better." Her sneer was clear as she raked me up and down with her gaze.

She wore a Chaos symbol on a necklace, the gold gleaming against her skin.

Oh, please, don't let this be Melanie.

"Are you Melanie?" I tried to keep nerves from my voice. Showing weakness was bad. I knew this.

"Oh please. Not. I'm Sherlyndie." She pointed at her chest and I registered she had a name tag there. "Well,

138

get in here before anyone else shows up."

"Normally we'd get you a key so you could come in the staff entrance, but you won't be here long enough for us to take that risk. Follow me."

Sherlyndie turned and headed into the back, not checking to see if I followed. As she weaved through, I tried to keep track of everything. Noting room numbers, the nurses' desk, vitals stations, all stuff our training indicated I would use as a medical assistant.

She stopped at an empty office with a pile of paperwork on the desk. "There. Fill that all out. I'll see if I can find the scrubs for you. Don't take long. People are probably already coming into the waiting room sure they are dying because they have a mosquito bite."

And she was gone before I could ask any questions. I dug in the desk for a pen and started going through the paperwork. It really didn't take long. Most of it was HIPAA, health information privacy forms. Acknowledgment I wasn't a medical professional, and a few other things to make sure I got credit for the hours that I worked there. Then I waited. My wet clothes clinging to me making me even clammier. I wished I could work without a bra, but while I wasn't endowed like Jo was, my breasts were a bit too generous to be able to work without one.

And I waited.

Glancing at my phone it showed that it was after seven-thirty. Completely unsure I stuck my head out the door, which I'd left open the entire time, but I didn't see anyone. I sighed and moved out into the hall trying to remember where the nurses' station was. Making my way back through the maze I worked again on trying to memorize where everything was.

Maybe I'll be lucky, and they'll have driers in the bathrooms.

Two women sat at the desk, one of them Sherlyndie. The other was middle aged, probably fifty, with short cropped brown hair. I didn't see any tattoos or jewelry, but that didn't mean anything. You weren't required to be marked at hedgemage rank.

"Who are you?" the second woman asked, her voice sharp, annoyed, and familiar.

"Melanie? I'm Cori Munroe."

She blinked, looked at me, then at Sherlyndie, who just smirked. "I see. What have you been doing?" She seemed more resigned than annoyed, which implied a lot about having a mage working there.

"I filled out all the paperwork."

"Excellent. Do you have any questions, and don't have any questions. We're swamped today. My other MA didn't show up."

Great way to set me up for failure. Thank you so much. I don't get paid for this, remember?

Even though the thoughts rattled around my brain I forced a smile. "Not really. But I do need those scrubs. And a place to change. As you can see, I'm a bit wet."

The office temperature was cool enough that I hadn't dried out much. I pulled the wet clothes from my torso with a soft slurp.

"What? Did you jump into a river before coming in? I swear." She huffed and stood up. I got the feeling she huffed a lot. "This way."

In short order I had scrubs that fit, barely. They were too big, but that was for the best. She also found a t-shirt that fit from one of their sponsorship things. It had a big heart walk logo on it. I didn't care. It was dry. Bonus was the towel and hospital socks that she handed me.

"Get cleaned up as best you can and meet everyone back in the central area. And hurry. We seem to be getting lots of traffic today."

I just nodded, slipped into the bathroom and gratefully out of my wet clothes. After I toweled off my hair and rubbed my skin briskly to try and warm up, I wrapped up my underwear in the towel and twisted it hard. That made them just slightly damp, not wet. The moisture-wicking underwear was proving to be worth what I paid for them. A few minutes later, dressed in the scrubs and my still damp shoes, I stepped out and headed to the central area.

"Is there a bag or something I can shove these in?" I held out my wet clothes and jacket. Melanie grabbed a plastic grocery bag from a drawer in her desk.

"Shove it in here. This is your area." She pointed to a corner with a computer. Then she handed me a checklist with a note pad. "Here are your duties. The system will tell you who to call and what room to put them in. You go get them from the waiting room, get their weight, height, temperature, blood pressure. Then in the room call up their record and enter what the complaint is. If it is serious and you think it might require immediate attention, grab Lyndie. Then come back, update, and grab the next one on the list." She paused and looked at me, a faint look of horror on her face. "You do know how to use the EPIC system, right?"

"A little bit?" Weren't they supposed to be training me? "They trained us on it and went over how to find all the stuff you just listed." And I wasn't lying. We'd had a week's training on it last semester. Over three months ago. I stiffened my spine. I'd figure it out. Though I looked at the computer with trepidation. I really hoped they had good anti-static protection. As wet as I was, hopefully I would be conductive enough to avoid zapping anything.

"Oh good. Here's your temp badge and your access codes. Remember the forms you signed prevent you from divulging anything you may see. Go. I've got to get someone roomed while I wait for you to get up to speed." Her frustration was clear, and I wanted to snap back, but I bit back my attitude. References were important.

I forced a smile and headed to the computer. Looking at the badge, I clipped it on my scrubs and managed to login to the system. Go me. It was the last thing that went right that day.

One lady was so large the scale couldn't weigh her and the other one was broken, so she yelled at me for being discriminatory against her weight.

Half the time the system refused to pull up patients for me and I had to go get Melanie to figure out why the system blocked my access.

A mage, Chaos from his necklace, came in for a gash across his arm and would barely look at me, though when Lyndie showed up he suddenly became polite and asked if she could take a look at his arm.

At least three people refused to tell me why they were there and then Melanie explained to me I need to work on getting the patients to communicate with me better.

One male patient got in my face, threatening me if I didn't get him pain drugs now, I'd be the one needing them. As I tried to explain that I didn't have access to anything, he swung his arm backwards, hit the oxygen valve on the wall and it pierced his arm, spraying blood everywhere. I screamed for Lyndie and my voice must have contained something, because she came at a run. He ended up getting his drugs, and I got to see a mage at work healing someone. That was fascinating, though she was pissed at having to offer up part of one of her braids for an idiot who was seeking drugs.

I hadn't realized I needed lunch, and I had nothing to

buy anything from the vending machine in the tiny vending area. I was starving by the time the day rolled to a close.

"Well, you sucked. But for a first day it could have been worse. Be better tomorrow," were Melanie's parting words.

The rain had stopped during the day and I climbed back on the bus just wanting to go home and cry. But I had reading to do and needed to get ready for the quiz on Monday. The only bright spot I could think of was only two more days until Saturday and I had Marisol's home cooking waiting for me.

That thought almost gave me energy and I clambered up my stairs to go into my apartment. Warm dry clothes that fit and hot food would go a long way to making me feel better.

I froze as I stepped into my apartment. Sitting on the couch were Jo and Marisol.

"Finally! I thought you'd never get home," Jo said, glaring at me.

Chapter 17

Over the years it has been referred to as branding, marking, creating ownership tattoos, and even discrimination. After the horrors of World War II, the backlash against it became even more severe, but no one has been able to think of a better way to identify mages to easily. Anything else can be too easily removed. The idea took hold back in 1876, when an irate husband, mad about his wife's refusal to obey him created a brand and seared her on the side of the face in an effort to let everyone know she was a mage, or witch at that time. He thought she'd be shamed and stay home, dependent on him. Instead she colored her scar with dyes and make up, and went out proudly showing off her powers, using it as an advertisement as to her skills. ~ History of Magic

CHAOS

She's here. What does that mean?

The thought matched the spurt of joy in my heart as Jo got up and stalked towards me. Her long dark hair cascaded around her, but there at the temple I saw her new tattoo. The colors didn't surprise me. Solid blue, the line in bright green, then hash marks in light blue. Unable to stop myself I reached up and touched her tattoo. The Order mage symbol bright. The familiar layout told me she was strong in Transform, pale in Air and Earth. Nothing that surprised me.

"What rank?" My voice came out as a whisper. I knew she wasn't a merlin, but anything else was possible.

Jo squeed. My laid back friend grabbed me in a bear

hug. Her strength and height had her easily picking me up and spinning me in a circle.

"An archmage! An archie!" Her words were so loud in my ear I flinched, even as I hugged her back. Happy for her. Her level crumbled what hopes I had. It meant college, probably a PhD. People that would fascinate her. And there would be me. Not a mage. No college. A memory.

She let me go, pulled back to look at me, and groaned.

"Merlin's cajones, Cori. Stop it. I know your parents left. But you're my best friend for life. I'm not going anywhere. Remember?" She pulled down her pants to expose her hip and the BFF tattoo. The one that matched mine. "You are mine. I'm still planning on growing old next door to you and letting our kids grow up together."

"Tattoos? Really?" Marisol's voice cut across our intense stares and Jo flushed, pulling her pants back up. "Both of you?" Her voice told me she wanted to see, and it was easy enough to tug down the scrubs to reveal mine. "Oh well. I suppose if that is the worst you two did as young adults I'm not going to complain. At least it isn't as tacky as it could be. Now come sit down Cori. Jo, tell her the rest."

I dropped my bag of wet clothes—they hadn't dried at all—on the floor and took my desk chair while Jo danced around the room, her excitement all but sparking off of her.

"They had to do lots of tests, which is why it took so long. And I'm sorry but I didn't want to just call you and tell you. That would be wrong. Then you weren't here, so I said I was going to wait and *Mami* said just as well, so yes." She paused and swallowed. "I'm going to GA MageTech. They are super excited about my skill set and babbling about all sorts of degrees. And if I do well, it will guarantee me access to the PhD program. The recruiters I talked to mentioned a job with the Army Corps of Engineers. They said Transform mages are really rare and there will probably be a battle between departments if I get a PhD and do well in my classes. But it means I'm staying here in Georgia. Atlanta is only an hour away. I can't start until the winter semester, but they will let me decide where I want to live and what I want." She took a deep breath and stared right at me. I tensed expecting the worse. "I want you to get a job in Atlanta. Near the college. And room with me. They said if you emerge it could be guaranteed. But if not, if you pay half the rent, they can do that."

"She was a bit insistent," Marisol said, her voice dry. But when I glanced over at her, there was only humor and love in her gaze.

"Hey, I'm not leaving you here. Not for anything. And besides, you like my cooking and someone needs to look after you."

"I love anyone who can cook. Which means anyone not me," I pointed out. But deep inside I wanted to cry with relief. Surely with all the skills I was learning, I could get a job in Atlanta. It would take a bit more money, as Atlanta was much more expensive. My brain stopped at that point and I realized if I was moving in with her, the government would cover the deposits required for an apartment. I wouldn't have to come up with it. It was a good thing I was sitting down, because my knees might have given out if I was still standing.

"Jo, I, I..." The words wouldn't come and she just grinned.

"BFF. That is what it is. Now we just need to get you to graduate with honors or at least certifications."

I groaned. "Oh, I'll graduate, but I tell you, whatever I

did in a past life I'm sorry for. The amount of negative karma is becoming ridiculous." I explained the day I had, and Jo growled in annoyance.

"Want me to go talk to them? That is just tacky."

The offer delighted me, and I wanted to hug her again. "Everyone would think you were my girlfriend, and frankly, I'm not in your class. Nah. I'll have to get used to dealing with this. But still, thank you. This means maybe I can afford the scrubs and everything else I need with my hours being all but destroyed." I brightened and told them about the other two groups putting me on, so I'd get some money.

"Excellent. I knew Laurel could come through with something. I swear there are days I wanted to just take you away from your parents, but every option would have made life so much worse for you." She sighed and I frowned. The chief had said something similar. Oh well, it didn't matter now.

"It's all good. I'm fine. I have the best best friend in the world, and now I think I can manage to get by for the next few months without living off ramen."

Marisol looked horrified at that. "I think not. No *hija* of mine is living off that *mierda*. It doesn't qualify as food. I'll make sure you have lunches and enough food that you don't need to worry about anything other than breakfast and snacks."

"Oh, wait that wasn't what I meant, you don't have to." My protests were probably weaker than they should have been. It really hadn't been what I intended. The idea of Marisol's food for lunches and most dinners removed my ability to truly protest.

"It isn't up for discussion. But we need to talk about your family." She made the statement the same way I'd expect someone to talk about dog shit on their shoes.

The lump that formed in my throat wouldn't go away

no matter how much I swallowed, so I nodded at her to go on while I got up to get some water.

"As you weren't here and I saw your parents were home, I told Jo to stay and I went to talk to them." I didn't know how to decipher the look on her face. Annoyance, pity, dislike? It was a strange look. "Apparently they had taken the day off to attend a school event and had gotten home with Kris. I told them I needed to talk to them about their daughter. What I find fascinating is Kris froze, looking at me as Estella and Rafael went pale. For a minute I thought they would pass out. They tried to get me out of there, but I wasn't having any of that. I pushed in and told them to sit. Rafael was so amusing." I'd never seen Marisol smirk before. It looked wicked on her. "He tried to say he would call the police and have me removed. I encouraged him, pointing out that Laurel would love to have a chance to address their treatment of their daughter with them. They both sat on the couch. Then they tried to order Kris to his room. That kid is going to be something else. He looked at both of them, shook his head, and sat on the far side of the room staring at them." Marisol sighed and took the water I brought her. Jo had shaken her head at me when I offered. Marisol sipped it, thinking.

"I won't bore you with the details, mainly because I still can't decide how I feel about them. Here is the bottom line. They never told Kris the lady living in the apartment was his sister and he wants to meet you badly. Preferably this weekend. But that being said, I let them know exactly what problems you were facing and that while you might be an adult now, they have not lived up to the spirit of having a child and had walked away when Stevie died." Marisol sighed and shifted in her chair. "I swear when I said that they looked like they were about to crumble in grief. I have lost a child, more than one. I get it, but *madre dios*, you don't quit on your other children. You don't walk away."

"It's okay. I don't need anything from them."

Marisol turned eyes on me that sparked with fire, literally. Her ability to control it, to make it obey her commands flicked in her eyes. I had no idea how that was even possible and pulled back a bit in surprise.

"Freaky, isn't it? We found out the hard way as kids when she spanked us her hand would get hot. Gave new meaning to the term hot ass." Jo's comment had me choking and Marisol heaving a sigh.

"It is not okay, and you and Sanchez were enough to try the patience of a saint. Well I chewed on both of them, pointing out that giving an apartment at what sixteen?..."

"Fourteen," I muttered, looking away from her.

"Fourteen?"

Marisol turned her gaze to Jo who shrugged.

"She begged me not to tell you." Jo looked at her mother with a steady gaze. "She was safe, had food. I didn't see a reason to break my word."

"Very well, but still. That was not parenting, it was forcing a child to be an adult. It is a credit to you, Cori, that you pulled it off. Got out of school with a 3.8 GPA. You are making something of yourself, and they deserve none of the praise. But I laid all that out and said you needed more money to be able to finish school. That you'd done everything by yourself so far. They came around to my way of thinking." Marisol dug into her pocket and pulled out a check, handing it to me.

I almost choked when I looked at it.

"It isn't enough, not by far. Money and things aren't a substitute for love. I wish you had told me more, but it took me a long time to realize exactly how much they

Mel Todd

had abandoned you. You put on a good show, Cori. And I'm sorry we didn't pry earlier." Marisol's gaze caught and held me, like a bug trapped in amber.

It took me forever to pull away from her eyes and look at the check. I choked when I realized what I held. "This is a check for five thousand."

Marisol snorted. It was a strangely inelegant sound from her. "It should have been for twenty, but they said it was all they can afford and I figured this would get you started, and help the two of you set up your new apartment this summer." She grinned at her daughter.

"Yes!" Jo jumped up, doing her hip shimmy. "Told you I had the best mom ever."

"Yes, you both do. Now come on, Cori. Let's go get you some scrubs that fit. Those look awful on you."

I gave in to temptation and went over and pulled Marisol into a hug. "Thank you, for everything."

She hugged me back. "Never forget how amazing you are. And take care of my daughter. She's a bit of a spaz." We both looked at Jo still doing a hip shimmy in my living room.

"I think I can do that. After all, she seems to want to keep me."

"Until the end of time, Cori. BFF. Learn it, love it, live it. Oooh, an apartment. This is going to be fun."

I started laughing, I couldn't help it. Her joy was contagious and some of the fear that had haunted me vaporized.

Chapter 18

The Chaos class of magic is a bit of a misnomer, and there have been strong lobbies to change it to Elemental or Variable class, but it has never changed. The branches within Chaos each have flavors that make sense and are often described as Chaotic, but even now, people think of evil when they hear Chaos and there is nothing in magic, or in any of the classes that has anything to do with good or evil. ~ Magic Explained

ORDER

I need to learn to work with people I can't stand. I need to learn to work with people who are jerks. Treat this as another test.

If I kept repeating that in my mind maybe I wouldn't lose it and strangle Lyndie. While technically you can't be discriminated against due to magic or the lack thereof, just like you can't stop someone from getting a job because of their skin color, none of that stopped people from caring. Lyndie was one of those "I'm a mage so I'm better than you" people. She flaunted it, making sure her tattoo was always visible, plus she usually wore jewelry that jingled and jangled and basically made so much noise I wanted to rip it off her.

But the worst part was that she was useless unless it interested her. Some weird medical thing, she was right there, acting like her Transform abilities meant she could heal anything. It didn't, by the way. While it helped, it also could create issues. Unfortunately, she was a skilled nurse. Just lazy, condescending, and a general pain in the ass. And Melanie ignored it all. She was aware of it, I could tell by her tightened lips every time something was left undone, but then she just assigned it to me.

I shouldn't care, but I did. I was the equivalent of a student MA. Which meant I shouldn't be doing anything other than the basics. But I was now muddling my way through returning calls, , giving shots, (that at least was easy), and being the chaperon for any gynecological stuff, which just made me uneasy.

I still didn't know if I was, or wasn't bi, straight, or gay, but the condition of some of those women's lower parts made my skin crawl and did absolutely nothing to make me want to be sexually involved with anyone. Male or female. Just ewww.

But as the weeks went by, I got better. They really needed to work on actually training people. I made it only because I needed to make it more than I needed just about anything else. That, and I had lunches made by Marisol with me each day. That helped too. Most nights I went home and studied and wrote the papers assigned and got ready for the tests. I also went through a few more EPIC training vids, but Friday and Saturday nights I was at the Guzman's. We apartment hunted, or at least apartment window shopped, argued degrees for Jo, gave her a bad time for her latest girlfriend, and for the first time in a very long time I felt like life was going really well. Even all the unexplained incidents had lowered in frequency. Saturday and Sunday mornings, I worked at Grind Down from six to two and then closed. My parents' money in my account made a huge difference.

I had two more weeks of MA, then I'd be on the police rotation, and frankly I couldn't wait, but that wasn't what had me tied up in knots that Friday. Via email, because calling me would have been too personal, my parents had agreed to let Kris come see me tomorrow after noon. In my apartment. I couldn't wait and the excited jitters carried over into work. Where there had been a respite in weird things happening, today saw them all come back with a vengeance.

My trek to the urgent care clinic was normal, at least it hadn't been raining, but the first patient set the tone for the day.

"Mr. Jones?" I asked as I stepped out the door looking around the lobby. I scanned, looking for who responded to that name.

An older man, late fifties at least, pushed himself up and moved towards me. His gait was odd enough that I glanced at his foot. Sure enough, the left one was a prosthetic. I made a mental note and opened the door a bit wider just as Lyndie walked by.

"See if you can do your job today without causing more drama," she said in a sotto voice I was meant to hear and did.

My shoulders stiffened as I tried to ignore her and focus on the patient, but my head itched fiercely in my normal reaction to stress. And she'd already given me a bad time about snow on my clothes—I didn't need any more grief from her today.

"Morning, Mr. Jones. Let's get you weighed and checked in." He nodded, his shaven scalp showing slight stubble as he moved down the hall. I pointed to the scale and when he went to step on it, his prosthetic snapped in half. With a half gasp I grabbed him and tried to support him, but he was a foot taller than me and we both went down. The chair there for people to sit in caught me in the shoulder as I fell, his weight on top of me.

Between my shout of alarm, cry when the chair slammed into me, and his yelp of surprise, everyone came running. I'm sure we looked a sight, his leg in two pieces and him laying on top me. Even Lyndie seemed surprised.

Everyone made sure he was okay. He was. The prosthetic had been old, he'd had it for over ten years, but still we all stared at it.

Once he was settled in the chair, everyone started drifting away. I lifted my arm to take his blood pressure and yelped in pain.

"Cori?" Melanie asked, looking at me. "What's wrong?"

"My shoulder I think." Now that the adrenaline had faded, pain radiated out of it. We apologized to Mr. Jones and Melanie grabbed one of the other nurses, Susan Carol, to examine me. In an empty room they pulled off my shirt while I tried not to cry out. Sounds of pain didn't make other patients feel safe.

"You did a good job. That is going to bruise and hurt like hell. You probably need to go home," the nurse advised. "I'll get you a prescription for some pain relievers. You need to ice it and take it easy."

"I can't." Panic caused my voice to spike. "If I get less than the hours needed here, I can't get credit. I have to stay."

"Oh come on, she was hurt on the job." Susan glared at Melanie who at least looked uncomfortable.

"She's right. It's to make sure they show up and not do a half assed job. I'll add it to my recommendations as what to change for the next round of students. I am sorry."

"Fine, but you get an ice gel on that now and take some ibuprofen. I'll get you the prescription before you leave. Tomorrow you are going to hurt. You'll need to take it easy."

I didn't say anything. Tomorrow I got to talk to my

brother for the first time. Easy wasn't going to be in my vocabulary.

The rest of the day didn't get any better. My shoulder was killing me, and I kept trying to reach for things, then gasping out in pain which freaked patients out. The three blood pressure machines died before I gave up and just did them the old-fashioned way.

The thermometer got stuck on 108 degrees no matter what, even for the others, so we all went to just asking if they thought they had a fever. Luckily only one person did.

The EPIC system locked me out twice. Even after Melanie and I verified the credentials I was using were correct, it still locked me out.

By the end of my day I was in pain, exhausted, and worried this would screw up my meeting with Kris. I gave in and called Jo as Melanie shut the door behind me. She looked as tired as I did, and she still had a few more hours to go. Even Lyndie hadn't had any energy to be snide as the day wore on.

"Yo-yo, Cori. You headed our way?"

"Jo? My energy level is gone. Today has been a Murphy day. How much do I have to pay Stinky to get him to come get me?"

"Ooh, that bad. Nah, I can come get you. Give me 20?"

"Thank you. I owe you."

"Darling, you can't pay what you already owe me," Jo replied in her best vamp voice, which was pretty good. "No worries. Be there shortly. *Mami* is making *quesadillas* with shrimp and steak."

"Yum. See you soon."

I hung up then bent over and gave my head a good scratch, sighing in relief at what I'd needed to do all day. The cascade of white left my scalp raw and aching, but at least it didn't itch anymore. I'd take what I could get.

But the scratching reminded me about my shoulder. I stared at the supermarket across the street. That Kroger's had a pharmacy in it. It shouldn't take too long to get this filled. I looked at it, Tylenol-3. The idea of just not hurting—the ibuprofen really didn't do more than smooth the sharp edges—sounded like heaven.

I texted Jo. *Pick me up at the Kroger. Need to get some pills*

Her reply back was immediate, telling me she hadn't gotten in the car yet. Texting and driving got you in big trouble, especially if you were a mage. They didn't bother giving you fines, they just tacked on how long you had to work for the government. The lowest amount I'd heard of was six months. Mages never texted and drove. It wasn't worth the price.

You okay? What you getting?

Explain when u get here.

I headed across the street. It was quiet for a Friday afternoon. Most business closed by five, if not earlier on Fridays. All I cared about was getting my pills and maybe splurge on a Coke.

Dashing across the street took the last bit of my energy. Barely aware of anything around me, I headed towards the front door.

"Hey, watch out!" A shout made me jerk my mind back into my surroundings from the haze it had been in and I stepped backwards, just avoiding getting clipped by a car speeding through the parking lot. The other person across from me wasn't so lucky. He jerked and spun to the left, his bag of groceries flying up in the air. Everything seemed to move in slow motion. I saw the man fall on his butt, the flash of red under the hat registering, then I focused on the groceries that flew up in the air and rotated. Again, it felt like I was watching a movie in slow motion, a strangely déjà vu feeling, as I watched eggs, flour, sugar, a box of blueberries, and a bottle of oil fly out of the bag.

In a move that would have looked unreal in the movies, yet I could see how each of them happened, the flour and sugar burst open and the egg carton opened as did the berries. I couldn't move, I don't know if that was because it happened so fast, or because I just couldn't look away enough to remove myself from what happened.

The eggs hit first on my head and shoulders, breaking open with dull splats, then the berries stuck to my hair and clothes. The coating of sugar and flour came next. I managed to get my eyes closed, and the whites of the eggs created a gluey concoction that made it hard to open them back up in time for the bottle of oil, glass of course, to land at my feet and shatter, spraying me with oil.

Time snapped back into normal speed and I stood there, covered head to toe with the makings of a pie, cake, muffins? I wasn't sure which.

People around me gawked, and the man who had all the groceries pulled off his hat, slamming it to the ground, to reveal a merlin tattoo and red hair.

Shay. Of course, it's Shay.

I took a deep breath, and instantly started coughing as I inhaled flour, making the pain in my arm flare to new levels. That seemed to kick everyone into motion. People ran towards me babbling, asking if I was okay. Shay stood up and stalked over to me, annoyance in every aspect of his body.

"Girl, you are a menace. Get that taken care of, get marked, get trained, before someone gets killed. Ronin are only romantic in stories." He clenched his fists, turned and glared at the driver who had stopped his car

157

and was staring at us, eyes wide. "And you!" Shay
headed towards the other man. The driver looked like
he wanted to jump in his car and speed away. "If you
move, I swear by the heavens I will drain every bit of
water out of your body and use it to quench my thirst."

Everyone froze, eyes wide. There was a reason
merlins were marked. They were lethal, and that symbol
on their face let everyone know it. The man stayed
quivering as Shay chewed him up one side and down the
other. The manager came rushing out and people tried
to clean me up. It didn't work.

Someone had mercy on me and got the pharmacist,
who took my script and id, then came back a few
minutes later. "The manager paid for it. I am so sorry.
How are you getting home?"

I didn't know how to answer that. Depending on
what Jo drove, she may or may not let me in the car. A
familiar engine rumbled and I sighed in relief.

"What by Merlin's hairy balls happened to you?" Jo's
voice high with surprise was the perfect end to a crazy
day.

Winston Churchill - While he was only a Time wizard, his ability allowed Britain to survive World War II. Some mages rose to prominence in showy ways like The Red Baron or the Desert Fox, but Churchill used his office to hide how hard he peered into the future to try and see a way to win. His hair was always gone, not due to male pattern baldness, but the need to offer it non-stop as he tried to see the future and change it. ~ History of Magic

SPIRIT

Two cups of Stinky's coffee before I get to work might possibly be a bit much on the caffeine level.

Jo had laughed herself sick before getting me in the truck and taking me to her house. There, after a long shower and borrowing clothes from Jo, I had an awesome dinner and promptly fell asleep on the couch. And they'd left me there. I slept fine but woke up with a kink in my neck and the feeling of being very behind.

On the bright side, Stinky made Mexican coffee for me that morning. Strong coffee. Very strong. Very yummy. And I had two large cups. Which was my normal amount, but apparently Mexican coffee has more of a kick. I need to learn to make that, the cinnamon was wonderful. I took my pills and that cut the pain down to a dull roar. Maybe it also made me more zen.

The over-caffeinated thoughts buzzed around me until I walked into the back door of the shop and found absolute chaos. Standing there, I sipped the coffee again.

Nope just coffee, cinnamon, a touch of chocolate syrup, and sugar. Nothing to change my perception of the world.

"Um, anyone want to tell me why this place looks like a bomb went off?" I called out, assuming that since the lights in the shop were on, someone was here.

"CORI! Oh, thank all the mages you're here. Help." I heard all this getting closer until Kadia slid through the door on the last words. Her normal neat braids were fraying, she looked exhausted and to my surprise, she threw her arms around me, squeezing hard. "Please come back. I can't handle Molly in the mornings anymore."

"Molly caused all this?"

"No, that was Lori, but Molly got so frazzled she called Lori in and she went home with a migraine. Lori can't handle morning shift." She said it the same way you would say espresso has caffeine.

"Where was Carl?" I was pretty sure he'd picked up all my shifts since I couldn't work mornings anymore.

Kadia threw up her hands. "You haven't even been here and things have been crazy. It all came to a head the day before yesterday, Thursday. That day he spilled a can of beans and slipped, breaking his leg, which meant Lori came in yesterday."

Lori was a sweet girl who did great in the slower afternoon crowds and loved making tea for the ladies. The harried morning crowds she couldn't handle.

"And that led to this, how?" I waved my free hand at the bags of roast beans, the stacks of cups and lids, the bags of sugar and bottles of syrups, all scattered and off kilter—not the normal organized place I kept it. It looked like someone had torn through it looking for a magic needle and not found it.

"Because every time we ran out of something, Lori or

160

Carl came back here to get it." She sighed. "Partially my
fault. I was used to you grabbing things, so I didn't come
back here after we closed yesterday. So, this morning I
found this. They never put anything away or kept it
neat. It's a disaster." Her lower lip actually trembled,
and she closed her eyes. "The front is worse. Our day
was so bad yesterday I thought I would have time this
morning to get it cleaned up and ready to go. I got here
at 5:30. But everything is such a mess."

I thought she might start crying. To prevent that I
spoke. "It's okay. We have almost forty-five minutes.
Let's get the front cleaned first and all the bakery goods
stocked. Are they here yet?"

She shook her head, trying not to fall apart. It struck
me she had emerged and been tested, how could she
look so young when I felt decades older than her. Maybe
mages aged slower? I knew I felt like I was at least thirty
lately with all the stress on me. That, or the pills were
the best thing ever. This wasn't as bad as someone being
snide to me. This I could fix.

"No. They should be here any minute," she admitted,
looking at her watch.

"Okay. We'll do that and in slow times I'll work on
the back. When is Molly due in?"

"She isn't. Yesterday was too much and she said
you'd be here today, and you could handle it all."

"Good. That gives us time to get to it. Now come on."

Maybe I was just good at cleaning up messes because
there always seemed to be one in my life or near me.
Either way we busted our butts for thirty solid minutes
and just got it mostly clean before the clock ticked to
seven and someone knocked on our door.

"Go open it, and I'll get beans to start grinding."

"You're the best, Cori." Her comment made me smile
as I headed on back. A minute later I returned with a

ten-pound sack of beans ready to go, though I needed to get them into the grinder.

Already there were multiple people coming into the shop. I set down the bag and started taking orders. The busyness of the morning had done a great job of distracting me of from thinking about this afternoon, though I really wanted time to drink more of my coffee. The cinnamon in it was excellent.

I looked up at the next person in line, a simple smile on my lips, and I froze with my mouth half open.

An older man, maybe late thirties, dark blond hair, dark brown skin, bright amber eyes. But what I couldn't stop staring at was the snake. Around the man's neck like a tie was a blue and green snake. Well it looked like a snake, but it lifted its head and flared out flaps on either side of it, like some lizards can. And I swear it laughed at me.

It wasn't a blue I'd ever seen on a snake; bright royal blue, and the green sparkled like emeralds. I snagged on the tie pin he wore, Spirit mage, strong in Soul. My eyes flicked up to this temple and it was there too.

Fighting the desire to babble, I continued with my rote saying. "Welcome to Grind Down, what can I get you?"

He looked at me funny, his head tilting, then for a minute his eyes unfocused looking through me. It was creepy as hell. Then he blinked back and shrugged.

"Large black coffee with vanilla syrup and room for cream, please." He handed me a card while the snake, or whatever it was, looked like it was talking to him.

"I see you noticed Elsba," he said as he took his card back.

"Hard not to notice her. Familiar?" I knew it was a stupid question, but I didn't know everything in the world. Maybe it was a snake I'd never seen before.

162

"Yep. All mine. One of the best things about being a mage. Thanks," he said as he headed over to grab the coffee Kadia had waiting for him.

Even with other customers waiting for me, I couldn't help but watch him walk away. Familiars were rare. I couldn't remember the stats but this was only the second one I'd ever seen. And you didn't have to be a merlin to have one, though it helped.

I shook it off and got back to serving customers, but I remained hyper aware of him sitting by the window drinking the coffee. Somehow it didn't surprise me when Shay came in and sat next to him. The fact that he refused to get his coffee surprised me, but then after yesterday I wasn't sure I really wanted to talk to him either.

"Kadia, make Shay his usual. Put it on my tab."

"Are you sick? Dying? Did he save your life?" She put her hand against my forehead, checking for fever.

"Very funny. No. I'll have to tell you about yesterday. But later."

I wasn't the only person watching the two of them, but Shay did flash a smile at Kadia, then a frown at me, said something, but handed her a five.

She came back, shrugged at me, and put the money in the till. I brushed it away, there were customers to serve and Shay would never explain anything to me. It wasn't worth worrying about. But I kept an eye on them for the next hour or more, and the number of times they glanced at me did nothing to allay my stress. I lost track of them when one of the grinders blew up and shot ground coffee everywhere. Kadia and I both looked like we'd been attacked by brownies.

Kadia glanced at me, started to giggle, then it became contagious and we were on the floor laughing like madwomen. Tears filled my eyes as I laughed, and I

163

tasted coffee in my mouth. I would miss this place.

I looked up to see Shay and his mage friend peering over the counter at us.

"Have you finally snapped? Should I be calling for an ambulance?" Shay asked, though he seemed more interested in my answer than actually worried about us. The other guy, and Elsba, seemed a bit concerned.

"Just a stress reaction. We're fine." I looked around and groaned. "Though we have a hell of a mess to clean up."

Kadia followed the path my eyes took and she groaned too. " I thought this place was bad before. And we still need to finish getting the back organized."

I wanted to rub my face, but right now that would have made everything just grind into my skin. I came home smelling like coffee on a regular basis, but this would be a bit extreme even for me. I hoped Kris didn't mind coffee, because I reeked of it.

We pulled ourselves to our feet and started to clean. The number of funny looks we got as people walked in would have garnered excellent ratings for a reality show. We just started saying, "coffee grinder exploded" before people could ask. Between making drinks we cleaned. When the place was mostly picked up, we took a lull in the crowds to run to the bathroom and give ourselves quick sponge baths. The number of towels we went through would make Molly wonder what we'd done. But we got it all cleaned.

Shay and his friend had left at some point, but between cleaning organizing, and keeping up with customers, I hadn't noticed them leave. I got the grinder fixed, dealt with two spilled coffees, and the TV refusing to get off Animal Planet, though that I didn't mind. I liked Animal Planet. All in all, Kadia and I were kept so busy there wasn't any time to clock watch. When I looked up at the clock, I felt my stomach twist.

"Kadia? Please tell me that the clock is wrong. Please?" She paused, looked at the clock, then her watch—I didn't wear one because they always went funky on me.

"Huh. Two-forty-five. We could have closed over forty-five minutes ago."

Today, why today?

"I've got an important meeting in fifteen minutes. The bus will take me twenty, we have at least thirty minutes of closing work, and I can't miss this meeting." I felt my heart starting to race. The first time ever Kris wanted to meet me, his sister. I couldn't miss it.

"Oooh, a hot date?" She teased as she shooed the last people out. I stood there locked in panic, trying to think of a way to get home. But I didn't have a car, and given the number of weird things that happened, driving had always seemed a bit risky to me.

"No. My parents are letting my brother meet me. I agreed to three pm." I'm pretty sure my panic leaked into my voice and Kadia's eyes went wide. While I didn't talk about it a lot, she knew that my parents and I were on the outs and that I'd never really met my brother.

"Oh fudge," she whispered and looked around the shop. It was a mess, but we'd spent so much time cleaning today it wasn't too bad. A knock on the door drew our attention. Her boyfriend Lawrence, never Larry, stood outside and waved at her.

Kadia grabbed my hand and dragged me to the door. "Lawrence, take her home, fast as you can. Then come back and pick me up. Cori, I'll get this mostly clean and we'll just deal tomorrow. Today has been insane."

"Thank you, thank you," I babbled, even as I hit the door at a run.

"Address?" Lawrence asked, not even asking why it was so important to get me home. Kadia had a good one here. He was pulling away from the curb before I even had my seatbelt buckled. I rattled it off, then closed my eyes. If I concentrated on breathing and didn't see or think about anything, maybe, just maybe nothing would happen to prevent us from getting there. I didn't even hope, I just focused on breathing and ignoring everything else.

The violent jerks of the car had me clenching onto the handle, but I kept my eyes firmly shut.

Breathe in, breathe out.

Nothing else.

The car came to a stop an eternity later.

"Wow, we made good time. And I don't have any lights flashing behind me. We're here, Cori. Did you get here in time?"

My eyes flew open and it took an interminable second to recognize my surroundings. But there was my apartment and the stairs leading up to it. Sitting there, looking small, grumpy, and the best thing I'd seen in a long time was a small figure. Even from here I could recognize the familiar hair color.

"Yes. Thank you so much. You're the best, Lawrence."

"No problems. Be good."

I scrambled out of the car and I didn't sprint to the foot of the stairs, but I moved fast, my attention focused on the small figure. As I stepped on the first step, his head jerked up and he looked at me. Everything stopped and I had to fight to keep moving. The emotions in his face and eyes cut me to the core.

"You're my sister?" His voice asked, tone full of wonder and disbelief.

"Yes. I'm your sister."

166

Magic has played so much in our recent history, a popular story trope is writing past historical events as if magic had been present, or had not been. The American Civil War finished just as more mages were emerging and there is an entire sub-genre of historical fiction that focuses solely on how the war could have been different. ~ History of Magic

CHAOS

Why didn't I make them include me in their lives? In his life. It hurts when I realize how much I had missed.

He'd followed me into the house, and no matter how badly I wanted to take a shower and get the ground coffee off that seemed to be all but embedded in my skin, I didn't. I focused all my attention on my brother. He was gangly, with the same eyes as my dad, and a mouth that reminded me of mom, but I couldn't remember the last time she smiled at me.

"Want a Coke?"

Kris's eyes brightened as he flopped onto the couch. "Sure."

From this reaction I suspected he wasn't allowed to have soda normally. Which just made pouring him a small coke even more sweet. Yes, I was probably being a pain, but I just let myself enjoy the mini-rebellion.

I poured the drink and handed it to him, then curled up in the chair looking at him, soaking up the presence of him here in my little apartment.

"Why do Mom and Dad hate you?"

His words sliced into my heart hard enough that I

physically flinched. Kris just looked at me, his head tilted in a birdlike look that reminded me of his brother, oh so many years ago.

"Do you think they hate me?"

Why in the world did I ask that? Do I think a seven-year-old knows?

But the words were said, and Kris considered them carefully, taking tiny sips from his glass. "Maybe. I mean they don't talk about you, but that lady said you were their daughter. They didn't say no. When I don't like someone, I pretend they don't exist. So why do they hate you?"

My eyes closed without me consciously choosing it and I thought about the question. "Want some more coke?"

Kris looked at his glass and drained it, then handed it to me. "Okay."

I went back into my tiny kitchen and opened the two-liter bottle of Coke. It exploded in my hands, soaking me and the kitchen.

"Oh wow! You okay?" Kris spoke from just the other side of the counter, looking at me, his eyes wide.

"Yeah," I muttered, my voice not quite a sigh. I reached for towels and mopped it up. I'd have to clean later because everything was still sticky. "So much for Coke for you. Sorry." My shoulder was starting to hurt, and I found that I really just wanted to cry. I pushed everything down and smiled at Kris.

"That was cool. Messy but cool." He'd grabbed a towel and helped mop up.

"That is my life. Messy but cool." I headed back to the sitting area, but this time perched on my stool, less stuff to clean up later. "I don't know if they hate me. I hope they don't. But I know, or at least I think I know, why I make them so unhappy."

"Why? 'Cause they make me happy. What did you do?"

"I didn't save my brother."

"Huh? You're my sister. You're not a guy, are you? Is that why they're mad?" His leap of logic caused a laugh to burst out.

"No. That might be easier." I frowned. "You're in second grade—how do you know about transgender?"

Kris shrugged. "TV, news. People are weird. So back to you."

The kid was like a dog with a really good bone. He wasn't letting go for anything. I kind of admired that. I got sidetracked so easily with all the drama that went on.

"I had a twin brother, Stevie. When we were almost twelve, something happened and he died. No one knows why. Estella and Rafael, your mom and dad,"—I clarified when he looked at me funny—"cried a lot. And I think they either blamed me for it or just couldn't stand to be around me because I lived and Stevie didn't. "

Or they hated me and even looking at me made them sick.

That I didn't say, trying, at least for Kris, to give them the benefit of the doubt. He didn't need to know my levels of guilt. Surely there must have been something I could have done. Maybe it was my fault? That secret guilt always ate at me.

"Did a drunk driver hit him?"

The question surprised me, and I looked at him. My face must have conveyed my confusion because he shrugged. "Tory had her big sister killed by a drunk driver."

"Ah. No. He just died. And I was there. I couldn't do anything."

We sat silent for a bit while he digested that. "So

Mom and Dad blame you?"

I shook my head. "I don't know. Maybe, maybe not. But I know it hurts them to see me. They've distanced themselves from me."

"But they don't do that to me."

"No. You weren't even an idea when all this happened. And before that they were pretty great parents." I didn't want to talk about this anymore. It hurt too much, seeing the happiness and how much he loved the parents that had turned their backs on me.

"So, tell me all about you. How do you like school? Who are your friends? What do you want to be when you grow up?"

His face lit up and he started to babble. I just sat and listened to him talk about friends, math, driving fast cars, and mostly him being a kid. Time disappeared as I got to know him. He was smart, stubborn, never let anything go, grudges or loyalty, and I hated how much of his life I'd missed.

The strident beep of my phone jolted both of us out of our daze. "Huh, let me check that. I glanced first at the time, as I had notifications hidden so they never said who was texting or messaging me. The time of five-fifteen surprised me. "Wow we've been talking for almost two hours."

His eyes widened. "Oh. I better get home. Was that Mom?"

I looked at the text. *Yo! How goes it? Want to come over for dinner?*

"No. It's a friend. But yes, you should probably get going." I stood up and he popped up off the couch. "I enjoyed talking to you. I'd like to do it again. Maybe a picnic?"

His eyes brightened. "Could you take me to the movies? Mom and Dad don't like comic book stuff."

170

I grinned at him and wrinkled my nose. "I love comic book stuff. As long as they approve I will." I walked down the stairs with him. "Kris. I want to get to know you, but I won't go behind their backs. They need to approve your spending time with me. If the past has taught me anything, it is that your parents' love is important. You don't want to lie to them or hide what you are doing. They are too important. I'd love to take you to the movies and get to hang with you. But only if they are okay with that." I tried to sound calm and logical, but I wanted to be a part of his life. "You know where I live. You are always free to come over."

We stopped at the bottom stair and he gave me a look that was a bit too old for him. "If I was older, would I still need them to say okay?"

I shrugged. "Maybe. Eighteen, no. Otherwise, I don't know. You aren't, so it doesn't matter." I looked over towards the house. Lights were on and I couldn't see them looking out the windows, but I could feel their gaze on me. "Go. I'm sure they're worried."

To my surprise he threw his arms around me and hugged tight. His head landed at chest level, and probably got sticky soda coffee mix on him. Tall kid. "I'm glad your friend's mom came over and yelled at them. I always wanted a big sister. I had one, I just didn't know it. I'll see you later?" he asked as he pulled back.

"I'll always be around if you need me."

"Cool." He hesitated, shifting from foot to foot, then, "Bye!" And he took off at a run across the yard. So much energy. Maybe when I was that age I'd had that much energy too.

A whiff of coffee, Coke, sweat, and just exhaustion rose up from me and I groaned.

He probably thought I stank. Shower first.

Climbing the stairs slowly, I texted Jo back. *need

shower, have homework. Tomorrow. Tell you about Kris.*

    KK silly. We have housing planning to do.

    I need a job first

    Pfft. I have faith. You're the awesomenest.

    Right now am coffee and Coke covered, talk later. I put my phone on the counter and headed into the bathroom. My clothes stuck to me. By the time I was clean I was almost out of hot water, but at least I didn't smell like a Coke/coffee mix anymore. The vanilla of my body wash was a definite relief, not to mention the five minutes I spent scratching my head until I couldn't feel any more build up. And I was starving. I couldn't gain weight, and it felt like I was always on the border of starvation. I totally envied Jo her impressive chest and curves.

Dressed in night clothes I ate first, sending silent blessings to Marisol as I inhaled two dinners. As I did that, I reviewed one of the textbooks on my e-reader. To my relief the cheap e-readers were tough enough to withstand my weirdness, so I read and ate, figuring out how to write the ten-page paper on the assigned topic. I connected myself to the grounding cord, then logged into my computer, moving carefully. Once I had everything secured, I started on the paper about ethical considerations compared to a patient in the clinic, in the ambulance, and as a police officer.

But my mind kept drifting to Kris's question. Had I done something? Or maybe not done something? I thought back to the time after Stevie died. I tended to focus on the moments surrounding his death, not the days following, but this time I did. Trying to remember what had happened.

I thought back. There were people in and out of the house, my parents crying a lot. People I couldn't put names to giving me hugs. But I had been so sick. That idea made me frown. Sick? Not sick really. I think everyone then had put it down to grief, but I tried to remember. Grief yes. It seemed there were days I couldn't stop crying. But I had felt heavy, swollen almost like a water balloon, overinflated, and about to pop.

I didn't remember telling anyone that. I just laid in my room and cried. It took about three days to feel well enough that I didn't have a queasy world off-kilter feeling, but even then I thought it was just missing Stevie. He'd always been there and his lack felt like a missing tooth I couldn't help but poke and prod at, as if doing that might bring him back. It didn't. In the days and weeks that followed, my parents and I drifted further apart. Looking back, I could see that now. Then I was so wrapped up in my own grief, and dealing with the weird feeling settling around me, that now I couldn't remember what I had felt like before.

Huh. That's an odd thought. I feel like me. Don't I?

I closed my eyes and actually tried to feel through my body and myself. My mind? Whatever. But I just felt like me. Nothing felt off other than a lingering headache from a crazy hectic day and the ache in my shoulder. I needed to remember to take another pill.

It must have just been grief and trauma. Training had taken us through the various ways shock can express itself. While lots of people went clammy and silent, others were hyperactive and babbled, still others wouldn't act different until they stopped, then it was like someone cut a puppet's strings and they just collapsed. Either way, what I felt then was probably shock, allergies, grief, maybe even a low-level infection from all the strangers touching me.

That led me back to the question - had I done

anything? Looking back over that time, I didn't think so. I'd just withdrawn, they'd withdrawn and neither of us had tried too hard to pull the other back into the fold. And by the time I needed them we didn't know how to talk anymore, so I kept just dealing and they leaned on each other. Me, I leaned on Jo.

No, I hadn't done anything. We just broke under the weight. One of my classes had a session on grief and lots of relationships broke under it. No big surprise ours had, it just had lingering effects.

The realization helped ease the pain a bit. Oh, it still hurt, they were the adults then. They should have tried or at least seen, but I don't think it had been on purpose. Just happened.

I finished the paper, really ethics were ethics, not that hard to do, though as an EMT I could see patient information getting out easier. You didn't have time to make sure no one could overhear you when a life was on the line. I did add a note that certain things that might be seen as socially impactful should get more consideration if in a public place, but the patient's life came first.

Chapter 21

Two of the abilities that relate to the more traditional idea of spells lay under the Relativity branch of Spirit. They are called Murphy's Cloak and Lady Luck. They are some of the few spells that can be actively cast on someone else. While they are normally short lived, as keeping them active requires constant offerings, they can be used to pester someone for short amounts of time and are hard to detect once the spell has faded. ~Magic Explained

ORDER

A quiet, normal day. I am so glad. I'm not sure I could have handled another Saturday.

Oh, I could have, but having Sunday morning be light enough for us to get the place cleaned up to sparkling, get the storeroom back to its orderly existence, and make some really good tips with extra nice service helped. In fact, the only weird thing that happened that day was no drama, nothing broke, no one had a fit, and no Shay. It was a nice change.

"So, lesson learned. I run the back, and keep Lori and Carl out of it," Kadia said, her beads clacking a bit as she nodded her head.

"That would be appreciated. But is Carl coming back? Thought you said he broke his leg."

"His leg is, but I'm pretty sure we can set a stool up for him and set him there at the counter. Makes my life easier as he won't be able to move much, but I'm getting more of the tips." She grinned at that last part and I laughed. "Besides, if Molly has to work the morning rushes, she'll be a basket case."

"No argument from me, but then Carl is the one you'll need to argue with. We've got, what, an hour until close?" I looked at the clock then my phone to make sure of the time. Clocks and I were always dicey, but they both agreed it was one in the afternoon.

"Yep. So, tell me how it went with Kris." It was the first time we had any down time to talk and she looked interested.

"It was really nice. I'm hoping to get to take him to the movies." I wanted to talk about it, but with Jo, so I changed the subject. "I like Lawrence. He's nice and didn't even get a ticket yesterday."

Her face lit up and her mage symbol gleamed from her earrings. "Yeah. I really like him. He's not a mage, but since I'm a hedgie it doesn't really matter. We're both going to get our food services certifications. We'd like to start a restaurant in a few years. He's an awesome cook. I'm just decent, but I can organize." She waved her hand around the shop.

"That you can. Hey, can I ask a question?" Kadia nodded at me as she tilted her head, watching me. "You're only a hedge, so why wear the jewelry. Why advertise? You already said you really won't bother getting trained."

She blinked at me, surprised by the question, then shrugged. "Oh, I'll train a little. Food service courses have an elective for us hedgies, though I'm totally owning the crone tag when I'm older. They teach us how to do the offerings in a way not harmful to us. And Fire is a good match, but most of the time the cost will be too high unless I'm trying to save a dish. One of the reasons I'm letting my hair grow so long is so I have lots to sacrifice as I learn how to do it. But as to why I wear it?" She shook her head. "From tattoos and jewelry you only know the following - someone is a mage, what type of mage and their strengths, and if they are a magician or higher, or if they're a merlin. But a hedge can be as deadly as an archie if they want. People tend to be nicer if they think you could do something very painful to them. So, I wear it because all they know is, I'm a hedgie or a poser. Either way people treat me differently."

There weas a subsection of people that pretended to be hedgemages. They pretended they could do magic.

"They do?" I was surprised. I mean it made sense, there was lots of discussion about equality in high school civics, but I'd never really noticed.

"Oh, it isn't obvious, but people are nicer when they realize you might be able to boil the blood in their veins." She flashed another smile as she boxed up the left-over pastries. "Granted, you do that, and you'll end up in government servitude or dead but still. People act nicer."

I thought back to the scene in the parking lot, and yeah people were scared of Shay. It had never occurred to me. That struck me as odd. Why had I never feared mages? Probably because most people including Jo were bigger than me anyhow. And well, too much death in my life. I didn't fear it.

"Makes sense. Sucks, but makes sense."

Kadia laughed. "You take what you can get. This is a lever I'll use to make my life better. No one needs to know that if I tried to do that, I'd have to go bald!" We both giggled at that and went back to finishing up. I'd miss this place.

I decided to walk home. I needed the fresh air, and a chance to clear my mind. The February weather was cold but clear, a nice walking temperature, and I enjoyed it. Thinking about the ethics segment, what Kadia had said, and wondering exactly what you could do as a mage. In high school they just mentioned the basics. Three classes with four branches of magic and each type had specific spells. Your ranking determined what you could do with it and familiars made you more powerful. That was it. They always said it wasn't worth worrying about. You could recognize the mage markings and know what they were, and if we emerged, college would teach us the rest. If we didn't, well it didn't really matter.

The ideas and thoughts looped through my mind until a yell pulled me out of my daze. I looked around. I was about a mile from my place. A familiar truck pulled up, with Jo in the passenger seat.

"Yo, Cori. I thought I'd have to ask Stinky to hit you with the truck to get your attention. Zoning that hard is a bit dangerous, ya know?" She grinned as she talked and I headed over to the truck.

"Yeah, school, work, and thoughts in my head. What's up?"

"Get in. You're coming with us. Mom wants to go over plans for this summer. The government has been shipping paperwork like crazy and they want me to decide on a degree path and what I want to do. They have so many suggestions for a Transformation mage. It's a bit overwhelming and I want to go over ideas with you. Besides, I need to show you Sophia."

Stinky groaned at that. "I can't believe you named the damn bike that. Who names their bike something dumb like Sophia? Sounds like a broken-down nag's name."

"Your bike?" That brought back a vague memory of the discussion Marisol and Henri had after she emerged. "Oh, your present from your parents."

"Yesssss," she hissed out the word, but glared at Stinky. "That is because some people don't know why I

178

named her Sophia."

I knew, I didn't even have to think about it. "Oh, let me tell him. It makes sense and Sophia would totally approve. You going to paint her?"

"Yep. White with silver and red details. She'll be perfect." Jo was almost bouncing in her seat, the excitement level was so high.

"Fine, tell me oh wise one. Why did my ridiculous sister give it an old woman name? No one is named Sophia anymore."

"Exactly. An awesome old one. Sophia from the Golden Girls. Perfect name for a motorcycle," I told him as Jo poked him in the ribs with her elbow.

His mouth opened, closed, opened again, then he sighed. "Point. Sophia is perfect. I'm just glad there are only two of you. Not four. If there were four, I'm not sure the world would survive."

"Oh, but it would be fun," Jo and I said in tandem then burst into giggles at his grin. By this point we were almost to their house. I glanced at Stinky. He was an Earth hedgemage, I thought, but I'd never seen him wear jewelry. Remembering the conversation with Kadia, I decided to ask.

"Sanchez, you're a hedgemage, right? Why don't you wear any markings? Mage markings, jewelry, something like that."

Jo fell quiet and I glanced over at her, worried I'd said something wrong, but she looked at Stinky with a curious look. "Huh, I never thought about it. You don't. Why? You emerged last year but decided not to go the college route. That must have upset *Mami*."

The truck slowed as he turned down their street. "Mostly I never think about it. I have the necklace *Mami* and *Papi* gave me. But, I'm not strong enough to do much without a good-sized offering." He ran his hand over his short hair, his hairline creeping back already. Henri had given up and shaved his head a few years ago. Baldness was the bane of male mages. "And I'm strong in Earth, while Paolo is strong in Water. We've talked about it. We could probably create a really good landscaping business, but mostly the personal cost is too high. They hand you all the calculations and offer to teach you how to learn what to offer, but without a familiar or lots of offering material you really only want to use it where the situation is really bad. For hedgies that don't want to do college they offer what is an 'In Case of Emergency' class that you take in the evening for a semester." He grinned. "Besides, it gives me a secret skill most people don't know about."

"Have you taken that?" Jo blurted out, looking at him, eyes wide. She hadn't known either. That did, in a weird way, make me feel better.

"Yep. Last fall. That was what I was doing most Wednesdays. It was interesting and I tell you, learning what I did makes mages really scary. What *Mami* and *Papi* could do if they wanted to."

"Ronin," both Jo and I whispered. The Ronin were mages who refused to abide by the laws of the OMO, which had a global impact on most rules. There were some merlins who spent their entire draft decade hunting them. Most lower-ranked mages didn't bother. When it would take a quarter of an inch of your fingernail to light a campfire, using a lighter was easier. Oh, they could still kill.

I pulled my mind away from that.

"Good to know. Maybe, Jo, you'll tell me what you're learning at college."

Jo snorted. "Please, I'm going to make you help me with my homework. You were always a better student than I was."

"If you cook, so we don't have to eat out all the time, I'll clean and help."

"Double deal. If you ate out all the time, even you would start to put on weight. I have no desire to prove the truth of the freshmen fifteen, *no bueno*."

The three of us laughed and traipsed into the house. Marisol had a stew going on the stove that filled the house with smells of spices. For a moment I just stood there and marveled at my own stupidity. Why was I so willing to walk away from the best things in my life? Thank the Merlins Jo would fight for me, because this just proved I wouldn't fight for myself. I needed to get better at that.

Even so, I walked in, absorbing every bit, as always scared I'd lose it in a heartbeat. Just like I lost Stevie.

Chapter 22

Nikola Tesla - An Air merlin. Known for his electricity experiments, what people didn't realize was that he was calling his own electricity via magic to test it and make sure it worked. Upon his death in 1937, a suspected attack by creditors, his notes were sealed and willed to the next Air merlin from Serbia. Unfortunately, this would not occur for another thirty years, and by that time his notes were no longer relevant. ~ Famous Mages

SPIRIT

I hope this class is more interesting than it sounds. And I swear, I'd better have gotten an A on this paper.

After getting home from Jo's last night, where I had eaten too much and Marisol sent me home with yet more food, I'd finished the paper, adding in aspects of ethics and magic that we hadn't discussed in class. If you weren't under HIPAA, were you required to keep your mouth shut? What if keeping your mouth shut meant the patient died? It would get hairy with some of the odd situations. And I'd been in more than one of them. The guy who fell from the sky kept coming back to me. That one could still give me nightmares.

I settled into an open chair—it wasn't a big classroom and the best ones were the ones near the heater. Only thing we could figure was the school tried to save money by keeping the experimental courses in the parts of the building where the heating didn't work.

I pulled out my notebook, focused, and cleared my mind. I'd already overcome the worst. This was the last week of MA and I couldn't wait. While I'd be glad to get the certification, I really didn't like dealing with the crap they had to put up with, and urgent care was nowhere near as bad as a clinic. There was nothing that made me want to become a nurse or a doctor.

Not that it would happen. I didn't have the magic to pay for the schooling or the brilliance to get the scholarship otherwise.

Monique glared at me as she walked in, a sneer on her face.

"That is my seat."

I looked at the seat then at her. "Obviously not, as I'm sitting in it. Next time, get your name put on it."

She flushed and stalked by me, knocking my stuff off the desk. I sighed and bent over, picking it back up.

Bruce walked in, handing out papers from last week. He nodded at me. "Interesting. The effect of experience to be able to make the right snap decisions. That experience with serious situations as a child/teen can provide a better balance at making them as an adult and using kids growing up in war zones as examples was excellent. Good job."

I flipped it over as he continued his routine and I grinned at the A in big red pencil on it. At least this was something I could be proud of.

"Okay peeps. I'm sure you've all been loving all this free time and having plenty of energy to get papers done." A groan of protest met him. The hours were as bad as working full time, but without pay. "See? Lots of free time. That should make the papers due next week interesting." He paused and looked around. "How many of you have high rank magic users in your family or close friends who have gone through the full training course?"

Only two people raised their hands and Monique was one of them. Most of us came from families with little to no magic. And while Jo qualified, she still had years of schooling to go through, so I kept my hand down.

"Hmm, about what I expected actually. For those of you who pay attention to the syllabus, you'll know this a section of the course is devoted to the responsibilities of magic users. While I am sure you all know about the Mage Draft, and the general rules, most non-magic users don't know the details. This is all stuff the government goes over with you in the first week of college. I can see you all shrugging. Why should you care about the legal requirements for mages? Well, here is one of the things that isn't spoken about much. Any tattooed mage, so generally any mage magician or higher, is required to render service to any first responder upon request." Half the class sat up straighter at that and I leaned forward, both worried and fascinated. I knew you didn't need to be tattooed if you were a hedge, at least hear in the United States. "If you are a merlin, even after you finish your mandatory service you must keep current contact info on file with FEMA. In the case of any national disaster or emergency, they can be recalled to assist." At this point the entire room was paying attention and I couldn't blame them.

Is this what Shay faces? If Chief Amosen needs him, he has to help?

I wasn't sure about that. Merlins were powerful, but there were always costs to doing any magic, even for merlins. A few hands went up. I resisted raising mine, I wanted to see what others asked first.

"Give me a bit before you start asking questions." Bruce nodded at the people who put down their hands. "If I don't answer your questions as I cover this material, I'll leave about an hour from three to four just for the question aspect. If you need clarification on something I'm saying, let me know."

My Luck

The people who'd raised their hands nodded their heads, and we waited for the next bombshell.

I'd always known about the mandatory service. I hated that Jo would be required to serve. Most people could turn it into an advantage, but there were always news stories about people who made it be the worst thing ever. Though if I thought about it, I'd never heard of a merlin saying that.

"Now, most of you know that to do magic of any type it requires an offering of your genetic material. For mages with familiars they can use material not attached to them anymore. How many people have ever seen a familiar?"

I raised my hand, and two other people did also.

"What about a familiar's hope chest?"

Only one person kept their hand up.

"Okay, then I'll cover that too. In response to an emergency, a magic user can be asked to use up half their available non-living organic material to assist first responders. They cannot be asked to offer up any living cells, though all mages can make the choice to do that. Any mage with a familiar can use material that is no longer attached to them. This is why most mages let their hair grow as long as possible. It is the best way to offer. Nails are next, then it follows to the outer layer of skin. Living cells have double the power of dead cells - so you will see many mages using blood as their offering, especially those who are very active. Blood is replenished easily and is very dense."

He took a drink of his water and looked at us. "Remember that the higher rank you are, the less the cost is. If you are a mage, you'll be trained in the costs and be able to calculate without thought. For some reason access to magic also gives you an exact knowledge of what your offering will be to pull

Mel Todd

something off. " Bruce shrugged. "None of that matters, but I want to make sure you understand it. A mage walks by and you ask them to stabilize someone you are trying to save, and their personal cost will be much higher than for an archmage with the same skills and strengths. People have been known to offer up body parts to save lives, but most people aren't willing to do that for a stranger - and you can NOT ask that of them." His voice stressed those last words.

"I need to make sure you are clear on this. While any mage is bound to assist you, if they say these words, "The cost is detrimental," you're done. You don't ask, you nod, and you do your best."

"But what if they're lying?" I was glad someone else blurted that out and not me, but I wanted to know the answer to that question.

"Not your problem."

Huh?

Most of the class had that reaction. And we all stared at him in confusion. He must have been prepared for this because he clicked his computer and the projector woke up with the words Good Samaritan and Wandering Mage laws written on it.

"The way the Good Samaritan Act works is if you - as a non or basically trained - civilian stop to assist someone and they die or get hurt worse because of your actions, you can't be held liable as long as there is no doubt as to your intent. Remember as soon as you graduate or get certified, you are no longer considered a civilian."

I flinched at that. I'd known it, but kinda forgotten. Up until now that law had protected me, though in most of the cases I couldn't have done anything to save them anyhow. But now if I failed, I could be held liable. It was a sobering thought.

186

"The Wandering Mage is a bit different." He clicked and another screen popped up. "The legalese of this law is a bit archaic and confusing. It was drafted and passed at the end of the 1800's, so it reads oddly. The gist of it is this - as long as the mage does not lose something that they are unable to regain, they are expected to assist to the full extent of their abilities. Now those are my words on this, but remember this phrase." The screen changed and a paragraph was highlighted there. "This sentence has been both a boon and a curse to many a mage who has run afoul of it."

I focused on the screen, reading the sentence slowly.

> In as so much that the lack of what would be offered by the mage does not affect either their health, appearance, or reputation; the request of any official from either the federal, state, county, or city government for assistance to prevent either the serious injury or death of any person or persons, whether known or unknown to the mage, must be granted until the offering boundary is crossed. At such time the mage may demure with the words, '"The cost is 'detrimental".

The whole class was silent for a while. Then someone spoke up. "Then why don't mages just avoid crime scenes or accidents?"

Bruce smiled a dry humorless smile. "They do. Think, how often have you ever heard anyone praising a mage's actions if they weren't directly involved in what happened? They don't want to get pulled into drama any more than most civilians do. Hence the law. But again, you can't ask a mage to sacrifice anything that might damage them. Back in the early 1900's, about 1929 I

187

think, there was a case. A young woman refused to help a carriage of immigrants from Ireland that had overturned. The injuries were horrific, it was documented extensively even by the reporters of that time. If you get a chance, look up the Irish Coach Riots in Detroit. But back to the point. She refused. Later she was brought up on charges of not being willing to sacrifice non-vital organic material to prevent over fifteen people from dying a very painful death."

He must have seen the questions in people's eyes, because he shook his head. "Nope, not explaining the case or the situation, go look it up if you want the details."

There was a flurry of people pulling up their phones. I just watched him. This was all fascinating and a much darker side of magic than what they talked about at school. But then, could you imagine a school full of kids with magic? It made my skin crawl. Kids sucked.

"Back to the point at hand. After the victims died, she was tried for refusing to adhere to the Wandering Mage law. Note, this is a federal law and the US, in fact most UN countries, have reciprocal agreements to abide by their countries' versions of this law." He took a drink of water, walking back and forth as he talked. "She, and I want to stress this, successfully argued that offering up her hair would have made her too bald to save that many and that would be detrimental not only to her social standing, but her ability to gain a husband, and violate the contract she had with her employer to not 'recklessly expend resources.'" Bruce smirked. "Think about that. She won because it might have made her less attractive to men."

The class sat there in silence, looking at each other. I kept my hair short, barely past my chin. Mages almost always had long braids or hair, most of the time with beads or strings woven in them. They never got their hair cut unless they had a familiar.

"Okay, so this is sinking in. What this means is you can request assistance from a mage. The odds are that in eighty-five percent of the cases it will be a minor offering from them, but it's that last fifteen percent where you need to accept the fact that they can refuse. You cannot force them." He gave us all a hard look. "Let me repeat that. You can NOT force them. Even the attempt is justification for them to kill you in self-defense. If they refuse, note it and move on. Let the legal arm of the federal government deal with the charges. It isn't your problem."

I sat there just blinking at him, unable to even conceive of a situation where I had the ability to help and I would choose not to, for my hair.

"So just to get this to sink in, by next week you need to dig up and compare and contrast two cases where mages were charged with not assisting. One must be a successful prosecution and one must be a successful defense. And no, you may not use the Irish Coach Riot as an example. Go find something new and interesting."

People grumbled and he ignored us. "Moving on. Police radio signals here in our state and in the local departments you will be working with."

The rest of the day was spent taking notes, doing pop quizzes on call signs, and then moving on to an anatomy refresher, something that never hurt. But I couldn't get out of my mind the idea of refusing, even if it cost you your life. I would have given my life to save Stevie.

Chapter 23

Magic is the worst type of drug, one that is freely accessible to some of us with the only limits being our imagination. Everyone should take vows of abstinence from magic and together we can create a world where everyone is equal. ~ From a speech by Freedom from Magic

CHAOS

By all the Merlins, please don't let this suck too much. I need to be able to work WITH the police.

I'd finished my last day of MA on Friday, and Melanie had graded me at 3.8, so I wasn't going to complain. Though I really wanted to take her to task about Lyndie, I knew she didn't want to risk not having a mage on staff. So for once in my life, I managed not to snark, got my grade, and left on good terms. Really good terms as she offered to hire me once I graduated.

Thanks, but I'd have to be really, extremely, over the top desperate to agree to that.

Even the thought made me nauseous. Dealing with people who whined all day long, even when no blood was spurting out of them, was not my cup of anything. Much less coffee. I'd pass.

Monday, after a class devoted to hands-on medical practicum, Laurel Amosen had called me, asking me to arrive by eight am today. If my calculations were right, I should be there by seven-fifteen.

The police station was only a ten-minute walk from Grind Down, so I'd left super early and grabbed three cups of coffee. Well, a refill in my mug and one to go cup each for Sam and the chief. I had no problem buttering up people when I needed to, and besides, at this point I knew for sure what they loved, and what they splurged on. They got their splurge drinks. And I still wasn't sure why they wanted me.

Cori Catastrophe.

The name hung in my mind as I walked into the station. We were a small town, but we still had an entryway to screen people. A cop I recognized but didn't actually know sat at the window working on something. He looked up and nodded at me, his eyes assessing.

"Cori Munroe, right?"

"Yes. I come bringing peace offerings for Samuel and the chief." I held up the cups of coffee and tried to smile winningly. From his smirk, I'm pretty sure I looked like a scared teenager, which wasn't far off. I felt like a scared teenager. Heck the last time I'd been in here I thought they were going to charge me with murder. It had not been fun.

"I'll buzz you in. Sam isn't in yet, but the chief is. You know the way?"

I didn't know if he was asking seriously or giving me a bad time, so I just nodded. A minute later I walked towards her office, this time paying a bit more attention to my surroundings. The walls were a boring beige that I really wanted to add some color to, and the desks all looked like they were refugees from old sixties television. I couldn't imagine how bad their backs hurt if they had to sit in those chairs for long. What made me bury my nose into my coffee cup and inhale the comforting smell of raspberry and mint was the odor of fear and sweat that seemed soaked into the walls. It made me want to run, even though I was supposed to be there.

They need a good steam cleaning. Or an exorcist.

The thought made me smile, imagining a man walking through with sage and incense, calling out all the bad odors and replacing them with good ones. Sage and rosemary would be a good start. If I had to work here, I'd so have those essence things on my desk.

With my hands full I couldn't really knock, but her door was open. "Chief?" I stood there as she looked up from her phone. Had I really caught her playing games, that would be awesome. Proof she was human.

"Come one in, Cori. Oh, is one of those for me?" Her eyes locked onto the tray I carried.

"Yep. One for you and one for Sam." I set them down on the desk and rescued my mug from it.

She glanced back down at her phone, and I realized a face was watching us from it, the fire chief. "Hey Martin. Cori's here so I'm going to go. Love you."

"Love you too, babe. Don't be too hard on anyone today. I'll have dinner ready when you get home."

The chief laughed. "I'll try. Mwah." With that she disconnected the video call and reached for the cup that had Amosen on it. "If this is what you bring every morning you'll make friends here fast."

I was still sitting there, mug raised halfway, looking at her in shock. "You told him you loved him? He told you that?" I blurted out the words looking at her. The expression on her face tore at me a bit.

With her cup in her hands she leaned back and looked at me, eyes serious. "Not everyone is like your parents or even the Guzmans. I don't think you've been around your parents enough as an adult to even know how they express love. And Henri and Marisol have been married for so long they probably have codes and actions that repeat those sentiments every day, you just have never thought about them. Telling people you love them is important. Especially when you are in our line of work. Every time we see them might be the last time."

A trail of ice followed by a slimly sensation ran down my back and I shuddered, taking an overly large gulp of coffee and then choking. The chief just watched me and I couldn't read anything in her expression. When I had finished choking, and somehow managed to not spit up all over myself, she spoke.

"You know I'm not your enemy, right? You're annoying and aggravating, and say things at the wrong time, but most of us in town have watched you with a bit of admiration and awe."

"Wait what?? Why in the world would anyone be impressed with me? I'm a nobody. Or did you watch for the entertainment factor? To see what catastrophe I got into next?" Bitterness coated the last part of my sentence.

Excellent, I went from incredulous to mocking in three seconds. New record. Someday I will learn to keep my mouth shut, or at least be polite.

To my surprise Laurel chuckled. It wasn't much, but it was enough to get my shoulders to unclench.

"Oh, part of it may have been that. You must admit you seem to go straight towards trouble or vice versa. If you had started this recently, I'd be pulling you in for mage testing. But I can't remember a time you weren't like this. So, I think it's just you."

"So what would the other part be?" I felt like a cat watching something, not sure which of them was the predator.

She sighed, got up, and to my surprise and discomfort, closed the door. Even more worried now, I watched her, waiting. But for what I didn't have the slightest idea.

"By the time you were a teenager, your parents had quit being a factor in your life. You took the bus everywhere or walked. You made your own lunches, even forged your own school notes."

I turned red at that. I hadn't thought anyone had noticed. But my parents just pretended they never heard me when I asked.

"The school called me, and stores called me. I think I found you and your brother about three months before I became chief." She brushed that away like it wasn't important.

"Why?" And I really wanted to know, why would anyone care, or was forging notes that big of a deal?

"Child neglect. Borderline abuse."

I didn't know how to react. Pretend like I had no idea what she was talking about? I tried, but my body reacted, sinking down and hiding behind my mug.

"It was abuse, Cori. Parents are supposed to support their child, care about them."

"So why didn't you do anything?" A year ago, even six months ago I might have shouted it. But right now I just asked, unsure I really wanted to know the answer.

"We almost did. A bunch of times. But," she sighed rubbing her wedding ring. "They would have pulled you from the house, put you with strangers, dragged all of you to court, and for what? It wouldn't have woken your parents up. If that would have worked, your teachers reaming them out might have registered. It didn't. So we let you be. You were smart, competent, healthy, and we figured any more disruption in your life would be worse than leaving you there." She paused for a very long time staring at me. "Were we wrong?"

Taking refuge in my drink, I closed my eyes, inhaled and thought. Maybe five minutes went by and she just waited. I appreciated that.

"I think a thank-you is in order." I started to say more, but a knock on the door behind me had me twisting in the chair and glancing around as it opened.

Sam stood there his eyes locked on the coffee. "Do I smell what allows me to work this early morning shift? And is it mine?"

"Well, your name is on it, but if the chief wants it, that's between you two."

The woman had the gall to smirk and start to reach for it. Samuel lunged and grabbed, whirling away protectively, and the lid popped off and soaked the cop that was walking by. All four of us stood and stared. Laurel started to laugh. It was a deep rich sound, not mocking at all, which surprised me for a reason I couldn't explain.

"You should've known better than do something like that around Cori. You're lucky it had cooled enough to not be dangerous."

Sam looked at his cup, a look of great remorse on his face; the other cop just looked up at the ceiling, sighed, and said, "I'm going to grab my car and swing by the house and change. Okay, Chief?"

"Go for it, Daniels. Sorry." She still sounded amused and I stood unsure at this new facet, or at least new to me, facet of the police chief.

"As for you, Clements. Get our intern into her outfit and get on your patrol."

The man whined looking at the empty cup.

"You know, there's a place that sells them. I bet you could get another one." I couldn't help the snark. "They even like me there."

"Yes, but it wouldn't be as special. This was done by you, for me." He sounded heartbroken and I had to fight not to roll my eyes.

"It was a bribe. I'll get you another," my voice dry.

He jerked his head up and smiled at me. "In that case, let's get rolling, rookie."

Chief Amosen cringed at him calling me a rookie. "Please try and remember she isn't a rookie, still just a civilian. And she has to fill out all the paperwork before she leaves this station." She handed me a folder at least a half inch thick.

"Then get hopping. I have coffee bribes to receive," he said, his voice had a false brightness that made me want to take a step backwards. You know, just in case he had lost his mind and was about to go video game crazy on us.

"Both of you, go," she said, a laugh still in her voice. "My coffee is just fine."

"Cruel, mean woman. See what I have to put up with?" He turned and headed down the hall, waving at me to follow him.

I paused at the door and turned back to look at her. "Chief?"

She lifted her head from the computer screen to look at me.

"You mind if someday I ask you about the day my brother died?"

Something dark and scared flashed across her face, but she gave me a soft smile. "No. Any time."

I ducked my head in thanks, then raced after Sam who was headed deeper into the station, not that it was that big. Twenty minutes later I wore a shirt that almost fit me, and had a bulletproof vest, a belt with a flashlight, handcuffs, a radio, a body cam, and not much else.

There were people in the class who'd complain about not getting a gun, or at least a taser. That didn't bug me at all. Shooting people held no interest for me. I wanted to help people, not take them down. Not kill them. For me, the radio would be my best weapon and the body cam a way to protect everyone, especially me.

Chapter 24

Familiars Hope Chest - in families where magic is common and familiars are often drawn to them, each person keeps what is called a hope chest - a small box much like a jewelry box, kept in the hope of attracting a familiar. Anyone with a familiar can use their own genetic material that is not attached to them. Hence the chest is used to keep nail clippings, cut hair, teeth, anything of theirs that someday could be used in an emergency. ~ Magic Explained

ORDER

I am so tired of signing paperwork. At this point everyone should know my social security number. If my identity gets stolen, I'll never know when it was taken.

"Ready for your first day?" Sam asked, after I'd spent fifteen more minutes getting all the paperwork signed. The best part of that was the paycheck. Not much, just minimum wage, but it was money I needed and made it so I could breathe a bit easier knowing I wouldn't have to be begging from Jo.

"I think so." The vest weighed a ton and I felt ungainly moving in it. "How do you guys run in these things?"

"Lots of training. If you wanted to be a cop after you graduate, you'd still have to go through the police academy. It just lets you go up the ranks faster as you have the degree and more knowledge of what most people learn the hard way." He gave me a sideways look. "If you were willing to stay here, you'd have a pretty good chance. Most small towns have a hard time getting good officers."

I followed him out to the squad car, looking at it with new eyes. "And you think I'd be a good one?"

"Oh, I know you would. Disasters follow you, but I've never seen you lose your composure, get upset, or freak at what happened. That is a good quality in a cop. You also think, too much sometimes, but it means you'd probably never shoot someone because you were startled. Your first instinct isn't to draw a weapon."

He paused as we slid into the car and he logged in, stating our location and what we'd be doing. With a grin he started up the engine and headed out. "Not drawing your weapon could be a bad thing in a dangerous situation, but if you made it through the academy, I have no doubt you'd be fine."

I looked out the window. I'd never really thought about this for a real job. I'd always been focused on being a paramedic.

"I don't know. Never really thought about it. But that doesn't explain you."

"What about me?"

"Why did you volunteer for this?" I didn't look at him as he drove, instead trying to see Rockway through the eyes of a cop. A different view than I'd ever had. Everywhere I looked I saw people and wondered who was about to break the law or do something that might get them or someone else hurt.

"Being a cop? Or risking my life with you?"

I jerked my head to glance at him, but all I could see was half a smirk as he looked straight ahead.

"Yes." If he was going to be a pain, I could match him.

"Point. I always wanted to be a Texas Ranger actually, but I didn't live in Texas and they have crazy requirements. So, I became a police officer."

Mel Todd

"Huh. Yeah, I can't see you in a Stetson. You'd look silly."

"Gee, why did I want to do this again?"

"That was my question in the first place. Why?"

He pulled into in a convenient parking space in front of Grind Down. Shutting off the engine, he twisted in his seat to look at me. "You drive me crazy. You always seem to be at the center of anything going weird or funky. But you never make the same mistake twice, and you are calm under even the weirdest situations. I want you to succeed. I wasn't a police officer when Stevie died." I flinched at that, but he continued. "But I knew about it. Everyone did. I couldn't imagine holding any of my siblings as they died. You did and then you dealt with everything else life has thrown at you by busting your butt and working hard. So why wouldn't I want to do this with you?"

My mouth had the consistency of damp cotton as it had fallen open in shock as he spoke. I closed it with a snap, looking at him and feeling my face heat up.

"I, I didn't know what else to do. I didn't see any other options."

Sam flashed me a smile as he opened the door. "And that is why you impressed people. You have always looked for a way to be better. To answer your questions, to solve your own problems. It makes people want to help you. Now come on. I believe you owe me a bribe."

I got out of the car, fighting the stiffness and weight of the vest. How in the world did they move in these things?

But leaving the heavy conversation topic behind was fine by me. It was a bit much to take. "To be fair, I already brought you the bribe. You are the one that spilled it."

"In a move that has never wasted a drop of coffee

before. So therefore, it is your fault." He held open the door to Grind Down with a teasing smile as we walked in.

"That is very unfair. How can I be responsible for your actions?" The teasing helped to remove the stress, but it flared back up at the wide eyes from Kadia and Carl as we walked in.

"Everything okay, Cori?" Kadia asked, looking at us. Carl just looked worried, which made no sense.

I looked down at myself. Polyester long sleeved shirt in the same style as Sam's but no emblems on it, black slacks, and black shoes. A bit monotone compared to my normal preferred style, but still nothing weird.

"Yeah. I'm doing my internship with the police for the next few weeks."

Relief flashed across both their faces. "Oh, yeah, I forgot. How is that going?" Kadia asked as Carl settled himself back down on the stool, the toe of his cast poking out from behind the counter.

"What did you think I was doing, Kadia? And can you make Sam here another drink? His got spilled."

"That isn't surprising around you." Carl's voice made the remark more stinging than it would have been from Jo, and I flinched.

"Stop it or I swear I will break your other leg," Kadia snapped out. "I don't know what his issue is. He's been a crabby jerk all morning." She worked on Sam's drink and waved off my money. I didn't argue—Molly liked us drinking the stuff and treating the cops well.

The bell rang and I glanced back, more out of habit than anything else, to see who was walking in. I groaned.

Shay scowled back at me. "Why are you here? You do not work here in the mornings during the week, only the weekends."

"Nice to know you care enough to follow my schedule." I pasted on a smile and said this all in a sickly-sweet tone. "Better watch it. I might start to think you're sweet on me."

The choked laugh from behind me matched the look of horror on Shay's face. I'd almost be insulted by how fast he stepped back, except he had to be at least twenty years older than me. Ewww. But it was made all the better when he slammed into the man behind him, knocking him down. The two of them fell to the floor in a tangle of limbs, coats, and a familiar flash of emerald green flashed up from them hissing in clear annoyance.

Clap, clap, clap.

I grinned as I watched them. "Excellent form, the legs were splayed nicely, and you took someone else down with you. Impressive. I'll pay for his coffee, Kadia. After a performance like that, he deserves a reward."

Sam snickered into his drink as the men extricated themselves from the tangle of limbs and stood up. Elsba, his familiar, hung in the air glaring at me.

"Hey, I didn't do it. Blame Shay. He's the one who stepped all over your mage. I had nothing to do with it." I spoke to the familiar, ignoring the men on the floor.

"Really, O'Shaungessy. What is it with you and your Spirit girls?" the man asked, his tattoo glinting.

"Oh, I'm not his." Though calling me spirited was amusing. "He, however, is the bane of my existence. Moving away will be a relief. I won't have to worry about running into him every time I turn around."

I loved tweaking Shay. Besides I really wanted to pet this guy's familiar, but you just didn't do that. Even I knew that, it was rude. Like petting a service animal. Besides, no one was really sure just how intelligent they were, and I knew I wouldn't have wanted people to pet me.

The banter probably would have continued, something I enjoyed, to be honest, but Sam's radio squawked. I froze and looked at him, frowning. The code that came across was public disturbance if I remembered correctly.

What really caught my attention, though, was Shay and his friend both froze too, looking at me with a weird expression on their faces. Even Elsba stared at me.

"Okay Cori, let's go. We'll walk. It's only a block from here." Sam headed to the door, his coffee left on the table. I trotted after him, his longer legs could eat up distance quickly.

"What's up? I caught a disturbance?" I tried to keep my breath even as I kept up. I'd have to start working out more. Too bad the gym idea hadn't worked. Not enough time to do everything I needed to do.

"Something going on at the bank." He darted a quick look at me. "You remember the rules, right?"

"Yes. Stay behind you and at the first sign of trouble radio for help." I rattled off the code for officer needs assistance.

"Good. Remember this job is always dangerous, but if you keep your head there should never be an issue."

"Isn't that just what you were telling me I'm good at?"

"Yep. Which is why I'm trusting you and not having you go sit in the car. Joy of a small town. Chief Amosen trusts my judgment."

"Lucky you," I muttered, then flushed again. Really, why were my memories so against the woman?

"Yep. I am." He slowed as we reached the bank. Sam turned and looked around, scanning the area. I mimicked his actions and looked. I wasn't sure what I was looking for, but I didn't see any idling cars, or suspicious-looking people lurking around. But then it was winter and what few people were out were bundled up. He frowned. "Nothing looks odd. Hang back. If I tell you to duck, you'd better be hitting the floor."

At any other time, I'd have made a snarky remark, but my adrenaline and nerves were too tight, so I just nodded. An odd jerky motion that didn't feel like me.

Sam winked at me and pushed open the first set of doors to the bank. I watched him go through the second and he walked over, looking calm, and talked to the security guard standing there.

Taking that as meaning it was okay, I pushed in through both sets of doors and stood on the opposite side of Sam and the guard trying to figure out the situation. There weren't many people in the bank. One older man, probably about Sam's age in the middle, his arms crossed, glaring at everyone. His dirty blond hair looked like he'd been running his fingers through it constantly and the bags under his eyes implied sleep was something he needed more of.

"That's him. He started yelling, so we hit the alarm. All I know is his name is Roy and he's pissed."

Sam nodded and headed that way, where Roy and one of the bank employees stood. I could see bank tellers behind their little screens looking a mixture of amused and nervous. There was one other customer who just looked annoyed at the entire situation as she wasn't being waited on while everyone paid attention to the man.

He dropped his arms to his sides, hands clenched in fists. I gave a quick scan of his clothes. They looked decent, but not designer. I'd been getting my clothes for so long from thrift stores, I knew how to tell if something was worth the money. And more to the point, if it could handle all the wear and tear I put on it. Roy didn't strike me as rich, but not poor either.

"I don't care what your records say. I filed all the forms. I didn't spend the money. I need it back in my account to pay my mortgage and get the utilities paid. It's too damn cold to have the heat turned off. I've got a family. You know I didn't take it out of my account." His voice would get calm then spike with anger each time he got back to the money and he got more agitated.

"So, what's going on here?" Sam asked, his easy-going attitude and charm oozing out of him. He excelled at defusing situations

"Mr. Saunders here says he's been the victim of identity theft. I don't have any police reports and I can't authorize returning the four thousand that was taken out of his bank account," the woman said. I couldn't see her name tag from my angle, but she looked and acted like a manager. Her attitude all officious and no sympathy in her tone.

"I HAVE BEEN!" His voice was a screech and I saw the woman take a half step back, worry flashing across her face. "I've filed with the credit bureaus, canceled my cards, filled out a police report, but work is still doing automatic deposits. This paycheck had our yearly bonus on it, and I couldn't get the money out fast enough before the crooks took it. I need it back. I'm doing everything I can. I'm following all the rules. Why am I the one being punished? I need to pay my bills." His voice cracked on that last part.

"I'm sure we can work it out. You said you filed a police report? Why don't we get it?" Sam kept his voice calm and light. "We can work something out."

"People think they can use identity theft as an excuse for bad money management. It was your transfer that took it out." The sneer in the woman's voice made me flinch and Sam looked at her in surprise. That moment of surprise and cruelty seemed to stretch out forever.

205

"You uncaring bitch."

My eyes jerked to the man, every hair on my body feeling like it was trying to stand up all at once. It was his voice. Before, he'd been angry and upset, with rage and frustration mixed in. He said these words in a flat, calm tone of voice as if he mentioning the time. He reached behind him, jerked out a gun, pointed it at the woman and in the instant he fired, my entire body went rigid.

Transformation - sounds like something out of a story book. Change lead to gold, spin straw to gold, make anything you want. The truth is, lead to gold is simple. Straw to gold is almost impossible unless you like wasting genetic material. It's one of the reasons the gold standard was abandoned before the 1900s and most countries moved to the US Dollar. ~ History of Magic

SPIRIT

He's shooting!

The thought went through my head, a mix of panic and disbelief even as I dropped to the ground and watched. Once again, time seemed to slow to a crawl and it felt like I could see the bullet moving, which was patently impossible. In a fraction of a second and an eternity, the bullet somehow missed the woman, there were three sharp sounds that were so close together I didn't know how I knew there were three. Then Roy dropped to the ground, the gun tumbling out of his slack hands.

No one else moved. It had happened so fast, then the woman started screaming and other people were freaking out. I just stared at the man.

Sam grabbed his radio, babbled about shots being fired, then went over to the man. He kicked the gun away and knelt down.

"I don't believe it. What in the world?" His voice sounded odd and after looking around I headed over to him. I still felt like time, like reality, was moving too slow, but it came back into focus as I went over.

"Is he dead?" I asked, even more detached than I normally felt.

"No. Just unconscious. Look." He pointed to ground next to Roy's head. A bullet, almost completely flat, lay there. Sam rotated the man's head a bit and at the temple was a red mark, bruising quickly.

"He'll need an ambulance. Probably subdural bleeding," I said, my voice abstract. I couldn't get past the feeling of seeing the bullet move.

"Oh, yeah, you're probably right." As Sam went to make that call too and handcuff Roy, just in case, I stood and followed my improbable thoughts.

From where he had been standing and the direction the gun had been pointing, I followed my silly idea of the path of the bullet. Over in the direction of his gun I stopped at one of the support pillars with a shiny metal insert for artistic reasons I supposed. There was an indent at one corner. I turned and walked at an angle away from the column and stopped at a heavy bronze nameplate by a door that had another dent. I turned again following a memory that didn't exist. I walked until I came to a bronze vase holding fake flowers on the little desk to sign checks. There was another wider dent there and I turned again walking back to Roy.

Huh. That shouldn't have happened. What is going on?

I didn't know if I was scared, or freaked out, but mostly curiosity rippled through my mind. How had that happened?

As I reached them, Sam stood looking around, with his hand on the handle of his gun. "You okay, Cori?"

"I'm fine. A bit curious."

"You? I'm trying to figure out how he shot himself. Unless someone else shot a gun?"

"No. At least I don't think so. I think I know what happened, but it doesn't seem possible." My voice trailed off as I thought. It wasn't impossible, just improbable. And the improbable had a bad habit of happening around me all too often.

Before Sam could say anything, sirens came to a halt outside the door, and two other officers came running in, guns drawn.

That devolved into a half hour of explaining the situation and waiting for an ambulance to get there and take Roy to the hospital. He still hadn't regained consciousness, but there were no other signs of damage outside the bruise on his temple. Sam sent one of the other cops to go with Roy to the hospital—he'd write up the charges and the situation in a little bit.

I had stayed out of the way, listening—it sounded like more paperwork than anything else. With my luck, I'd probably be involved in that.

"Hey Cori?" Sam said, walking over to me. I looked at him, having made sure I stayed out of everyone's way. "You said you thought that you knew what happened. Can you tell me?" He didn't seem dismissive and in all the years while he'd treated me like a careless idiot occasionally, he'd never disparaged my comments or thoughts.

"Well, still not sure I know why. But I think I can show you what. It's pretty weird."

The look he gave me wasn't anything I could read. Half serious, half something else, but it made me shift my stance, suddenly uncomfortable.

"Show me."

I walked him through everything, the dents and then back to where Roy had laid. "I didn't touch anything, and I can't swear that I'm not making it all up because there is no way for me to follow a bullet's trajectory. But it makes sense."

Sam stood, his head following the path over and over

again. "You ever think about getting tested?"

I sighed. This was becoming a theme. "No one in my family is magic. There hasn't been anyone for a long time. And if I had emerged, it was so mild no one noticed - including me. It isn't required unless I turn out to be higher than a hedgie."

"True, but if you are a mage it might explain some of the weirdness."

"Except you always emerge after puberty ends, and I've always been a trouble magnet. The chief commented on it earlier. I'm just weird or so low it means I could never do anything."

"Maybe." He shrugged. "Either way I'm glad no one got seriously hurt. The manager was being purposefully insulting. I'll see if I can get him off on minor charges with community service. I checked and he did file identity theft papers. One of the detectives will verify the information. You, however, need to fill out a report. Saying what you discovered and all of your impressions of the scene up to and after the shooting."

I groaned. "Why is everything paperwork? I thought you actually did stuff."

"We do. Paperwork. Coffee. Donuts." He smiled. "But that's later. Now we get to go do patrol, and if you're nice, I'll let you use my computer to start on your half of the report."

The rest of the day had no excitement, not even a speeding ticket, and I did get my report written up. Sam even gave me a ride home, which meant I'd have lots of time to work on my paper for class. As I climbed the stairs, I glanced over at the house. It had been really busy the last few days, but I hadn't seen any sign of Kris. Now it lay quiet and dark. Maybe a late night or school function. I shrugged and finished climbing the stairs. I unlocked my door and stepped in, then came to a sudden halt. Sitting on the counter was a manila envelope and the key to my door.

Sweat beaded up on my body. As far as I knew Jo and my parents were the only people that had extra keys. I didn't breathe as I walked over and picked up the envelope, the key tumbling off to the floor. I pulled out the letter and another piece of paper tumbled out as well. With my heart beating hard enough it sounded like the crash of thunder in my ears, I read the letter.

Corisande Munroe –

This is to let you know that we, Estella Munroe and Rafael Munroe, have sold the house and this apartment. The new owners will not be taking possession until late June. At that time, you are expected to have vacated the premises. Please turn over all copies of the keys at that time. The new owners are a management company, Pinewood Realty Management. They will contact you when they plan to start remodeling the main house. The contract states you have the right to stay until that time.

We have moved out of state and there will be no further contact. Enclosed is a money order for ten thousand. This ends our responsibility to you.

Do not try to contact us or our son. We will not respond to any attempts at communications.

Estella Munroe
Rafael Munroe

It was signed by both of them. I just stood there looking at it, my body flashing hot, then cold, as sweat broke out all over me. I read it twice more before I bent over and picked up the other piece of paper. It was a cashier's check. I now had more money than I'd earned in the last six months.

211

Mel Todd

I looked at the check and then slipped it back into the envelope. I walked over to my couch, ignoring the sound of something either falling in the bathroom or exploding in the fridge. Sinking into my couch I stared at the wall, processing.

It took a while, and when I finally came out of my haze, I'd decided a number of things.

- Jo and the Guzman's were more a family than my parents had been in a long, long time.

- If Kristos ever reached out to me, I'd respond, but until he turned eighteen, I would not search for him.

- That I was relieved. This was the proof they didn't care, and it meant I could quit trying.

Feeling an odd lightness, as if something that had been weighing down my soul had been cut away, I went make some dinner. I turned on the hot water and waited, and waited, and waited. Still icy cold. I shut the water off and cautiously opened the fridge. Sure enough one of the cans of soda on the top shelf had frozen and exploded everywhere. Sighing, I hung my head and looked for anything else that had gone haywire. Maybe from here on life would become normal?

I headed out the door, making sure my keys were still on me—the last thing I needed was to lock myself out. The water heater for the apartment was in the garage area, where I could have parked a car if I had one. I rarely went in there. I had a tub of summer clothes that I swapped out once it quit being cold. But mostly it was empty. The fuse box, the water heater, a bench with my box of clothes, and the washer and dryer. One step in and I knew there was a problem. The cement floor of the garage shone back at me when I flipped the overhead lights on. Water spread out in rippling waves as it poured from the heater.

Shaking my head, I walked over and shut off the

212

water valve. That much I knew how to do. But fixing the water heater? The people I would have put in a request with were no longer here. It was just me. I waited for a wave of panic or stress and nothing came. Just acceptance that I'd always been alone.

Climbing the stairs seemed easier than I expected. That burden I'd carried without realizing it had vanished. I almost laughed. Apparently when you no longer cared you were free. I'd have to remember that.

I picked up my phone with an abundance of care. Even with money, the last thing I needed was to get yet another new phone. Maybe they sold them in bulk.

The person I needed was number one in my favorites list, and I hoped she always would be.

"Yo-yo, Cori. How was the first day of exciting police action?" Jo's bright voice came through the line and wrapped around me in a wave of warmth. She was my joy.

"More exciting and boring than I expected. I'll tell you all about it if you come over, but can you bring Stinky?"

"Ooh, you decided to go slumming and date my brother?"

"Ewww... no." I shuddered. Sanchez was great, but no way. I'd become a merlin before I ever dated him. "Are you insane, do you feel good? Besides do you really want me dating your bother?"

"Well, if you got married, then you'd be my sister-in-law and you'd never be able to escape my clutches, so it does have its benefits."

"Yes, but that would mean I was having sex with your bother."

"Oh... ewww... yeah no. You're stuck with me as BFF instead. So, what's up?"

"Well, all the water from my hot water heater is

Mel Todd

currently spilling out over the garage floor."

"That would qualify as a problem. Yep, I'll grab him. Need me to bring anything else?"

"Well, I've got a lot to tell you, but I think I have chips and salsa your mom gave me, so we should have snacks."

"Hmmm... we'll see. Be over in a few." Jo hung up and I went to clean up my refrigerator. It didn't matter. I had family, chosen family, and I was starting to believe that just maybe they would be there for me always.

Chapter 26

Rasputin – even to this day his name can cause shivers of horror in those who knew of his reign of terror. Even though he worked with Lenin, it is speculated he drove Lenin's desire to control all mages. From what he was seen performing, most figure he was a Spirit merlin. Proof that the school of mage you have access to has nothing to do with the type of person you are. ~ Famous Mages

CHAOS

I need to convince them to install speech to text on their computers. They spend way too much time writing reports.

After the last two weeks of doing a ride along with Sam, I'd come to a few more conclusions.

Cops had to write lots of reports.

Most people were idiots.

I didn't mind the investigation part but dealing with people was annoying.

That conclusion surprised me, to be honest. I thought I'd gotten good at letting people's little quirks and being obtuse slide off of me after all my years working at Grind Down. I'd had to argue with someone that an eight-ounce drink and a cup were the same amount of fluid. I even had to prove to someone that our medium at ten ounces was less than the large at sixteen ounces.

All of that meant that I thought I'd be able to handle people being silly or stupid in the line of enforcing the law.

I was wrong, very, very wrong.

The proof of that was a woman Sam pulled over for weaving across the lanes. It was about three in the afternoon and we were headed back to the station on Friday to finish paperwork and kick me out. I was ready to go home. It had been a long week.

"Stay by the car and watch. I want to make sure there isn't anything dangerous going on. Most likely she's looking at her phone and I'll be writing a ticket."

I nodded. So far, he'd written at least five tickets for using a cell phone while driving. I could barely manage to walk and use one, so driving and doing that seemed reckless to me.

Sam got out and I did too, my radio at the ready. That was the best part of having me there, I could call things in, call for back up, or whatever was needed. Half this week we'd spent going over all the call signs. I was surprised to realize the variation of signs between different departments but learning them wasn't an issue.

He walked up to the driver's side of the cute little sports car. It was bright blue, with only room for two people in the front. A two door, and I wanted it with an odd wistfulness.

"Ma'am, please lower the window," I heard him say as he stood by the car door. From my angle I couldn't see the window come down, but I could hear the radio on in the car, so I assumed she had complied.

"Ma'am have you been drinking?" He'd reeled back a bit as the window came down. I titled my head back a bit, but nothing caught me. In this instance it would have been excellent to be an Air mage and have the scent swirl to me, but it didn't.

Whatever she responded with I either I missed or couldn't hear, but I heard him next. "Ma'am, I'm going to have to ask you to step out of the car."

The door opened as he stepped back from it. It was a

woman about Marisol's age, her business suit a shade too tight, and she had a full head of fake blond hair in a tight cut against her head, so most likely not a mage, not with hair that short.

I moved to the driver's side of the squad car so I could see better. and to make sure I didn't miss if Sam needed me to get help.

"Ma'am, may I see your identification, please?"

"I already told you, I only had one drink. I'm fine," she protested, her hands on her hips, even as she swayed back and forth on heels that were taller than a medium coffee. I knew if I tried to wear those I'd hurt myself, badly.

"I still need to see your ID, please." Sam stayed calm and professional even as she bent over to get her purse out. Even me, with my almost famous obtuseness to sexual innuendo didn't miss her tight skirt and the way she waved her ass at him. Granted she had a good figure, but when she came back up I saw her face and blinked. I hadn't seen that much makeup on a face since I went to the circus and got freaked out by clowns.

"Here. See, I'm legal. I just need to get back to my job." Even her speech slurred a bit and I wasn't sure why she'd even tried to drive. "I only had a martini, well maybe two, but I'm fine." She leaned forward and slurred a bit. "I'm a functioning alcoholic. Have to be. Only way to survive the stress. I don't get drunk."

"Ma'am, can you walk on the line between here and my partner standing over there?"

I had a giddy reaction to being called his partner and stood up a bit more. Stupid, but it felt good.

"Fine, but I'll have your badge for this." She started walking towards me swaying like a flag in a stiff breeze. Personally, I was glad there was very little traffic here, given how badly she stumbled and weaved.

Mel Todd

"Cori, will you please get the breathalyzer out of the back?" He'd followed her, watching with an annoyed expression. I was getting good at reading Sam.

"Sure." A minute later I had the kit for him. It rather reminded me of a stud finder used in construction. He put a clean cap on it and had her breathe into it.

"I'm not drunk. You'll see. I've barely had a drink."

"Of course, ma'am." He looked at the numbers and held it out to me. I raised my eyebrows. Driving while under the influence rates were one of the things we went over. And anything over a blood alcohol content .08 in Georgia was legally drunk. She was at a .31 BAC.

"How in the world did she drink that much and still get served?"

"Ma'am, please put your hands behind your back. You are under arrest for driving while under the influence." Sam, at this point, had passed into really annoyed.

"I told you, I'm not drunk. Now let me go."

"Ma'am, please."

"No!" She turned and swung a fist at him. As she did, she fell backwards, her heel snapping, and she landed on her ass.

"And now I'm adding the charge of assaulting an officer."

The next hour, all through the ride back, the booking, and the blood test she continued to protest that she wasn't drunk That she hadn't swung at Sam and that she must have been drugged.

By the time we were done it was six P.M.

"Are all people that stupid?"

Sam laughed. "You be amazed at how many people ignore what is in front of them. They don't want to admit they did anything that might get them in trouble. Or worse, change how they view themselves. We lie to

218

ourselves more than anyone else."

"Maybe. But still, that scares me."

"Good. It means you'll pay more attention to people and think about what lies they are telling themselves. Like, I can have one more drink. Or, no one will notice if I just steal one thing. People need to protect their view of themselves more than most things."

I had thought about that over the weekend a lot. By the end of this I might be even more cynical than I already was. That was a sobering idea.

But outside the drunk driver and the exciting start of the first week, it had been relatively routine. I suppose I should have expected the universe was just saving up energy to mess with us the next week because it started with a bang. Monday had been a normal class day with more practice in medical stuff, which I loved, and I was feeling pretty good about passing all the tests on medical procedures. So that hadn't worried me much.

Tuesday, I came in with my normal coffee for me and Sam. The extra money from the Munroe's had made it so I didn't mind doing this little splurge, plus next week I'd get another paycheck. That excited me as much as anything else did. Maybe I could get some nice clothes for Atlanta.

"Hey, Cori, thanks" His response was abstract and distant as he accepted the coffee. "Ready to go? We're going to have a busy day."

"Sure. What's going on that makes this different from last week?"

"Big rally in town for a motorcycle club. They are out at the fairgrounds, but historically they've drifted out of the zone a bit. So, we need to make sure they don't cause any issues." He headed to the car and I followed trying to remember if I'd ever heard about this.

"This happen every year?"

"No. Every four. They rotate out to different areas—apparently they are a pretty big group." Sam looked worried as he slid into the car.

"What aren't you telling me?"

"The club is called Bad Ass Mages. Or BAM. To even apply to the club, you have to be at least a wizard. And even the girlfriends or wives have to meet that rank requirement."

I buckled in and looked at him feeling my stress ratchet up a bit. "You're telling me we have a biker gang made up of nothing but mages here in town?"

"Yep. And it means we need to be extra cautious. While true rogue mages are rare, if only because the people that hunt them don't allow them to ever serve time, asshole mages are common."

"Oh. So, be extra polite?"

He gave me a cynical smile. "It means yell for help if you think you need it. No one is going to criticize you for over-reacting. There are some archmages coming in for extra shifts. Their call codes are here." He said that as he taped a piece of paper to the dash. "If anything goes sideways, you get on the radio and yell for these people."

Working with the cops had just gotten more real. Up until now, I'd still felt a bit like an actor in a boring movie. But that was the goal of the police, to be bored. I suddenly got that being bored was an excellent goal. Maybe I should try it more often.

"Absolutely. So, what's the plan for today?"

"Mostly patrolling, but the schedules have been changed so we all go by the fair grounds to make sure we have a strong presence there and keep an eye on things. The last thing anyone wants is to provoke them, but at the same time we don't want them to think no one is paying attention."

"Sounds like a delicate balance to keep."

"Welcome to the exciting world of police work." Sam smiled at me and he seemed less tense than a few minutes ago. "But I think this day will require extra coffee." He reached back and pulled out a large travel mug. "Nothing fancy this time, just black coffee with a couple squirts of syrup. Enough to enjoy the flavor."

"I think that can be arranged."

We drove out and I watched the city, the areas of fields and trees, wondering if lurking behind one of them was danger. I'd always liked the idea of dragons or some of the other magical creatures that occasionally appeared but working with the police was making me realize that people were the worst dangers of all. It didn't really surprise me, but it was a mindset adjustment. Most of the bodies or people I found were freak accidents, almost never were other people involved. Just fate.

After a quick stop at Grind Down, we headed out. We hadn't even made it more than a half hour into our day when the first call came over the radio. The code sounded familiar, but I couldn't place it immediately.

"Which call is that?"

"Suspected overdose. They'll have an ambulance on the way too, but because of where it is, they want me to go in first and make sure it isn't a danger."

"Where is it?" That confused me. Rockway didn't exactly have a bad side of down, or places where it was dangerous to go. So where would it be happening at that they wanted cops there first?

"Where else? The fairgrounds." With that, he flipped on his lights and we took off. My stomach had tightened into a knot of worry with the sirens and lights announcing our presence to the world as we pulled into the fairground. The back area was covered with RVs,

Mel Todd

motorcycles, tents, small campers, and sometimes just a cot near a bike. We were waved down by a man in leather who looked like a stereotypical biker, but the Chaos symbol on his temple gleamed out at us, reminding me exactly what we were walking into.

He didn't look threatening. If anything I'd say he looked exasperated.

"Officer," he said leaning down. "George is over there. No one else is around for the most part. They went on a scenic ride. Bus coming up behind you?"

"Yes. Where is George, you said?"

The man stood up and pointed down the road to a tent that looked like all the others with a big three wheeled motorcycle outside it. Sam nodded at him and drove down there slowly, watching everything. He'd shut off the siren, but still had the lights going. Once he reached the tent, he opened the door.

"You know the rules: stay watchful, yell for help if we need it."

I nodded, but as I looked around this all seemed so normal, not really scary like we were about to be attacked. Maybe just false confidence, but it still seemed odd to have it be so normal after how much I'd worked it up in my mind.

Chapter 27

Spirit is the rarest of the classes and its branches possibly the most misunderstood. Everyone knows that a Psychic mage can read your mind and a Soul mage can see ghosts, but as science understands the skills that isn't accurate. A Soul mage can see, feel, and hear imprints of emotions and some of those emotions are solid enough to form ghosts. But no evidence has been presented that the soul can be manipulated at all. ~ Magic Explained

ORDER

Never, ever think it is boring and routine, 'cause that's when it bites you.

The thought seared into my mind as I dove back into the car, slamming the door as a huge dog that wasn't a dog came bounding out of the tent growling at us. It stood about three feet at the shoulder and if I'd seen it in the woods, I would have thought it was a werewolf. Even if they only existed in fiction, that's what I would have thought it was.

"Dahli, down. They're here to help George." The man who'd met us at the turn in yelled at the werewolf, Dahli, as it stood in front of Sam, growling loud enough that I could feel the vibrations in the car. Sam had his hand on his pistol, but there was no way to pull it before Dahli could have ripped out his throat.

"Dahli, I mean it. Or we'll just let George die like the idiot he is, then where will you be?" The man had gotten closer and had quit yelling.

The growling stopped and the dog—oddly it almost

looked like a dog now—whined and went over to the man, collapsing at his feet, huge head on its just as huge forepaws.

"Ignore Dahli. She's George's familiar and is a bit protective. I swear if it wouldn't kill her, I'd kill him for causing her so much stress and worry."

Sam, whose face had gone pale, nodded. "In the tent?"

"Yep. Not sure why they sent the cops out for this, though." The man sounded bewildered as he crouched down and rubbed Dahli's ear with one hand.

"Standard protocol for drug overdose in a potentially dangerous situation," Sam said as he cautiously stuck his head in the tent, then backed out. "What'd he take?"

"Drug overdose? Take? Things really do get corrupted as it travels from person to person. George is diabetic. He took too much insulin. I've got him stable, but I can't do anything more without the right drugs. Normally he monitors it better, but he couldn't resist the cinnamon rolls this morning, then tried to balance it out. Took too much. Really need the bus here."

"Crap," Sam muttered and I opened the door cautiously, watching the not-dog as I did so. Sam jumped on the radio. "Escalate the bus to my location. Diabetic coma, not an OD."

I heard the response and went over. "Want me to get him out so they can help faster?"

"Yes, please." It only took a minute to pull the man out from the tent on his foam mat. Older, obviously overweight, with a spirit tattoo bright on his temple. The whine of the sirens coming up the drive let us know help was almost here.

"No, you can't go, Dahli. Let them take care of him. You freak out too many people." The man paused, looking at the dog and sighed. "Then next time be a cute cuddly cat or a Pomeranian, not something from most of our nightmares."

"I thought," I stopped myself from saying werewolf—barely—"Dahli was George's familiar."

The ambulance came and two people I didn't recognize jumped out, headed over, and immediately started working on George. I stayed out of the way, since I wasn't allowed to jump in and help no matter how much I kept running through all the procedures in my head for a person in a probable diabetic coma. They really shouldn't have gotten the call messed up. The time might make a difference in his survival but then again, mages tended to be tough.

"Oh, she is. But familiars can talk to anyone they want to. If they want to. That is usually the catch. They seem to find only their chosen mage worth talking to."

"They're intelligent?"

Dahli sniffed at me in a disparaging manner, but she kept her eyes on her mage, now being loaded onto a gurney.

"Very, but they aren't human, so their reactions and thoughts don't always make sense to us. Sometimes they freak us the fuck out." The man laughed, but his eyes tracked George. "What hospital will they take him to? He's got VA coverage, did his four years then another decade in the army."

"Kennestone," one of the paramedics said as they buttoned him up. He glanced at Dahli. "While she can come see him, it would be nice to wait until he's in a room."

"Thanks." The man stood and looked at us. "Thanks for the help, officer, ma'am." Then he walked away with the werewolf trailing after him, tail between her legs.

I didn't say anything until we were back on the road. "That was both more and less than what I expected it to be."

Sam laughed. "The BAM can be scary and a pain in the ass. But they aren't ronin. They are still subject to rules. They are just a pain in the ass because it's the equivalent of walking through a room of ticking bombs. You never know when one, none, or all of them might go off."

"Did you know the guy who waved us down?"

"Know him, not really. Know of him, yes. Name's Scott Randolph. He's an archmage. Started out as a research scientist for the DoD, he got re-tasked and did multiple tours as a Rogue Hunter. Tough man." Sam sounded almost admiring.

"Renegade group? That the group that goes after ronin?"

We headed out on one of the state routes, and I could see just the slightest hint of green on the trees. Spring was starting to creep in.

"The official name is Rogue Rapid Response Team, but Rogue Hunters is how most people know of them," he commented as he drove. We dropped the topic after that, getting distracted by a downed tree call.

The rest of the day faded into routine and I had come to cherish it. I talked to Sam a lot about the papers I wrote, and he gave me different viewpoints I'd never considered before. I found that I rather liked him as a friend.

When I got off work, Marisol waited in the parking lot. I saw her because she stood by her car and even from the door, I could see her rage.

Oh fudge, Jo must have told her.

I walked over, dreading an explosion. Jo took after her mother in being happy and easy going, until you crossed a line, at which point they both went nuclear.

"Hey Mrs. Guzman," I offered with a tentative smile

hoping she'd correct me. Instead she went in for the kill.

"It is true? What Josefa said? They left you with a letter and some paltry money, disavowing you?"

I shoved my hands in my pocket staring at the ground. "Yes," the word came out. I was more upset about Marisol being upset than the Munroes walking away from me. The last thing I wanted was Marisol or Henri to start to hate me too.

There was a weird sound like she had started to say something. I hunched my shoulders as I tried to figure out a way to make it better.

"Cori, look at me." Her command caught me by surprise, and I looked up at her, then wanted to die when I realized Sam had come over too. "I am not mad at you. I am furious at those worthless people that gave birth to such a wonderful young woman, not at you. I should not have asked you that here. At your work. It was - rude of me. I'm sorry. I had just been stewing on it all day since Josefa told me this morning."

Marisol reached out and lifted up my chin, looking me in the eyes. "You are as much one of my children as my own. More, as I don't feel the urge to strangle you anywhere near as often. You never need to worry about calling or asking us for anything. Anything. Is that understood?"

I nodded a jerky nod, both happy and intimidated. Marisol Guzman in a rage was scary. I almost imagined I could see her magic crackling around her.

"But I have changed my mind about something." I froze, watching and waiting. Still too unsure to guess. "You may not call me Marisol. I know Mom might be too raw, too sore since yours was not a mother. Instead call me *Tia*, aunt. I will be your *Tia* and Henri your *Tio*."

The smile that spread across my face was so wide it hurt, and I didn't care. That felt right in a way I hadn't expected.

"Gladly, *Tia*."

"Good." She pulled me into a rough hug and kissed my forehead. "I expect you for dinner Friday." She pulled away and nodded at Sam. "Good evening, Samuel."

"Marisol," he replied. Neither of us said anything as she left.

"Do I want to know what that was?"

I smiled back at him. "Me finding my family."

He arched an eyebrow at me, then smiled. "Good. Come on. I'll give you a ride home. I have some thoughts on your paper about mage responsibilities and why it isn't always in the first responder's best interest to ask them for help."

"Oh good. I've been struggling with that."

"I figured. Your nature is to give when at all possible. You haven't learned to see from other viewpoints. Yet."

"You saying I'm naive?" That stung almost. I wasn't naive. A stab of pain flashed through my head and I winced, but it had already faded away.

Stupid headaches.

A screech from a hawk caught my attention and I looked up. Out of the corner of my eye I saw Sam do the same. The hawk had a dark colored snake at least four feet long in its claws and the snake was not happy about it. But what really caught my attention was the flying flash of green that darted in and attacked the hawk, which was why it had screeched.

The green lash darted back and forth until the hawk dropped the writhing snake. I couldn't see more than the colors and the movement, not details. I would have bet my entire paycheck that the green flying snake was Elsba. She darted in and grabbed the falling snake in her jaws. Then in a move I'd only seen done by crocodiles on TV, she flipped the snake up and pulled it down into her gullet. In the time it took me to hiss out a startled breath, half the snake had gone down her throat.

"What by Merlin's Beard?" Sam hissed out. As I watched, Elsba, ate the rest of the normal snake. Then, with her belly obviously enlarged, she flew away. The hawk had disappeared.

I looked at Sam, who looked just as stunned as I felt. I shook my head. "Nope. Don't know. Not discussing. I didn't see anything or know anything."

Sam glanced back up at the disappearing green thing. "Agreed. I know nothing. College papers, let's discuss that."

The rest of the drive the two of us worked very, very, hard to pretend we'd seen nothing that might have qualified as watching a dragon eat a snake. Or maybe a wyvern. Heck if it was Elsba what exactly was she? Either way, that way led madness.

The rest of the week was drama free. Just the normal tickets and shoplifting calls. There was this feeling of impending doom that was a bit creepy, but nothing happened. No drama, just normalcy.

Waiting for something to happen was exhausting.

Chapter 28

The Empress's Handmaidens are what Japanese female magicians are called for Japan's version of the draft. While over the years the mandatory robes have faded down to just wearing a traditional kimono while working on behalf of the Empress. However, they the mandate that all mages, even hedges have their faces tattooed. This has created an odd war of beauty standards that clash among Japanese youngsters. There are two views, one that the tattoos should be highlighted with the use of make up to make them sparkle and snap, and the reverse that they should be down played and treated as no more than an unfortunate birthmark. ~ History of Magic

SPIRIT

Okay, maybe I'm in danger of becoming an adrenaline addict. Or I'm just twisted. That could be it too.

I found myself sulking as I finished cleaning up Saturday at Grind Down. Nothing strange, or even odd had happened today. Well, I never saw Shay. That was odd and a bit disappointing, which confused me. Did I really need that much more drama in my life that I missed sparring with Shay? Or did it really prove I was more than a bit twisted, or Murphy cursed, whatever Shay meant by that?

Marisol had issued orders to me when she dropped by this morning. She expected me to show up after work. There would be dinner, talk about housing, and she would make sure I was doing okay. It felt very odd, but I enjoyed her caring. Besides, I hadn't had any downtime to spend with Jo for a while. Once the clean-up was done, I headed home, showered, then started walking. I'd see if I could talk Stinky into driving me home, but for now I enjoyed the long walk to stretch out legs that had stood all day. My thoughts wandered as I walked, mostly thinking about the police ride along. I wasn't hating it as much as I thought I would. The Criminal Justice Associates degree might end up being useful.

I saw her coming. I wasn't that lost in my thoughts, and the electric blue with green trim was impossible to miss as she came to a stop in front of me. Quiet roads in small towns did have advantages.

Jo pulled off her helmet, dark braided hair tumbling out in what I could recognize as sexy, but all it did was make me glad I didn't need to fight with combing it out. My own short bob was bad enough.

"Yo, Cori. Wanna ride?"

I didn't know how to answer her. Yes, it looked awesome. No way, we'd both die.

She grinned at me, reached into the saddle bag, and pulled out a helmet. "I got you something." She handed it to me, and my eyes suddenly got wet and I blinked rapidly. The helmet she held out to me was a deep ruby red, the color I always tried to get my hair, but the capper to everything was the Gothic print on the back that said 'Cori'.

"When?" I couldn't get anything else out. The cold air stung my face.

"Believe it or not, Stinky got it for you. Said you'd ride with me one way or another, so you might as well be safe."

I blurted out a laugh. "Remind me to thank him. For that I may need to start calling him Sanchez instead."

"Oh, don't do that. With your luck he'd develop a crush on you."

I rolled my eyes. Jo loved to tease me way too much about him. Mentioning that I thought he was cute when I was fourteen had nothing to do with how I felt about him now.

"Promise you'll drive"—I paused trying to figure out the right word to use—"conservatively?"

Jo laughed, her deep rich laugh as always making me feel wrapped in warmth. "I won't be reckless." She patted the tank of the bike. "Not risking my Sophia with any crazy driving."

I didn't even try not to grin at the name. I pulled on the helmet then climbed onto the back. Wrapping my arms around her waist, I leaned into her as she put her helmet back on.

"Hold on." Her muffled voice came through the helmet and I grinned to realize they had speakers so we could hear each other.

"I'm ready." I'd ridden occasionally with her and Paulo on his motorcycle. But it wasn't something I did often. Either way, I held on tighter than I probably needed to, but I knew how to lean and move as she revved it back up and turned the bike around.

True to her word, and I had seen Jo drive like she had a wasp's nest in her bra, she drove sedately. We didn't talk much, just enjoying the drive.

About a mile from her house, her sharp intake of breath had me jerking my head up to look. A deer had bounded into the middle of the road.

"*Madre Dios*!" Jo hissed and tried to turn the bike. The world slowed and I felt my skin burn as I broke out in a cold sweat.

The deer looked at us coming, Jo couldn't stop in the time we had, and the deer leapt up as if it thought it could escape by jumping over us. Jo cranked the handlebars and squeezed the brakes as we turned. The

motion was too sharp, too fast, and in crystal clear time
we spun too sharp as we lost traction on the wet March
road. As we spun, the motorcycle slid underneath the
belly of the deer, her hooves barely clearing Jo's helmet.
The bike completed two full three-hundred-sixty-
degree rotations, then rotated another one-hundred-
eighty degree's. We faced the deer that stood there in
the middle of the road looking at us. Then it calmly
walked to the other side, as if nothing had happened.

"Holy...," Jo's voice trailed off as I held on. My fingers
wouldn't unlock from around her waist. "Did that?"

"Yes," my voice squeaked out. I suddenly itched as if
someone had brushed me raw.

"You okay?" She half turned in on her seat to look at
me, but I knew all she could see was helmet.

"I'm fine. That was close. Too close." My voice shook
and I fought to get my heart rate back to normal.

"Yes, it was," she muttered. Slowly she turned the
bike around, and we finished the trip to her house at an
even more sedate pace. I climbed off first, ecstatic to
have both feet on stable ground.

Jo pulled off her helmet and hung it on the bike. I
pulled mine off and tried to discretely shake it out—I
could feel my scalp itching again—then I handed it to
her. She was peering back down the road in the
direction we had come.

"Cori, are you sure you aren't a mage?" Her voice
stopped me, and I looked back at her.

Why in the world does everyone ask me that?

"You don't think I would have told you if I emerged?"

Jo frowned at me. "Of course, you would. But you
know that not all emergences are big and splashy. What
if you're a hedgie like Stinky? I think you should just get
tested. It could be interesting."

I didn't roll my eyes, but I really wanted to. Time to

change the subject. "What was it like? Getting tested, I mean."

"Weird." The answer was immediate and definite.

"Thank you so much for the illuminating answer. That explains everything," I replied deadpan, crossing my arms to look at her.

"What? I'm not sure how I was tested. It was weird."

"So tell me what they did." I paused, struck by a sudden thought. "Or are you not allowed to talk about it?"

"Huh? No. Or at least if I'm not supposed to talk about it, they forgot to tell me." Jo twisted one of the strands of hair in her fingers, an old nervous habit I hadn't seen in a while. "Come on out back and I'll try to tell you. Though it did blur a bit."

We headed to the backyard and she glared at the wet chairs, then sighed, dumped the standing water out of one and sat down. I copied her, ignoring the dampness on my rear as I sank into the chair.

"So, when I woke up, I was more than a bit confused, and even though I vaguely remembered you talking, I couldn't focus. They gave me some soda, the full sugar and caffeine version, and it helped. They explained I'd emerged, and I was there to be tested and registered. They gave me time to let it sink in, saying they couldn't force me." Jo snorted at that. "Yeah, like I wanted to go on the run. It took a bit for me to get clear headed and stable enough that I could walk."

"Wait — stable? They said you weren't hurt." My heart rate ratcheted up with worry.

"I wasn't hurt, just—remember when we found that vape pen with pot in it stashed in Marco's bag?"

The change of topic took me a minute, but I nodded. He'd been playing with pot about two years ago and being the stupid eighteen-year-olds we were, we'd been unable to resist. "Yeah. Made your head go all fuzzy and everything just seem kind of off kilter."

"That's how I felt. From how calm they were, I get the feeling it is a common reaction. That took a good thirty minutes to wear off. But after that they had me step into this room. Kinda reminded me of airport body scanners."

I nodded. We'd gone to Florida on a class trip to Disneyworld. They had scanned all of us in those weird things.

"Well it looked like that. I felt like things were pushing at me, like wind or pressure, but there wasn't anything there. Just me standing in a tube with invisible pressure. Was just odd. When I stepped out a woman smiled and said I was an archmage. She seemed overly happy. Me? I freaked out a bit at being such a high rank. But she just smiled, they have super fakey plastic smiles that were more creepy than anything else." Jo shivered. "Really fakey. Like they were painted on. But they waited until I calmed down and ushered me into another room. This guy stood there. And I should say every single person had mage tats on their faces. I don't think I've ever seen so many mages in one place before."

Jo jumped up from the chair, pacing, and rubbing her hands on her jeans. "So, this other room had three balls sitting on a table. One was smooth, ordered, like a round Rubix cube, the second prickly and jangly, like steel wire in a ball with yarn caught up in it. Then the third which was the one that I really didn't like, it looked like a crystal ball, but I swear there was something in it. He told me to pick the one that I liked the best. That was easy. I reached for the one with all the blocks." She smiled. "It reminded me of something soothing and orderly, like when you click that last puzzle piece in. Then they said room one and escorted me to another room. I still had no idea what was going on, so I followed." She wrinkled her nose. "I think they keep you off balance like that to ensure compliance."

I watched as she fell silent and paced more back and forth. "The last one is both obvious and makes no sense at all. There they had a series of blocks scattered on one table, a pile of earth in a sandbox, a fan on another table, and a bunch of growing crystals on the last table."

She shrugged. "The rest is kinda obvious and boring. The crystals called to me. I walked over and stroked them, and they changed direction following my touch. Then the fan turned and blew air at me. Last was the blocks. I just had to arrange them. I knew, just like I know how to put a motor back together."

They then announced my skills and let me talk to the tattoo artist and sign the draft paperwork." She shrugged and lifted her hand to touch the tattoo. It had healed nicely and the blue and green were pretty against her skin, the design of Pattern looking stylized. "So other than affinity to different objects, which could have been anything, I really don't know how they tested me."

She didn't talk for a while staring up at the sky. "After everything is done, the tattoo is added, they tell you not to access your magic until you get into classes. Only the fact that I had parents that were both marked mages let me put school off until next semester. They really wanted me to go now."

"Why didn't you?"

Jo turned and looked at me, her eyes catching me. "I'd never leave you. And you need to finish school. I must have presented a convincing case."

A thought struck me. "Did you see a merlin while you were there?"

The question pulled her out of her thoughts, and she looked at me confused. "No, not that I remember, but I wasn't paying much attention to the tats only that they had them. Why?"

"No specific reason, but I wonder if mages put out a magic field they can sense." What I didn't say, I was wondering about Shay's odd comments. I couldn't be a mage. It made no sense. Or if I was, I was so useless as to not have power. "Doesn't matter. Come on. Your mom is staring out the door at us."

Jo turned to see Marisol standing there, looking worried. "She is a worry wart. But come on, I'm hungry. And remember, no mentioning that."

"Not a chance," I agreed. The last thing I wanted was to think about those breathless terrifying moments anymore. We headed home where warmth and love surrounded me, removing some of the stress. So much still loomed ahead I just needed to do my best and I'd make it.

Chapter 29

Mages can determine what cells are used for spells. Hair and nails are the cheapest—great workings cost appendages. All-over sunburn is a hallmark of young users who haven't learned to direct the cost. Most mages at the magician rank and above can direct the cost without conscious effort. This is part of what you learn in school. It becomes automatic, knowing how much you will offer—the same way we learn to walk or run or drive, it ceases to be a conscious thing. Large scale offerings will often be planned. The sign of a mage missing a finger or something else often means they had to do a major offering, usually involving healing. ~ Magic Explained

CHAOS

I got my paper done, nothing blew up, and even work was good. Maybe, just maybe, life is looking up.

I had sent my paper in the night before and even got to class a bit early. Monique just sneered at me and stomped by. I didn't even bother to let her know I'd noticed.

Though not seeing Shay at the Grind Down also meant I didn't see his weird friend. I had wanted to see Elsba again and try to decide if I had really seen her fight a hawk and eat a snake.

I wonder if that counts as cannibalism?

Waiting for class to start, I pulled up the syllabus and looked at the topic for today. I had reviewed them all at the beginning, but really didn't remember the order they were being presented. This one sounded either very interesting, or boring as all get out. Laws, social strictures, and warnings about unregistered mages.

Huh, didn't think you really could be. But then Sam mentioned the Rogue Team. I thought that was for mages who didn't want to serve.

The obvious hole in my logic made me glad no one could hear my thoughts. If you were never registered and were higher than a 4, well then you were rogue. But what did they expect us to do about that?

Bruce walked around handing out papers from last week. He didn't' say anything when he dropped the paper on my desk, but I grinned at the A+ written on it. The conversation with Sam had helped add some details to it. The bubbly feeling in my chest intensified.

"Decent job on the papers. Some of you are doing exactly what we hoped and are talking to the people mentoring you about these topics. Remember, they have been doing this a lot longer and don't have an optimistic attitude for the most part. This is a good thing. You want the cynical view. It will prepare you for what you see in the field. You can be positive, however, being falsely optimistic will get people hurt."

He turned and clicked on the projector. "Today we get to talk about what you are required to do if you come across an unregistered mage. Now we all know hedgemages are not required to register, though most of them are, just as a side effect of knowing what their rank is."

There was a murmur of huh's in the classroom, but this answer I had at least figured out.

Bruce shook his head. "If you get tested you get registered. The act of signing in registers you. The standard statistic is thirty-five percent of humanity are mages or at least have the ability to tap into magic. Many of researchers that believe it is closer to seventy-five percent."

Another murmur went through the classroom and I frowned. That many people? But why didn't anyone talk about it or teach more magic stuff?

"The thought is most mages are hedgemages. They will probably never know they have magic. If they go to get tested, they are instantly registered, but if you never think you have magic..." Bruce shrugged. "So our current statistic stands. But the question is, 'What are you required to do?' When you get your EMT certification, part of that certification is agreeing to uphold the laws governing magic users. It is a generic agreement that locks you into upholding OMO regulations. Those regulations state that any mage over hedge must be registered."

"Okay. So how do I know the person next to me is a mage or not if they aren't registered?" I glanced to see who had said it, male I knew, but no one jumped out at me. I turned my attention back to Bruce. I wanted the answer to that question too.

Bruce gave a wicked smile. "And there is the question and the escape clause in most of this. It boils down to basic common sense. You see someone with no markings doing major magic and the offering isn't obvious or immediate, such as they go bald or sluice off multiple layers of skin, they probably need to be reported. And honestly, err on the side of caution. If you report someone who is a hedge and never got tested, or has registered, one of two things will happen. The OMO will run their name, verify their identity and say they are registered, thanks for checking. Or they will arrange to pick up the person—note this is their problem not yours—and have them tested. If they test out at the low rank, then they get registered, and gently pointed towards the hedgemage magic classes and it is done. How many of you know there are three aspects to registration?"

This time only two people raised their hand as I scrambled to try to remember. There was the obvious, the tattoos. Oh, that's right the OMO guy had mentioned a new id. But the third I couldn't think of.

"Marcy?" Bruce pointed to a woman who raised her hand. I'd talked to her a few times. In her late twenties, one kid, and... that's right her husband was a mage.

"Tattoo, driver's license is updated to show you are a mage, and mandatory draft enrollment."

Once she said that it was obvious. And I groaned at myself, annoyed at not thinking through all the complexities.

"Correct. Now when you test you are also registering, but really all it does is note that you tested and the outcome. Here's a fun question. How many of you know how testing is done?"

There were lots of exchanging glances and I frowned. Jo had told me easily enough, and it just seemed mostly silly more than anything else. Part of me doubted that was how they tested. It made more sense to have a merlin there with super magic sense. The rest would just be for show.

No one raised their hand and Bruce nodded. "Even mages who have been tested aren't sure. They know they are asked what pulls at them, and it is a weird selection of objects. But they never cast spells or even do anything. And if you ask two mages on the same day, the items they list are completely different. I'm sure the OMO knows how it is done, but they aren't saying. However, the testing is consistent in every country. And they never get different types of magic skills even if you are tested by different people in different countries. That being said, worst case is that a non, or low rank magic user is tested and let go. But if it is an unregistered mage, here is where it gets serious." His voice had flattened out and took on a serious note, his body stiffening. "If you have proof someone did magic and by your inactions allow an unregistered mage to injure someone and you do not report it, you will be considered an accessory to the crime as well as aiding and abetting. The worst thing that happens for reporting a mage is they waste a few hours. The worst thing for not reporting a mage is you will be enrolled in the draft, even if you don't have magic."

His words fell like lumps of sticky tar in the classroom. Splattering us and making us shift unconsciously as the reality of this settled in.

Fear gripped me and I worked it through logically. I had never emerged and after Jo's display, any emergence above a hedgemage would be obvious. I was just weird, as usual.

Bruce sighed. "Yes. It is taken seriously, though few magic users ever report anyone. Most feel they have done their duty by serving in the draft. And worst case, if they don't report someone, they serve a few more years. This is why the government leans so hard on non-magic users to report anyone suspected of being a high-ranking mage. If you don't think you can report someone, don't sign your certificates."

"It isn't fair we have to be stooges and turn people in if they don't want to serve," came a nasally protest from the classroom. This time I knew the voice. Monique Kinnison. She whined. All the time. And everything was unfair and stacked against her. I had to resist the desire to strangle her on a regular basis.

"That is a discussion for a philosophy classroom, not here. But I will ask you this, you really want a merlin running around without training? A merlin that can cause an earthquake at a ten or higher on the Richter scale without meaning to? Part of the mandatory registration is mandatory training." Bruce looked like he was about to say something else, but just shook his head. "So, just do yourself and everyone else a favor and report it. We tried to make it mandatory that all people taking this class went and got tested but that idea was shot down."

He clicked the next slide and we spent ten minutes going over the various laws that governed mages. One of the sub-bullet points caught my attention.

"What is that sub-clause about leniency granted for people under twenty-seven?" I asked, trying to figure out why there would be leniency after how harshly he had talked about unregistered mages.

"Ah, that applies more to self-reporting. Twenty-five is the latest age a mage has ever been recorded as emerging, so they added two years to it. And it has been made clear that not all people realize they did emerge if it happens while sick, intoxicated, or unconscious. So, there is a window where you can get tested years later when you figure out that you are a mage. Any high-rank mage self-reporting at thirty will suffer the consequences, which is doubling the draft for them. Personally, I disagree with that, but I don't make the laws."

"Consequences?" That was me again.

"The penalties for committing a crime using magic are higher for a mage pretty much always. Simply because they are required to train to make sure they KNOW how to use their magic. That is what half of their classes are."

He got blank looks from me and I guess a bunch of others. "When you go in for the draft, AA is the least amount of education required. Bachelors is the most common, and masters and doctorates are encouraged at wizard and higher. You will always have a minor in mage studies. This teaches you how to do offerings that don't kill you, how to use the spells in each class, and how to live and deal with the draft. It is a lot of course work and more than one mage has gotten seriously hurt completing it."

I'd heard all that, but also knew there was something about immediate draft service for those who couldn't handle school, but the consequences were harsh. Not that it mattered to me. I tuned back into what Bruce was saying.

"Generally, most mages you meet that are out of control will be during their emergence. That is where you contact the OMO as soon as you realize it is an emergence and can identify the person. If they are not seriously injured, which is rare, you transport them to the nearest OMO office or wherever they direct you."

"Emergences are not dangerous? The ones we saw on video were scary and people got hurt," Monique protested again.

Really, can't she learn to talk without whining?

Bruce waved his hand in a so-so motion. "Those were old, camera filming wasn't the greatest, and they were usually prisoners. Believe it or not, catching emergences is relatively rare. There are one or two good online videos of them, but how much was real versus excellent film editing is anyone's guess. In the twenty years I worked in the NYFD I only saw two mages die during emergence."

"See, they are dangerous," Monique said, her voice triumphant.

Bruce turned and just looked at her, and his look was so cutting I flinched back, though I had no sympathy for her. Monique paled and sank down further into her chair. I saw a hidden smirk on more than one face. She

244

had not made herself well liked.

"As I was saying, I only saw two deaths. One was a young man who was working a summer job doing windows and emerged thirty stories up. He fell when he emerged and didn't survive the impact with the ground. The second was more tragic. A young mom, only twenty-two, with a one-year-old, emerged while driving across the Brooklyn bridge. Killed her, her daughter, and two other people in the car." He shrugged. "Most of the time it is weird and scary, but not really dangerous. Usually magic seems to sense that the people are not in a life-threatening environment."

A sudden evil smile flashed across his face. "Though there is one incident where the emergence did kill someone. Look up the Rachel Simons case. She emerged while an asshole was raping her. She drained all the water out of his body. So, I guess there are some examples of emergence being dangerous."

His grin was rather scary. I needed to learn to smile like that. It was intimidating.

Chapter 30

All colleges have a magic minor in the AA and BS degrees.
Double majors are common at the archmage rank. Experienced
teachers are sought after because you need to be an archmage
or higher to teach some of the more nuanced aspects of magic.
You are taught how to control, isolate the cells to offer, and how
to use the spells. Entire classes will focus on a single spell.
While it is possible to learn on your own, years of trial and error
have found a solid understanding of physics, biology, and math
is required to be effective. ~ Magic Explained

ORDER

*This job goes from boring and nothing ever happens, to
"Oh Merlin, I'm going to die in the next thirty seconds." If I
make it through this without gray hair I'm going to be
impressed.*

Sam handed me the radio as he drove. "Radio in
those call signs I taped there." He peered out the
window again in the direction we were going, and you
could see a fireball shooting into the sky. "We're going
to need them."

A simple disturbance call, trouble at the fairgrounds.
And when you started seeing lightning and fire when
you were still ten miles out, you know there was going
to be a problem. For the first time in a very long time, I
wished I was a mage. I also hoped I'd make it through
the week. Dying like this would be a bit silly after
everything else.

Holding onto to the handle near the roof I called it
in. I used all the right words. "Unit Edward Alpha

headed to Rockway Fairgrounds. Disturbance reported at BAM site. Visual confirmation of large amounts of magic. Requesting back up. Specifically, Mike Three and Charlie Four. ETA to fairgrounds twelve minutes." My voice stayed calm and smooth and it dawned on me I wasn't scared. Exasperated, nervous, but not really scared. I played with that thought as we careened around corners. Maybe it meant I'd be a good cop after all. Or I had gone insane. Either one seemed likely.

The nearer we got, the weirder the air felt. I couldn't explain it, but it seemed similar to what it felt like when lightning was striking like crazy. Sam didn't seem to notice anything, so I just kept my mouth shut. I was all too aware that in many ways I was a liability for the department, and I didn't want to ruin the good relationship we had. Maybe that we had always had.

Siren screaming and lights flashing, Sam tore around the last corner before the straightway into the camping area of the fairgrounds. A huge, oddly straight, bolt of lightning hit the ground in what seemed like the middle of the camping area.

"Shit, shit, shit. Check with backup. Where are they?"

"This is Edward Alpha, where is our backup? The situation seems electric." I smirked to myself at my pun and Sam groaned, but didn't say anything.

"Edward Alpha, ETA on dispatched officers is four minutes," the sterile voice of the operator said. The 911 gals never sounded so robotic. I didn't know how they handled their dispatcher sounding like that. What was odd was that she had a super bubbly personality in person with a voice that expressed her current mood.

"Rodger." I released the mic button as Sam came to a stop where the road ended and tents and campers took over. The same man was standing there waiting for us. No huge not-dog by his side. I felt let down. I really wanted to see more familiars though I wasn't sure why. They'd never talk to a normal person.

Sam got out of the car, hand on his weapon as he scanned. "Randolph. We've got mage backup on the way."

I got out of the car, peering at the man. Scott Randolph looked so mad I was almost surprised he didn't have steam coming out of his ears. "Those gods be damned idiots. This is why mages don't drink, 'cause you get stupid. Leon thought his wife Julia was hitting on Ivan. And Ivan, that stupid braindead Cossack, thought Leon was dissing his girlfriend Carol. Now I've got a Fire mage throwing down against an Air mage. At the rate they're both going they'll be bald or dead. If they were just going to kill each other I wouldn't care, but you see that?"

As he said it, another bolt of lightning came searing through the air to impact with a boom that rattled my brain. The hair on my arms stood up with the energy in the air.

"Thought you were an Entropy archmage." I stared at Scott in surprise. Surely he could be our backup.

Scott started walking and we followed, getting closer to the commotion. I could hear whooping and hollering and men shouting.

"I'll sear all the hair off your damn head if you even look twice at my wife!" one man hollered. Old, older than Chief Amosen, he had long matted dreadlocks that looked like someone had chopped them off unevenly. With dark hair but pale skin, he almost glowed as he raised his hand and fire danced along his fingers.

"Like I'd want anything to do with that slut. Every man who's had her said she's a shitty ride," another man spat back. He stood in an easy pose, a big guy at least a few inches over six feet. His white blond hair and build screamed Slavic ancestry.

A woman sitting on the side sucked in a sharp breath and jumped to her feet. "Ivan, are you saying I suck in bed?" Her voice high and indignant and Scott groaned again.

"Shit. And she's been doing coke. Why do I hang with these idiots?"

I watched all this in disbelief as the one woman, Julia I guess, launched herself at Ivan. Another woman, Hispanic with half her head shaved interfered with her attack and they started rolling on the ground.

"See what you did? If my Julia gets hurt, I'll see how you taste roasted."

"Randolph, can't you stop them?" Sam hissed.

"I don't have the damn education to pull off that trick. Power sure, but I'd need to know exactly what I was doing for which molecules. My strengths are in Time and Water besides. I did all my education in theoretical physics and quarks. I don't have a damn idea what the alcohol molecule looks like, much less how to break it into harmless components." He glared at the people on lawn chairs watching all of this and drinking beer. I thought I even saw some people placing bets, but I must have been wrong about that. "You want them dead, that I'm very good at. I have lots of experience at that."

"Well, killing them might be an option," Sam muttered as another wave of fire burst out and I swore one of Fire mage's dreadlocks was shorter.

"Oh, Leon is still posturing. He'll have to get close to bald. My worry is if he gets pissed and starts boiling water his control sucks. He'll kill everyone in the area without realizing it. And I don't give a damn how good Ivan is, controlling lightning is chancy at best. If it goes sideways, he'll hit one of the RVs and we'll have a real explosion. Damn near about ready to shoot both of them, but then I'd have all of them after me." He waved at the crowd cheering them on. "I swear I'm raising all their dues next year and I'm pointing back to this incident when they whine." He flinched as a huge gust of wind toppled one of the tents. "And doubling their bail deposits."

I looked at him, completely lost. Everything he said raised more questions. I really wanted to talk to him and figure out what he meant. And maybe see Dahlia again.

"Can't blame you." Sam turned and I heard the sirens that must have grabbed his attention. "And here comes backup." Another shriek grabbed my attention and I spun as someone started batting at the lawn chair that had caught fire. The person spun—from this distance all I got was skinny with dark hair—and the earth under Ivan's feet wrenched open and he stumbled into it, cursing.

"Shit. This is what I was scared of. Why can't the idiots do pot? No one starts fights; all they do is talk about metaphysical crap and eat too much." The venom and stress in Scott's voice was stressing me out more than anything else. "I really hope your backup knows how to do crowd control over magical idiots."

I glanced at Sam, expecting a confident answer, but as he looked around, he just nodded. "Me too."

Running feet and clanking belts—I'd never realized how much noise the belts made when you ran—came up behind us, telling me who they had to be before I saw their faces.

A man with tight curly reddish-brown hair on skin that was a toss-up between an Americano and a latte, trotted over to us. On his other side, with a figure I knew Jo would have been drooling over, was a woman. She had to be at least six feet tall and was all muscles and curves. Her nose and straight black hair mixed with skin that reminded me of chestnut wood hinted at a Native American background.

"Oh good," said Randolph. "Please tell me at least one of you can do something to stop this before it becomes a full-fledged riot? I can go in and kill them easily enough, but people get very upset when I do that unless sanctioned by the US government. And I don't see federal badges on any of you."

I made a mental note to research who the heck Scott Randolph was.

The two new cops glanced at him and then at the situation.

"How many people? Just the ones here, or are there others on the campground we need to worry about?"

Scott got a funny look on his face and took a half step back, which caused Sam to look stressed, which I found exceedingly odd. Weren't the cops on our side?

"No. Just the people here." He flinched as the tires on an RV seemed to dissolve as a woman continued to screech. More and more people were getting to their feet, anger radiating in their body language.

"Good, about what, twenty-five?"

"Roughly," Scott's voice was wary. "Psychic mage?"

Her grin held humor and maliciousness mixed together. "Archmage. You might want to get behind me."

"Move, Cori." Sam had grabbed my arm and was pulling me back. The other cop backed up too, but he didn't have the odd look on Scott's face. Scott's look was something between envy, respect, and fear.

"What is she going to do?" I asked as we backed up.

The woman turned and looked at me, and I swore I saw power glowing in her eyes. "I'm going to knock them all out. They'll have hangovers from hell in about an hour, but none of them will even be thinking about throwing spells." She turned back around, and I itched to grab her and make me understand. There was so much I didn't know. I needed to know more. The list of things to research got longer and longer. Maybe I needed to pay more attention to what mages could do.

"We should be safe here. Jada is good at this. Doubt it will even cost her a quarter inch of hair. I'm George Thompson, that's Jada Simons." George smiled at us as he talked, his gaze flicking over the three of us.

I gave him a smile but then my eyes were drawn back to her. For some reason I expected something showy and comic book worthy. Instead she closed her eyes and took a deep breath and then let it out. As she did people dropped like flies. One moment they were standing there yelling, the next they were crumpled on the ground.

"What the hell was that?" I asked, shocked.

George grinned, watching Jada. I didn't detect sex or lust in that look, just respect and admiration. "Psychic archmage. KO spell is something only they can use. It's devastating, but effective in small groups."

"That was small?"

"Merlins can do up to two hundred, but in full scale riots with thousands, it's useless. 'It's an excellent ability for a cop, 'cause it doesn't matter how much speed or booze you have in your system, you go down. Handy. Reduces shoot outs. Too bad it's limited to line of sight, but nothing's perfect."

I looked around, stunned at how something I was starting to think we wouldn't make out of alive had just ended so simply. "Yeah, impressive," I said still looking.

"Yeah, but he didn't tell you what else Psychic Mages can do." Randolph's tone was sour and he watched Jada with a look that told me he would trust a charging rhino before her.

"Believe me, sir, the last thing I want to do is read anyone's mind," said Jada. "It is never pleasant, ever. Frankly, it is the skill I use the least. Truth, at least, is useful if not annoying. Do you know how frustrating it gets to get a constant feedback in social niceties? I can't shut the damn thing off." Jada glared at him as she spoke. "So put your prejudices away, unless you have something to hide."

"You know damn well everything I'm hiding isn't mine to say. And if you know who I am, you know you don't want to read my mind." He turned and looked at the unconscious group and the few coming in from further afield to look at the crumpled BAM members. "I swear, if any of them had actual planning abilities they might be dangerous. As it is, I'm stuck running an adult day care. Oh well, at least they pay me well. Now I'm going to dump all their booze and pretend I don't have a damn idea what happened to it. I hope the headache is hell."

"It should be. I added a bit of extra umph to it."

He gave her a long look then a sharp nod. "Good job. Send me the bill. I'll pay it." With that he walked away, collecting liquor bottles and dumping them on the ground as he went. Before he'd done more than a few the huge not-dog joined him. I could hear low level murmuring from people as they wrestled friends and loved ones up and away from the area.

"If only all of them were that easy. At least they aren't trying to knock over banks," George said with a laugh. "Need us for anything else, Clements?"

Sam shook his head. "Nah. Thanks. If I'd been stuck, things would have gotten messy."

"You related to Samuel Clemens?" Jada asked and Sam groaned.

Mel Todd

"No. My parents just had a very bad sense of humor, but I figure I got off lucky."

"Oh?" Jada had crossed her arms across her chest, looking down at him. She could really pull off the imposing warrior act.

"They named my brother Mark Twain Clements."

George and Jada choked then started to laugh. "I'll agree. Let us know if you need anything else, but we're more than ready to get back to Atlanta," George said with a wave as they headed back. "This place is too quiet for us."

We saw them off and I looked back at the quiet campsite. I'd always known mages could do amazing things, but I'd never realized how useful they could be for important stuff that didn't rate news stories and movies made about them. I'd have to remember that.

Chapter 31

Emergence: Contrary to what most people thought about magic in the Middle Ages, where magic resided in the domain of women (generally crones), magic emergence tends to occur after the cessation of puberty. With the hormones in the body settling down into defined routes, it is then that if the person is so blessed, they will emerge. Most people admit that teenagers with magic would be hazardous at best. ~ Magic Explained

SPIRIT

Holy shit, I didn't realize this had been based on a real person. And I met him? Holy moly. And he was so contained. But now his comment about killing everyone makes sense.

I'd gotten to class early, so I took the time to look up Scott Randolph and almost dropped my phone. One of my favorite movies was The Rescue of Stranthorn. It had been an action adventure block buster and won two Oscars and multiple Golden Globes. The Oscars had been for Movie of the Year and Best Screenplay. As a teenager I'd watched it so many times I had entire sections of the movie memorized. It had also cemented in the public consciousness just how deadly a pissed off mage could be.

The incident had happened before I was born. A small mall, Stranthorn Park in upper New York, was taken over by magic extremists. They felt that mages should be the ruling class and were going to execute one person an hour until the US government was dissolved. There were twenty mages, all determined to make sure the world knew that mages would never be kept in servitude again. A researcher from a small lab was also caught in the hostage situation. Scott Randolph – though for the movie they had changed his name to Steve Randolph. After they killed the first person, he single-handedly went up against all twenty and killed them. In the movie they had killed five more people, but according to the news story it was only two more, though by the end of the movie the mall had all but been destroyed.

I tried to remember the various ways he had eliminated the bad guys, but in the movies it was always spectacular and visually stunning. The man I'd met seemed much more subtle. I quirked my head. In the movie he'd had a familiar. Digging back through I found it. He had one but it was killed in the battle. In the movie his familiar lived. In the movie it had been a beautiful dog, a husky or something like that. From the news story it had been much smaller with six legs, but still vaguely canine.

Ouch. Losing your familiar must hurt.

I didn't know much about the connection, but still anything like that would hurt. Wouldn't it? The rabbit hole of learning more about the man, and the trying to figure out why he was in Rockway, Georgia, beckoned but the door opened and Bruce came in.

He cleared his throat to grab everyone's attention. "We won't be in here today. Everyone to the practical labs. We are all going to take the CPR-BLS Healthcare provider exam, the cognitive Exam, and the Psychomotor exams. You must pass these tests to graduate. But by taking them now, it will allow you to assist while riding in rigs during your last rotation instead of being dead weight. Your exam costs are covered as part of this program."

There were groans and grumbles, and a few panicked looks, but I grabbed my stuff and headed to the practical lab. This, at least, was useful. Maybe I could test first, but it was still hours of tests. Either way, no paper due next week. That made me happy.

They had a refresher available for the CPR aspect, but I knew I didn't need it. The CPR-BLS or Cardio-Pulmonary Resuscitation: Basic Life Support test itself I, at least, was ready to take immediately. I cranked through the practical and multiple choice aspects of the test to the beat of Staying Alive in the background. I'd never get the darn song out of my head now.

As soon as I'd cleared the CPR-BLS, I jumped on a computer and started the next one, the cognitive exam. I'd been studying the material for months. The better your scores were, the better your chance of getting a good job. And I needed this. Drug names were the hardest for me, but I'd been focusing on that via the practice tests. Psychomotor exams would be harder. They were done on a 'victim' and you were judged on how you did everything. It would help me to be sure I was ready for the ambulance ride along.

Five hours later I was done and had passed everything. I wanted to dance. I just needed to finish the course to get my EMT certification.

I walked out, one of the first people done, to glares of annoyance, especially Monique whose eyes radiated with hate I didn't understand. But I was just about dancing at my scores and the possibility of certification. If I applied when I got home, I'd be able to have my certification by the ride along. I had a bit more to get the paramedic certification, but step one was done.

The ringing of my cell phone pulled me out of my euphoria, and I didn't even glance at the phone just answered.

Mel Todd

"This is Cori, successful passer of EMT exams." I expected it to be Jo, Molly, or maybe Kadia. And my joy had to be visible in my tone. I wanted to dance.

"Congratulations are in order then?" There was a question in Sam's voice.

"Yes, that is exactly what is in order. I got past the first hurdle. I can legally help now. And it justifies me getting paid!" That part almost had me shrieking. After everything, I could see a light at the end of this long journey.

"Well then, we will need to celebrate. But first, you interested in working today? Would mean you'd take off Friday. We could use the help." He didn't sound stressed and the BAM had left two days ago. I considered the offer. With no paper tonight I didn't have anything else to do except personal research and that was just to satisfy my curiosity. Maybe if I worked, I could ask him about Scott Randolph.

"Doing?" I at least wasn't going to sign up for anything truly awful. That question warred with the side of me that wanted to just say yes to the money aspect. But still ask questions, you never knew what people were trying to sign you up for.

I could hear his amusement as he responded. "What? Don't trust me? No worries, nothing drastic. There's a game at the stadium this afternoon and we're short officers to do security. With the manpower from Atlanta last week we had to return the favor this week. I could use someone else to do security checking: wanding people, checking bags, and acting as authority to campus security."

Laughter escaped me. "I'm supposed to act as authority to guys more than double my age and my weight?"

"You've got good instincts. You don't overreact. I

really think you should become a cop, Cori. I'd have you in my car any day. But yes. You get authority, and an official police vest." He said the words like he was dangling a carrot under my nose.

"Sure, I can work." I looked around and shrugged. "I haven't actually left campus yet, so I don't have a uniform with me. "

"Okay. I can swing by, pick you up and take you home then we can go to the stadium and get ready?"

"Oh, that would be great. Thanks." I told him where to pick me up and headed that direction. Fifteen minutes later I was in my apartment changing clothes. Ten minutes after that, having fortified myself by zapping a *quesadilla* Marisol had made for me, we were headed back to the college and the stadium.

I'd never been a sports person so in the few years I'd attended, I'd never been to the stadium. With all the game day flags flying and people milling, it held energy that was almost seductive. Even I felt the desire to be part of the excitement.

We parked and Sam grabbed a bag from his trunk. We headed to the stadium entrance, with me in an official police vest and my belt, but still no gun or taser. Part of me almost felt like a poser without them, but that wasn't something I had delusions about being able to use, though I had gotten much more comfortable around them.

"This is pretty easy. For the most part we are looking for weapons. We don't care about a pocket knife, but no guns or batons. Check coolers and bags for booze. Sodas are fine, and it if is a single beer or something, use your judgment. Mostly I'm concerned about the hard stuff. Let me know if you see anything that sets off your alarm bells and I'll handle it."

"Sounds easy enough."

Mel Todd

"It should be. Good way to spend a nice spring day."
Sam grinned as he said it and handed me a wand and a
bunch of zip ties, just in case.

I was glad we were there early, as it gave me a
chance to get into the groove of wanding and checking.
The people coming in now were laid back, chattering
about the game as they let me wand them and give
cursory checks of their coolers. In the first hour I only
had to confiscate one six pack of beer, which the person
shrugged over and let go with grace, much to my relief.

The flow sped up as the crowds grew thicker. I had
to concentrate to not get over complacent, which was
tempting as more and more people showed up. People
got a bit more annoyed at having to wait to be wanded,
but it didn't upset me. I got really good at that look
Laurel gave me, the officious "I can make you regret
your decisions'" look. To my amazement it worked,
though I caught Sam glancing at me and fighting back a
smile more than once.

There was about fifteen minutes to the game start
according to the start time being blared over the speaker
system every five minutes. And really, they needed a
better speaker system, the voice distortion was so bad I
wasn't sure it was a human speaking.

A man approached mixed in with a herd of others.
He was older than most, but there were lots of parents
and other relatives, so the age didn't make me look
twice. I wanded him with fast efficient moves, and
nothing pinged. I gave him my quick customer service
smile. "Enjoy the game."

"Oh, I'll enjoy the reactions."

I froze, his words not stopping me so much as the
tone and the sneer. Turning I followed him with my
eyes as I held my hand up. His odd gait pulled at me. I'd
seen lots of people over the years with various

disabilities when it came to walking but his way of moving seemed wrong.

"Sam?" I said, leaning over a bit so he could hear me over the sounds of people around us. He looked up at me, raising his brows. I nodded at the man hobbling away. And "hobble" was the only way I could phrase it. "Something is off about him."

He followed my gaze, eyes narrowing. "I see it. Stay here." He headed after the man in a ground eating stride I didn't have the height or the weight to pull off. Some things just required a certain amount of physical mass, that I, at five-six and one twenty, just didn't have.

"Sir, can you halt a moment? I need to talk to you."

How Sam made his voice boom like that, I had no idea. But lots of people turned back to look at him, including the guy.

"Yes, you, sir."

The man started to run. But his odd gait made it so he didn't get very far before Sam was close enough to step in front of him. "Sir, can I see what is in your pants?"

"Fuck you. Fuck you and the rest of your mage-loving idiots. Everyone thinking the world is so good. Can't you see you're all slaves?"

Before Sam could stop him, not that I thought he had any idea what the man was about to do, he fell to his knees. Liquid shattered, soaking his pants. "I'll free you all."

"Get down!" The words tore from my throat before I could think. The ground underneath him split, causing him to fall forward as an explosion rocked me to the ground and blew Sam over. Nearby people screamed out as shards hit them, but the man lay still.

I climbed back to my feet and raced over to Sam, cursing myself softly at not having my med bag with me.

He lay there shaking his head, eyes unfocused. I did a quick safety check on him, but other than some minor cuts he was fine but dazed. I checked him for a possible concussion, but his eyes dilated correctly, and he could answer my questions as he sat up slowly.

Verifying he was fine I headed over to the man, I didn't want to move him, but I needed to check his pulse. I reached down under his hair to check his pulse and got nothing.

"Sam, help me roll him over. I need to see the damage." I didn't see any flames, but the ground under my feet felt funny, crumbly almost. Sam got up and on three we carefully rolled him over. Gasps and the sounds of a few people heaving surrounded us at I stared at the man. Whatever he had strapped to his legs had blown down creating a crater underneath him. He'd obviously had more things strapped to his torso. His legs, pelvic area, and abdomen areas were messes of red gore. There was no chance of him surviving or even still being alive.

"I'd say he blew up all his chances at freeing anyone," I muttered.

Sam just glared at me as sirens approached our location.

Chapter 32

Information rules the world, and the OMO is well aware of this. As one of the few independent agencies in the world, on par with the World Health Organization, their inner workings are shrouded in a great deal of secrecy. Only mages archmage or higher are ever hired there. They only contract with companies that agree to have all employees tested and only those with zero magic are allowed to work there in a service capacity. This is just proof they cannot be trusted. ~ Info on the Freedom from Magic website

CHAOS

I'll be happy if I never see anything that gory again.

The images kept flashing in my mind, even by Saturday, as I wiped down the counter. Other cops had showed up, then Blaise, the medical examiner, but this time he had only enough time to cast a quick glance at me before he was pulled into the scene.

Was it a crime scene? Did that qualify?

I'd spent the next hour in a tent scratching my head until it bled. The pain had been a nice distraction from the memories. Too bad it didn't work now.

The rest of the crowd had been very subdued and our team losing didn't help. Either way I was glad to be home that evening.

To my relief, my second to last week of police duty went quietly. We agreed to let me have next Friday off, though Laurel reminded me to come and turn in my equipment that day. Either way, I'd get the luxury of sleeping in. I was looking forward to that.

No matter how hard I tried to focus on the upcoming practicals, or customers, or cleaning, the blasted images wouldn't leave my mind. Made it hard to eat and I really didn't need to lose any more weight. My clothes were falling off again. Thinking about it made me reach for another day-old muffin. I didn't really like the muffins, scones were better, but they almost never lasted to get old enough for me to justify eating.

The jangle of the door pulled me out of my thoughts. With a sense of relief, I'd even take Shay at that moment. Instead, I looked up into a green ribbon.

"Elsba!" I don't know why I said it or why I sounded so excited, but at least when I looked at the strange creature, I didn't see the remains of the man's body. I'd never even learned his name.

I shook myself and forced a smile. "Hi, what can I get you?" I managed through a force of effort to say it to the man she rode on, not to her. And I didn't understand why I thought of her riding him, not him holding her. I really needed a life that didn't involve dead bodies.

"I'm meeting a friend here, but I'll take a large mocha. And can I get Elsba a herbal tea, cool?"

That sounded reasonable to me, especially as I was pretty sure she ate mostly meat. "Sure. Is green tea okay?"

"Perfect."

Kadia was taking a break down at the bank dealing with some paperwork, so I made the drinks and walked them over to them. I'd poured the tea over ice then strained it into one of our larger cups, figuring it would be easier for her to drink out of.

"Thank you," he said as I set the drinks down. Elsba slithered off of him and I watched, fascinated. She had tiny hands that normally leaned up against her body. They looked like bird claws as she latched onto the rim

264

of the cup and licked at the liquid.

The jangle of the door interrupted my fascinated focus, and I resented having to drag my eyes away, but froze as Scott Randolph walked in.

"You live here? In Rockway?" The words came out shocked, and I felt my face heat up. I had a sudden wish for the earth to open up and swallow me. For a second, in my embarrassment, I thought I felt the ground tremble, but that was just me being an idiot. I recovered with, "Hi, what can I get you?"

He'd paused just far enough in that the door had closed behind him and looked at me. "You were with Sam dealing with crap out at the fairgrounds. What are you doing working here? Police can't pay that little. And why aren't you marked?"

The questions threw me off my practiced patter and annoyance slipped out. "I'm not marked because I'm not a mage, duh. See the short hair and lack of tattoo? And I'm not a cop, I'm an intern. You noticed I didn't have a gun or badge? Or was that too subtle for you in your state of rage to catch? After all, you seemed more concerned about how to kill people than what the people there to help were doing." It wasn't exactly fair, but he'd annoyed me. What was it with people and marking? I was no more a mage than I was the president of the US, who couldn't be a magic user due to the twenty-eighth amendment.

Elsba's mage choked on a laugh. "You being a jerk again, Scott? Seems to me she isn't all that intimidated by the great Scott Randolph."

"Well I had to look up who he was, so not really." I was so lucky my nose wasn't growing from all the lying I was doing. "Besides the actor that played him was better looking."

At that the man at the table gave up and just laughed,

Scott looked both embarrassed and annoyed, and finally sighed. "I'm sorry. I was being a jerk both times I met you. And I just assumed you were a mage, you-" he broke off and shook his head. "Never mind. I'm getting old. Too much time spent manipulating quarks." He dug into his pocket and pulled out a ten. "Could I get a large coffee with a splash of hazelnut in it? Please?"

"Sure." I took the money and went to make his drink, though I tried really hard to hear what they were talking about. But mostly the other guy just seemed to be teasing Scott. Even the familiar laughed at him. When I brought over the drink and set it down, I tried to give him the change.

"Keep it. You earned it."

"Thanks." I started to turn away, but the need to know once again was an urge I couldn't ignore. "If you don't mind, I would like to ask you a question." My voice came out more aggressive than I intended, but I held his gaze.

"As long as you don't want an autograph, go for it," he replied, his voice gruff. I watched his friend snicker and I swear Elsba was laughing too.

"Why would I want your autograph? I didn't even know you were a real person until this week."

"Merlin, I need to keep her around to burst your ego." I glanced at him, I really did need to figure out his name, but oh well. "Please ask, young lady. I'm ecstatic to see what you prick his self-inflated pride with next."

Scott shot his companion a dirty look, which only made the man laugh harder. Holding up his hand he offered it to me. "I'm Sloan Michaels. Long-time friend of this reprobate here. And you are?"

I fumbled for a minute, then shook it. People didn't usually introduce themselves so formally. "Oh, Cori Munroe. And reprobate? At first, I thought he was the head of a mage biker gang. Then I found out he was a scientist. Now I'm not sure what he is." I looked at Scott, head tilted. "What, or who are you?"

He glowered, but it didn't have much heat. "I don't usually have to justify my existence to wait staff." He paused and looked at me. "But I guess you aren't that." He frowned again peering at me. "You sure you're not a mage?"

I wanted to groan. This was getting old. "If I am, I'm barely a hedige as I'm not old enough to be a crone. I haven't emerged or experienced anything that might equate to emerging outside a sneezing fit. So yes."

"Huh. I'm probably just tired. Dealing with those idiots all week is exhausting." He narrowed his eyes at Sloan. "And don't get me started on you or that legless menace you seem to like."

Elsba just laughed at him, then went back to lapping at her tea.

"Oh sit. Your hovering over me doesn't help," he snapped, waving me to a seat. I looked around; the store was quiet, and Kadia would be back any moment, so I grabbed a chair and swung it over. "Not sure why I'm telling you all this, but might as well. Not like it's a big secret. Yes, I am, or was, a scientist. With a PhD in theoretical physics. The DoD had me working in a small lab on stuff for the space station. All hush-hush stuff, boring really, but being able to monitor and manipulate quarks to create some new elements was kinda cool. What that meant is I knew how to use my magic to move very small things and make very big differences with a minuscule offering." He stopped and looked at Sloan. "Tell her your degree."

Sloan laughed. "He just wants to put me in the spotlight. I'm a chiropractor by trade. But while I got the medical degree, I'm not good at the mental high-end stuff. If I can't see it, I can't manipulate it. Scott here can manipulate what he only thinks exists. I prefer bones and muscles. They're at least visible." He shrugged. "My draft was served doing basic clinic duty on a base in the middle east. Elsba loved it. The heat and lots of creatures to eat."

The creature nodded her head up and down. There was no escaping that was what she did. Me, I tried to resist scratching my head. It would wait until I could step out back and shed another layer of dandruff.

"So, working with imaginary particles gave you the knowledge of how to kill people?" I expected him to avoid the question or be obtuse. The movie and reports made it sound like he'd been very good at killing them. If it was a bit over the top in the movie, I blamed that on Hollywood.

Sloan choked on another laugh. Scott got a funny look in his eye and Sloan quit laughing, leaning back and holding his cup. "Do you know the real reason they require education for mages over hedgies, and try to encourage mages at any rank to attend the training classes?" Scott asked as he refocused on me.

I shrugged. "Control over mages."

They both barked out laughs that had no humor in them.

"Your cynicism isn't far wrong but that's only part of it. Magic is vast and we don't understand it all yet. Did you know that we theorize the emergence and the strange things that happen with it are your body instinctively learning how to make offerings, how to control what magic they have available to them?"

I shook my head mute, surprised by this idea.

"It's true. Do you still teach about the Age of Awakening in high school?"

"Sure. But it's only a month, mostly talking about the

appearance of magic and all the mages that died trying to learn how to control it. There's lots of focus on the greats of that time. The people who worked out how to use it." I shrugged. "For the most part they expect us to memorize names. Who did what. Like Enrico Fermi setting out the conservation conversion of cellular energy to magical energy. Mentions of the Franco German War and the first Mage war. How different commanders used mages as shock troops."

Scott sneered. Or at least I think that was what it was. It sure wasn't a smile. "They don't mention all the people that died from mages playing with their new powers. It was a lot. Most mages only get the dark secrets if they go for their bachelors, then they are required to take the course. Write papers and learn just how horrible we were. It's one of the reasons every government in the world has such strict controls and the rules of using magic users in battles..." He trailed off and shook his head. "That doesn't matter. The answer to your question is you need to know how science works to use magic. A Fire mage doesn't just create flame, he actually speeds up molecules to make them burn. A Water mage has an affinity to the H_2O molecule, but if they don't understand how it works, they can accidentally create H_2O_2 instead. Many have. It's why all mages have hard science degrees. The more you know the more dangerous and efficient you are."

Sloan sighed. "It's also why the government requires more draft service from merlins. It isn't so they can do awesome and great things." He waved one hand through the air in a flourish. "It's so they completely understand how easily they can kill or destroy without meaning to." His smile was bitter. "Welcome to the reality of being a mage."

That threw me and I leaned back, considering. The

odd idea that maybe Stevie had been killed by a mage, a merlin, seeped into my head. The sound of the door opening and a customer coming in pulled me away for a bit.

When I had dealt with the customer and did a bit more cleaning up, I came back over. They didn't welcome me, but they didn't object when I sat down on the chair. "Okay. I can understand that. But what was the whole BAM thing? You aren't the leader of a biker gang?"

Sloan snickered, hiding his face in his coffee. Elsba had disappeared, probably under his coat. Was she cold or warm blooded? Or did that even apply to her?

Scott sighed. "I guess technically I am, maybe. More accurately, I'm the CEO and CFO. I try to keep them out of trouble, pay bail, hire lawyers, and occasionally manage to keep them from getting in major trouble. Really, they would have been better finding a spirit mage like that lady cop." He shrugged. "Most of them are people who did their time and came out scarred or broken and have a hard time with the day to day world. Some just are tired of the grind and walked away. The few that are really broken only rarely come in for the big events like that." He snorted. "They pay me good money to play babysitter a few times a year when there's any level of organized event." He cast me a sharp smile. "So, if I'm done baring my soul to you?"

I rose. "Sure. I was just curious. Thanks for answering. And I'm glad no one got seriously hurt the other night. We'll be closing in about an hour. Next drink is on me." I headed back to the counter wondering where in the world Kadia was as I finished stocking stuff. I needed to scratch my head like crazy and I didn't want to leave the counter uncovered.

Chapter 33

The twenty-eighth amendment limits the president to no more than two terms and prevents him from being any rank of mage. To even run for president, you must be tested by the OMO and they must verify you have no magical power. This was made necessary by the actions of Franklin D Roosevelt after it was found that he had read the minds of German officials, knew about the Holocaust, and purposefully hid the information as well as information that could have prevented Pearl Harbor. ~History of Magic

ORDER

This time the craziness didn't happen to or around me, but poor Kadia.

Lawrence called as I was about to shut down early and go find her. A trip to the bank should have taken her about fifteen minutes, but she'd been gone over an hour and a half before he called. Turns out she'd tripped walking out of the bank, twisted her knee, fell, and slammed her head into a column which had caused her to be so disoriented she started making crazy offerings and setting things on fire, like her clothes. It had taken EMT's to get her calmed down and sedated. Then they took her to the hospital to get her knee worked on. She'd be out for another week, then back with a brace.

Molly agreed to let me run the place myself, which suited me just fine. Carl and Lori made more work than they were worth. Besides, Sunday mornings were usually quiet.

I'd gotten tired of the normal fare on TV and had it

playing old episodes of Law & Order: Mage Unit, which at least was never boring though surely most of it was an exaggeration of how powers worked. That, or they all had familiars and chests of genetic material.

The morning had been quiet, Sundays were, so I'd worked on studying for the exam. The paramedic certification test would be the week after I graduated, but I'd gotten back the scores on the test for my EMT certification. I'd passed. Not perfect, but darn close. Meds were the only thing that I had trouble with, so I was going back over all the variations of meds and making sure I was good at spelling and pronouncing them. So many were so close that you needed to be careful.

I looked up, standing as I did so, to assist the next customer. When the chief stepped in with her husband behind her, I frowned.

"Morning Chief Amosen, Captain Martinez. What can I get you?" I knew what she would probably order but I didn't think the fire chief had ever come in. I'd seen him a few times, but I had no idea what he drank, if anything.

"My usual please, Cori. Martin, you want your hot chocolate?"

"Yes, with a shot of mint in it," he replied, his soft voice almost funny out of such a thick man. Where Laurel was all wiry muscle, Martin was only about two inches taller than her 5'7" but he was at least six inches wider, all muscle. I had no problems believing he could carry a man out of a burning building.

Laurel paid for the drinks and looked around the empty shop. At ten-thirty church was still in session. Most of the customers would show up around eleven and then I'd be busy until two, when I would shut down. At least working by myself the tips would be good.

"I was wondering if I could talk to you. Seems pretty quiet."

My stomach twisted hard into a knot, but I nodded. "Sure." She headed over to the table where her husband sat. Oddly enough it was the same one that Scott and Sloan had been at the other day.

I cleaned up from making the drinks and headed over, sinking into the chair. "If you're telling me I'm fired you could have just told me not to show up Monday." I tried to make it into a joke, but the churning I my stomach didn't let me make it as light-hearted as I tried.

"Do you really think I'd do that to you?" There might have been a note of hurt in her voice, but what did I know?

"Expecting the worst is easier than hoping for anything good," I observed, sidestepping answering her.

"True. But no. If you were interested in going through the police academy, I'd sponsor you. But now this is about Harold Court."

It took me a second to place him. It had been months ago, and I had managed to dismiss him from my mind. "The private investigator?"

"That's the one. A detective in New York following up passed on some more information. Something I felt you at least needed to know."

"Okay..." Was I interested? Worried? Apathetic? I really didn't know, but either way, I did want to hear the information.

"Apparently the search for Kory Monroe was his only open case. And it's a case that over ten investigative firms have taken on over the last eight years, all looking for a mage with a name similar to that. A Spirit merlin. They wouldn't give me details, but everyone seems to think it's very important this merlin is found."

"Huh. Okay. Sounds odd." I pointed back at the TV. "They never seem to have any trouble finding people. Heck, some of the Pattern mages can recreate an entire crime scene with an offering of a nail or two."

Laurel snorted. "Not quite that impressive but yes, missing persons usually don't stay missing unless they want to. Psychic and Pattern mages do manage to find people quickly. But either way, I wanted to let you know about their request. Note this is a request, not anything they can force you to do."

I looked at her confused.

What in the world is she talking about?

"They are requesting, whoever is hiring these mages, that anyone with a name even similar to that of Kory Monroe go in for mage testing if they haven't already."

"Huh? Why?"

She shrugged and her husband just looked vaguely amused. "I'm not sure, but there seem to be some pretty high-powered people behind the hiring of these PI's. I don't like giving in to the whims of powerful people for spurious reasons. You've never emerged, or at least not at a rank that either you or anyone else has noticed. And I understand not wanting to get on the government radar more than we already are. But I was obligated to inform you of their request."

I rolled my eyes. "Everyone lately keeps asking me to do this. I'm not a mage. Or if I am, I'm barely a hedge. No thanks. I think people test just because you get the education for free. I'm not high enough to qualify so why bother? Besides, I'll graduate soon. I'm almost there."

My skin all but crawled and I felt like I was having a panic attack as I fought to keep a straight face.

"I get that. So, I asked. You said no. It's done." She

really didn't seem to mind, but the idea of government people having their fingers in my life freaked me out.

"And you really don't know why they're looking for this mage?" I didn't know why I asked. My eternal need to know why probably, but it didn't make sense. All mages were registered when they emerged. Why would someone not register? The consequences were bad.

Laurel sighed and peered into her coffee. Martin on the other hand seemed to smirk at his wife. He caught me giving him a look.

"I told her you'd want explanations. And it isn't a huge secret. Mostly I'm smirking 'cause now she has to make dinner tonight."

She huffed. "I should have known better. You've always wanted to know everything. Here's what I was told. A powerful merlin put out the call for this search right before he died. The mage they're trying to find supposedly had a huge emergence that was felt all the way to New York about oh, nine years ago around April."

I frowned at that and she must have seen it.

"Yeah, about the time Stevie died."

He was killed.

My mental rebuttal was instantaneous, but I didn't say it. I'd never wanted to face the possibility he died of natural causes.

"And yes, I thought about it. But neither of you were anywhere near finishing puberty. If I had to guess, you had just entered, and he would have soon enough." Laurel shook her head, not looking at me. I felt oddly grateful for that little bit of privacy. "Either way, the call went out for an emerged merlin. Apparently, there is a will and a fortune at stake. Plus documentation and research about how spirit magic works, and until this merlin is found, it's all locked away. Spirit's still one of the least understood branches. That's probably why they're asking this and grasping for any straw. But really, the person would be in their late twenties if not early thirties by now. Heck with a name like Kory it could be a male as well."

I nodded, feeling my tension drain from me a bit. It didn't make me happy. Too bad the name couldn't have been something like Gerald or Samantha.

Outside, there was a huge crack, the squeal of brakes, screams, and a loud bang even as my head began to itch like crazy and my energy depleted like someone had punctured a bag.

Laurel and Martin were up and running for the door. It took me a minute to stand up, the wave of dizziness making my knees wobble. I blinked it away reminding myself to eat better. I had food, good food in the fridge, and money to buy groceries. I really needed to quit skipping meals. It took another few seconds, but the dizzy faded and I followed them out the door.

The old Bartlett pear that stood near the intersection had snapped in half and fallen in front of a car. Laurel and her husband were talking to the people in the car.

How long did I sit here?

I watched for a few minutes, but no one was hurt and as soon as the EMTs got there and a squad car pulled up, Laurel and Martin headed back towards me.

"I told those blasted city planners Bartlett's are a safety risk. They're brittle and you never know when they're going to break. I wish we'd pull them all, but every time I suggest it, everyone whines. If I win the lottery I'm donating the money and trees to replace all of them. Menaces, I tell you." Martin's voice carried clearly as they walked up to me.

"You okay, Cori?" Laurel asked. "You looked a bit gray when we ran out, and not too much better now."

"I'm fine. You and Molly are just working me to death."

She tilted her head looking at me. "This is what you want, right?"

"It is. A good degree. A way to make a solid living, and a backup plan. I'm good." I reassured her, nerves flashing through me again. I couldn't risk losing this. I was more than ready to graduate and start working for real. The internships had been more fun than I thought they would be. I had learned a lot. I'd be able to work with the police and medical personnel with a bit more clarity.

Huh - maybe the designers of this new course aren't as big a bunch of idiots as I thought.

"Good. Well, I'll see you in the morning. Last week. Let's hope it's quiet and uneventful."

"Always and never," I replied, a joke I was quickly learning that cops used. You always wanted to be bored and never were.

"Truth there." She paused looking back at the tree then at me and shook her head. "Never mind. Have a good rest of the weekend, Cori."

As soon as she and Martin had left, I locked the door and rushed to the restroom, glad for the lack of customers. My skin itched and when I pulled off my shirt, I found patchy spots of dried skin everywhere, peeling as if I had the world's worst sunburn.

I stared into the mirror. One of the first clues to an emergence was a sunburn all over the body, but even as I stared in the mirror, I didn't look red or burnt anywhere. My hair never seemed to grow, my eyes didn't look dilated and the patches of skin were in odd places. Nothing concrete.

See, stupid, you're not a mage. Even if you were, you'd be a terrible one.

Giving into the urge, I scratched my scalp, and ignored the fine white powder that drifted down. It felt so good to get it off. This time I managed to quit scratching before I drew blood. Glancing down, I saw the white all but disappeared on the tile floors. I heaved a sigh. That was why I usually did this outside. Not in any place I now needed to clean up.

Once back out in the main area I saw that more time had passed than I realized and I shrugged. Closing thirty minutes early wouldn't make a difference. I sent Molly a text and started closing up, making sure to vacuum and mop the restroom. It had been a long weekend.

Chapter 34

The draft was put into place immediately after World War I. Education and control of mages was treated as mandatory by the US, and many other countries adopted some form of it. For mages, wizards, and archmages, they were required to get a college degree, then work in government service for one year for every year of college paid for. The average is a bachelor's and four years of service. ~ History of Magic

SPIRIT

If I strangle Monique, I wonder if people would donate money to get me out of jail?

Class on Monday sucked. From nine am to four pm we were in a morgue practicing medical techniques. I did great but was about to kill the others with their whining. Variations of "This is gross, who wants to work on dead bodies?", "Oh they stink" were solid for the entire time. Even Bruce looked ready to strangle a few of the students. Monique was the worst. Complaining about the smell, the stiffness of the flesh, that they were all old and ugly, and on and on.

My temper snapped. "Monique, suck it up or quit. If you can't handle doing this, I don't want you in the field where I might ever need you. There's the door, use it."

A whispered round of "yes, please", caused her to shut up, but the constant glares at Monique from the rest of class were just about as distracting.

Anatomy I had down cold, and I could slip a needle in without anyone realizing I had done it. Performing tracheotomies wasn't an issue. Mostly it was just the meds and making sure I had them all grouped together. And I had three more weeks of practicals. I wasn't sure everyone else would make it out alive. Monique, the rest of us might kill. And I didn't know who was going to strangle her, Bruce or my classmates.

Back at the police precinct Sam seemed preoccupied, but he said it wasn't anything, so I didn't push. Heck, for all I knew he was fighting with his girlfriend. The week sped by and to my delight and regret, it was quiet, nothing more exciting than one drunk and a fight at the shopping center. That incident and the aftermath reminded me why I never wanted to be popular. The popular girls' nails should be regarded as lethal weapons.

I couldn't figure out my disappointment as I walked in late Friday morning to return my belt, shirt, radio, and other supplies. Being a cop or even any sort of law enforcement had never been anything I'd thought about before this experience, but I had enjoyed this. The solidity of the law made a nice backdrop to lean against. To know what was and wasn't right, or legal, felt comforting. I had never realized how much I missed or needed it.

The desk person looked up as I buzzed in. I'd be giving up my card today too. That was another tiny cut in my soul I didn't want to look at too closely.

"Go on in. The chief asked you to head back to her office."

"Thanks," I replied, heading back. I had a whole day to myself. I tried to keep that in mind. A true day off. What did I want to do?

I knocked on the door to her office. She looked up and smiled as she saw me.

"Cori, come in, and take a seat. Sam will be here in a few minutes. You're early as always."

Worry churned in my gut as I sat. Someday maybe I'd quit expecting the worst, but I doubted it would be anytime soon. I sat gingerly, setting my uniform and equipment on her desk.

"Thanks." Laurel leaned back, lacing her fingers together and looking at me. "Tell me, what did you think about the experience?"

Oh, she just wants to get feedback. That I can do.

The relief that washed through me was ridiculous. I needed to get my worry in check. "Honestly, I had expected to hate this. Preconceived notions, I guess, but I enjoyed it more than I thought. I felt useless a bit too much, but there's more to law enforcement than just being a jerk."

A burst of laughter from behind me caused me to grin as Sam walked in.

"You trying to say I was a jerk?"

"Not now, but when I'd run into you prior? Sometimes."

"That was only because this young girl kept being in the middle of crime scenes or dangerous situations and it scared the hell out of me. Getting to know you has helped with that." He dropped a folder on the desk and nodded at the chief.

"You weren't useless. Having someone to call for help is always a good thing. We've done police explorers and ride along for civics classes for years, but we wanted to try this. Our rate of people quitting after less than a year as an officer has been over sixty percent. The common reason is that being an officer wasn't what they expected. It's part of the reason we had you write so many reports and fill out everything. We are trying to give people a real glimpse as to what it's like before the police academy. Do you think we succeeded?"

I leaned back to think about that. The boredom, the terror, the endless paperwork, but there had been parts I thought were neat. Parts that made the other parts worth putting up with.

"I think so, though voice-to-text software would make dealing with all the reports so much easier."

To my amusement Sam gave a little arm pump and Laurel sighed. "I'll take that under advisement. Thank you for that feedback. Your grade will be turned in to the college, but I'm giving you a 4.2 out of 4. You handled the incidents you found yourself in with poise and I want to make sure that is noted in your college record. And just to reiterate, Cori, if you ever want to apply for the police academy, I'll sponsor you. Hell, I want to sponsor you. I think you'd make a damn good cop. Put me down on your reference list for when you start job hunting."

"And me," Sam added, winking at me.

The smile that crossed my face almost hurt my

Mel Todd

cheeks. At this rate maybe I would be able to get the good job I needed and to live with Jo in Atlanta. Just knowing the chief of police thought I'd be good at any job helped a lot, but the glowing reference would help even more. I'd been worried about getting a good enough job as Marisol had narrowed it down to three apartments. Any of which would be incredible, and larger by at least twice than what I lived in now, but my portion of the rent would not be insignificant.

"But that brings us to the next part." Her words grabbed my stomach in a vise once more and I hated how I reacted to her. She was the one who told me Stevie was dead.

The memory slammed into me and everything snapped into place. I'd never remembered that before.

"You. You told me he was dead." I'm sure my words seemed to come out of nowhere, but they were said before I could think to control them.

Laurel blinked at me and then nodded slowly. "I did." She tilted her head, looking at me confused.

"There were parts of that day I've never remembered. That memory just coalesced into my mind. I think that's why I always expect the worst from you."

"Ah." There was a world of understanding in her tone and she did understand. I could see it in her eyes. Something in me healed as I realized what my issue with her was, and I relaxed. She'd already told me the worst thing in my life; nothing else would even begin to measure up.

"Well, what I want to give you now is nowhere near that traumatic. I know your parents sold the place and moved. The grapevine let me know they told you no contact with your brother." Laurel growled. "For the record, your parents are broken idiots, but as he is

282

seven, I can't override their wishes and he is in a household that loves him. From what anyone can see, they dote on him." She shook her head. "But that doesn't mean I approve of what they did or how they reacted. So here." She handed me the folder.

"We decided you and Kristos should have options in the future," Sam said, his voice serious. "We'll let you know over the years if the information changes."

"The chief of police where they live is someone I know. We've worked together occasionally. He'll keep me informed."

With fingers that I couldn't stop from trembling, I opened the folder. There in black and white was their new address, who they worked for, where Kris went to school, and their phone numbers.

"When he turns eighteen, if you still want to make contact, we'll get him your phone number." Laurel's voice was soft as I tried to read the paper that blurred as I looked at it. No matter how much I blinked, it still remained blurry.

"I don't have words," I managed after staring at the information for too long.

They both grinned. "Don't worry about it. Regard it as an early birthday present. We have the information in the system and reminders on our calendars. Someday maybe you'll get to know your brother."

I nodded and carefully put the paper back in the folder, clutching it to my chest like it held all the answers to every question I'd ever asked.

Sam rose. "Come on. Today I'm buying you a coffee and then giving you a ride to anywhere you want."

He remained true to his word. He got me a large raspberry mint latte and then gave me a ride over to the Guzman's shop. He waved as he left, and I watched him go.

Why did I ever think he was a bit of a jerk?

I needed to remember to get to know people before I made judgments about them. Who they were was often different than who I thought they were. Yet another lesson I needed to learn. Life was full of them.

I headed into the garage. I saw Stinky and Paulo working, but didn't see Jo immediately. With a shrug I headed into the office. Henri looked up from the desk and gave me a smile.

"Cori. What brings you here today?"

I ran his tone through my head, but all I got was a bit of worry, which made sense as I could count on two hands how many times I'd shown up at the shop in the middle of the work day.

"I've got the day off and was wondering if I could steal Jo for the day. Maybe go shopping or figure out how to survive *Tia*?" Calling Marisol aunt for the first time felt right and wrong at the same time.

"Wanting a chance to go play hooky and enjoy being young?" His voice held humor and affection. "It's good to enjoy being young. You are both too serious for your age." He looked down at the schedule and nodded. "She needs to finish up the oil change and tire rotation she is working on, but our schedule is light. And I need to get used to not having her here in a month or two anyhow. Go on back and let her know. You two girls have a good afternoon. To live. You don't do enough of it."

"Thanks, Henri."

"Cori." His voice stopped me, and I turned to look at him. "Marisol is *Tia*. I am *Tio*."

I ducked my head feeling my face heat, then I lifted it back up. I refused to be ashamed for being loved. Maybe my parents hadn't been able to get past it, but others thought I was worthy. "Thank you, Tio." The word rolled off my tongue and he winked at me.

"Now go. Enjoy."

I headed back with a spring in my step. Twenty minutes later we were on the back of Jo's bike and headed out of town. There was a nice place by the lake that we wanted to visit, and we grabbed sandwiches from Publix on the way out. An hour later we sat on the picnic table looking at the water of Lake Allatoona.

"Chief Amosen really said that? That she thought you'd be a good cop?" Jo had finished her sandwich way faster than I had.

"Yes," I mumbled around a mouthful of food. I forced down a swallow and continued. "But she also thought I should get tested."

"Yes! Way to go, Chief!" Jo did a little hip wiggle of joy. "When are you going?"

I groaned. "I'm not. Why does everyone want me to get tested?" It was a whine, I know it was a whine, but I was so tired of people wanting me to go waste my time and my hopes on getting tested.

Jo glanced at me then out towards the lake, her face serious. "I just think weird stuff happens around you. A little too much. Maybe you are a mage and if you get tested you get access to classes."

"Jo-jo-"

She interrupted me. "No, I'm serious. You took all the classes. You know the consequences of being an unregistered." Her voice was heavy with worry.

"Yes, for magician rank or higher. I've never emerged. And given what you went through and the few videos I've seen, it would be noticeable if I came in at a significant rank. You know I've always had the weirdness. So it can't be that I'm a mage."

She chewed on her lip, her body hunched as she looked at the sparkling water, the sun creating spikes of light across it. "So, just do it. Then you'll know."

"Know what? That it is another thing I'm a failure at? Prove to myself there is one more thing that I'll never be. I can't be a good daughter. I'm not date worthy, hell I still can't figure out if I even like boys, girls, both, or neither. I'm a hazard to the people around me. And you want me to prove once and for all that I'm such a low mage that I can't even do anything useful with it? I don't need any more proof of how much a failure I am." Bitterness leaked out, coating my words and I winced at how it sounded. I sunk further into my jacket, shoulders hunched, ashamed at what I had revealed.

"Corisande!" Jo almost yelled the word as she jumped off the table and faced me. "Your parents are idiots. You're not a failure. You've taken care of yourself for years. You've created a career for yourself. You paid for school by working hard and doing it slowly. You have the respect of the police chief. My parents love you like you're one of their own. You are driven, creative, caring, and all you do is try to help others. I never want you to think that. You are my best friend. You're sexy as hell, cute, and anyone - male or female - would be lucky to get you. Never forget that. EVER!"

She yanked me off the picnic table and pulled me into a hug so tight it almost hurt. But it felt so good I never wanted it to end.

"You are my best friend. Never forget that," Jo murmured as she held me tight.

I sank into her arms and for a few moments I pushed everything away and just reveled in being loved for being me.

Chapter 35

The wise man treads carefully around dragons and mages. Both are touchy and can kill you with little effort. ~ Chinese proverb

CHAOS

I really wish I could fall in love with Jo, she'd be like the best girlfriend ever.

After the emotional scene at the lake, Jo and I spent the weekend hanging out, going to different places after I got off work. Molly kicked me out at noon each day, giving us the time to go and enjoy the area. We took an afternoon trip to Helen, Georgia, where she delighted in making everyone think we were lovers. I played along because it amused me, though even with Jo pointing out men and women to me I didn't get that thrill of interest she talked about. I could see they were cute, or sexy, but I was more drawn to boots way out of my price range or to the chocolate that made both Jo and me moan. When she declared it was better than sex, I figured I could just live with chocolate then. It seemed like less effort.

Overall, it was the best weekend I'd had in years. All my papers were done. The last few weeks were in-depth practicals, application usage, and then tests. And Tuesday my EMT rotation started. I would be working as an EMT. I'd received my certification that Monday at the end of class. About half of us had passed the first test. Bruce chewed on those who had failed it, including Monique.

I had to resist smirking as he did that. Some days I

was a not very nice person. Mostly I had my sights set on Tuesday and my first day in my chosen profession.

The night before I tossed and turned, haunted by dreams of me failing, or worse, hating every moment of it. By the time I woke in the morning I felt like I could have just stayed up all night and been more rested. It wasn't a good way to start the first day on the job.

As I trudged to the bus stop, clinging to my coffee as if it was a life line, with the heavy med bag dragging me down, I mused that at least I was getting good at first days on the job. A figure stood waiting at my stop, which surprised me. Usually I was the only one there, but then it had been a few weeks since I rode the bus on a Tuesday. The police had been close enough to not need the bus.

The person turned and looked at me as I approached, the bright red of his hair peeking out from under the hat. The April air was still chilly in the morning, but the glimpse of red was all I needed.

"Morning, Shay." He grunted at me but didn't look away. "What?" I asked after a minute of his intense stare.

"You will need to make choices soon. But you have time. Hopefully, we have time for you to learn enough to make the right choice for all of us."

"Huh? Shay, what are you talking about?"

He sighed and shrugged. "Possibilities, probabilities, options, paths. The future is less clear than the past, and you are confusing. Sensing has never been something I was good at and you are cloaked in swirls and eddies that confuse and mislead, but Elsba is never wrong. Besides, if I'm wrong, the cost is low. If I'm right and you are the point, the cost is high. Twists and turns, choices and decisions, everything flows and nothing is certain. Emergences to be and those that have been are shifting points."

I stared at him. Out of everything he had said the only thing that actually made any sense to me was Elsba. Lack of sleep, not enough coffee, and stress about the day, drove my tongue.

"Shay, the snake makes more sense than you do. Maybe you should learn how to speak English before you go and confuse people with meaningless words."

He growled and muttered something that I really didn't understand. Long liquid sounds that changed into short harsh sounds.

"And now you're cursing me in tongues? Because if that is something I'm supposed to understand, I don't."

Shay looked up to the sky—it was looking like it might be a gorgeous morning.

"Corisande, never change who you are. Your very being you is all that can be asked. Hold on to that. What others expect is not your problem." The rumble of an engine interrupted him, but as the bus pulled up, he cast me a quick smile. "Jo is true. When all else falls at your feet, she will never falter. Her nature is to assist, her heart is yours."

I didn't have a chance to ask anything else. He climbed up into the bus and I followed hurriedly, but it was full enough that I couldn't sit near him, which I think he planned on purpose. Sitting in the back I sighed, annoyed and confused by his random words.

A merlin talks to me and all I get is weird comments and attitude. Or statements of the obvious. Yes, Jo is true. But I don't plan on falling so far that I need to lean on her. Ugh. As always, my best path is to ignore him.

To my surprise, the distraction of Shay's words made my stress over the day disappear. When I disembarked from the bus and headed to the fire station where Sally was stationed, all I had was curiosity about the day ahead. Maybe his reminder that Jo would always be there made the difference, though we did need to find her a girlfriend everyone liked. Otherwise, her serial dating might drive us all crazy.

Sally had told me to go into the bays—they'd probably be open—and stick my head into the area. Someone would be up and around. I didn't even need to do that. Martin stood there, cleaning the windshield on one of the fire trucks as I walked in.

"Cori, morning. Come on in. I've got paperwork for you to sign then we'll track down Sally."

I mock groaned. "At this point I'm pretty sure I've signed my soul away. Question, who is going to get it? You or Laurel?"

Martin flashed a smile at me. "We're still trying to decide. I keep pointing out she has more opportunity to get souls than I do, so I should get you. Beside I've got you last."

I laughed, shaking my head. "Not sure I'm worth that much. One beat up soul? You may want to hold out for a better offer."

"Pfft. I think I could get a great deal of use out of you. Trade it for magic favors."

I burst out laughing as I followed him into the office. "I can see there is much about magic I didn't know if they are offering favors for souls."

"Hey, dark alleys and shifty ronin—surely I can swing something." He winked as he sat down at the desk and handed me the paperwork. "I'd trade almost anything for someone else to do paperwork for me."

I looked at the pile and sighed. "Yes. I've decided that hell would be making people fill out paperwork for all eternity."

He winced. "That does sound very cruel, but this, at least, you can convince yourself is necessary."

"Uh huh," I said unconvinced. I picked up the pen and started reading and signing. But it really wasn't anything that I hadn't already signed before. Mostly disclaimers, privacy, acknowledgment of rules and regulations. I paused when I got to the last few pages, the signed stack flipped over on my left.

"Sir? What is this?" I held out the pages to him.

Martin arched an eyebrow at me, I knew it was at the "sir", but he looked at the papers.

"Oh, standard paperwork for a short-term contractor. We are working through an agency. We got all your paperwork and test exams, so that is the W-2 and everything. 'They'll take out taxes, etcetera. And this lets you work overtime if needed without having to change your hours." He flashed me a smug grin. "Welcome to the wonderful world of working for the county as a first responder."

I stared at the employment contract and the hourly wage. "Meaning if I sign this, I get paid as an EMT level one, and this company can place me other places if I don't get a job? I can float as a fill-in?"

"Yep. We figured for a lot of you, companies don't always want to hire people with shiny new licenses, but if you have some experience and get good reviews, it makes getting a job a bit easier. Doesn't pay as much as a full-time employee, but even working a few days a week should make it possible for you to pay rent. Even in Atlanta." I caught his smile as he turned away.

I refused to start my first day of work crying like a silly child. The dollar amount sitting there would ensure I had time to job hunt. At the rate they were paying me, I'd be able to really buy new furniture and find a job I wanted. I had to fight to blink away tears. The town I had been trying so hard to get away from turned out to have been supporting me more than I ever realized. For the first time I wondered if maybe I could come back here.

"Cori?"

I lifted my head to see Martin looking at me.

"We want you to spread your wings and fly. You've never let anything stop you. Go, explore the world out there."

I sniffed hard and finished signing the papers. I didn't say anything as I handed the bureaucratic stuff to him. My face said it all.

"Go on. Through that door. She should be in the day room. She's got a kit for you, and you have your bag?" It was a redundant question as it lay next to my feet. But I stood, grabbing it.

"Yep."

"Good. Have a great experience, Cori." His words followed me, making me smile, though not really with humor. My experiences were rarely great. Often crazy and stressful, sometimes entertaining, but rarely great.

His office had three doors and was a big open room. One door led into the bay where I'd met him. Glancing through the other I saw a big country style kitchen. I went to the right and found a living room-like area but with tables to work at as well as a TV and couches, and what looked like multiple video game consoles.

Sally stood at one of the tables, a bag similar to mine spread out right where he said she would be. She looked up as I walked in. "Hey, Cori. Congrats on the exam. That was a great score."

"You saw it?" By some miracle my voice didn't squeak—I counted that as a win. I looked around the room, not seeing anyone else in it, but the ambulance, paramedic truck, and both fire trucks were present in the bay.

"Yep. Was sent to us as we're your sponsors for this

round. I wasn't surprised at all." She had a smug smile on her face.

"Were certain people surprised?" I had a feeling there was more to her expression than just being sponsors.

"Oh, Jeff might have lost some money to me." Her smug look grew brighter if possible.

I looked around, unsure what to do. "Where is everyone?"

"The boys are working out. Kat and J are sleeping. Come on. Set your bag up here and we'll go through it. The way they ship it is almost useless for when you really need stuff and if you go with the default layout, you'll spend way too much time digging through it. Did you remember to fill out your voucher?"

I looked at her not understanding what she was talking about.

"For your bag?"

"It was part of my required school supplies." I suddenly wasn't sure. Had I missed something? I'd never been sure why they wanted us to get it especially if we had to use it—it was a lot of money to spend to have to constantly refill. I didn't think you were supposed to spend your own money to do that, but what did I know?

Sally looked at me surprised. "Didn't they explain it? It was supposed to be on the curriculum."

"No?" I racked my brain, frantically trying to think if I'd missed something. But other than required equipment, Bruce hadn't mentioned it.

Sally groaned, pulled out her phone, and typed something on it. "There. I made myself a note to follow up on that aspect of class. Those things are too bloody expensive to expect people to pay for them out of their own pockets."

My confusion must have shown on my face. "No worries. Come on, set it up here." She patted the table she had her own bag set on, all torn apart.

I hefted it up there and she looked at me. "Let's get you dressed, then I'll explain. Come on and I'll give you the two-cent tour." We stuck our heads into the fitness room, waved at the men, and walked into the dorms. They had three sets of bunk beds that reminded me of old movies and Pullman cars. Each bed had a curtain you could pull across it, making a little cocoon for yourself.

"Here's your locker. " My name C Munroe had been written on it, right next to S Chang. She opened the one with my name and pulled out a jumpsuit in bright red with yellow fluorescent tape down the sides. Two more lay in the locker, waiting to be needed. "Not the most flattering things ever, but you'll be amazed at how warm they keep you and that they ignore most damage and soiling. If something actually stains this stuff, it probably would have left burn marks on your skin." She glanced at my boots, the ones I had bought in Helen, not the ones I had actually lusted over but the practical boots that should serve me for a year or two.

"Yep those will do. Usually I wear leggings and a tank top under this and keep a few in the locker just in case. Colder weather, it's a turtleneck. We don't have as stringent rules as some of the bigger cities. Here, wear the jumpsuit and you're good."

I took the suit and disappeared into the bathroom. There was a full shower and a toilet, along with a pile of huge fluffy towels. I changed quickly and made a mental note to buy some leggings asap. They weren't what I normally wore, but I could see how much more comfortable they would be than the slacks I wore right now.

When I stepped out of the bathroom Sally stood there, waiting for me. "Good. They fit. They'll deduct them from your paycheck, but you can keep those. Now let's go look at your bag." She spoke as we walked back into the day room.

"This is my backup bag, it's an excellent chance to show you what they were supposed to talk about."

"Ambulance Rockway Three, collapse at Third and Main. Please respond." The disjointed voice blared over the speakers and Sally flashed me a smile.

"Too late. Let's go."

Offerings are mysterious and simple at the same time. All magic must be fueled by genetic material of the mage. While living cells can be offered, the most common are nails, hair, and external skin cells. There are numerous mages who use blood to offer as it is easily replenished. If you have a familiar, you have the ability to use genetic material not attached to you. It is interesting that blood, if it is still "alive", does not need to be attached to the mage. ~ Magic Explained

ORDER

I really am certifiable, but since Sally is just as wired as me, I guess I'm in good company.

Sally had taken off at a run and I followed her, leaving the bag there when she shook her head as I started to reach for it. I jumped into the passenger side of the ambulance even as the big garage door slid up.

"Pay attention. This will be your job on the next run," she said.

I nodded, but she wasn't paying attention as she buckled in. She started the engine and picked up the radio all in less than fifteen seconds.

"Rockway Three, over. In route, details requested."

A laptop sat there, and she flipped it open as she started out of the garage. The app popped open and details appeared. "Take notes as they talk. You'll see, this should be like the stuff you've seen in class?" Her voice ended in a question and my heart seized.

I glanced at the laptop and saw with relief it was exactly like one of the apps they'd had us practice with last week. I knew this software.

"Got it."

She flipped on the sirens and tore out of the driveway and down the street. As the radio squawked, I recorded the information.

"Male, approximate age mid-thirties, collapsed walking out of the supermarket. Manager is waiting. Male is breathing but unresponsive. What's your ETA?" The dispatcher was talking so fast I could barely keep up. I glanced at Sally.

"Under three minutes," she responded, not looking at me but the traffic.

I repeated the information into the radio. There wasn't anything else for me to do. "How do you know where you're going?"

"There's a GPS there," she nodded at a part of the dashboard I hadn't paid much attention to. "But Jeff and I spend a lot of time memorizing maps. We make a game of it, blocking streets and providing addresses and we have to get there without looking at a map. Granted Rockway is pretty small, but in the big cities it's even more important. You need to know the roads if you're the driver. Freeways can be shut down and in bad weather roads might be closed. Always take time to study maps. You never know when it might be important. GPS isn't always there."

The vehicle slowed as she turned into the parking lot of a Food Depot. "Follow my lead. I would have preferred to go through this a few times, but I have faith."

I kept my self-doubts to myself, instead I jumped out after her once the bus stopped. Getting the gurney out of the back proved to be more complicated than I thought, but Sally didn't seem upset as we got it out. I would absolutely be practicing that. It looked like it might eat my fingers if I wasn't careful.

She grabbed a bag and threw it on the gurney then headed over. Three people were standing around the man lying on the ground.

"Cori, go start basic assessment." She handed me a stethoscope, flashlight, and blood pressure monitor.

I nodded, grabbing what she handed me, and knelt by the man's other side as she started asking questions and taking notes.

I listened to his chest, the heartbeat steady. His blood pressure was a bit high at 132/85, but nothing alarming. I peeled back his right eyelid. A blue iris appeared. The pupil contracted as I shone the light into it. I then peeled back the second one. The wide pupil told me what was wrong before I even flashed the light across his eye.

"Sally?" She paused in what she was doing to look at me. "Breathing steady, BPM is 132/85, but his left pupil is blown and unresponsive."

"Pain stimulus?" she snapped out, but I was already doing it. A sharp hard knuckle to the sternum usually roused response from even unconscious people.

"Negative."

I didn't hear her curse as much as sense it. She jotted something down quickly and stood up. "We need to get him to the hospital asap." It took a bit—we needed to practice moving unresponsive people onto the gurney, especially when neither of us weighed more than a hundred fifty pounds.

But we got him strapped in and in the bus. "Stay back here, hook him up to the monitors. I'm going in hot."

I gave her a look—if I was right about what had happened, he was already dead. But I said nothing, instead hooking up pulse-ox , blood pressure monitor, and EKG. There wasn't anything to give him, so I kept him comfortable as Sally tore through town. I'd had the week-long class to get my driver license notation for ambulances and paramedic trucks scheduled for two weeks after graduation. Something else I'd stressed about before finding out I'd make some money plus the money my parents gave me. I almost felt rich. Or at least I knew I could afford it without going into debt.

Sally could hear me in the front of the bus, and I wished she was in back with the patient. "Can't you help him?" My voice didn't shake, but I knew mages could do incredible things. Which meant Sally should be able to do something.

She did me the honor of not pretending to misunderstand me, but she asked me questions first. "What is your diagnosis?"

"Brain aneurysm." My response was immediate and blunt. It sucked, but everything pointed to that, though I could be wrong. I didn't think I was. The fact that his EKG was starting to wind down supported my hypothesis. Without thinking twice, I put him on oxygen. It would help keep him alive longer or preserve the organs for transplant.

"I suspect that too. If I knew exactly where the blown vessels were and what areas of his brain had been damaged, I might be able to do something, but in reality, a merlin couldn't save him. That's why many of the best doctors who are mages are surgeons. You need to see something to be able to affect it. There are very few aspects of magic that allow you to work blind. And few people who can work with what they can't see. One of the reasons they push education so much."

That was the second time someone had told me that and I filed it away, wondering what Jo would be able to do with even more knowledge than she already had about mechanics. Scott had said that was a skill of his, and Sloan admitted he couldn't do it. So, not just power but innate abilities. I'd have to remember not everything on TV was true.

We didn't have any more time to talk as she pulled into the emergency room bay and nurses ran out to meet us. "I'll take it this time, you listen and learn." She snapped out the words as she threw open the doors in the back and then started to pull the gurney out.

In fast concise words, she laid out the situation. A doctor grabbed him, peering into his eyes as we walked through the ER to one of the rooms.

"Let's get an EEG on him."

The machine to read brain activity wasn't one that I had seen in the ambulance. I'd need to ask if that was something I had missed or if they just didn't carry it.

It took the experienced nurses less than two minutes to have him hooked up, even as another nurse took his wallet and personal effects from me. I had recorded his name, age, and address on the forms. He had a phone on him, and I'd verified there was emergency contact information on it, but that wasn't my job to do. That fell to others.

"EEG active," someone said, and I turned to look. The brain waves showed exactly what I had expected, low level basic readings and they were fading. There was no higher brain wave activity. For all intents and purposes he was already dead, his body just hadn't caught up with that knowledge.

"Donor?" a doctor asked, her voice neutral.

"According to the license, yes."

"Good. Hook him up to life support and get his family notified and in here. They have choices to make. There is nothing I can do for him." Her voice wasn't cruel, just matter of fact and I watched her walk away.

I couldn't take my eyes off the dead man, standing

there with my hand still on his ankle. Things I had never seen, created from my imagination, flashed across my mind. My parents coming in only to be told their son was dead.

"Cori?" Sally's voice broke apart the images that I'd never seen. Instead, it was the man, looking at me. His eyes wide and surprised, blinking at me, then staring at his body. He looked around wildly, then at the body again—already nurses worked on keeping it alive though the man, the person he had been, was dead.

"Cori? You okay?" Sally's voice again, right in my ear. I jumped and the man faded away, leaving me with the body a man who'd never laugh again.

A hand touched my shoulder and I turned to look at her. There must have been something on my face because she frowned. "I know you've seen dead bodies before. Something wrong?"

I shook my head, chasing the strange images—all of them must have come from my imagination. I shrugged and forced a smile that I'm sure looked as fake as it felt.

"I've never come with them to the hospital before. It just hit me, I guess. Made me think about things I've never thought of before. Kicked my imagination into overdrive I guess."

The last thing I needed was to tell her I thought I'd seen the dead man looking at his body. That wasn't any more real than my parents standing by Stevie's body and crying, begging the doctor that it couldn't be true.

"The first few patients that die on you are hard. In some ways this one was easy."

I wasn't shocked by her words, not exactly, but I did give her a look.

"He was dead before we even got the call. You don't need to ask yourself if you did the right thing. Would he still be alive if you had moved faster, been smarter, done

301

something else? I'm sorry you got this as your first call, but at the same time it could have been worse."

My mind flashed back to laying in the car, my hand on the boy's face as he died. Yes, it could have been much, much worse.

"So now what?" Though I suspected I knew. Paperwork, then back to the station to repack and clean the rig.

"File the reports and get back. We need to go over your bag so it's useful, and then, since you have your EMT cert you know the law?" she asked as we headed over to the admin portion of the ER.

"Yeah, but since I don't have a car and I can't carry it with me, I haven't worried about it."

"Point. Create a mini bag with things you can use to do what you can. Then get a decent one once you get a car. You'll hopefully never need it. But if you do, you'll thank all the stars in the skies."

Once again, I found myself smothered by paperwork, but soon enough we were back at the station. The rig didn't take long to clean or set back to rights, then she went over the bag with me.

"As I was saying, the point was for you to have a couple weeks with the bag, organize it, figure out what works for you. Every medic is different on how they like it organized." She handed me the voucher. "This is to be filled out so you get reimbursed by our department, as you'll leave the bag here. Normally techs only buy the bag and the department or agency provides the supplies. But to be good at this job you need to know everything in this bag intimately. Know what you prefer, how to use it, and most importantly how to know when you need to restock."

With that, Sally launched into reviewing the bag and everything in it. Needles, gauzes, pressure bandages—

all the things I would have sworn I knew how to use.
Turned out I barely had a clue.

The rest of the day was spent on two more calls, the
first a diabetic who had slipped into a diabetic coma, the
second a kid who'd managed to trip and break his arm.
By the time the day was done, my brain thought it might
explode with the new knowledge.

I caught the bus home in a daze of information
overload and worry that I'd made a huge mistake.

Chapter 37

**While almost all governments have signed legislation and
other affirmations that there is no preference for mages in their
country, mages still tend to be mostly upper middle class and
higher. Even most hedgemages tend to be in better jobs and
better paid than the equivalent non-magic users. ~ Magic
Explained**

SPIRIT

*All I want is a night of solid sleep. I'm starting to
understand the attraction of drugs. If I could get eight
hours of dream-free sleep it would be wonderful.*

Nightmares followed me through that first week.
Jumbled up things that weren't possible mixed with
images that might have been memories of Stevie's death,
or just my subconscious deciding to torture me.

By Friday I begged off seeing Jo and just collapsed
into bed, trying to convince myself I'd make it through

work tomorrow. Jo had accepted that, but only after I promised to go out Monday night. She was determined to celebrate my birthday. Part of me had a hard time realizing it was April already. I'd graduate next month.

Then the Paramedic test. I needed to refresh the meds section again but working with Sally and admitting that was my weakest area had already helped me leaps and bounds. I felt like by the end of May I'd be ready to take that exam.

By some miracle I got six hours of sleep Friday night. Which meant I dragged myself into Grind Down almost functional. Kadia popped in the back door minutes after I unlocked, making me suspect she'd been waiting for me.

"You're back!" she squealed, wrapping me in a hug so tight I felt faint by the time she let me go.

"I take it that you missed me?" I said when I could draw in enough air to speak.

"You have no idea, though I ran the back room, so it isn't a complete disaster. Walking with a brace is a pain in the ass." She gestured at the brace on her jeans. "But I'm still better off than Carl. I have no idea what Molly is going to do, but she needs to replace you and me soon. She is worse than the other two combined. I get she wants to make more money, but seriously, I start my own classes soon. I can't take her social awkwardness." Kadia's familiar babble made me smile and soon we were in our groove, the shop clean, customers satisfied, and lists of what stock was getting low created.

But for the first time I felt discontented doing it. Getting caffeine didn't really make a difference in someone's life. It might make their day better, but it didn't change anything. I wanted to be back in that bus, making a difference in people's lives.

But could I do it? Would I ever be as good as Sally or

Jeff? Oh, I hadn't made any horrible mistakes in the last week, but looking back, I could see things I should have done better, or faster, or known.

Stop it. You're doing it. Sally would tell me if I shouldn't do this.

The self-pep talk broke off as three men walked in. They didn't fit my normal Saturday crowd, as all three wore suits and had self-important attitudes. My skin crawled as they came in. Only one of the three was a mage, a Spirit mage, but I treated them the same as everyone.

"Morning. What can I get you?" Long experience let me project humor and friendliness, even though my body wanted to back up and run away.

"Are you Corisande Munroe?" the mage asked.

"Yes," I answered, though I really wanted to play dumb.

He reached into his coat pocket and pulled out a thick manila envelope. "You've been served." He handed me the envelope and I took the envelope with numb fingers. Before I had a chance to even look at the envelope, much less figure out what this was about, he continued. "And this is a restraint order preventing all communication via yourself or other parties with Estella, Rafael, or Kristos Munroe." That piece of paper was added to the pile. He then smirked at me. "Have a great day."

I looked at the papers as if they were written in Russian, unable to even figure out what this meant. Before I could open the folder and pull out the papers one of the other two men spoke.

"Corisande Munroe, you've been accused of cheating in the EMT certification exam, as well as the cognitive test. There is also an investigation about your relationship with Bruce Marxin and possible unethical interaction." He handed me another sheaf of papers. Glaring out from the top page was the crest of the school, proclaiming its authenticity.

"What?" squeaked out of my throat. My hands went icy cold as I took the additional papers.

"Read them. The charges are listed out in the attached documentation. There is a hearing this Monday morning to address these charges. Please note if these claims are upheld, your ability to work as an emergency technician in the state of Georgia will be rescinded, you will be expelled and blacklisted from retaking the test for five years. Failure to appear will be seen as an admission of guilt." He rattled this all off as if the words weren't causing my life to crumble into pieces at my feet. "Have an excellent day." He and the other man traded a half laugh, as if they were performers nailing a show.

The added smirk of contempt with the swirl of coats as they headed out the door slammed another icicle into my soul. In two hands I held papers that felt like they weighed tons.

"Cori? Cori? Can you hear me? You've gone really pale. Here, sit."

A huge commotion arose outside, yells, and shouts, but I couldn't focus as Kadia led me to a chair. I sank into it.

"Oh, by Merlin," Kadia gasped. "The entire traffic light pole came down, took out the cars of the guys that were in here. What is going on?" She shifted her focus back to me, but I could only stare at the papers, not knowing which one to open first. Indecision gripped me and the ringing of my cell phone came as a relief. Something, anything else to focus on than this. Besides, from the ring I knew it was Jo. She'd make it better. Just hearing her voice would make it better.

"Hey Jo-Jo. What's up?" I knew my voice shook, but I clung to the solid person that she was. When her voice came over the phone, that thin control shattered.

"Cori? Sanchez is hurt. They're rushing him to the hospital now. A jack snapped and the car dropped on his leg. It's bad. The bone broke really bad. I-" Her voice broke and everything else pushed away.

"Where are you?" I headed to the door as I spoke.

"Going to the Healthstar Hospital in Rome. Cori, if he loses his leg..." Her voice trailed off and she fought back a sob. No magic would be able to grow him a new leg. It meant prosthetics and a long hard road ahead of him.

"He won't. I'll meet you there. Jo, I will be there." My voice hard and sure.

"Thanks. I need you," she admitted and hung up.

"Kadia, I've got to go." I pulled up the ride share app as I spoke. "Jo's brother was hurt. I'm going to the hospital to meet her there. Sorry, you're on your own. Call Molly."

"Cori, here." She shoved all the paperwork at me, with a binder clip holding them together. "Call the school while you go there and find out what this is about. I'm sure he'll be okay. I've got this."

"Thanks, and sorry." I grabbed everything, shoving it into my bag. I'd look at it later.

I managed to schedule a ride, and they'd pick me up at the corner in a minute. "Thanks," I said over my shoulder heading out. The commotion outside surprised me as I looked at the huge light pole that had fallen, pulled by wires and guidelines across the two cars parked in front of Grind Down. The men who had come in and tried to shatter my world were yelling and gesturing at a police officer that stood there. Utility crews had already shown up and were dealing with the snarl of traffic and people.

On any other day I might have stood and watched the action, trying to figure out what had happened. Today that didn't matter. Jo was first. Then school, then when I had time, I'd look at the stuff from the Munroes. I refused to even call them my parents anymore.

Maybe I should legally change my name?

The idle thought kept me distracted as I turned the corner and walked away from the chaos. A car pulled up and I matched the info, sliding in. "Healthstar Rome, emergency room."

The young man scanned me with a startled look. "You aren't hurt, are you?"

"Huh? No, meeting a friend there. Her brother was taken in."

"Oh, good. I don't need blood in my car."

I nodded, not paying much attention, as I focused on the papers from the school. There in black text on heavy white paper the charges were laid out. Monique Kinnison said I had cheated. The tests we took were too hard for anyone to get a nearly perfect score. That my consistent high grades and praise from the instructor pointed to both cheating and a bribing of the teacher for this course. That made me blink. The subtext was that I was sleeping with Bruce for good grades, though it wasn't bluntly said.

I should have strangled her; it would have made life easier for everyone.

I scrolled through my phone and pulled up Bruce's number. As the car headed, not fast enough, to the hospital I looked at his number. He had handed it out when the semester began. Finally, I shrugged. I never talked to him outside of class that I could remember. I didn't even think he lived in town as I never saw him at Grind Down. What evidence could be presented to make it look like there was anything between us? With a sigh, I hit call.

"What?" His voice snapped out and even my numb worry couldn't prevent my slight flinch.

"Bruce, this is Cori Munroe. I had a visit from some people about me cheating and apparently sleeping with you?" The numbness came through in my voice, and I calculated how much longer until we reached the hospital. At least twenty minutes. More than enough time to get some traction on this.

"That little bitch. I should have kicked her out the first week." His voice was a low snarl and I could almost feel the rage coming out of it.

"They said my license would be rescinded if I didn't prove on Monday that I didn't cheat." I flipped through the papers until I found the details. "I'll have to answer charges that I suborned my instructor to give me special treatment and assist with my grades."

"So, she is stupid and blind. One, I would never date a student. Two, you're the wrong gender for me. And three, I prefer my dates a few years older than I am. You're young enough to be my daughter." The contempt in his voice stung, but I figured it really wasn't directed at me.

"So, it says Monday. Is there any advice you can give me, or did I mess up just by calling you?"

"Oh Monique, the administration, and the social groups can kiss my ass. I have nothing to hide and I refuse to act as if I do. You were right to call." His voice smoothed out and his tone became more matter of fact, less emotional. "Come prepared on Monday to take all the tests again. And study anything you didn't do perfectly on. The test will be held in a trial-like atmosphere, and Monique will have to present her case. You can get a lawyer, but her case is so flimsy that I

Mel Todd

wouldn't unless you are really worried about it."

A spiral of worry wormed its way up my throat. "If I pass the test, will my license remain untouched? I mean this won't affect my standing with the licensing process? I can't continue the internship if it has been suspended."

"I'll make sure it stays intact. I am bringing a lawyer, and I'm about to make Monique and her family very sorry they ever messed with me. I have a college friend who owes me a favor and I'm calling it in."

"Okay. I'll study and be prepared. Thanks." I sounded distant and hollow, but too much had happened today for me to even care all that much.

"Hey, Cori?"

I paused as I'd been about to hang up. "Yes?"

"The only thing you did wrong was to be a damn good student. You showed her up and she had every advantage. Don't worry about this. It will all work out for the best. I promise."

"Okay." I didn't say if I believed him. Right at that moment I didn't believe in anyone or anything, not even myself. "I'll see you Monday."

"Yes, you will. Try and have a good weekend." He sounded resigned and reassuring at the same time.

My sob of bitter laughter rang in the car. Bruce had already hung up, or I had. I didn't know which of us hit the button first.

"Miss? You okay?"

The driver's voice pulled me a bit out of my haze, and I focused on where we were. About five minutes out from the hospital. I'd been there once or twice over the years. It must have been serious if they brought him here instead of the local hospital.

"No. But I'll live. Thanks."

His dark eyes caught mine in the review mirror and I saw the glint of mage jewelry. I just turned my head.

Nothing mattered right now. I started to open up the
pile of papers that represented the Munroes and their
issue with me, but then didn't bother. I read over the
school stuff again, making a list in my head. But most of
the charges were so fake, I couldn't figure out why they
had even listened to her. Cheating maybe, but usually a
retest was the extent of anything that was asked of
people.

The car slowed down and my eyes caught a sign,
'Kinnison Bone Therapy' and it clicked. She must be
related to Gerald Kinnison. He'd funded a lot of medical
and college buildings in the area. If that was the case,
they might have been worried about losing money. I
couldn't remember anything on campus called or
attached to the name Kinnison. Before I could pull up
my phone and dig into the campus map the driver
pulled into the ER. Jo first. The Guzman's were much
more important than a Kinnison could ever be to me. I
slipped out of the car, paying the driver on the app, and
headed into the ER.

Saturdays were usually crowded and today was no
exception. I looked around the room, frantic to find her,
or any of them.

Chapter 38

Saving a life or taking one are the most common tropes in any story about mages. The dramatic rescue or last minute save by offering up the last thing they can spare. The number of mages that give up fingers and toes in the movies would make you think half the population is always saving people. The reality isn't that selfless, or that simple. ~ Magic Explained

CHAOS

Where are they? They should be here somewhere. Unless...

I broke off that train of thought. Jo had said broken leg, not death. While not impossible to die from a broken leg, if your femoral artery was hit, it would have been unusual. The moving mass of people made it difficult, but after getting out of the way of the automatic door, I saw them in the far corner.

Marisol was in a chair, not moving. Her face looked pale, even at this distance. Jo sat next to her, perched on the chair as if waiting for a chance to fly and do something. Henri leaned against the wall. I didn't see Paolo, but Marco was pacing back and forth, and staring at the far doors of ER, the ones that led back to the various treatment rooms and OR's.

I made a beeline to them, weaving around crying children, sniffling and sneezing adults, and pale, sick teenagers. I couldn't help but assess as I walked through: colds, hangovers, a nasty wound that needed stitches but wasn't life threatening. The normal ER stuff from what I could see.

"Cori!" Jo all but shouted and launched herself at me. My arms were open and this time I comforted her. Even with me being two inches shorter, I provided the strength and solace this time. We stood there until she sighed, and only then did my arms relax to let her be.

"*Tia, Tio*, is there anything I can get you?" I asked, as Jo stepped away. Marisol had risen, looking at me, her face pale. Her arms opened and I stepped into them, still trying to offer comfort rather than take it, but Marisol knew too well how people felt and we shared the support this time.

When she pulled back, I dropped to the floor, refusing to think about what every surface of this place must be coated with. "Tell me what happened. What has the doctor said."

He has to be alright. No one needs to lose a child. I don't want to see that happen again. I can't.

I felt my body itch as I sat there, every bit of me feeling wired and strung out. Just stress and me being unable to help yet again.

Henri answered. "I'm not a hundred percent positive of what happened, and I figure they'll get an insurance adjuster out there, one with Pattern or Time to replay what happened. All the lifts were full with oil changes and repair work, and someone came in that just needed the spare removed and their new tire put on. Nothing difficult. Sanchez said he'd do it and grabbed one of the standard tire jacks to lift it. Next thing I heard was the customer shrieking like a mouse had run up her pants. I went out there as if I had wings. He was laying under the car with the tire on his leg, crushing it. His heart was beating, so I called 911, and got the boys there. We didn't move it until the emergency personnel showed up. I was worried about causing more damage."

I nodded at him. It made sense. The tire applied

pressure and the damage to his bone would have already been done, so better to wait and make sure if there was blood it could be dealt with.

"They said it was broken in multiple places, a very bad break. They didn't know I could hear them, because they were worried about it needing to be amputated if the bones were shattered badly enough."

Marisol and Jo hissed in unison and Henri mumbled something under his breath.

"Well the good news is you did everything right. Leaving the tire there until help could arrive was smart. It probably prevented a worse outcome."

As I spoke there was a man that rushed into the ER area, carrying his wife. Even from there I could see she was having trouble breathing. The nurses grabbed her and whisked them both back in minutes. With a shake of my head I turned my attention back to them.

"Marisol, Henri? You want something hot to drink. It may be a while depending on what they needed to do."

They started to protest, but I rose up. "You want tea and Henri wants hot chocolate. Let Jo and me go get it. It will keep her from pulling down the walls." They both glanced at Jo, who all but vibrated with the need to do something.

"That sounds good. Here," Henri said as he pulled a twenty out of his pocket. "You already know what we want, or at least need."

"Come on Jo-Jo, you need to get out of here for a bit." With obvious reluctance mixed with her desire to do something, Jo let me pull her up from her chair. "There's a chain coffee place about two blocks away. You want anything, Marco?"

"Large coffee and some sort of pastry," he muttered still pacing. "Thanks."

I simply nodded and dragged Jo out of the place. My

body still twitched, and my head felt like ants were marching over it. As soon as we were outside and a few steps away from the hospital, I gave in and bent over, scratching my scalp like it was a pan that needed scouring.

"One of these days you're going to need to do something about that dandruff. Seriously, it should be better by now. You've tried every shampoo ever produced."

"Ha! That would be too easy. The last doctor said this is my stress outlet. Either I need to have less stress, or I need to deal with it better." I moaned a bit in pleasure as the last of the flakes scrubbed off. "At this point I'm just glad all my hair hasn't fallen out, though it would be nice if it ever grew." I tugged on my bob a bit mournfully, though the majority of the time I was just glad that it was easy to care for. Jo had to keep hers in eternal braids because it grew so fast. If she undid it completely it would probably hit her knees.

"Hey just think - I'll be able to learn how to use my hair to do magic. Soon it might actually be at a realistic length." She fell silent then looked at me. "Thanks," she said, and I looked at her. A smile touched my lips and I hip bumped her.

"Nothing to thank me for. Family?" I hated the tremulous note in my voice as I said that, but she grinned and bumped me back.

"Always. You're stuck with me until after the sun goes nova."

"Oh? What happens then?"

"We turn into star dust and form new stars of course. Maybe we'll be the source of life."

Walking along the sidewalk towards the glowing green sign I smiled. "That would be nice, but I hope they don't have my luck. It can be a bit exhausting."

"Meh. You have great luck. You found me."

"You sure it isn't the other way around? You found me? Though that would mean you have horrible luck too," I pondered in mock heavy thought. "So maybe my good luck gave you bad luck?"

"Neither. It was fated, written in the stars," she ginned at me. "We will always be together."

I laughed as we walked into the coffee shop. A few minutes later we headed back. Chocolate for Henri, a large passionfruit tea for Marisol, coffee for Marco along with a chocolate croissant. I wasn't in the mood for coffee, but Jo went for their sugar iced chocolate thing. Mostly I just wanted time to read the papers. I'd left my bag with Marisol and wasn't worried about it. Later tonight I'd focus on it. Right now, it could wait.

Walking back into the ER waiting room, I froze. The atmosphere had changed, taut and dangerous. Half the volume had dropped, and everyone was looking back at the corner where Henri and Marisol were standing talking to a black woman in a white coat. From her stance and the way she held herself it was obvious she was the doctor. Henri had his arm tight around Marisol's shoulders, all but supporting her as she leaned into him.

We moved through the room, arrowing in on Jo's family.

"We don't know what we can do. To not have to amputate we need a specialist, and the only one in the area at Grady is already in an operating room doing spinal surgery. We are hoping we can wait long enough for him to recover and be able to work on your son, but the fact that the transport here didn't kill him is a miracle. The bone shards are so close to his arteries, one good jolt and he'd be dead before we knew anything was going wrong. We're trying, but right now I don't have any good news to offer you." The pager went off on the

break you. He's one of the best. Tell him you're contracted with us. I'll grab your jumpsuit and badge. Go." She hung up.

I whirled to Jo. "Keep this for me. I'll get it from you later." I shoved my bag at her and took off at a run out of the ER. The bay was to the right of the ER and it was a hive of activity as people frantically stocked their ambulances. Others were diving in and lighting up lights and sirens.

Inhaling as much oxygen as I could, I bellowed out, "Darryl?" I looked around as people glanced at me. Someone leaned into a bus and a minute later a man stepped out, a man that made most men in my life look like toothpicks. I wasn't positive how he could get in the bus and drive. The other person pointed at me and he moved towards me at a pace faster than I could run.

"You have five seconds," he said in a disconcerting English accent. I shook my head trying to reconcile my expectations with his voice. "Three." He started to turn away and I quit worrying about it.

"Sally Chang said to come with you. I'm contracted to the Rockway Fire Department as an EMT."

"Get your ass in the vehicle then, we need to get out." He headed back as others finished loading up and headed out. "Ride in back. Leo's my partner." He wasn't rude or angry, just matter of fact and I scurried to keep up. Diving into the back and sitting on the bench as the other man, late twenties with a chaos tattoo on his head, shut the doors behind me.

Seconds later the ambulance pulled out and I braced myself as the lights and sirens flipped on. When we hit the freeway, I lifted my voice over the road noise and sirens. "Do you know what the situation is?"

Leo turned to look at me, his tattoo, a bright yellow against his red-brown tan skin, complimented his light

Mel Todd

brown hair. "Bus carrying kids to an away band competition, followed by parents. Another car hit them head on and the bus flipped, taking out other cars. Count is ten cars involved and at least thirty victims. Unknown complications at this point. Two confirmed dead, but others expected." He rattled it all off in a way that made it seem more normal and common—it let the information hit me without emotion and I appreciated the matter-of-factness.

"Got it. How many units responding?"

"Ten. We've got all the local county ambulances and at least two of the private ones coming. They've requested two life flights already." If anything, the ambulance had sped up as he talked. I braced my feet and went with the jerking and shaking.

"Who's incident commander?"

"Your fire chief, Martin Martinez. He's ordered SMART triage." I nodded at his sharp look even as I felt my heart triple thump in my chest. START stood for Simple Triage and Rapid Treatment. That meant we'd very probably be making the call on who would live or die. Red meant emergency, get to hospital; yellow indicated that they were seriously injured but had a little time; green, injured but could wait; white meant minor injuries. But black meant no medical attention could save them and to move on to the others. That would be a decision I'd have to make.

I ran the process through my head, but it was one of those they only covered briefly. Every department had their own flavors, though the color breakout was the most common. I swallowed, nerves landing in my belly and twisting it into a knot of worms riddled with spikes that sent me into frissons of panic.

What if I screw up? What if I triage wrong? What if I cost someone their life?

322

Nausea swarmed me and I closed my eyes trying to breathe.

"Get on your game face, people. We're coming in now." Darryl's voice intruded on my attempts to keep my stomach where it belonged, but I couldn't keep my eyes closed. I had to see. I leaned forward and tried to see out the window. But the sun, flashing lights, and moving vehicles created a jumble of broken images that didn't make any sense.

The ambulance jerked to a halt and the two men flew out of the doors. Before I could get to the back door, it flew open.

"Out girl. Find your boss and do your best." Darryl spared a half second to nod at me before he grabbed a bag and headed out.

I swallowed down my nerves and stepped out of the back, and the world seemed to slow to a stop. Even the moving people stopped as I stared, my skin burning as I took in what lay in front of me.

This area of Georgia had roads that snaked through the mountains with sharp drops on one side and a rising cliff on the other. A yellow school bus lay on its side across the entire two-lane road. It had apparently rolled, from the dents on the top, and came to a stop at a wide pull over meant for slower vehicles to get out of the way. At least six vehicles were scattered around it on this side like a child had thrown down his Hot Wheels and stomped away. They lay on their sides or had slammed into the underside of the bus or crashed into the side of the mountain. From the bent and twisted guardrail, I assumed at least one car had gone over the side.

The ambulance I rode in was at the edge of the responders. Fire, police, ambulance, state patrol, and sheriff were all there, the lights still for that eternal second as everything I saw burned into my brain, into my soul. Then I moved, my foot crunching on gravel, and everything snapped into motion, people rushing towards the mass casualties.

I spun, looking for Sally or Martin. I needed my equipment and gear to be any use to anyone, otherwise I was a civilian creating problems for them.

Black hair in a shining sheet caught my eyes and I spun, laying eyes on the familiar logo and lettering. I took off at a run towards them. As I got closer, the voices started to make sense amid the sirens, the shouts and the screams and sobs of the victims.

"All of you, start triaging. I have the tags here, grab them when you head out. Use your best judgment. If you have a black or red summon me, Jordan, or Chang to verify. Otherwise Chang and Laurent will be getting people down this mountain to where the choppers are. They have a park about five miles down where the copters can land. We have three red already and we'll need to bus them to the helicopters stat. Your job is to stabilize people and keep them alive until they are taken from you into a bus. Chang, Laurent: I expect you to drive like sane maniacs, transfer your patients, then get your asses back up here. All of you, your job isn't done until the only people left are the dead and the responders. Move," Captain Martinez's voice bellowed like trumpet causing the hair on my head and the back of my neck to raise with its power.

I stopped next to Sally. "I'm here."

She glanced at me, nodded at the ambulance that she drove. "Good. Your gear is there. Change and do your job." She didn't take even another second, just grabbed her gurney, and raced away with it. With my mind alternating between panic and assurance, I headed over to the ambulance. I pulled open the door and sure enough, there were my jumpsuit and my bag waiting for me. We'd packed and repacked the bag over the last few days so I knew where every item was and could find what I needed with my eyes closed.

Glancing around I realized I was being an idiot. I stripped off my jeans, they really didn't work under the jump suit, and my coffee imbued shirt. No one had time to worry about a half-naked woman. I stepped into the suit, and she'd even grabbed my boots. I slipped them on, and it felt like something else coated me as I pulled up that outfit. I don't know what it was, but my heart rate slowed. I felt lighter, and the panic that had been building at the back of my mind stepped back. I grabbed my bag and moved over to Martin.

He thrust a handful of tags at me, giving me a long look. "You're the green one here. Don't be scared to yell if you need help or a second opinion. Go."

I nodded and swallowed down a lump of nerves, then headed towards the person nearest to us that had no one attending them. Most of the closer victims had people around them, but they had started at the opposite side of the scene from me. Which meant there were people that needed me. Part of me kept waiting for the panic, for me to flounder, but instead I just rushed to the side of the closest person laying there and dropped to my knees. Her breathing was thready, and her skin was pale and clammy.

Shock, low respiratory sounds, pupils responsive but sluggish.

The diagnosis went through my mind as I continued. Everything pointed at internal bleeding. Pulling back the woman's shirt, and it really only registered to me when I was cutting the straps on her bra that she was a woman, the bruises were red and livid, pooling with blood.

"Ma'am, can you hear me?" She groaned something

that might have been taken as a yes, maybe. "Let me know if this hurts." I pressed gently at the area of her spleen, and she almost convulsed.

Major internal bleeding. Definite red, they'll need to operate, and soon, if they want to save her.

I grabbed the red tag, attaching it to her wrist, which seemed uninjured. I stood and looked, catching Martin's eye. "ETA on next trip to life flight?" I yelled, but there was no subservience in my voice.

He moved over and looked at her. "Tell me your diagnosis," he snapped as he glanced at his watch. "First one is due back in five, and the next copter should be here in fifteen."

"Major internal bleeding. Stable, but decreasing rapidly." I took her blood pressure and heart rate again, and it was lower. "Time is critical. Internal injuries, probably a ruptured spleen."

He moved closer and scanned the notes I'd made. "Looks right. I'll flag her next. Rip off your notes and leave them here. Get to the next person.'"

I froze for a moment, looking at the woman I had no more ability to help, who might very well die no matter what I did. For the first time in a very long time I wished almost desperately for magic. Magic to heal. Magic to save. But I wasn't Sally or Jo. My world didn't work that like that. I gave a sharp nod of my head and stood, looking.

There about ten yards to my right was another person, younger and writhing on the ground. The erratic movements and the soft whimpers indicating extreme pain acted like a beacon. I headed right for the boy. Nothing else mattered—what mattered was helping him until he could be made stable or transported.

Kneeling next to him, I checked the young man wearing a band uniform from my old high school. He looked at me eyes wide, breathing rapid.

"Hey, can you hear me?" I asked, my voice soft and soothing as I pulled out the stereoscope, placing it on his chest.

"Yes. Am I going to die?" he asked, his speech as rapid as his breathing, shallow with a bit of a gurgle, but not much.

"Nope. I'm here to prevent that. It hurts to breathe?" I felt along his ribs, finding the broken area pretty fast at his sudden intake of breath.

"Yeah. Hurts to take a deep breath."

"Hmmm." I checked for concussion signs, going on through the checklist. "What instrument do you play?" If I could keep him talking, he'd focus more on me than on what hurt.

"It's stupid," he muttered, but it broke off on a half sob as I got down his leg.

"I doubt it. At least you play. I can't do anything musical." I cut open his pants, exposing a bad break with the bone jutting out, but bleeding was sluggish, which meant no major arteries were severed. I pulled the inflatable splint out of my bag and put it on his leg. "Looks like you did a number on your leg. You're going to be able to get people to sign it for weeks. Bet you can get them to give you their desserts too if you play it right. " I kept up the chatter to distract him as I got the splint secured and inflated.

"It really hurts." He tried not to whine, but it slipped through.

"I know. You want a shot to help?"

He looked glassy eyed but nodded. "Yeah, it really hurts."

We had limited amounts of morphine to give, and I would need to stay for a minute or two to make sure he didn't have an allergic reaction, but I pulled out the vial

Mel Todd

and needle, pulling in 1ml. He wasn't a big kid, but that break was nasty and the more stressed he was, the more he had a chance of making it worse. I gave him the shot and filled out the card, tying it on his wrist.

"Hey, this card is important. It says you are hurt pretty bad, and they need to get you to the hospital quick like. So don't remove it, okay?"

"Got it. Means I go to the hospital. Will they call my mom?"

"Absolutely. See all the first responders, the police, fire fighters, they are all here to make sure everyone is okay." I checked his vitals again, but his breath had stabilized as the morphine kicked in and he was calming down. "So you just lay here and close your eyes. Someone will be by to get you to the hospital pretty soon."

"Okay. Thanks lady." He closed his eyes, exhausted from the stress.

I tapped his head. "Someone will be here pretty soon. Just rest."

I got up and grabbed my bag, heading to the next person. A blond girl, her band uniform a mess of blood and dirt. But she sat against a vehicle, watching everything with alert eyes.

"Hey. How you doing?" I asked as I knelt next to her.

"Better than most. Arm's broken." Her eyes tracked well as I ran checks on her.

"Sure is. Let's get that splinted." I got the splint on it and she sighed a bit as that immobilized it. I dug out a sling. "You in pain?"

"A bit, but I don't need anything. I'm fine. I've done this before." She nodded at her arm. "I'll live." Her eyes tracked and I followed them to one of the people laying there with a jacket draped over their faces, her mouth set in a grim line.

328

"Okay. I'm going to hang this tag on you." I showed her the tag and the green. "It means you need to see the doctor, but you'll be fine waiting a while. You good with that?"

"Yeah. Go. Help the others." She swallowed convulsively. "I'll be fine."

I gave her a reassuring squeeze and moved on. The afternoon disappeared in helping, tagging, comforting, and moving to the next person. The first black tag I filled out didn't even shock me and I didn't bother to ask for backup. It was the bus driver and his body was cooling by the time I reached him. I tagged him, closed my eyes for a brief second, and moved on. The living needed me, he didn't.

Chapter 40

The hardest part about being a mage is knowing what and when to offer. Offering is easy, offering wisely is a challenge. ~ Pattern Merlin Thomas Edison

SPIRIT

I think I missed someone, there has to be someone I missed.

The idea nagged at me. I kept turning around and looking. But every person I saw still in the area had a tag, and most of those at this point were black—waiting for the coroner, or white—just waiting for a ride back to town. One of the cars had been rolled right side up and was drivable and the whites were going to head to an urgent care facility to get their treatment before driving home. But they weren't what called at me.

I kept turning, exhaustion clouding my thoughts. The sun had sunk down and cast red and yellow light everywhere, creating a canvas that would have rivaled anything painted by Bob Ross, except the red and blue lights, the garish scars on the vehicles, and the bodies draped in black on the ground.

"Cori?"

I'd heard Sally approach, but something kept pulling at me. I thought I almost knew from where.

"Yeah?" Distracted, I started to walk to the side of the road.

"What's wrong?" Sally sounded as exhausted as I felt. I didn't know how many hours we'd been up there—I knew I wanted my shower and bed—but that tugging wouldn't stop. I glanced at her and saw her hair was shorter by a good ten inches, giving her almost a bob cut look, and her long nails were gone to the quick. She'd spent a lot of magic today keeping people alive.

"I don't know. I feel like we missed..." I stopped talking and turned, as a sudden silence fell. Most of the first responders had left. They were starting to tow out the various vehicles, the bus would be last. But in that moment of silence I thought I heard something.

Ignoring Sally, I headed towards the front of the bus where it over hung the edge, just a past the doors, but it was enough that you couldn't walk around that side of the bus. That brief moment of silence ended with the beeping of tow trucks backing up, engines turning over, and just the noise of people filled the area.

Something still pulled my attention over here and I knelt on the side of the road, the guard rail blocking my view.

"What am I missing?" Sally didn't sound dismissive, just curious, and ready to go home. But I couldn't turn away.

"Give me a second," I said, my response abstract as I wormed my way under the guardrail and looked. It took a minute in the low light and shadows here to figure out what I was looking at. The glass of the bus accordion door had broken out in a single big pane and was laying against a tree, which probably helped the bus from sliding down any further. Crumbled at the base of the tree, wedged between the tree and the cliff, and hidden from almost every view by bushes, lay a figure. Blood covered most of the exposed skin, but I could just barely hear and see the rise and fall of the chest.

"Sally, I've got another victim. I need a basket and supplies, stat." I rattled this out as I wrapped one leg around the railing support and made a quick wish it wouldn't give and tumble me down the slope.

"Hello? Can you hear me?" I looked for a way to get down. There were a few pines there and I might be able to brace myself, but if I missed it would be a long painful fall to the bottom.

The head lifted, turning the tiniest bit towards me, and I heard a pained sound. "Help? Please?"

My throat tightened at the sound of that voice. The amount of pain and terror in it threatened my own composure.

"Cori, help is on the way. Here." She thrust a rope with a carabiner already attached to it. "You probably haven't done the courses, but loop and get down there. You're smaller than me, and I'll need to direct them. I'll send one of the guys to you once we can get some support. Probably from the other side."

I tied off in clumsy movements, and she tightened my knot. "I got it. Go."

She handed me a bag, not mine as it was about empty, still, supplies were good. I slung it over my shoulder, then half crawling, mostly trying not to fall, I worked my way under the bus and over to the person.

When I got close enough, I braced myself on the tree next to the victim and made sure the rope was clicked to the hook in the waistband. I knew I really should have a full harness on, but time and training were lacking. Sally would probably have to radio to get the help we needed. Baskets weren't standard issue for most ambulances.

"Hey, I'm Cori. I'm here to help."

The figure gave a broken sob. "I tried to scream, but no one heard. I thought I'd die here. Thank you." The voice suggested female and young, probably one of the students from the bus.

I didn't dwell on her comments, there wasn't anything I could say to address them, so I focused on what, at least to me, was the important part. "Can you tell me where you are hurt?"

I heard the sound of another sob being swallowed, then her voice, what little strength it had starting to fade. "Everywhere, but I can't move one leg. The other I can wiggle my toes, but I can't get my left leg to do anything. I think I'm bleeding somewhere. I felt it tickling for a while, but now I can't tell you where. My head hurts. There is only one of you, right? Or is there someone else with you?"

Probably concussion, bleeding, possible spinal injury.

"Just me for now. But I've got other people coming." The constant itch of my skin and head were distracting me. Probably allergic to something with as badly as I itched, but I pushed it all down to focus on the girl. She must have been about fifteen, not much older.

"I'm going to get closer and see if I can find any other injuries, okay?"

"Okay," her voice had gotten even smaller. I moved around, grabbing trees and roots sticking out of the cliff. The entire time I hoped they didn't give way.

Moving around took forever, but I got a look at her and cringed. She'd impaled herself on a branch and it was at the edge of her spine. But when I craned around her body and pulled back her shirt it wasn't distended, so it hadn't gone all the way through.

"I'm going to touch you a bit. I want you to tell me if it hurts really bad or just uncomfortable. Okay?"

She made a sound I took as an agreement, the silent clock in my head speeding up as to how much time she had. I pressed gently, no obvious response, I pushed harder and she moaned a bit, but I didn't hit any resistance.

"Sally?" We had run out of radios and there was too much chatter on them anyhow, so I just yelled.

"Yep?"

"I need a hacksaw. She's got a branch in her, but it doesn't seem to have pierced her abdominal cavity, or if it has, it is just barely, but either way we need to cut her loose and get her to the hospital asap."

"Okay, Darryl is coming down. We have him anchored. He'll bring the saw."

I glanced at the area around us and kept mental fingers crossed that he was more graceful than me, and that they really had him anchored well. I finished my examination, finding a long laceration on her thigh that had bled a lot, but was now sluggish. That worried me. "Hey. What leg did you say you couldn't move?" I asked as I prodded the wound and didn't get any reaction.

"My left," she mumbled. I checked her pulse. It had slowed even more and the clock sped up.

"Sally, I need her out of here stat. The clock is racing and I can't exactly give her an IV here," I barked out, panic and worry making my voice sharp.

"I'm coming down now." The incongruent British accent told me who was coming down without me needing to look up, but I did. Darryl made his way down, a full harness on him, a stretcher basket attached to the rope a bit beyond him, and a hacksaw in his hand.

"Thank Merlin. You aren't a mage, and I don't know any other way to do this. Do you?" I hoped maybe he'd be a mage that could just dissolve the wood.

"No. And Sally is spent. Besides, it would take her too long to figure this out." He peered at the situation then nodded. "I'll brace her and the wood. You saw fast and smooth and I'll try to keep it from moving."

He'd brought down a neck collar and we got that on her and taped her arms together. Her head almost lolled, but her eyes would open and focus on us every so often and she'd almost smile before fading back down.

I nodded and waited until he was in position. It wasn't a big branch, only about an inch in diameter. But an inch of wood in your body was still an inch too much. At his nod I started to draw the blade back and forth across the branch where it connected to the tree, making sure I was clear of his hands. It cut easily, but it still took me a solid minute.

She moaned as I sawed, and I realized I didn't even know her name. That bugged me for some reason, but I kept at it, until with a sudden snap it broke, and she sagged into Darryl's arms.

"Got her. Can you pull the basket over here

From our angle we couldn't get a backboard on her, and with the wood in her we couldn't take the risk anyhow. Having her on her side would be safer. I moved over, slipping twice, giving my heart a reason to try and explode out of my chest. But I moved the basket and Darryl, in a move only someone with his height and strength could have done, lifted her up and laid her on her side in the basket, all while keeping her from moving barely at all.

The next few minutes seemed to crawl as we secured the basket and people up above began to heave her up. Both of us came up with her trying to keep her from moving more than was unavoidable. I was drenched with sweat by the time I crawled over the guard rail onto safe ground. An ambulance sat backed up right to the edge, waiting for us. They had lifted her in by the time I crawled back to my feet, Sally at my elbow. "Get in, Cori. You're going with."

I looked at her, confused. I'd been here the entire time.

"She's the last one, and you've earned this. Go with her. Be her advocate until you get to the hospital." She was pushing me toward the ambulance, and too tired to argue, I crawled in, sitting on the bench. I looked at the young woman lying there in the light for the first time. Her dark curly hair was full of leaves and dirt, her band uniform torn and dirty, and her skin so pale she looked like a vampire from any popular movie.

We started to move and I reached out to hold her hand. "Hold on. We're headed down. You'll get to ride in a helicopter. What's your name?" As we hurried down the road I hooked up monitors no one had taken the time to do. Her heart rate was sluggish, but still beating. I didn't like her pulse ox, but right now there wasn't much I could do about it.

"Courtney," she whispered and it took me a minute to realize she was telling me her name.

"Hey, we're both 'C' names. Must be why I found you." I put humor and a smile into my voice, knowing she'd hear it.

"Hurts."

"I bet. But you're super brave to have hung in. And now you'll get to fly to the hospital. How cool is that?"

"Heights bad." Her voice so thin there wasn't even a tremor to it. I glanced back at her EKG, but while slow and her blood pressure sucked, she was holding on.

"Maybe, but you'll be safe inside and we'll get you to the hospital as fast as can be." I felt the bus start to slow. "In fact, I think you're about to go on your first helicopter ride. Something to tell a prospective boy or girl friend."

Her mouth tilted up at the corner.

"You're funny."

"Nah. Just me."

We came to a stop and I heard the front door open. I disconnected the leads and got in position to help lift her out as the doors to the back flew open.

"Ready?" Sally asked, Darryl standing next to her.

I nodded and less than three minutes later we were ushered towards the passenger area of the chopper, the rotors whipping my hair abound like a vortex.

"Hey, Cori?" Sally shouted, and I paused in the doorway, still overwhelmed and exhausted.

I looked back at her, my brows drawn together.

"You did damn good today. This job was made for you, and I'll have you as my partner any day."

Her words rang in my ears and I climbed in, my mind a whirl. But the primary thing was the smile that spread over my face.

This was what I was meant to do. I'd be damned if anyone would take that from me. The school would have a fight on their hands, and so would my parents. This was my dream and I'd earned it.

The rise of the helicopter matched the rise in my heart, and I smiled all the way to the hospital.

Mel Todd

Epilogue

We are all masters of our own destiny—magic is but one aspect in our choices. In the end, who you are still matters more than what you are. ~ Merlin James Wells

CHAOS

Take that, you little whiny bitch.

I seemed to be getting less forgiving and more vindictive as I experienced life. I was strangely okay with that.

"Monique Kinnison, you are charged with falsifying statements to the board and conspiring to slander and libel two people with fabricated evidence. These are serious charges and after deliberating we have decided to expel you and place a mark on your record barring you from taking the EMT or Paramedic certification test for the next five years."

The words rang like a death knell, and Monique started crying, big hiccupping tears that I thought might be real.

They had interviewed Bruce and me individually and while that had been uncomfortable, it had been painless. They then asked, just to settle any possible conflict, if I would be willing to take the tests again with a third-party instructor.

I shrugged and said yes. At this point my morning in class was shot, but after Saturday, my confidence in my own abilities was high enough that I didn't mind missing my practice exam.

I aced the test. All three parts, topping my previous

338

score. I took the exam in a classroom with one instructor, wearing only a tank top and jeans. I used the pencil they provided. Unless I had telepathy, I couldn't have cheated.

Maybe it was petty of me, but I enjoyed watching her fall apart and seeing the look of disappointment the older couple with her had on their faces as they walked out. I had spent Sunday reviewing all the paperwork and figured I would show up and play it by ear. I didn't know what else to do, as hiring a lawyer was well out of my league. To my delight, I was free with an even better score.

"I am sorry about all of this, Cori," Bruce said as we walked out. "You're a good student, if a bit weird, but I knew you would never have cheated."

"It's a stupid test to cheat on. If I don't know the information and get in the field, I could kill someone by accident. That is not acceptable. Why would anyone be stupid enough to cheat on a test like that?"

He smiled a bit sadly. "Not everyone feels that way, but I'm glad you do. Some people need to pass the test, not caring about who might pay the price for their laziness; or maybe it's arrogance. I've never been sure which. You have an A in the class, no matter what, and I have faith you'll do just as well in the paramedic test as soon as you graduate. Go enjoy your day."

I gave him a smile as he walked off, but it faded quickly. The day off was what I needed, as I had to go talk to someone else.

The bus ride gave me time to review the documents one more time before I got to the police station.

"Hey, is the chief in and does she have time to talk to me?" I asked the front sergeant.

"Let me ping her," he said with a smile and I nodded. Willing to wait. A minute later the door buzzed. "Head on back, she's in her office."

I walked through the now familiar space with none of my original discomfort.

What else can you get used to, simply by learning about it?

That idea occupied my thoughts as I walked back to her office. There were a few things that still made me uncomfortable. Maybe I should go learn about them rather than just fear them. I'd learned more than I expected from this. I tried to let that lesson sink into my mind. You only feared that which you didn't understand, so I'd have to try and understand more. My never-ending quest to learn and figure things out sharpened. Maybe someday I'd get the answers I craved.

Laurel looked up before I could even knock. "Hey, Cori. What brings you by? You decided you really do want to go to the police academy and are looking for a reference?"

The amount of hope in her voice surprised me. "Um, no. Still liking the EMT gig, though Saturday was a bit intense."

Laurel sighed then waved at her chair. "I heard. I also heard you did damn good. They usually avoid pulling newbies into that. It tends to rattle them, and I hear you didn't get rattled."

"Oh, I got rattled." I nodded vigorously. I couldn't remember the last time I'd been so worried about failing. "But the patients were what were more important and I tried my best." I shook my head, already feeling uncomfortable. "But that wasn't what I wanted to talk to you about. I wanted to talk about this." I slid her the envelope and the restraining order.

"What's this?" She asked even as she picked up the paperwork and began to read. A frown creased her face deeper and deeper as she read. "Well, fuck," Laurel muttered and I blinked. I couldn't remember ever hearing her cuss. "I'm sorry about this Cori. It never occurred to me they would trace it back to you. Give me a minute."

She continued to read, and I settled back in the chair looking at the photos that adorned the room. Most of them were of her and Martin, though there were one or two of her with a younger man and one with an older woman. I wanted to ask why she had never had children, but I managed to not blurt that out. Even I knew that wasn't my business.

"I swear, Cori, your parents are pieces of work. But here's the good news." She looked up, stacking the papers back up and putting them in the envelope. "Go to court, it's in June. Agree to not send anyone to spy on them or try to contact them in any way. Also agree to not try and contact Kris while he is a minor. But only while he is a minor." Her emphasis on this. "After he is eighteen, he has the right to decide if he wants to contact you."

I looked at her, confused. "But I didn't ask anyone to spy in the first place."

Her grin would have made a shark envious. "Exactly. Which is why you can say that with perfect honestly. What other people do isn't your problem. You always knew he would have to make the choice to contact you prior to eighteen without interference. Maybe he will. But either way, you can go to court and agree to every one of their terms. Don't even bother with a lawyer, just agree to their terms. They have to prove if you break them and since you won't," she glared at me and I shook my head, "it won't be an issue."

She slid the papers back to me. "Bottom line. Don't worry about it. You didn't break any laws or even try to find them. You didn't do anything wrong."

Mel Todd

The stress that had wrapped around my spine like kudzu released a little and it felt like an electric shock raced own my back. The picture frame on her desk fell backwards. We both turned to look at it and Laurel rolled her eyes then looked at me.

"You're sure?" I asked, trying not to look at the picture of her with the older woman, that now obviously had a crack running through the glass.

"Yes. Go to the meeting. Agree not to try to contact them or Kris until he is an adult. Refuse any agreement where you don't speak to them. If they contact you, you can talk all you want. And then let it be. They aren't worth knowing and you have a decade before Kris can make his own choices."

I nodded. It made sense and at this point I just didn't want to deal any more. In a decade, and didn't that seem like forever, I would start trying to see if he wanted to talk to me.

"Thanks. I just wanted to make sure." I rose from my chair, the paperwork in hand.

"Not an issue. You do have friends here, Cori, even if it seems like catastrophes follow you." She shot a wry look at her picture.

"Thanks. I'll get out of here before a tornado strikes."

Laurel cringed. "Don't even joke about that. I'm too scared it might happen." She was both serious and teasing at the same time. "By the way, Happy Birthday."

I ducked my head but smiled. "Thanks. See you later."

I walked out of the police station, my whole being feeling lighter. I'd file everything when I got to the apartment. I had little doubt I'd pass the exam, and Bruce told me I'd graduate. Sally had agreed to start letting me practice in the back lot driving the ambulance to help with the course after I graduated. And best of all,

I was heading over to the Guzman's for my birthday dinner.

Pain flashed through my skull and I groaned for a second, then it faded. I shook my head. Where had that come from?

A strange sound up in the sky made me look up and there Elsba hung, wings beating like a hummingbird, a strange ripple behind her. Before I could focus too much she darted down behind buildings and disappeared as did the ripple in the air.

Magic will never make sense to me, or be anything I use, but it sure is fascinating.

I laughed and headed home. My next challenge would be to find a job in Atlanta so Jo and I could start our lives as true adults. My faith in happy ever after was higher than it had been six months ago.

Finally, my life was on track and no one would be able to tell me what to do. And I'd leave behind all the oddities that followed me. My life was about to begin.

I still had questions. Who was Cori Munroe? How was Kris? Why did Stevie die? What did my strange dream/memories mean? But with a good job and time, I'd be able to find all my answers. Right at that moment, I just wanted dinner, *flan*, and time with my chosen family.

Everything else would wait until I had to deal with it.

Appendix: Magic Symbols

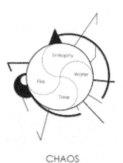

Chaos:
- Entropy
- Fire
- Water
- Time

CHAOS

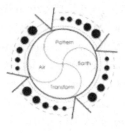

Order:
- Pattern
- Air
- Earth
- Transform

ORDER

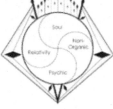

Spirit:
- Soul
- Relativity
- Non-Organic
- Psychic

SPIRIT

Final Thoughts

Wow, what a ride. But that was just one story in this series. You can find the rest of series on Amazon. The Twisted Luck series has 5 books out and 3 novellas. You can find all the information on my author page here.

Remember if you enjoyed this book, please leave a review. Amazon, Goodreads, Bookbub, they all link and help authors like me sell more books which means you get more stories to read.

Don't forget to sign up for my newsletter and join the Facebook group. Can't wait to get to talk to you.

If you would like to follow me somewhere else, check out all the places you can find me here.

Mel

Mel Todd

Mel Todd has over 20 stories out, her urban science fiction Kaylid Chronicles, the Blood War series, and the new Twisted Luck series. Owner of Bad Ash Publishing she is working to create a place for excellent stories and great authors. With over a million words published, she is aiming for another million in the next two years. Bad Ash Publishing specializes in stories that will grab you and make you hunger for more. With one co-author, and more books in the works, her stories can be found on Amazon and other retailers.

Made in the USA
Las Vegas, NV
12 May 2022

48800181R00208